I0762533

THE SECRET WORLD OF BRIAR ROSE

CINDY PHAM

Kokila

KOKILA
An imprint of Penguin Random House LLC
1745 Broadway, New York, NY 10019
penguinrandomhouse.com

This book was edited by Zareen Jaffery, copyedited by Diane João, proofread by Rob Farren, and designed by Asiya Ahmed. The production was supervised by Rye White, Madison Penico, Natalie Melius, Misha Kydd, and Vanessa Robles.

Text set in FS Brabo.

Library of Congress Cataloging-in-Publication Data is available.

First published in the United States of America by Kokila, 2026

Manufactured in China
RRD

ISBN 9798217113026
1 3 5 7 9 10 8 6 4 2

The authorized representative in the EU for product safety and compliance is Penguin Random House Ireland, Morrison Chambers, 32 Nassau Street, Dublin D02 YH68, Ireland, https://eu-contact.penguin.ie.

To my eleven-year-old self, who started wishing she could sleep forever and never wake up. I'm glad you stayed.

AUTHOR'S NOTE:

This story is inspired by my experience with depression and suicidal ideation. If you find the subject matter to be difficult to read, please take care of yourself first.

CHAPTER 1

THE LAST WORDS Elly said before she disappeared were "I hate you."

To Corin, the sentiment was nothing new. Saying "I hate you" was a universal language between sisters, and their tongues spoke it fluently.

Elly yelled it whenever Corin stomped over her chalk drawings and wiped them off the concrete. Corin hissed it whenever Elly hummed songs in the middle of her sleep and woke them up. They went to bed angry yet huddled for warmth every night. After the warplanes destroyed their homes and soldiers seized their family's belongings, the only thing they had left was each other.

But this time was different.

This time, when Elly said "I hate you," Corin knew she meant it.

Her sister had vanished as swiftly as any other resident come sunrise. Anyone living within the dilapidated buildings or rubble-filled streets of Gyldan knew their home wasn't forever. There would be a few years of normalcy and routine, if their factions allowed it, before the rumbling sound of bulldozers came to tear down the walls. A century-long turf war between rivaling countries meant constant itinerance: new military, new flags, but never any warnings for the families who lived in Gyldan. Houses were simply strategic locations to be secured, and people like Corin and Elly were just collateral damage, about as insignificant as roaches that were crushed to death if they didn't move out of the way.

As Corin wandered through the city center in search of Elly, she could hardly imagine these same streets bustling with trade and people a century ago. Her grandparents had risked their lives seeking refuge in the prosperous kingdom surrounded by forests, but those dreams were quickly dashed when the royal family abandoned its people, leaving an ungoverned country to descend into chaos. Warring groups divided into territories, and with soldiers patrolling the borders, Corin knew Elly couldn't have left their faction.

She pasted posters with her sister's likeness around soup kitchens, town squares, even shops that had closed their shutters, like the burning bakery she had looted for bread after the last round of warplanes came. Her stomach rumbled with hunger by the time she circled back to the marketplace, a deserted area with ramshackle storefronts and stragglers sorting through trash. She approached a few of them to ask if they had seen the girl on her poster, but their eyes glazed over the image, or they muttered a noncommittal response, or they cursed her out, which always resulted in her cursing them back.

Mostly, though, she was ignored, like another body rotting on the street.

Her appearance probably didn't help. Hunger had whittled her limbs to bones and hollowed her cheeks. Swaths of crow-black hair stuck to fresh bruises across her face. Tattered pants and ripped sleeves revealed grime and mud, the stains blending with her dark skin and old scabs. At eighteen years old, she already looked dead.

She nailed her last poster onto a wooden pole and took a step back, examining her work. She had recreated Elly's face in charcoal with all the details she remembered. Every freckle on her dark skin, every birthmark on her long limbs. Her short, choppy hair, which always curled behind her ears. She had a small, rounded nose, wide cheekbones, and two large pools of eyes the color of summer soil after it rained. While Corin inherited their father's broad shoulders and strong nose, Elly carried their mother's features, soft and feminine like a black-eyed daisy.

The longer Corin stared, the more she hated the drawing. The sketches were too crude and badly smudged. They looked like Elly but couldn't capture her. They didn't show what it felt like to hold her hand, to feel the stickiness of her palms from all the times she broke dandelion stems and marveled at their white milk. They didn't show the light in her eyes whenever she heard a new story, the cuts on her fingers from plucking weeds in the cracks of sidewalks, the dirt under her nails from digging into soil and shouting that there was another world underneath that they couldn't see.

"She's still asleep down there," Elly would insist in rushed breaths, "the princess from long ago—"

Corin shook her head, dispelling her sister's foolish enthusiasm for fairy tales. Even at the age of twelve, Elly still latched onto bedtime stories she'd heard as a child when they had lived with other artisans. Corin thought leaving the commune last year would, at least, let Elly outgrow childish interests and forget their friends. In the end, it was only Corin who wanted to forget them.

Before she dwelled longer, the sound of footsteps approaching made her reach for her belt. She turned to flash a dagger at the stranger's throat, then pulled back as the elderly woman before her gasped.

"I'm sorry," the stranger stammered, her voice frail and light. "I wanted to see your poster."

Deep wrinkles etched the woman's face like a crumpled plant. She wore a faded shawl that thinned above her wrists, showing a wedding ring that glinted from her finger. Corin handed her the crinkled paper and watched the woman squint at the drawing of Elly. Her lashes nearly brushed against the charcoal as her face pressed closer to the parchment. White clouds that surrounded her pupils shifted, her eyes straining to scan every detail.

"The shading on the girl's face is excellent," the woman murmured. "You're very talented."

Corin counted her breaths to restrain herself from cursing at the stranger. She felt foolish for hoping Elly would be recognized and angrier that the woman would waste her time by prattling compliments. She was not here to show off her technical skills in some pitiful act of panhandling. But why would anyone care? Even if people knew Elly had been missing for a full day, they would assume she was simply another street rat who faced the early mercy of death.

But Elly wasn't dead. Corin knew this, because there was no body. She had checked the usual places her sister loitered: the soup kitchens filled with lines of gaunt figures, the root cellars they hid in to shelter from rain, even the riverfront where their old friends had built their commune, a now-destroyed home that she swore she would never return to again.

No, it wasn't that Elly was dead. It was that she was nowhere to be found. As if she had disappeared into thin air.

"You remind me of the artists that lived by the river," the

woman observed. "People only remember the insurrection, but before then, I used to see them paint and build. Tragic, really, what happened to them."

Corin steeled herself to shut out the sound of bullets, the smell of burnt flesh, the muffled scream that burned in her throat whenever she imagined that day. It had been a year, and still the scene came to her in nightmares and woke her in sweat and tears. There was no point in picturing how even the autumn leaves died that night, crumpled like the bodies strewn over the debris. She had not been there, after all. She needed to focus on the opportunities in front of her, here and now.

"Are you an artist?" she asked.

"Yes. But it's difficult now, as you can see." The woman's disfigured hand gestured to her cloudy eyes. "My husband used to describe a scene to me and I would draw it. Before he died, we drew so much together."

Corin imagined the woman and her husband, hunched over an easel, splatters of paint dripping over the canvas edges. Their voices were soft murmurs, an echo of her own parents'. *See this, Corin?* Her mother's hand steadying Corin's fingers over a brush. A round smear of orange paint, bright like apricot, messy like juice. *You just made the sun.*

"My parents were artists too," she said. "My mother was a painter. She taught me everything."

"Oh, that's wonderful. And your father?"

"A sculptor. He liked making pots, the tiny ones you grow plants from. I'm better with a brush, though, so sometimes I'd paint them after he finished."

The woman cracked a smile.

"You must keep painting, then. Sometimes art can be the only refuge in this world. These soldiers take our loved ones, but they cannot take this. That's how we keep a memory alive, even if it's gone."

Corin thought of patchwork quilts stained with paint, clay pots drying by the window, a tiny cottage made of lime-washed brick, and a roof so low she could kiss the thatch. Her father's calloused palms, her mother's belly pregnant with Elly, the low hum of a song they'd made up. She could paint the memory into permanence, proof that there was once a home where love overflowed.

She took the elderly woman's hand. This was someone left with no family, just like her, searching for a way to bond with another human being. Corin would give her that connection. She would let the woman know that, despite their despair, at least they had crossed paths with one another.

"Thank you," she said. "I won't give up on my dreams."

The woman crinkled her eyes and nodded with conviction, as if her heart turned a little softer from their brief connection with each other. They bid goodbye, and Corin watched the woman leave before dropping her smile. Her hand dug in her pocket, where the edge of a wedding ring pressed against her palm.

It was smaller than she would have liked to barter with, but she could still make some decent money from it.

Maybe it took a mind deteriorating with old age to fall for a trick like this, believing in the dreams of a starving artist. But the truth was that dreams were never enough. Her mother died when she was ten, her paintings and clothes discarded by leering men who wanted to put their own marks over her body. Her father changed after that, stewing in liquor and regret until he finally gave in to his darkest desires and drowned himself a year later.

No, if Corin painted a memory, it would be this: A raging river that took three bodies. A baby wailing as the water drowned them. A girl who only had the strength to carry her sister, not the weeping man who brought them there.

It would be a portrait of survival, because in the end, that was what mattered. Not the fleeting love of a mother gone too soon, not the strength of a father who'd lost too much. Not even a makeshift home that once opened itself to an orphaned teenager, only to disintegrate before she turned eighteen.

She had no capacity to focus on something as meaningless as art. After the insurrection took her friends, there was no one else but Elly and her.

Now, there was only her.

Because even as she kept searching, Elly never returned.

CORIN WOKE TO the sound of soldiers seizing her home. It wasn't much of a home to begin with, but she had depended on the deteriorated building as a roof over her head, even if that roof was composed of wooden boards and cobwebs.

Troops barged in clanking metal and heavy guns, stomping up a creaky stairwell that led to an alcove blocked by a rotting wood door. When they kicked it open, she'd barely made it out of bed. Their eyes fell upon the pile of burlap and moth-eaten sheets, their noses wrinkling at the rotting odor of trash and unwashed clothes. She felt naked under the gaze of these strangers, like a roach found belly-up in a sticky trap.

"No squatters," one of the men yelled. "You're on our turf now."

The distant roar of bulldozers made the floorboards rumble. The walls trembled, as if they could tell another man-made machine was coming. Her pulse raced as she rifled through her bags and fished out crumpled documents.

"I rent under Woodbine," she spat, as if the name of a rich landlord meant anything. Her pointer finger stabbed the bottom half of her papers where both of their signatures were scribbled beside last year's date. She had recalled the day she met the old man with as much regret as getting talked into holding a knife, even though she'd never made the cut. His pale eyes had locked onto her first, sensing her desperation even from across his shop. His smile had chipped incisors, like a wolf baring its teeth at his next prey. She knew she'd made a mistake shaking his hand and it had haunted her ever since.

The only consolation from their deal should have been the new roof over her head, even if it was in a decrepit building. But the soldier barely glanced at the document she presented. His disinterested expression felt like a rock sinking in her stomach. She understood, even before he spoke, that any prior agreement she'd made was for nothing.

"Woodbine sold ownership of his land and left Gyldan. Demolition orders call for any illegal housing to be claimed under Zilar military."

The soldier stamped the Zilar flag, a striking blue marked by an eagle and a coat of arms. He raised the pole high enough to puncture the boarded rooftop. She watched the flapping cloth in the sky with shaking anger. Her curled fists wanted to smash Woodbine's pallid face. He'd put blood on her hands the day they traded favors, and the desolate excuse for a home she was about to lose had not been worth her sacrifice.

The barrel of a gun pressed into her back, forcing her to move. She couldn't even walk a clean path to the door as hordes of men swept the home for valuables. Metal detectors crawled the floorboards like mechanical spiders, hunting for hidden gold from a once prosperous land. She sneered at their pointless search. Greedy men who already had everything always wanted more. Her family had escaped Zilar for refuge in Gyldan, only for their home to be stolen once again.

If they had asked, she would have told them there was nothing to seize. She'd sold Elly's old toys and baby clothes for a pathetic amount of bills after her sister outgrew them. She'd already thrown away palettes and brushes when she gave up on art. At least when they took her parents' home, there was furniture to overturn and memorabilia to destroy. Old paintings and cracked pottery and things that could have mattered if she still had a family.

They couldn't take from someone who had nothing left now.

Yet something floated behind a tattered sheet, small and round and strung by a metallic chain nailed to one of the scorched beams. Instinct crackled her heart and made her lunge for it. The sudden movement caused a soldier to knock his gun into her head and force her knees to the ground. He pressed a boot to her back and grabbed the chain. The pendant, a hollowed ring where a gemstone should have been, dangled between his narrowed eyes. He let out a snort, dropping the necklace to the floor where her cheek pressed against wood.

"Worthless," he muttered.

He was right. Her grandmother's pendant held no monetary value, the lack of gemstone turning the necklace into nothing more than a misshapen copper band. There was no practical reason for Corin to keep it like a family heirloom. And yet, his disgust at the ornament, as if it were as insignificant as the rest of her ancestry because they weren't gilded by fortune, made something snap inside her.

She snatched the chain before standing.

"You're wasting your time," she spat. "There hasn't been gold on this land for centuries. The only thing you're digging up are the graves you've made yourselves."

She had already braced herself for the soldier's retaliation when his gun barrel swung down, metal crushing against her eye.

CHAPTER 2

103 YEARS AGO

PRINCESS AMELIA DID not believe in true love, but her faerie godmothers thought she did.

The three of them floated behind the painter, who had been toiling over the royal family's portrait for hours while Amelia sat with her father and stepmother. One faerie pressed her fingers to both corners of her mouth and flashed sparkling teeth.

"Think of the true love you'll meet someday," she said, "and how excited you'll be to fall for him."

Ah, yes. A handsome man to provide reason for her to smile. This was the motivation to keep living, despite the curse that promised she would sleep forever when she turned eighteen. Clover had granted the gift of true love's kiss to break the curse, so of course the godmothers believed in it. Their entire credibility depended on the cure, lest their reputation be tainted.

Amelia forced her lips into a smile. The godmothers clapped for her like she'd performed a magic trick.

Still, she felt nothing.

She possessed a face that every painter loved: bright eyes the color of sea glass, waves of golden hair rolling past delicate shoulders, porcelain skin with blushing apples on her cheeks. Her face had the symmetrical shape of a heart that pinched to the dainty point of her chin. The smile she wore highlighted the pink blooming from her lips. People compared her to roses, even though she never cared for them.

The painter could add as many shades as he wanted, but she was still a blank palette behind the face her godmothers had gifted her. Only a pastel dream of a girl to soothe people's ideas of what beauty should look like.

If she had any ugly, gnawing thing inside her, no one would ever know.

THE PORTRAIT HUNG as a centerpiece in the castle's grand hall. Dark oils streaked across the canvas, the paint bleeding together to make three figures.

The first thing Amelia noticed upon its undraping was the gold glittering on her father's throne. He sat tall and broad-shouldered in his chair, casting a wide shadow on its crimson velvet and lacework. A gold finish had been added to the crest rail, and his crown glinted under the light like a halo. Either the painter took creative liberties, or King Victor had ordered it himself, for a crown made of gold was impossible. Throughout the kingdom of Gyldan, not a single ounce of gold existed in clothing, furniture, or jewelry. The mineral had been wiped from the land for centuries, so rare it had become nearly extinct.

Instead, the only remaining gold lived in the royal family's blood.

She grew up with the story retold to her several times, a teaching tale for why her family was extraordinary. Gyldan had once been nothing more than barren land isolated by surrounding forests, where wild faeries and creatures attacked any human that trekked through the foliage. That changed when her great-grandfather, King Samael, found an orphaned faerie named Oleander. To display his gratitude for the king, queen, and their son, Oleander enchanted their blood with gold so that Gyldan would become prosperous for the rest of their ancestry's rule.

Oleander was the only faerie who possessed the ability to create gold, but he limited his magic to one family so that their exclusivity would hold power. Still, rumors swirled throughout the land that he'd hidden the last treasure in a secret place within Gyldan. People climbed mountains surrounding the river valleys, traveled to other colonies for clues, even fought with wild faeries in the forests to excavate trinkets from tree hollows. They failed to discover any hidden fortune, and would never receive the answer from Oleander, who crossed death as an act of loyalty when King Samael died.

Amelia glanced down at her wrist. Beneath pale skin, the faintest hint of gold shimmered in her veins. The ancient magic still worked, but the bloodline wouldn't continue with her. She was fifteen now, a ticking clock set to stop working in three more years. Her father deciding to marry was understandable. Broken parts should always be replaced, therefore King Victor needed to produce a new heir. Preferably a son, but if not, at least a girl who carried a stronger legacy than sleeping for the rest of her life.

She just didn't expect the new queen to be so young. Lilith looked more like an older sister than a stepmother. Barely eighteen years of age, the woman had married Amelia's father only yesterday. This painting finally allowed Amelia time to observe her.

Lilith didn't have the pretty and delicate bearing of most noblewomen. She was strong-jawed and muscular with dark olive skin and a sharp aquiline nose. Her long hair was tied into neat, knotted locks, streaming down her back like rope. A set of pearls wrapped around her throat like a choke hold.

"The pearls simply ruin the whole thing, don't they?"

Her godmother's voice made Amelia startle. Iris had sneaked behind her like a shadow, so quiet that even the flap of the faerie's delicate robe barely made a sound. She gazed at the portrait and shook her head in disapproval.

"She didn't listen when I told her they wouldn't match the wedding theme. Some nonsense about wanting to keep a piece of home with her."

"Which home would that be?" Clover chimed. Thick coils of blond hair bounced as she entered the hallway. Faeries were known to be lively spirits, and as the youngest sister, she embraced that reputation with a spritely voice and natural sunny glow.

Amelia couldn't blame her godmothers for their distrust. Being fiercely protective of the royal family was their job, and having a stranger live in the castle introduced too many risks. Especially when that stranger came from disgraced nobles and carried a reputation for spending time at brothels.

"I overheard her trying to convince King Victor to set up camps," Iris whispered. "More places to take in runaways from Zilar. Dangerous criminals who would eagerly stab the king for a fraction of his golden blood."

"Madness!" Clover cried.

"Why he chose a woman with friends from whorehouses, I'll never know."

"Well, you are the company you keep—"

A new voice interrupted their hushed conversations. "Enough with the gossip, ladies. Let's have a little more tact, shall we?"

The two sisters parted, making room for their eldest. Dahlia wore a ruby gown with a high neckline that accentuated the sharp point of her chin. She tucked a curl of brown hair behind her ear and turned to Amelia with a practiced smile.

"Welcoming another woman into the castle must be difficult. You miss your mother very much, don't you?"

Amelia didn't respond, because she couldn't miss someone she never knew. Her mother had died giving birth to her. She held no animosity toward the new queen, nor did she react with any of the tantrums that one would expect from an adolescent. Instead, she felt about the situation like she felt about most things: indifferent.

Where her mind often wandered as her godmothers gossiped was a different road entirely. One far away from ancient castles and limestone towers and talk of golden bloodlines, demons' curses, even true love.

"Godmother Dahlia," she murmured, "will I still become Briar Rose?"

She waited for an answer as the faerie pursed her lips. Long ago, the godmothers discussed plans to disguise her as an orphan. They feared that the demon Malicine would visit the castle and trick her into pricking her finger on a spindle. It might be easier, they suggested, if she lived as an ordinary girl among the other forest nymphs. A girl by the name of Briar Rose.

"No, my dear," Dahlia said apologetically. "Your father didn't think it would be a good idea."

Amelia held her breath so that her chest would not deflate. Hiding her disappointment, she bid the faeries goodbye and retreated to her bedroom. For the rest of the evening, the godmothers would likely chatter about the new queen or potential suitors who could break her curse. They wouldn't know that such matters were far away from her mind.

In her head, she had already envisioned this life they planted long ago, watered the seeds and watched them grow into a cottage nestled deep in a far-off forest. It would be a fraction the size of the castle, but there would be a garden of sunflowers, a front porch where she'd share tea with forest animals, and windows that let sunlight cast in sideways.

In another life, she would rise with the sun and sleep with the stars and never feel alone.

She would be happy, rather than someone only pretending to be in their portrait.

CHAPTER 3

COLD WATER STUNG Corin's skin as she splashed her face beside the river. Fat bruises the size of berries bloomed on her cheeks, and her left eye was swollen shut after the soldier had beaten her. But she was used to looking like crap, and really, she was more concerned that Elly had nowhere to return. If her sister tried searching for their ramshackle house behind the railroads, she would find only a mountain of rubble and an army of soldiers who would sooner protect land than their own people.

When most of the blood and grime washed off, Corin limped down the rocky path by the river's edge. The water had turned to a muted gray, reflecting the dull clouds of a washed-out sky, though most of the riverbank was covered in dead leaves and weeds that grew along the edges. Autumn should have killed her memories of this place like the trees, yet reminders lingered on every corner. The soft murmur of stream that once lulled Corin and Elly to sleep in their tent. The patch of grass where their friends lay freshly washed clothes to dry under the sun. The gritty pile of rocks that children collected to skip across the water. That time felt like the closest thing to peace, which was why she shouldn't have expected it to last at all.

She passed by the area where she had last seen her friends, marked now by churned mud and shattered stone. The commune moved their tents along the river trail throughout the seasons to avoid capturing soldiers' attention, but she remembered the place she'd visited the night she left for good, the gentle slope of wildflowers her boots had crushed to death when she fled under the moonlight. A year was enough time to turn her friends to dust, but she couldn't stop smelling charred flesh as if she'd been with them.

She quickened her pace to leave them behind. Dryness thickened her throat like the scream she swallowed every morning after waking up. When she thought it would come up again like bile, she steadied herself at a wooden pole. Her blurred gaze fixed itself to something simple: The mud on her boots. The scattering of gravel. The curved lines of chalk on the rocks' surface.

The familiarity of it struck her. Most of the drawings had faded from rain, but she recognized the rough scribbles of white and the uneven bumps of paint. She had taught Elly to soak chalk in water to create a paste and seen her sister cover sidewalks with drawings. The day before they left the commune, despite Elly's protests, she had stamped them out. At least, she thought she did.

She knelt down to turn over the rocks. Each drawing revealed underside was a tiny stab of betrayal. There were ruffled petals colored in white, as if in mid-bloom, and broad circles that spiraled around a stem like full moons. A few of the stems turned into wavy lines, which she guessed were locks of hair, a childish depiction of a flower crown worn by a girl. Except, to Elly, these were not ordinary flowers, and this was not an ordinary girl.

Anger pulsed against her temple as she kicked the rocks into the river. She had told her sister to stop listening to fairy tales. That stories were shared to placate and distract from reality, but they would never be tools to survive in it. All this time, she feared Elly would die in the crossfire of soldiers, be snatched by men with leering eyes, or keel over from hunger and poverty. But she hadn't lost her sister to any of those things.

In the end, the girl had run away to chase the most dangerous thing of all: hope.

SUNSET BLED INTO the mountainside by the time Corin reached Gyldan's borders. She understood then why a castle had been built here centuries ago. The rocky terrain overlooked the surrounding forests, and if any god had favored her to make her born in wealth, she would have wanted her windows to oversee the towering trees and changing leaves as well. But the castle was long gone, rumored to be buried with its sleeping princess, and the only sight left was dead foliage and patrolling soldiers. They stood along the border with rifles and sharp eyes, as keen to pull the trigger if they spotted her as they would be for any animal.

She stayed away from walking trails, ducking behind a boulder to evade a passing military tank. Once the roar of the vehicle faded, she continued stalking along the mountainside as she had for the past hour, tearing down vines that wrapped around the rocky walls and rubbing mud over her clothes for camouflage. Thorns ripped holes in her gloves, and her palms prickled with splinters.

When she thought her chafed skin couldn't handle more, her fingers dug into a rock crevice that finally felt different from the rest.

Cold air wafted through the small cracks. The change in temperature raised bumps on her skin. She cut through the thick vines with her dagger, shearing the tendrils that twisted around each other until a gaping black mouth opened before her.

She stepped back, staring into the darkness. The wind whispered around the rocks like a secret. She thought about the ones that would never be uncovered by the world, lost in time.

A century ago, refugees from Zilar dug tunnels connecting to their neighbors in Gyldan while evading the dangerous forests that surrounded the kingdom. Her grandmother had been one of hundreds who survived traveling for miles by foot. But monarchy dissolved into war after the royal family died out, and as neighboring kingdoms fought to take over the land, military forces found and demolished several passageways. Now desperate travelers used the remaining network of tunnels for a different purpose: to find the princess who fell asleep one hundred years ago.

She knew the story well, because it was Elly's favorite. The other artists from the commune had told Elly about the legend, and she loved repeating it to Corin. On rainy nights when they hid inside their tent, Elly would whisper in Corin's ear the tale of a princess cursed by a demon. As midnight struck on the princess's eighteenth birthday, the girl pricked herself with a spindle and fell into eternal slumber. Her faerie godmothers gifted true love's kiss as a cure, yet when time came for the prince to kiss her, she never opened her eyes.

"That's why Gyldan is so terrible now," Elly had whispered.

"Because some princess pricked herself with a spindle?" Corin remembered saying. "That's stupid."

Elly had shaken her head. Her face had been tucked in the crook of Corin's neck, her hair tickling under Corin's chin whenever she moved. Corin had retaliated by tickling her stomach. Elly had shoved her elbow into Corin's face with a huff.

"There were people who visited her tower before the castle was buried. In all their drawings, she wore a crown of moonflowers. Those only bloom every hundred years, and they did on the night she fell asleep."

"Is there a purpose to this story, or are you just rambling to annoy me?"

Corin had known the flowers were Elly's latest fixation, their concrete surroundings etched in clumsy chalk recreations. She didn't like the way the story clung to her sister like false hope.

"I counted the years. They're going to bloom again in three days' time," Elly had said, wide-eyed and breathless. "What if that's when the princess will wake up?"

Corin had diminished her sister's beliefs by stamping out her chalk drawings and reminding her of reality. No one could fall asleep for centuries, let alone be the savior to a kingdom overthrown by war. Desperate travelers who ventured inside the tunnels chased after a fantasy, where skies were filled with magic and faeries instead of warplanes and smoke. Not only were these ideas foolish, they were also dangerous. Despite hundreds of people attempting to find the princess, no one had ever made it out of the tunnels.

Corin stared at the abyss and pictured Elly walking into the darkness, motivated by inane stories and imaginary flowers. As she rolled up her sleeves, gripped onto the rocks, and climbed down into the hole, she thought about how she'd underestimated the gall that a child of twelve could have. She would not let her sister pay the price of stupidity with her life.

The tunnels turned colder the deeper she traveled. Goose bumps prickled her flesh even as she massaged her arms with muddied gloves. She tried marking each turn she made with lines of gravel, but there were other stones in each corner, trails left behind by those who'd inevitably become lost.

"El?" she called out.

No one responded but her own echo. She inhaled a deep breath and gritted her teeth.

"When I find you," she called again, "you're going to be in so much trouble."

SHE DID NOT find Elly.

Corin lost count of the hours, her awareness of time ebbing and flowing like the wash of a tide. Blisters oozed between her toes, each step in the endless tunnel laced with pain. Rocks cut through her gloves and scraped her skin.

At first, the excitement of following Elly's trail had propelled her forward. She'd recognized the chalk drawings of moonflowers on the walls and the clumsy scribbles that could have only been etched by her sister's hand. But as the hours stretched along endless passageways and wore down her body, she wondered how Elly could have survived this far. She dreaded turning a corner where the chalk no longer remained and finding her sister's body instead.

A jagged stone cut her back as she leaned against a wall. Even breathing was difficult, the stale air thick with dust and dirt. She wanted to give up and cry. Not because she was tired, but because she could only imagine Elly walking this same path, her body hollowing from the inside out until she was nothing but bone.

"We can't survive without each other," their mother had told her when Elly was born. "You have to protect your little sister."

And she'd tried, hadn't she? After their parents died, she'd kept Elly out of trouble, steered her away from open streets when the warplanes came, traded favors with other artists from the commune so they'd look after Elly while she looted shops during air raids. She threw herself into destroyed homes and threw fists at strangers who gave her broken ribs and black eyes while calling her a low-life thief.

That was what eldest daughters were supposed to do. Their survival was her responsibility, because she was born first.

"Hmm . . . I don't think that's the full story, Corin."

A familiar voice echoed through the cavern walls. A young woman with a greasy ponytail sat on a rock beside her, the stray strands of her chestnut hair strewn over her sunken cheeks and black eyes. Her skin was summer brown, and her mouth set in a hard line, the way Corin remembered her a year ago. The woman picked at dirty nails through her fingerless gloves, a matching pair to the set she'd gifted Corin when they first met.

"I don't remember you being so responsible when I found you," said the woman. "Or have you already forgotten?"

Great. Corin was so hungry she was hallucinating the dead. She clenched her jaw, trying to shut out Harlow's figure, but ended up drawing the memory closer instead. Corin was barely a teenager when the artists found her beneath the bridge that spanned the river, her body curled around a shadowy recess where concrete jutted over the ledge. They'd tried getting her attention, but she couldn't lift herself from the ground to tend to the dirty child beside her, couldn't even bother responding to Elly shaking her shoulders and whining that her head was itchy from their filth.

They'd carried Elly across the river, while Corin had to be dragged like a corpse. They'd cut Elly's hair and massaged soap into her scalp. After, they'd ripped pieces of bread and hand-fed Corin while she sat blank-eyed and silent.

She was twelve, and her parents had been dead for a year, and she couldn't muster the strength to try anymore. It was easier to tune out Elly's crying and pretend she was no longer a person, but a ghost.

"You were a wreck," Harlow said. "Maggie told me your body was there, but your mind wasn't."

Corin hadn't bothered learning everyone's names those first few months, because they didn't feel real. She saw herself living among them as if she were a distant entity, watching from above. There was her body, carrying tables along the riverbank, washing berries to share with the others. They were a group of ten to fifteen vagrants, some young, some old, and a few came and went throughout the seasons. Memories of her new beginning and acquaintances were a blur. They didn't crystallize until the morning she woke to Elly and Harlow's laughter, the two of them skipping rocks down the stream.

Seeing Harlow's gentle gaze toward her sister, Corin had realized it wasn't that she resented her parents for making her the eldest daughter. She just wasn't cut out for it.

"I've thanked you countless times for everything you did," she muttered to the empty space beside her. "But I'm better now, and I don't need you anymore."

She forced her aching bones to move, if only to ignore Harlow's ghost. The flame on her torch was nearly dying, but she saw enough of a path ahead and touched the rocks beside her to feel the wide artery of granite. The passage covered with Elly's drawings turned lower, forcing her to crawl. A rotten-egg smell struck her face, rank and pungent. The longer she crawled, the stronger the stench of decay wafted in the air.

She dragged her match across a rock and lit the torch brighter, raising it to the ceiling to illuminate the rest of the path, only to discover she was no longer alone. Skeletons lined the narrow passage, draped in yellowed bones and ragged clothes. Her nostrils flared at the foul stench thickening the air, as if death had been sealed in a jar for years and she had twisted the lid open.

She buried the back of her hand against her teeth and muffled the urge to scream, letting it die in her chest. None of these people had made it. They could have been her. Or Elly—

No. Corin's eyes scanned the dead, searching for details to identify her sister. The shape of her body, the jut of her bones, the fabric of her clothes. They did not match the bodies here.

"C'mon. It's nothing you haven't seen before," Harlow drawled. "Oh, wait. You weren't there."

Corin fought the urge to vomit as her imagination brought forth familiar bodies strewn across the rocks. She had not been there, but that didn't mean she couldn't picture it. Their hands tied behind their backs. Maggie howling like a feral animal whenever she was threatened. Rowan using his broad torso to shield the women. And Harlow, that damn, stubborn rebel who had planned everything, shouting at the soldiers until gunshots silenced her forever.

Corin knew, logically, that this was not the same passageway where her friends died. The army had sealed the tunnels after their capture. She didn't know what was worse: if she had been a rebel foolish enough to join her friends and die with them, or being the coward who abandoned them to save herself instead.

She paced in the tunnels, frantic eyes searching for familiar relics to identify her sister. Dehydration and hunger overshadowed her senses, turning her vision dizzy as darkness closed in. She kept seeing it. The wet mess of Harlow's open skull. The white sheet of

Maggie's sunken face. Rowan's stiff limbs, unable to shield everyone from the bullets. She stopped at someone's foot and cursed the memories that kept flooding to her mind, warping the bodies in front of her. The tunnels shrank, the walls caving in from the corners. She couldn't breathe. Faces blurred together, strange and familiar. Blue lips, sallow skin, maggots crawling beneath eyelids, digging into her skin.

She had told Harlow not to go to the tunnels. It wasn't enough. She had warned Elly not to chase after fairy tales. Now she would lose her sister too.

The weight of her grief became too heavy. It forced her to her knees and made her give in to her hallucinations. Crying, she bent over a body and let the small shape fit itself in her arms. She kept saying she was sorry, so sorry, as she rocked back and forth, despair consuming her like a tidal wave. Her head pulled back too far, and then she felt the wet patch of rock, the hard *thud* of her skull against the low ceiling, the loss of gravity in her limbs.

Her body tumbled backward. Darkness took her like the bite of teeth. Even as she disappeared, she was still screaming.

CHAPTER 4

103 YEARS AGO

A SCREAM CAME FROM the library. Amelia burst through the doors to find Queen Lilith standing on a table. Their eyes met, and the woman pointed a trembling finger toward the bookshelves. Yellow scales covered a thick length, and three lines of dark brown spots ran down its body. A common garter snake, Amelia recognized, likely one that had wandered in from the greenhouse.

She picked up the snake and cracked open a window, letting the animal slither outside. Meanwhile, Lilith's legs continued trembling atop the table. Amelia reached a hand to help her down. In her grip, she felt warm skin, lean fingers, and a sweaty palm that, surprisingly, had calluses. Their proximity made her notice the freckles on Lilith's sun-kissed cheeks, the birthmark on her chin, and the gleam in her wide brown eyes, one slightly smaller than the other whenever the woman winced or smiled.

Amelia became aware, then, how her presence had its own

absence. She herself had no crooked features or unusual birthmarks. Her gift of beauty was a blank slate. She didn't shine the way Lilith did.

"Thank goodness," the queen sighed with relief. "I was about to whack it with a book, but that would've been a waste of good literature."

Amelia examined the array of tomes splayed over the table. Handmaids dusted each shelf to keep the books pristine, but she had never seen anyone read a single page. Even *The Book of Samael*, rumored to have been a journal left behind by the late king, was just for show, its contents completely illegible.

Lilith's collection looked different. There were cracked spines, pages flipped open, scribbles of ink across dense notebooks. All bookmarked and carefully curated even amid chaos.

"What are you doing?" Amelia asked, following Lilith as the woman pushed a rolling ladder down the aisle. Books wrapped in leather and cloth spilled from floor-to-ceiling cherrywood shelves.

The queen fiddled with her pearl necklace, her eyes scanning the room before they stopped and lit up. She climbed the ladder, plucked a book from the top shelf, and tossed the tome to Amelia to catch.

"I'm drafting a proposal to open Gyldan's borders and establish resettlement programs. I figure the king will listen if I dress it up in more formal language. People in high positions love to use lengthy words for such simple things, don't they?"

Amelia pictured her godmothers' disapproving faces. In council meetings with her father, they had stressed the importance of maintaining the kingdom's borders and protecting Gyldan from invasion. It didn't matter that their neighbors in Zilar were fleeing persecution. Foreigners brought diseases, stole jobs, and took resources away from natural-born citizens. When a nobleman was caught having an affair with a migrant woman from Zilar, Lilith was the babe who had been born from scandal. Amelia assumed the woman would distance herself from her family's reputation when she married the king. Instead, she was doing the opposite.

"Why should we welcome outsiders? Is it not better to take care of ourselves before risking our safety for strangers?" Amelia parroted her godmothers' words, for this was the code that the faeries followed. If Gyldan had not offered them wealth and status, the Fae never would have mingled with human affairs at all. She wondered how quickly they would disappear from the human eye if they no longer had such enticements.

Lilith pursed her lips, which were no longer painted dark like her portrait. She looked more vibrant now that her face was stripped to natural colors. This, Amelia thought, was what the artist should have drawn.

"When I was a child, my mother told me about how Gyldan used to be nothing more than sand. Before it turned to gold, the land was a barren desert that stretched for miles. I liked that idea: that something can be made from nothing."

Her heels clacked against the patterned wood as she slid down the ladder. The momentum made her rush to Amelia with such smooth speed, it was almost as if she was floating.

"I think people can do the same," she said, "and we start with each other."

Up close, Amelia could see how the dark hues of Lilith's eyes flickered under the sunlight like wine. The queen was not pretty in the delicate way in which the godmothers had blessed Amelia to be. Yet there was something radiant about her: the strength in her jaw, the sharp point of her nose.

Perhaps this was supposed to be what beauty looked like, Amelia thought. To care so deeply about something, it brought life in you.

SUNFLOWERS BLOOMED WHEN summer arrived. Amelia kept a fistful of seeds in her pocket. She liked to pluck them from the greenhouse and replant the flowers in glass jars around the library. When sunlight hit the windows and spilled through the jars, the flowers turned their heads and looked up at the sky, following the sun like admiring children.

She mimicked their behavior when it came to Lilith as well. They spent slow afternoons in the library, occupying the space as if it were their private oasis. She learned phrases in different languages from beautiful countries that were torn apart by war. She listened to stories about Lilith's mother fleeing to Gyldan through secret tunnels and working in brothels to survive. Every time, she stared at Lilith, watching the pages of books flutter between her slender fingers, the furrow in her brow, her soft pursed lips.

One day, the queen didn't visit the library until late evening.

Amelia had curled into an armchair and fallen asleep waiting for her. She dreamed of a cottage house, clean sheets drying in the breeze, and a garden of sunflowers that germinated in late spring. The cottage was made of misshapen stone. Forest animals visited the porch for warm tea and nonsensical conversations. It was a silly dream, quick to dissolve as she awoke to Lilith shaking her shoulder.

In the candlelight, shadows appeared beneath the queen's puffy eyes, as if she had been crying. "I didn't think you'd still be here," she whispered.

Had Lilith wanted time alone in the library? Strands of dark hair drifted loosely from her knotted locks. Amelia wanted to brush them away from her face. "Are you all right?"

The woman's gaze was distant, too complicated to discern. A moment of deliberation passed, as if she were evaluating her words carefully.

"Amelia," she said, "do you think I am capable of deception?"

Amelia stared at her, trying to make sense of the puzzle in Lilith's expression. She could not fit the pieces together. She decided it didn't matter. "Of course not."

Then the doors flew open, and she soon realized that whatever she believed didn't matter either. Heavy feet stomped across the room, and candlelight flickered with seething rage under a new presence. Lilith turned around in time for King Victor to strike his palm across her face. Her hip knocked against one of the tables, its legs scraping the floor with an ugly sound that made Amelia wince.

"How long were you going to keep this a secret?" He pronounced each word with a hardened voice and a spray of spittle.

Lilith placed a hand on her bruised cheek. Her jaw was clenched, and in the crevices between her fingers, Amelia spotted tears. "I've told you before," she said. "This time, I didn't want to make you angry again."

"And did you think the midwife would hide this from me as well?"

As they argued, the candlelight grew too bright in Amelia's vision. Wooden shelves stretched and blurred in every corner. She tried to tune out her father's voice, but it was too loud, as if he could shake the books with volume alone.

"The godmothers were right. You are nothing more than a grifter vying for the crown."

"That's not true," Lilith protested. "I want to build Gyldan together. You know that."

"Your barren womb will help me build nothing."

Lilith drew back, as if his words struck harder than his hand.

"Don't look so surprised," he said. "Your father was my closest friend. I did him a favor by marrying you so that you wouldn't be left in disgrace after he died. I at least expected your fertility to be as rampant as your whore mother."

Pieces of their conversation scraped Amelia's ears as she put together the ugly truth. Lilith was never supposed to be her stepmother, nor a proper queen for Gyldan. She must have known this too, as shame warmed her cheeks and made her fists bundle the fabric of her dress into a white-knuckle grip.

Victor's shadow grew taller under the candle flames. "I can tolerate your overzealous ideas, but I will not accept you lying to me. For your deception, you will be exiled from Gyldan by dawn."

The threat knocked the weight out of Amelia's body. Fear charged her forward, the bright reality of Lilith snuffed out like a flame. "No!"

She jumped between them and splayed her arms wide, standing like a shield. Despite her shouts, her voice still trembled, hardly a buffer against the looming figure of her father.

"Please, Father. There must be another way."

His blue eyes crinkled as they settled upon her. The expression only deepened the wrinkles on his face, the sagging skin that betrayed the time he fought so hard against. Gray hairs had spread across his beard, and he could no longer hide them.

"The prosperity of Gyldan rests on its ruler having our blood. If they do not have it, the kingdom will be doomed."

She swallowed hard. She thought about the gold that shimmered in their veins, how she had to strain under the light just to see faint traces of it. Their family's lineage was too fragile. Her father was growing older, his coughs sounding sicker. He was running out of time.

Then again, so was she.

"I will marry a prince," she declared. "Before I turn eighteen, I will find someone to rule after you. He will be brave and strong and smart. I will give him a child, so that the next heir will have our blood."

She steadied her breathing, counting the short future ahead of her. Her mind suppressed the image of a swollen belly, an entire life bursting inside her while she was robbed of her own.

"I will do all of this, but only if Lilith remains queen."

Lilith tugged Amelia's arm, urging her to stop. It was too late. Since Amelia's curse at birth, her fate kept being sealed, over and over again. She stared at her father and silently pleaded with him to give in. He ran a hand down his black hair, stopping where the streaks of gray ended.

"It's not that simple. There needs to be consequences."

"Please," she begged. She wanted to argue that Lilith was good for their kingdom. That no matter how many princes she met, it was Lilith who she thought was brave, and strong, and smart. But according to her father, trust had been broken, and she knew such pleas would be ignored.

She knew, too, there was another thing the king cared about.

"I want her to stay, because she's the only mother I've ever had."

The lie tasted foul on her tongue, but she needed her father to believe it. If Lilith could stay, Amelia was willing to pretend that the only reason she wanted the woman beside her was due to familial attachment. There would be no other explanation, no deeper feelings she could have explored. Nothing that was complicated or wrong.

She would bury the truth so that it would never see the light of day.

King Victor's crinkled eyes turned sympathetic. A long sigh hissed through his gritted teeth. After a tense silence, he turned to Lilith. His hand raised like a threat before she could speak.

"You are lucky my daughter cares for you. But mark my words: If you deceive me again, there will be a steeper price to pay."

Lilith squeezed Amelia's hand, a silent thank-you. Amelia could hardly feel it. Her whole body had turned numb. The candles surrounding them burned too hot. Her mind lifted away from the wax and drifted to the edge of the room. Beyond the windows, the night was pitch-black. She thought of sunflowers perched on sills, the way they stretched toward the sun, as if aspiring to become stars themselves.

But there was no future where things could be different. Darkness always came, and the sunflowers would never become what they dreamed of being. Her feet stayed rooted to the ground. If she tipped any farther, she would sink below the earth.

CHAPTER 5

"SHE'S TRAPPED BELOW the earth," Elly often insisted, her ear pressed to the ground. As a toddler, her tiny fingers would claw garden soil, dirt caked beneath her nails, all in search of a girl who the world was uncertain ever truly existed.

Corin said that even if the fairy tales were true, sleeping comfortably in a big castle was no nightmare for a princess. Still, Elly believed the castle remained underground. On the eve of the princess's eighteenth birthday, the queen brought hired men into the kingdom to assassinate her husband and stepdaughter. The invaders murdered the king while the princess escaped into the forest, only to cross paths with the demon who had cursed her as a baby. The demon tricked the princess into pricking her finger on a spindle and doomed her to eternal slumber. Among the roaring flames of their battle, the prince killed the demon and saved the princess. He brought her back to their castle, only to find it was too late. Even with true love's kiss, she remained asleep forever.

Despite being the successor to the throne, the prince was so consumed by grief that he asked her faerie godmothers to bury the castle underground. He would sink alongside the walls, so that he would never live in a world without his true love. Even when rivaling kingdoms tore down Gyldan's borders and erupted into war, they would never be seen again.

A hundred years later, Corin would disappear with them.

She woke with a scream clawing at her throat, as if she'd emerged from a nightmare. But she hardly remembered her dreams, and soon enough she forgot what she'd seen.

Sharp rocks stabbed her spine like tiny knives as she lay flat on the ground. Dust particles stung the back of her eyelids, as if ants had crawled through the slits and were nibbling the skin underneath. Her eyes were so dry they burned, like she had been crying. Yet all she remembered was the darkness taking her when she fell.

Yes, that was it. She had fallen. Slipped over debris and slid farther underground. Her head had slammed against a rock, rendering her unconscious for what must have been hours.

She rolled over to her side, but the movement shot flashes of pain down her back. Her neck and shoulders had been locked in the same position for too long. A gagging noise burbled from her parched throat. She hunched over, trying to vomit the invisible sand that piled in her mouth, but there was nothing to heave from a hollow stomach.

There was nothing left inside of her. She was empty.

And she was going to die.

She had imagined herself dying before, pictured hundreds of gruesome deaths in her mind, but nothing like this. Stranded after wandering endless miles, buried beneath stagnant air and soil, it seemed too uneventful.

Harlow's laughter echoed through the tunnels. "No, compared to your eighteen years of living, it's too gentle a way to die."

Corin groaned. Even in near death, she couldn't escape Harlow's ghost. She supposed Harlow would have loved the irony. By the time their commune busied themselves making posters and protest materials, Corin had distanced herself from the artisans out of self-preservation, complaining to Elly that these efforts only made them look like criminals putting themselves in harm's way. They'd wanted to send a message to the army, but there was no point risking their lives for a war that would never end.

Now here she was, dying like the rest of them.

Darkness engulfed her in the tunnels. Her coiled body shivered in the cold as she waited for death to wrap her in its box and tuck her away. Surrounded by dust and debris, she would become part of the ground, a skeleton whose bones didn't deserve to be unearthed.

The last words she'd hear from Elly would be a simple truth.

I hate you.

For a moment, there was nothing. Then a new thought emerged from her drowsy haze, like a dim light peeking through the dark clouds of near-death. Her hand roamed over her chest, fingers twitching for the ghost of an object. After her palm came up empty, her fingers jammed into the soiled pockets of her trousers and sifted through dirt.

Her necklace was gone.

Panic triggered her body to roll over. Splinters bit into her palm as she found the broken half of the torch that had slipped from her hand when she fell. She sucked out the splinter, blood dancing on her tongue. Bitter, it tasted. And alive.

She lit the last match in her pocket and held it to the cloth. The small flame radiated an orange glow over the walls. A shadow stretched above her head, inviting her to turn around and meet a skull staring straight into her eyes. The black grains that stripped the skull's translucent skin looked like rotten sand had washed over his corpse. Nausea swirled in her stomach. Flashes of bad memories, blue lips, maggot trails. A familiar body in her arms. An echo of a scream.

She bit back her bile and focused on one point of clarity. The skeleton's brittle finger glinted in the shadows and dangled her necklace, which had been caught on bone. She snatched the chain and wrapped it around her neck. Her palm pressed against her chest as she counted the rapid beats of her heart and wiped the flashbacks from her mind. It was easier if she could focus on the cold metal against her sweat, the smooth touch of her mother's hands when she'd given Corin this pendant, the story she'd told about Corin's grandmother crossing these tunnels to Gyldan.

The necklace was the only reminder Corin had that a future was possible. And she couldn't picture any future without Elly.

She pressed her palms flat on the cavern walls as she crossed deeper inside the tunnels. The torch's dying flame turned fuzzy in her blurring vision. Perhaps it was better she couldn't see clearly, so she could avoid staring at bodies draped over the jagged rocks. She wouldn't think about Harlow or how she'd let her other friends die. She would leave them behind with the rest of the corpses in the tunnels, shutting them out, like her mind did with everything else.

By the time the bodies whittled down in numbers, the sour smell wafting under her nostrils died down. A new scent permeated the air, musky with mildew and notes of copper. Then came an invisible spark, something alive and tingling. The shift in the air remained even as she reached a dead end, the path stopping at a dirt wall that appeared to be a landslide.

It seemed too sudden, too abrupt of an ending. Dizzy from dehydration, she rocked back and forth and deliberated what to do next. When she looked down, she was shocked to find a torn piece of cloth stuck to her boot. Her fingers snatched the maroon cloth so she could inspect the bright blue stitching that clumsily ran along the inseam. She recalled how the needle had pricked her fingers, her annoyance at Elly for tearing a hole in her pants, forcing Corin to practice her shoddy sewing skills before Rowan called her hopeless and fixed it himself. The stitching was an exact match to the clothes Elly had worn when she ran away.

Elly was here. More importantly, she was alive.

Corin dropped to the ground in a panicked frenzy and started digging, searching for traces of her sister to follow her path. A stone floor exposed itself beneath the soil. The concrete had to be paved somewhere. She stared at the dead end of the tunnel, then grabbed the wall, clawing her way through the dirt. Her hands dug for several grueling minutes until the fabric of her gloves thinned to strings and her skin turned raw. She searched until, finally, she found a wooden door on the other side.

She stepped back in disbelief. People came and died searching for a buried castle, waiting to be stirred awake. She couldn't explain what stood before her, how the stories could have possibly been true—just as Elly had said.

THE CASTLE FROM the fairy tale shouldn't have existed. At least, not in this condition. Most of the structure remained intact, but large, gaping holes peppered the sepia-washed wallpaper, as if gnawed by a monster. Velvet drapes had turned maroon from old age, covering cracked windows. Corin tried parting the curtains and coughed from the dust. Outside, the glass revealed dark soil surrounding the castle.

Surely, she was hallucinating. Hunger could do that to a person. Yet the air tingled with something peculiar, like a cold wind that had trapped itself inside and now howled in mourning. Goose bumps prickled her skin, and she clutched the torn cloth tight in her fist. No, it didn't matter how this relic came to be. What mattered was that she needed to find Elly.

She pictured her sister walking through the castle, imagining what might catch Elly's attention first. In answer, watercolors jumped from the hallway. Corin crossed the faded carpet that unfurled rows of paintings along the wall, where kings and queens of Gyldan's past sat decorated in gold. Their bloodline was supposed to prove they were special, untouchable. Yet here they were, strings of parchment hanging off the edges of their destroyed features, every portrait slashed like an open wound.

She stopped in the middle of the hallway where one person remained unscathed. A tall woman sat next to an elderly king and a blond child. White pearls clasped the queen's neck. The bloodred fabric of her gown brought the same color from her pursed mouth. Her auburn hair was tied in knotted locks, and her sharp nose pointed to the air. She looked like someone posing to be royalty, resulting in a stiff upper lip and a set of unsmiling eyes.

Corin pressed her palm to the bumps of paint, drawing a line between the stiff queen and the blond girl whose face was destroyed. She kept hearing her sister's stories about the royal family, doomed by curses and wicked stepmothers, and how this fate had brought them to ruin.

"El," she murmured, "what if you were right?"

Light shone through the door from where she'd come, followed by a crash. She stomped out her torch and tossed it aside. Shouts echoed through crumbled walls, forcing her to scramble toward the opposite end of the hallway.

She burst open doors to an empty ballroom and scanned for a hiding place. Dusty chairs had broken down and lay crooked, bleeding beige filling and feathers over the cracked marble floor, but there was a long sofa that still stood on four legs. As footsteps came closer, she rolled to the ground and ducked behind the sofa's tapestry.

A group barraged the ballroom, stumbling over the marble.

"Ezran! You need to sit down. You can't move too quickly after a ritual."

She peered behind the sofa's tapestry. A limping man barreled forward, followed by three women dressed in satin robes and laced veils. Light sparked from one of the women's fingertips as an armchair mended itself together and stood upright to catch the man when his knees buckled over.

Corin held her breath, forcing her body to freeze like a statue so her shock wouldn't give her away. There'd been rumors that faeries once existed in the forests surrounding Gyldan, some even holding positions of council among the royal family. But since the monarchy's collapse, no faeries had ever been witnessed by human eyes. To Corin, this meant they were never real. Now she couldn't explain the sight before her. Chairs did not move on their own, and ordinary people could not create light from their hands.

If faeries were real, and they had chosen to leave behind a dying kingdom after it no longer served them, there appeared to be at least one human who had convinced these faeries into providing him aid. The man named Ezran struggled to keep balance over the chair, as if the room were spinning and he had just landed in it. He looked pale and sick, the color of his skin matching his steel-white armor and cape. A breath hissed from his lips.

"We need to visit the tower now. The moonflower's going to bloom."

"We still have time before midnight," one of the women said. "You need to preserve your energy before you cross over. We don't know what will be in her subconscious until we arrive."

The others nodded. "You've waited a hundred years for this. What's a few minutes more?"

Ezran looked at them, jaw clenched.

"It's a hundred years and a few minutes more without her."

A heavy silence hung in the air. One of the women placed a hand on his cheek. Color slowly filled his pale skin, as if fighting for its place.

"You protected her when she needed you. Tonight, she'll need you more than ever," she said. "We will bring her back. I promise."

"You know how I feel about promises, Dahlia. I don't break them."

Corin strained to make sense of their conversation, but none of them mentioned seeing a child. Either they hadn't crossed paths with Elly, or they already caught her. The fear of that paralyzed Corin, preventing her from escaping even as the strangers left for another room. Elly was always good at hiding, but Corin didn't know what these people were capable of.

She waited a few minutes after the room cleared before following their path. The door where they'd exited opened onto a winding staircase. She pressed her back against the wall, allowing her to glance in both directions in case more people came, as she climbed sideways along the stairs. The next floor revealed a shorter hallway filled with bedchambers.

She rummaged through each one in a frenzied rush, tossing aside sheets, opening every wardrobe, checking beneath bed frames. Every turn, she found nothing but dust and disappointment.

"Damn it, El," she hissed, "where are you?"

Footsteps came closer from the hallway. She swiped a sharp toothcomb from the vanity before climbing inside a wardrobe. Her hand gripped the tool so tightly she could almost see the whites of her knuckles in the darkness cloaking her.

The door creaked open, and she held her breath. There only came silence. Yet, if she strained hard enough, she could sense a presence on the other side.

His voice spoke, a low sound made of lilting ink that seeped into her core. So smooth and calming that if she could taste it, she wouldn't even realize it was poison leaking down her throat.

"Let me guess what you are," he said. "A peasant hoping to wake up the princess so she can fix your miserable life. A thief scavenging for whatever treasure you can find in old ruins."

The wardrobe felt too small, restricting her breath and closing in on her. His footsteps clacked louder, closer, and suddenly there was too much dust inside her space, too many cobwebs hanging from corners that itched her skin and taunted her to make a sound and betray her hidden fear.

"But I've lived in this castle longer than you've been alive. I've searched every crevice, every place, and still the treasure cannot be found. Which leads me to one conclusion: Amelia has hidden it in her dreams. And I made a promise that I would protect her treasure with my life."

The sound of a sword being unsheathed sliced into her ears.

"She won't be sleeping for long," Ezran said. "But you will."

His sword plunged through the wardrobe as Corin jumped to the side and barely missed the blade. She kicked the door open to

Ezran's chest and lunged forward, slashing his face with the metal handle of the comb. She felt like she'd cut hard marble, some precious art that had been preserved for centuries, one so valuable that her life would be taken as penance for tainting it.

Blood spurted from his cheek as he reared back, buying her a fraction of time to escape the chamber. She ripped off the door handle behind her and jammed the comb into the hole to trap him inside.

At the staircase, she glanced back and forth between both directions, her mind screaming to make a choice. Go downstairs and run away. Go upstairs and find a sliver of a chance that Elly would be there.

She chose when Ezran's sword smashed through the door.

Spiral steps spun in her dizzying vision as she ran up the stairs. Her body was failing her, too weak, too starved. Ezran's boots slapped against concrete, charging close. His sword slashed her heels when they reached the top. She let out a cry as she rammed open a wooden door, the entrance bursting under the weight of her collapse. The three women inside the room gasped at the stranger bleeding before them, as if uncovering a malformed creature lunging from the dark. Corin had bruises and open sores everywhere, blooming like ripe plums over a wretched face. She looked worse than an intruder. She looked like a madwoman.

Maybe she had gone mad after all. Because as she looked up, she swore the girl sleeping inside the tower was the princess herself.

Satin sheets tucked the girl's pale body in a billowing mattress. Blond hair spilled over pillows and lace, while a vine of flowers wrapped around her head like a crown. The flowers were the color of bruises, wrinkled and small and yet to bloom, too ordinary of an accessory compared to the extravagance that surrounded her.

In contrast, a garden of roses covered the wooden frame of the bed like a blanket. The largest one bloomed on the left side of the girl's chest, bright red like bloodstain.

Everything was alive, while the girl looked like she was already dead. Her skin was ashen, her lips more gray than pink. One of the women had lifted the girl's arm, and at the tip of her finger, a drop of blood gleamed under the light. Instead of dripping down her hand, the bead floated in the air as a small, swirling orb of red.

Corin's attention snapped to Ezran as he grabbed her by the collar. The slash she made across his face had already disappeared. She didn't understand how marble could restore its cracks, while her broken body retained every wound in permanent memory.

His pristine face came closer to her broken one. His breath was cold as he snarled, "You don't belong here, thief."

Ezran swung his arm back, his sword ready to plunge into flesh, as she braced for the pain. It came not as darkness, but a blinding white flash. Instead of a blade puncturing, her skin tingled under light. The sound of a distant bell shook the tower, followed by the crackle of air being torn apart.

A hole opened like a glowing mouth. Not on the floor, or the wall behind the bed, but in the empty space above the girl's head. The flowers in her hair lifted in bloom. Their purple bruises washed away into pure white. Petals swirled in the air, the smell of florals mixing with blood.

Then, from the other side, Corin heard her sister.

Elly's voice came from inside the hole, breathy and far away. It reached for Corin's skin, gripping onto her bones, tugging her veins like invisible string. She could recognize that voice anywhere, even as a distant echo. Her sister was there. Somehow, she was inside, calling for Corin.

Suddenly nothing else mattered. Not the cluster of women shouting, not the tightening grip of Ezran's hand on her collar. He tried pulling her away, but she would not let him take this from her. She swung her fist and barely felt the hard crack against his face or the dent in his cold skin. Her legs sprinted forward, chasing Elly's voice, as the tether between them tightened. She leapt to the opening and let light swallow her body. Ezran's presence dissolved behind her like grains of sand slipping through an hourglass. The sleeping princess vanished. The women's shouts turned to echoes. The room spun in a blinding blur. Her vision filled with white, burning so brightly that she could not tell if she had met or escaped death.

As she crossed over, Elly's voice turned clearer.

She's real, Corin.

Corin could have sworn she heard her sister laughing.

I told you so.

CHAPTER 6

102 YEARS AGO

AMELIA TREKKED THROUGH the forest, her boots sinking into snow. White coated the bare trees surrounding her while bits of crystal fell on her cheeks like teardrops. In the distance, the sun barely rose over the castle, hitting her eyeline. She blinked hard from the winter light, pulled the collar of her wool jacket to her chin, and winced at the air nipping her face.

A bulky figure walked beside her, cloaked in bear fur to blend with the towering trees. His muddy footprints were so large they could swallow her own feet. She didn't understand why her father took her to the woods. Winters in Gyldan were so cold that even wild faeries hibernated in the forest, refusing to come out unless humans tantalized them with jewelry and coins. She had asked her godmothers to accompany them on their trip, but they preferred lounging around the castle, content with their crackling furnace and wool blankets made from rabbit fur.

"We worked hard for this life among royalty," Clover harrumphed. "Don't mix us with common nymphs."

"Were the forest nymphs and animals not your friends?" Amelia had asked.

"Worrying about others who no longer serve you, my dear, is a waste of precious time. I choose to be with those who can bring good to my life."

Amelia had assumed Clover meant this literally, as the faerie beckoned another servant to pour wine into her goblet.

And so, Amelia joined the trek with her father alone. All morning, he wore a dour expression and flat mouth. She remained silent to avoid worsening his mood and instead sought distraction from the nature surrounding them. A sweetly whistled warble of a bird played across the passage of white trees. Her eyes followed the sound before stopping at the movement of a new creature in the distance.

Speckles of white covered the deer's light-brown coat. His large ears twitched as falling leaves grazed his head. The tip of his nose pushed around a pile of twigs, and his soft pink tongue flickered as he ate a woody portion of leaves and stems.

The small pleasure of his meal made something flutter in her heart. She wanted to sit beside this deer and brush her hand through his coat, counting the star-colored spots that blanketed him.

"Good find. This one can be your first."

Her father's blue eyes fixed on the deer. A sense of dread filled her stomach, like he'd uncovered a secret she didn't want to share without tainting it. He handed her a bow and quiver that held a dozen arrows.

The purpose of their journey to the woods sliced her like the bitter nip in the air. She pushed the weapon back and shook her head frantically. He ignored her, slinging the strap around her shoulder, and positioned the bow in her trembling hands.

"I can't," she whispered.

"Yes, you can." He kept his voice low so that the deer would not run. "To hunt is to prove you can conquer. It's a reminder we have power."

"I don't want to conquer anything."

"You are the future queen, Amelia. This is what it means to be a ruler."

She gripped the bow as realization sank into her bones. This was the real test she needed to pass. Not whether she could make a good wife or mother, but whether she could stand tall and become a woman worthy of a crown.

Perhaps there were girls who dreamed of conquests and power, but not her.

Her father lined her body perpendicular to the deer. He muttered directions about drawing an imaginary line to the target and standing upright, but she hardly heard him. Her knuckles clenched white over the bow. She stayed trembling, her arrow pointed askew to the ground. Her father leaned over her shoulder to ready her hand and hold it upright. The hedgerow of his beard prickled the side of her cheek like an animal scratching at her.

"I will not be raising a princess." His breath was low, quiet. "I will be raising a warrior."

The tip of the arrow pointed straight at the unsuspecting deer. She breathed hard as she imagined the arrow piercing the deer's flesh, staining the stars on his coat and turning it red like a bloodied sky.

Her hand let go of the arrow only after shifting the bow to the side.

They watched the arrow strike a nearby tree. The deer jumped and scattered into the distance, disappearing before she dropped the bow.

She broke down crying, wiping the drip from her eyes and nose with her sleeves. Silver clouds cloaked the weak sunshine as cold air bit her wet cheeks. Her father bent down on one knee and brushed a thumb over her tears. In her blurry vision, she saw the gray hairs that stemmed from his temple.

"It's all right." His jaw was clenched. "Let's go home."

"IT WAS HER first time, Your Highness. You know she loves animals far too much to harm another living being. That's what makes her so sweet."

Amelia overheard her godmothers talking in the dining room after dinner. She peered from the doorway, where a long oak table stretched from one end of the hall to the other. King Victor stabbed a fork into a piece of venison. The meat had been roasted, a pink hue on the inside exposed between each slice.

"She cannot fend for herself," he muttered.

Dahlia, who had been speaking, shifted her chair legs across the tile floor.

"Perhaps she does not have to. We can still return to our original plan of disguising her until she's safe from Malicine."

"That's not the issue."

"Then what is it?"

A long silence pulsed between them. Candlelight made the blood around the king's plate gleam a sickly shade of red. His eyes took in the wine swirling inside his goblet, retrieving a distant memory from its murky waters.

"When my first wife was with child, we didn't think the baby would survive. Then Amelia came out, kicking and screaming. I was too amazed to even be disappointed that she wasn't a boy. The way she emerged into the world so defiantly, I thought she would grow up to be a fierce woman. Spunky and loudmouthed, just like her mother."

There was fondness in his voice, tinged with a foretelling of defeat. The king drank from his cup, his throat bobbing up and down until he eventually set the empty goblet on the table. He leaned forward and pinched the bridge of his nose, squeezing his eyes shut.

"But she couldn't have turned out more different from what I imagined. She talks to animals and inanimate objects as if they are her friends. She stares at the sky longer than she can look into another human's eyes. She's there, but she's never present."

He pushed the chalice farther away from him. Drunk eyes roamed across the wolfskin blanket that lay scattered in front of the fireplace. Preserved skulls and animals sat on the mantel. The room had been decorated with relics from his younger days, a time when he was a hunter before he became king.

Amelia had heard stories about his own father taking him to the woods, shooting the creatures that inhabited the wild, and coming home to make fresh stew. He had shared his childhood tales with pride, his chest puffed, his face flushed with glory. This was what it was like to be a man, and wasn't that what made a person stronger than all?

"I'm not afraid of my daughter dying," he said. "I'm afraid of her growing up to be a coward."

Murmurs shifted among the godmothers, but their responses faded in her ears. Her feet slowly backed away from the door before sprinting down the hall. She reached her room and dove into bed, burying her face in pillows and hiding from the rest of the world.

That night, she understood the cruel irony of her birth. When Amelia was a baby, her godmothers had blessed her with three gifts: beauty, song, and true love's kiss. Beauty proved itself whenever men ogled her pearl face, golden hair, and long lashes. Song revealed itself as handmaids fawned over her voice echoing down the corridors, sweet and light as a hummingbird's. True love's kiss promised itself to be the cure to her curse, the answer for whenever she needed a reason to wake up and keep living.

She was born a beautiful girl with a beautiful life.

They told her she could become anything.

And so, she became nothing.

CHAPTER 7

LIGHT SWALLOWED CORIN, scattering pieces of her into fragments as fine as windblown sand. Stars exploded around her ears. Their debris peppered her skin and sank beneath to set her veins on fire. Rays broke through every particle in her body as she punctured through an ocean of bright blue.

Water filled her lungs before it turned to air. Bubbles burst from her feet and then transformed into clouds. Her limbs flailed forward, her body hurtling between ice crystals in the atmosphere. Wind whistled through her hair and whipped her face as she descended through an endless sky. A white flash ripped into her bones before she came together again, the tiny particles of her conscience clustering together to form a body landing softly in snow.

The wind slowed to a stop.

Then the world waited in silence for her.

She opened her eyes to a hole filled with light in the sky, its rims swirling in a thin coat of red. Blood slipped from the fringes and scattered into pieces. One fell in her palm like a snowflake, drying like a scab, before it dissolved. The hole closed above her, as if it had never existed at all, and the sky returned to normal as a portrait of pure white with saw-toothed trees. One branch bent beneath her weight, its wooden arms cradling her in a blanket of soft snow as if she were a newborn.

Across from her, between another tree's limbs, someone was watching.

The stranger was different in an otherworldly way. Pearls glistened across her cheeks like teardrops and embedded her porcelain skin, dappling around her chin and forehead. Snowdrop flowers intertwined her silver hair, spilling over a pale lace dress with nightingale embroidery and beaded feathers. Her eyes looked like sea glass, narrowed and glaring, as if Corin were an intruder that she would kill with her bow.

Corin should have retreated at the sight of the weapon, but she couldn't move. The stranger's gaze pierced into her skin, as if she were peeling the layers underneath to look inside. Their eyes held each other for an infinite moment, the soft fall of snow blurring in the background, clumps of snowflakes catching in their lashes. The quiet gripped her, bit into her skin, left her feeling raw.

Because the stranger didn't just look at her. She didn't speak to her, spit at her, or even pity her, as if she was a ghost who had already passed.

This person *saw* her.

And that was the most dangerous thing of all.

Then a breeze came, and the stranger's expression shifted into softness. Her eyebrows raised, her lips parted, as if realizing something Corin couldn't pinpoint. She lowered the bow and tucked away the unused arrow. Her silver hair flickered in the sunlight as she fell backward, disappearing into the snow like a mirage.

Corin lunged forward and tried to peer below the branches, but the girl's lace dress and powdered hair vanished in a blanket of white. Not even the slightest sign of footprints marred the earth. She disappeared as quickly as she'd appeared.

Corin's eyes darted around the tree in panic. Her leg stretched to another branch as she tried to maneuver herself on to it. She hooked her arm over one of the limbs and thought she had a good grip, until the wood snapped.

She yelped when she fell, but the landing was soft and rendered her quiet. Bits of crystal fell from her hair as she turned around and scanned her new surroundings. The sun barely rose from the mountains in the distance, rays of light shining between the cracks of trees. The bright colors were too overwhelming for her senses. She rubbed her eyes before stopping at a disturbing realization.

Her hands, once shattered, were now whole.

She took off her gloves and flexed her fingers, waiting for something to crack, yet every bone remained in place. Her fingers ran through her coarse hair, nails digging for dried blood and open wounds that no longer existed.

No. This wasn't right. Her breaths quickened, panicking. She wanted to scream that this was a trick, some trap to catch her off guard. She should have been dead, but the fact that she was alive scared her. The gentle snow of this place was more frightening than the bitter cold of Gyldan. It told her that she did not belong, because she was not suffering.

She jumped at a sudden movement from the corner of her vision. Behind a wide tree trunk, a fox appeared. The animal was small and wild, his pointed ears twitching upon sight of her. His tail whipped around as black, beady eyes stared into hers. A lump formed at the base of her throat. Something unsettling swirled in her stomach, a familiar burning sensation at her fingertips. Before she could make sense of it, the fox moved closer.

She took a step back. "What are you?" she hissed.

The fox tilted his head.

"I am breakable." His voice was distorted, as if his lungs had been damaged. "But you already knew that, didn't you?"

Her hands scorched in response. She reached slowly for his fur, her fingers stroking through hearth-spun browns. Beneath his coat, she felt it: The cracks in his skin. The shards in her hands. The memory cutting into her like a knife.

Then something hit the back of her head, hard and cold. The fox ran away and disappeared behind the trees. She spun around and prepared to defend herself against the attacker until she saw the spikes of black hair and the small silhouette of a young girl. Corin's heart stopped in her chest. Flecks of snow turned the child's hair into a salt-and-pepper halo, and her dark eyes gleamed with recognition. The girl tossed a second snowball in the air, catching it expertly with her palm, as a mischievous grin tugged at her lips.

"Took you long enough to get here," Elly said.

Corin didn't move, afraid that the slightest movement would make Elly disappear. But her sister stood in front of her, solid as the truth. Every scab and scar that lined her kneecaps and elbows, every dark freckle that stained her cheeks like stars.

"El," Corin breathed, "what are you—"

A second snowball struck her face. This time she fell with her feet kicking off the ground. She shook ice out of her eyes in time to see her sister running through the trees, her laughter fading in the distance.

A strangled sound ripped out of Corin's throat. "Stop!"

She caught up to Elly and barreled her to the ground. Their

bodies collided in the snow, her sister's small frame pinned underneath Corin's heavy chest. Corin wrapped her arms around Elly so tight their bones could have fused together.

"Don't ever run away from me again." Desperation cracked in Corin's voice, stilling the small body beneath her.

In the silence, she held her sister close. The familiar smell of musk and sweat wafted under her nose as she buried her face in Elly's hair and let the short spikes tickle her cheeks. Elly's breath was warm against her skin, and she took comfort in hearing it. These were the sounds she needed to fall asleep back home: the familiar drum of Elly's heart, the pulse of her veins. Proof that they were still alive, bright and beating.

Elly's voice was muffled as she said, "You still need to say it."

"Say what?"

"That I was right and you were wrong."

"What the hell are you talking about?"

Elly pushed herself off Corin to stand. She placed her hands on her hips in indignation.

"I told you the tale of Sleeping Beauty was real. You saw her in the tower and jumped through that portal, didn't you?"

Corin tilted her head to the sky. The portal of light had closed and disappeared with the clouds. The smell of blood and flowers had already vanished from the air.

"Her godmothers said they were going to cross over to her subconscious," Elly said. "That must be where we are now."

"How did you hide from them and find your way here?"

"Because I'm smarter than you, obviously."

Corin scowled. "No, you ran away just to prove a point."

"You still haven't admitted I was right."

She opened her mouth to argue, then stopped. She couldn't give another explanation for what happened in the castle. She didn't even understand how Ezran hadn't found and killed them already. The path had closed after she jumped through. Somehow, no one else could open it again.

Elly had predicted everything. The castle buried underneath Gyldan, the sleeping princess hidden from the world, the moonflowers set to bloom. And yet, even so—

"It doesn't matter if you were right. That was the stupidest thing you've ever done. You could've died, El. That man would've killed you. You're lucky you escaped, or I would've found you rotting in the damn ground."

Corin tried to ignore the ache in her chest and strain in her throat. She didn't want to picture a stiff body in the tunnels, the limp shape of her sister and her withered skin. How Corin would have had to hold her and feel the weight of her hollow stomach and stiff bones. It was easier to replace this feeling with anger instead, to yell at her sister instead of admitting the gut-wrenching fear of losing her.

Irritation simmered between them, infecting Elly as she jabbed a finger in Corin's direction.

"If I hadn't looked for the princess, you wouldn't have done anything. You'd have stayed exactly where you were, and we would've been stuck and miserable in Gyldan. I don't want to live a life where nothing changes."

The pit of Corin's stomach filled with shame. So it was true. Elly *had* hated her life with Corin. She hated it so much that she ran away to chase after a fairy tale.

Elly stormed off, heading toward the frozen lake. Streaks of light purple tinted the pool, a pastel color that mixed like paint from weak sunlight and pale skies. Corin ran across the ice and grabbed

Elly by the wrist. On the lake's surface, their reflections were a blur, hardly distinguishable as two silhouettes instead of one.

"Stop running," she snapped. "We can't get separated again."

Elly spun around. "Then why didn't you stop me before?"

Cold air stung Corin's cheeks. A crack formed in the ice, and it sounded like it came from her chest. She let go of Elly's hand and opened her mouth to speak. Once again, nothing came out. It was becoming harder to provide answers to her sister. The last time she did, Elly ran away.

At her silence, Elly scoffed. "You were glad I was gone."

"That's not true." Corin's assertion sounded more like a plea. It was easier to pretend they had just gotten into another fight. But this was different. She remembered Elly's last words to her, the pain that laced her sister's throat as she said it.

I hate you.

She reached out for her sister until a violent gust of wind ripped her fingers from Elly's cheek. Their feet were torn off the ground, their bodies lifted in the air, tugged like puppet strings by some invisible force. Elly's back struck against tree bark while Corin's body was flung in the opposite direction. Wide cracks burst open in the lake like an open mouth about to swallow her. Corin's legs fell into freezing water, shocking the rest of her limbs. She shouted for Elly, but her sister looked dazed, as if the girl were fighting off unconsciousness.

Corin climbed over the ice with chattering teeth and frozen limbs screaming in pain. An earsplitting screech rang in the air and forced her to look up. The world peeled back branches as a winged creature tore across the sky, landing in the snow and rumbling the ground. A long neck craned around the edge of the lake before slitted eyes fixed on her.

Poison-green irises narrowed into sharp slits. The creature charged forward, shaking the ground with each step. As fire broiled inside its mouth, she realized this was no ordinary monster, but a dragon about to kill them both.

CHAPTER 8

136 YEARS AGO

ONCE UPON A time, on the coldest night of the darkest winter, Malicine was born.

Bright white stars gazed upon snow-frosted trees. Clusters of nymphs gathered in the forest, their bodies cloaked in silk gowns and fluttering between branches. Their excited whispers disturbed the forest's silence before bells chimed in celebration.

A newborn faerie was arriving soon. A little girl, one who would surely be small and wide-eyed and beautiful, just like them.

The naked moon smiled upon them in the sky, but it especially shone for three faeries. They pushed each other to the side so that they could get the best view of the newborn. Dahlia, the oldest faerie of twelve years, walked ahead of the other two, her chin held high the entire journey as if to prove a point.

She shot a dirty look at the middle child of ten years, Iris, who kept collecting snowflakes in her knitted gloves and getting her hands wet. But it was the youngest sister who Dahlia lectured the most. Clover, despite being eight years old, had yet to learn manners. Her teeth chattered loudly in the frost, and steams of breath blew out of her pouted lips whenever she complained about the cold.

Someday, when they visited the king of Gyldan, Clover would have to learn how to make a proper impression with human royalty. The winter nights were bitter, but if they secured a spot in his council, their new, luxurious lives would become the envy of the other nymphs.

Still, an unspoken silence cloaked the three of them like a patch of ice fog. A new faerie meant the king's attention would be further divided. Already the three sisters together felt stifling.

They stood in the inner rows of the circle that gathered around their mother. Sweat slicked across her pale forehead as her back leaned over a bed of moss. She took refuge underneath a willow tree, where nymphs gathered a barrier of twigs and leaves, casting magic to prevent snow from falling inside. A few faeries brushed moist strands of hair away from her face. Others counted her deep breaths and extended glowing palms, keeping her warm.

Dahlia's heeled shoes tapped against the snow. She told herself the gesture was from impatience, not dread. Yet she couldn't help but replay the past few months in her mind. She remembered the wails of pain and several times she watched their mother nearly collapse, tears streaking from bloodshot eyes. Their mother described the pain as a beast clawing its way out of her womb. She would squeeze out a few words before reeling forward and clutching her stomach, shrieking at the sharp kicks against her insides. On her worst days, when the three sisters clamped their hands over their ears to shut out her earsplitting wails, Clover would cry in fear that their mother was dying.

Tonight, her screeches made the saplings shiver around them. Dahlia had witnessed the birth of her two sisters to earn this intuition, but this birth felt different. A bitter wind nipped their ankles, like teeth scraping against flesh. She sensed the baby emerging soon.

With their mother's final push, the head of the baby came into view. But rather than a round head of flesh, a pair of horns tore through their mother, ripping her apart.

The nymphs screamed. The baby had sickly skin, green as old spinach. Its cries pierced their ears, a wail that turned garbled as it began choking on their mother's blood. Sharp nails grew from tiny fingers, gnarled and twisted like hooks. The sisters recoiled in disgust as the baby slithered out of their mother, who remained limp in her bed of dead leaves, the frail fragments of her life draining.

Dahlia jumped forward and thrust her open palms to the creature. Moss slipped away from the ground like melting ice. The barrier of twigs and leaves flew toward the monster and stacked itself into a makeshift cage. The other faeries dragged their mother's limp body away from the creature, but she had already taken her last breath, a life lost for a monstrous one. The stench of death and life mixed together in unholy matrimony.

Inside the cage, the newborn's screeching sounded like knives scratching against plates, a sound so horrible that Dahlia wanted to scream to drown them out. She saw Iris curled beside a tree trunk to retch the contents of her stomach, while Clover fell to her knees, crying until her face turned red in the snow.

Slowly, Dahlia paced toward the cage, where the creature's wailing turned hoarse with each passing minute. She looked closer beyond the foliage of dead leaves. Blood and sweat slicked over the baby's green skin. Black horns protruded from its temples, the same ones that had torn apart their mother.

The faeries recoiled upon sight of the grotesque creature, for their mother had not given birth to a baby sister.

She had spawned a monster.

CHAPTER 9

THE MONSTER STOOD at least twenty feet tall, the color of rotten grapes washed over its scales. Long claws scraped against the ice with a sickening sound that made Corin clamp her ears after getting out of the lake. A bloodred gem in the dragon's chest flickered in the corner of her vision. Inside swirled a cloudy liquid, the familiar scent of iron wafting through the air. She tried to pinpoint where she remembered the smell from, but everything else was too foreign. The colossal creature flickered its forked tongue between its teeth, as if anticipating the taste of her flesh.

Instead of Corin's direction, the dragon charged toward where Elly was draped over a tree and snatched the girl in its mouth. Her body dangled in the air, the collar of her shirt barely held within the monster's bared teeth. She shrieked Corin's name, and Corin could feel it then, the crack in her heart, like ice breaking apart the lake.

Corin chased after them by cutting into the snowy path, but with each flap of the dragon's wings, gusts of wind pushed her backward. She dove to the ground to stay flat and grip mounds of snow for leverage. She wanted to scream for Elly, but her voice was too muffled by the snowstorm, her body as insignificant as an ant in a sheet of white.

No, Corin thought fiercely. She'd just found her sister. She would not lose her again. She sprinted forward and leapt off the slope, hurtling into the air at the same time the dragon took flight off the hill. Her body smashed against the monster's tail. A pained gasp escaped her lungs as pain rippled across her abdomen. Her stubbornness had to override the pain as she forced her arms to wrap around the tail's spikes and cling on tight.

The wind howled as they soared several feet above the trees. A fierce blizzard washed the world in white. She locked her elbows and crawled over the monster's scales to get closer to Elly, still trapped in the dragon's mouth. She grunted from the ice pellets raining on her face, pushing forward as if it didn't feel like a hundred tiny daggers were stabbing into her skin. What she wasn't prepared for was the creature circling around a jagged mountain, swiveling its back, and smashing her body against the rocks.

Sharp gravel tore through her skin. She screamed as she let go.

"No!"

She barely caught onto the end of the dragon's wing, her body flailing in the snowstorm. A blast of wind turned over her torso. A sharp rock nested itself at her side, stuck like a knife. She felt like she was being split open. Even as she forced her legs to latch onto the dragon's wing, her arms burned as she pulled up the rest of her weight.

The pain was too much. One of her hands slipped, and soon the other one would follow. She couldn't let this be the end. She'd lost too much, and if she were to fall, she'd take everything down with her.

Her free hand pulled the rock from her side and plunged the jagged end into the dragon's flesh. The stone punctured the monster's wing like a stake. The dragon emitted a wounded screech and dove into the peak of a mountain. The world turned upside down as they toppled into the snow. Panic forced her to roll herself upright and locate Elly's collapsed figure at the edge of the cliff.

"El!"

Her shout only caught the dragon's attention as it whirled its head in her direction. The black slits of its eyes thinned as it stomped closer. She dove into the snow, frantically digging for another sharp rock to use. Her palm brushed against something hard as the snow uncovered a hilt instead.

She blinked in disbelief. The hilt was not the leather-skin grip of an old dagger, but a crescent-shaped pommel with a blade the length of her torso. Snow slipped off the steel, and its shiny reflection showed her own bewildered expression, a pair of widened black eyes that could not believe she'd stumbled across a warrior's sword.

Both her hands attempted to lift the weapon, but the blade was so heavy it strained her arms. She swung with her full body weight and stumbled forward. The movement was slow and clumsy, giving plenty of time for the dragon to rear its neck and dodge. The creature snapped its jaw forward and towered over her. She choked under its hot breaths, her skin burning from sparks that flickered from its mouth.

The bloodred gem on its chest glowed, and there it was again, the familiar scent of iron. She stared at the fork-shaped tongue that slithered over its teeth, the mouth that opened so wide she could have disappeared in one breath. She braced for the tear of flesh, the plunge of teeth.

Then a blur of white smacked the back of the dragon's skull. The snowball was so tiny in comparison to the creature that it would have felt like nothing more than an itch on impact. The sphere slicked off the dragon's torso and melted, the interruption turning into a measly puddle.

She spun around to the edge of the cliff, where Elly stood wide-eyed and shaking. Crumbs of snow stuck to her trembling hand. Corin cursed her sister for doing something so stupid.

The dragon turned to Elly. An orange glow smoldered over its stomach, the low hum of a growl shaking the ground. Heat radiated across its scales as flames scorched inside its body, swelling, bursting, until they exploded in a fiery ball.

"El, run!"

The scream that left Corin's body strained with terror as she sprinted for the cliff's edge to outrace the fire's rolling tide. She jumped in front of Elly, one arm wrapped around her sister's head for cover, the other thrusting the sword like a shield. Flames hit hard against the steel, licking her hands, the sting of burns biting into her skin.

She waited to be consumed by flames. Instead, the fire twisted around her sword. Steel gleamed as heat ricocheted and shot back at the dragon in a fiery whirl. Scales ignited in waves of bloody red. The creature screeched and recoiled, caught in its own fire. Its silhouette danced in a wall of vermilion before shrinking into a black figure. Her eyes strained to make sense of their silhouette, but the shadow keeled over the ledge of the cliff before plummeting down below.

The howling halted when the dragon hit the snow. A hard *thud* echoed throughout the mountains before the land returned to quiet.

Snow drifted softly to the ground with the blizzard stopped. She dropped her sword and fell to her knees.

She'd done it. She'd protected Elly.

Relief washed over her like the sweat slicking her forehead. Her shaky breaths struggled to outpace her frantic heart, and she had to remind herself that, through some miracle, they were safe.

"Why did you come back?"

The question stunned her. She turned to Elly and took in the widened look in her sister's eyes. Elly appeared genuinely confused, but surely the girl was in shock. She barely caught her own breath as she continued.

"You didn't have to save me. You could have run, and you would have been safe."

Corin punched Elly's arm, ignoring her sister's yelp.

"That's for asking stupid questions," she snapped. "I'm always going to be there for you, whether you like it or not."

Elly rubbed her arm with a grimace, then lowered her gaze to the snow, taking a sudden interest in her shoes. Corin knew the silence meant her sister was putting together the right words to say. She waited for a thank-you, even a childish dismissal. Instead, Elly finally met her eyes.

"I didn't mean to be gone for so long. When I ran away, I knew it would be okay, because you would find me. You always do."

Corin's heart clenched. She wanted to run her fingers through Elly's bristly hair and pull her into an embrace so she could feel not only her warm skin, but the veins pulsing beneath it. Smoke hung off their lips, thick and white as the clouds that parted above them. Snowflakes drifted slowly, melting under their lashes. A full sun emerged from the sky and tingled their skin with warmth.

Then laughter echoed from the cliff, breaking their reverie.

Corin grabbed Elly's hand as a figure with green skin appeared from the edge of the rock. Black horns protruded from the cliff-side like gnarled hooks as the figure grew taller. Their crimson lips twisted into a sharp smile with fangs jutting out. The cloak over their shoulders trailed behind like a black river. Their crooked fingers curled around a wooden staff where, at the top, a familiar bloodred amulet was embedded in the wood.

A raven soared through the sky and perched on top of the staff. His eyes were red and cloudy, matching the haze trapped inside the amulet.

"Bravo," the horned figure said. "What a hero you are, flinging around a sword and defeating such a scary beast. Don't you feel so special?"

Their words slithered like a snake, dripping with venom. Corin pulled Elly behind her and stepped forward. "Who are you?"

The stranger clicked their tongue, a fleshy pink organ in the shape of a fork. Their dark lashes fluttered, and she recognized the black slits in their pupils, like a cut that had been reopened.

"You don't recognize me?" A twisted smile split the creature's face. "I'm Malicine, the dragon you killed. Or, at least, you thought you did."

She took in the stranger, towering at six feet tall, and recognized their features. Dark purple scales ornamented their cape, and the black horns on their skull were the same as the ones that protruded from the dragon's head. Even the jewel encrusted in their staff glowed the same way the amulet did from the creature's scales, a strange fog swirling beneath the surface.

She grabbed her sword and charged ahead. Malicine pivoted as the blade swung, watching her stumble over the snow. She lunged for them again, but when they waved their staff, the sword froze into ice so bitingly cold it slipped from her hands. The frosted blade shattered into pieces.

"Enough fooling around. I swear, what is it with humans and big swords? You aren't the first person I tricked into thinking they killed a dragon, you know."

"Why did you attack us?" Elly demanded.

The black slits of Malicine's eyes thinned as they studied Elly. Veiled thoughts passed behind their face like shadows. They exchanged glances with their raven in shared scrutiny.

"Your sister wanted to protect you and feel like a hero. I was merely playing along with her whims."

"How would you know anything about what I want?" Corin snapped.

Malicine's cape spun in the wind as they stepped to the edge of the cliff. Their arms gestured toward an endless stretch of white, where infinite rows of saw-toothed trees surrounded chalky mountains in the distance.

"Because this is the dreamworld, where your subconscious desires come to life."

A snowflake drifted to their face. They held up their finger, the sharp tip of their nail barely grazing the crystal before the jewel in their staff glowed. The crystal froze in mid-motion. Even the snow falling around them stopped, suspended in the air. Birds stilled in the sky like puppets dangling from invisible strings. Then, in a fraction of a second, the snowflakes hardened into floating icicles. Malicine pointed their finger, sending shards to Corin and Elly's faces like flying daggers.

Corin covered Elly with her back and flinched. A moment passed and she didn't feel the cold stab through flesh. She looked up and sucked in a breath, refusing to blink. The crystals hung in the air, a width of a needle away from pricking her eyes.

"Now it's my turn for questions," Malicine said. "Who are you and what hole did you crawl out of?"

She still held her breath, afraid that if her head moved forward, she would slice her eyeball against the ice. Through gritted teeth, she hissed her answer.

"I'm Corin. This is Elly. We come from the kingdom of Gyldan."

Malicine cocked an eyebrow, as if she'd misspoken. The crystals melted and hit her face with freezing water. She reeled back, spitting out ice.

"You came from the most prosperous kingdom in the human world, and you look like that?"

Annoyance slipped through her chattering teeth. "It's not prosperous. It's a rotten place filled with soldiers who'd kill any child if it meant claiming a piece of land."

"That's not the Gyldan that I remember."

"Well, whatever you remember, that's not where we're from."

Despite the bitterness in her response, Malicine's expression shifted into contemplation. They stroked their jaw in thought before their gaze locked onto Elly like a target.

"You, child. Tell me the truth."

Elly froze in place, paling under Malicine's stare. She opened her mouth to speak until Corin jutted her arm between the two. "Stay away from—"

Sharp nails carved into Corin's throat as Malicine hoisted her body up like a rag doll. She choked under their grip, boots dangling in the air. Impatience made the green of Malicine's eyes bubble like acid.

"I wasn't talking to you. You have a liar's spirit. I can see it in you. But children do not lie." They looked down at Elly. "You, little one, may be the closest thing your sister has to honesty."

Elly's throat bobbed, but the rest of her body did not tremble. Instead, she straightened her back, lifting her chin as she looked Malicine in the eye.

"Let Corin go, and I'll tell you whatever you want to know."

Malicine tossed Corin into the snow as easily as swatting a fly. She gasped for air, kneeling over the ice while Elly rushed to her side to hold her.

"Aw. What a protective pair of sisters you are." Malicine hardly sounded touched. "I'll take your deal, child. The two of you will come to my castle and explain how you arrived from Gyldan. Then I'll decide what to do with you."

Elly agreed at the same time Corin said no. Malicine smiled, as if catching Corin in a lie.

Corin hissed to her sister, "That monster's going to kill us."

"Trust me," Malicine said, "if I wanted to kill you, you would have been dead the second you landed here."

Elly didn't look at either of them. Instead, her gaze drifted to the mountains, the fresh fall of snow, the bright-red cardinals that chirped from white-coated trees. A quiet solitude that brought peace, unlike the hollow cold of Gyldan that strangled its people with frost. She glanced down at her worn-out shoes with the dirtied rubber soles nearly falling off, how out of place they looked in the clean sheets of white.

"Is it much of a life if it feels like we're already dead?"

An answer lodged in Corin's throat. She wanted to say yes, that there was more to their lives beyond this, that they had suffered for a reason. But nothing came from her lips. They both knew it would have been a lie. The truth, one that she'd learned time and time again, was that sometimes people suffered and died and there was no good reason for any of it.

She nodded while silently cursing the illusion of choice. Malicine waved their staff to take the sisters away. Above, cardinals scattered across the blue sky, wings beating with freedom once denied to them in another world.

CHAPTER 10

122 YEARS AGO

BEFORE MALICINE BECAME a dragon, they dreamed of becoming a bird.

They dreamed it so often that they would awaken to the thud of their body hitting the ground. Then their eyes would open, and reality would sink in like the heavy weight of their heart. They were not a bird, but a child trapped in a cage. The enclosure was tall and narrow like a cabinet. Instead of a hinged front, their sisters crafted iron bars to reveal slivers of the world around them. The smallest ray of light leaked from the sole window of the cabin. A bitter taste of what they would never have.

A trickle of blood streamed down their forehead and stung their eyes before they blinked. They had reopened their wounds from striking their horns against the iron bars, trying to tear the spikes from their head. But the horns stayed where they were, a deformity that sprouted from their temples like weeds they couldn't rip out.

The more the horns grew, the more Malicine grew. It became harder to believe their cage used to be as small as a chest box. In the fourteen years following their birth, their sisters had enchanted the size of their crate to grow along with their body. The iron bars expanded just enough for them to stretch their limbs, but never enough to spread their wings.

They swallowed dry saliva and counted the number of times they watched the sliver of sunset through the gap in the crawl space.

Three times.

It had been three days since their sisters left for Gyldan.

The faeries didn't bother to refill their empty bowl, like they were a neglected dog. Malicine wanted to rip their sisters apart and feed their flesh to every starving creature in the forest. They imagined the three faeries dining in a lavish castle with the Gyldan king, feasting on wide plates of venison and bowls of rabbit stew, the very same animals that lived among them in the wild. How ironic it was to be a faerie from these forests, wanting so badly to be chosen by a king who killed animals for sport.

It was their sisters' dream to serve the royal family of Gyldan. Ancient tradition tied both species together: The royal family offered wealth and status, while the chosen faeries extended magic and wisdom in return. Dahlia, Iris, and Clover wanted this prestige more than anything. Meanwhile, the thought of serving anyone made Malicine want to heave the contents of their stomach, if they had anything left.

They were hunched over cold ground when a shadow blocked the light from the window. Perched on the broken sill stood a raven with eyes as red as blood. He had a broad neck and unkempt feathers at his throat, yet the tip of his beak was sharp as a knife.

Here they were, a weak little child shriveled up in a cage, while this bird stood free. Malicine wondered if the raven understood the cruel irony.

His curved beak opened, and a deep croak rumbled from his throat.

"You have his blood. I can smell it on you . . ."

Malicine's pulse hummed. His voice was clear and crisp, sinking into their green skin.

"How can I understand what you're saying?" they demanded. "What are you?"

The raven moved across the ledge with a two-footed hop. Malicine spotted blood staining his black feathers. His head hung weary.

"Oh, I am so hungry," he moaned. *"I don't suppose you have an extra pair of eyeballs for me to eat . . . it would be too strange to taste his blood from you . . ."*

"Answer me," they snapped. "Whose blood are you talking about?"

Red pupils glinted in recognition. An ugly and harsh sound rippled from his chest, almost like he was laughing.

"You do not know, even though you are the spitting image of him," the raven mused. *"You are the descendent of my master, the Demon King."*

"There's no such thing. Only humans become kings."

"Ah, but there does exist a king in the Otherworld."

Cold sweat slicked their palms. They swallowed hard and asked, "Where is the Otherworld?"

The raven croaked under his breath. *"I have wandered so long in this world that I hardly remember what the other one was like."*

Malicine scowled. "Some useful raven you are."

They had wondered about their heritage before, but saw only a corpse in their mother's death and a shadowy figure in their father's absence. Half of them was Fae, and that half alone was why their sisters never killed them, for it was against principle for faeries to murder their own. The other half of Malicine remained a monstrous enigma, one that they wore on their green skin.

Malicine watched the raven's wings hover in rigid motion. The blood from his wounds had dried into scabs around his throat. His wingtips looked burnt at the ends, like a match long left out.

"He left you behind too," they murmured.

His gaze flickered in an unreadable expression. Weak legs hunched him forward, old and weary from wandering a foreign world for too long. Malicine felt a strange sense of solidarity with this creature, so unlike the demon's fair-colored predecessors who made their differences repugnant.

"I have tried to return to my world for centuries, but I cannot find a way to cross over. But you . . . you are a part of him. You can find the portal to the Otherworld."

Malicine twisted their lips. The iron bars surrounding them closed in. They wondered, in the raven's dreary efforts to survive, if he had turned blind enough to not notice their entrapment.

"I don't know how to find something like that. Even if I were to figure it out, I can't break free."

"Ah, but yes, you can."

"Because I have his blood?" they spat. "Clearly, that has benefited me well so far."

The raven's eyes shone like beads. He looked intensely at them, like he could peer beneath their skin. *"Because I can feel the anger boiling inside of you. And where I come from, you can do many things with anger."*

Malicine went quiet. A rock sat at the pit of their stomach, one they hadn't dared to uncover. A distant rumbling buried inside their chest and threatened to burst.

They jumped at the scraping sound of a wooden hinge opening. Moonlight spilled onto the floorboards. Three shadows emerged from the door, laughing in unison. Pale women with cheeks flushed in feigned demureness and footsteps as light as the fresh air they breathed from outside.

Clover slapped a hand over her chest in mock surprise, as if she hadn't the faintest idea that they'd trapped Malicine down here for years.

"Oh, what a shame you missed our trip. Our meeting went exceedingly well," she bragged. "I wouldn't be surprised if the king asked us to live in his castle by next sunrise."

"Let's not be presumptuous," said Dahlia, trailing behind her. "The official ceremony won't be until his daughter is born. Then our gifts will be put to the test."

"The family already adores us. Why wait for something we know will happen?"

A pair of keys jangled in the air. Brass rings twirled around Iris's finger as she let the skeleton key rattle in her hands. The toothed end smiled wickedly at Malicine.

"Don't worry. When we move into the castle, you can still live with us. Maybe your new cage will be made from gold."

Raucous laughter scraped Malicine's ears like the dead trees of winter nights. They felt the rumbling in their chest again, a heat of molten lava threatening to erupt. As Iris turned to the cage, Malicine leapt forward and shot their hand through the iron bars. Sharp nails scratched across their sister's pale face. Fresh blood spurted in the air as Iris screamed. Malicine's fingers curled into fists, bits of flesh wedged beneath their nails.

"Any kingdom ruled by your advisory will be in shambles," they said. "Those humans deserve the devastation that's coming to them."

"How dare you!" Iris screeched. She shot a burst of light through the iron bars. Jolts of electricity flared across Malicine's spine like they were struck by lightning. They seized on the ground, sparks biting into their skin. Flames burst from their ribs and spread across the rags of their clothes. They pounded their fists against their chest, but fire kept reigniting. They couldn't even gasp. The air was getting sucked out of them.

"Enough! We have to keep it alive," Dahlia snapped. "Put the fire out, Clover."

As flames licked Malicine's ribs, they spotted in the corner of tear-stung eyes Clover's figure turning around to fetch a bucket. She filled a wooden pail with water, but as she stood back up, her gaze met the raven perched at the window.

Screeching, she hurled the bucket at the creature. The raven flapped his wings and dove forward. His sharp beak drilled into Clover's eye as she erupted into a glass-shattering scream. Dahlia thrust an open palm to the walls and pulled splinters from the wood so that they pierced the bird midair. He collapsed to the ground, spitting out Clover's eyeball. Limp on the floorboards, the raven gave a low, gurgling croak as he writhed in pain. Dahlia crushed his wing under her heel.

The crunching sound of bones snapped Malicine to their senses. The fire had burned the last remnants of their pain away, and they choked out a scream. "Get away from him!"

The world spun in the heat of their rage. They breathed in the fire, letting it become a part of them and swallow them whole. They didn't realize they had torn through the iron cage until they were already on top of Iris, the gnarled claws of their nails digging so deep they could see exposed bone in her cheek. Her shrieks were muffled in their ears. Dark blood dripped from their claws and crystallized into a dim shade of violet, transforming from skin to scales. Their wounds tingled and tightened, prickling from their shoulder blades until wings sprouted from their back.

They rose higher, towering over the faeries, their body stretching like a snake. Their head smashed through the ceiling of the cabin, splinters stabbing into their scales, but their wrath was too strong to feel anything else.

Malicine craned a long neck to take in their peripheral vision, wide and vast. They saw a world covered in snow, the tops of the trees in the forest, and the specks that were their sisters, so tiny and weak against the volume of their rage. The faeries cowered under Malicine's immense shadow, and they understood then why they had been contained in a cage, kept small and frail, the fire dampened inside of them.

The faeries had been afraid of what Malicine was. Of what Malicine could be.

Fire boiled in their stomach, warm and tingling. They twisted their long neck around a cluster of trees like a serpent hunting its prey. Sharp teeth bared, fire building in their throat. Malicine's scream came out as a monstrous roar. A tidal wave of fire spewed from their mouth, tearing down every tree in its vicinity. Branches burst in walls of crimson. Snow melted as the entire surface of land collapsed into ash. The world lit itself into a burning hell, and it was so delightfully warm, Malicine could make a bed within the flames and sleep in it.

They twisted back to the pile of debris, hulked over the raven's body, and clamped their wide mouth over him. His heart pulsed faintly inside their snout. Black feathers drifted out of their teeth as they carried him into the sky. The two of them blended into the night, leaving behind a trail of menacing laughter.

Even after he healed, the raven stayed beside Malicine. Perhaps the bird had been drawn to them for a reason. The two of them were kindred souls. Ravens were special creatures because their grudges burned deep. They never forgot those who had wronged them.

Like the raven, Malicine did not forget. And they certainly did not forgive.

CHAPTER 11

CORIN GASPED AS the terrain surrounding her shifted under Malicine's magic. Mountains sank below the ground and drifted toward the horizon, dipping lower until it hollowed itself out as a valley. At the same time, the ground they stood on lifted higher, transforming into a hill. Blankets of snow slipped away like grains of sand. Her boots sank into solid surface, a winding pathway slicked with ice and cobblestone.

The shifting landscape ebbed and flowed like the sea, making Corin dizzy. Her knees hit ice as she lost balance. She clasped a hand over her mouth and tried to quell the nausea.

"Ah," Malicine said. "I forget you're not used to this."

Before Corin could retort, a glacier rose like the waves of an ocean. They were already at high elevation from the hill, but the ice expanded even taller, chipping away until it built itself a translucent castle. Stout trees sprung around the footpath, glittering with cyan leaves and ice-coated apples. White gemstones dappled frozen fountains, their hushed waters reflecting colors of pale moonlight.

Malicine approached the double doors and waved them open. Under the flurry of snowflakes, Corin grabbed Elly's hand for balance as their shoes glided along the ice sleet. Flowers carved underneath the floor. Icicles shaped like water droplets dangled from chandeliers. A spiral staircase cascaded around the end of the room, edging over walls the color of a robin's egg.

Elly let out a breath of smoke in awe. The corners of Malicine's lips turned upward in an expression that unnerved Corin.

"It's fine to admit you're impressed. I've always wanted to have my own castle and rule over people."

"But there's no one here," Corin said.

"That's because I realized I don't like people."

Malicine crossed the spiral staircase, motioning for the sisters to follow. At the top floor, a long glass table stretched from one end of the room to the other. In the center sat a snow-encrusted fruit arrangement, blooming like an icy bouquet. Malicine pulled one of the frozen skewers and snapped the stick in half. The skewer melted, drenching the bowl in water. Vibrant reds and yellows leaked into the fruits and brought them to life. As Malicine reached the end of the table and waved their staff, the entire table's surface filled with food.

The sudden appearance made Corin jump against the wall. The volume of colors and aromas was so overwhelming that her eyes jerked across each plate, not knowing what to focus on first. Garlic and tomatoes topped over slices of warm bread. Small plates held brie tarts that oozed with raspberry. Bigger dishes sat in the center and displayed billowy circles of pasta drenched in squid ink and cheese.

Saliva threatened to drip from the corners of Corin's mouth. She licked her lips as discreetly as she could.

"In the dreamworld, eating is a pleasure, not a necessity," Malicine said, pouring a bottle of wine into their goblet. The scent of black cherries and dark rich earth filled the air. "Whatever your stomachs desire, it is yours."

"How do we know you're not trying to poison us?" Corin hissed.

They rolled their eyes. "Of all the ways I've thought to kill you, it never crossed my mind to waste food. Indulge yourself already. You look like a bunch of ragged children in the state you're in."

Elly reached for a plate of roasted squash and lentils until Corin smacked her hand. The girl knew better than to take food from strangers, especially ones that had almost killed them earlier. But a deep grumble came from Elly's stomach, and that was the sound that Corin hated most: her sister going hungry.

"I'll taste first," Corin said. "If something goes wrong, run."

She glanced at a plate of bell peppers. They were as orange as the sunset, sliced open and stuffed with mushrooms. Too many colors, too many ingredients, too many chances to die in vain for a luxury that was never theirs to begin with. She stabbed one of the mushrooms with a fork and bit into the buttered caps. Flavors burst on her tongue, each grain of spice dancing on her lips. Creams melted down her throat, and a small fire lit the inside of her stomach, warm and comforting.

Elly and Malicine watched every movement of her jaw, every swallow that bobbed her throat, until eventually, Corin had to admit defeat.

"It's good," she muttered, staring down at the plate. "It's really good."

"Better than anything you've ever eaten?" Smugness tinged Malicine's voice as Elly dove in to join the feast, slicing a layer of chocolate cake.

Corin remained silent. It was true that they had never eaten anything as extravagant as this. But she was not some hopeless peasant who had never enjoyed a warm meal. Her eyes gazed over the ornate table as she remembered a smaller one years ago, built from a fallen tree trunk. Mismatched plates stacked atop as her friends had bundled together in the winter, small candles and patchwork blankets keeping them warm.

Those nights had become a winter tradition, where everyone brought their own ingredients for the communal stew. Corin had looted turnips and carrots from farms. Harlow had traded favors with the butcher, bringing steak and chicken. There was Rowan, a weaver who grew his own mushrooms, and Maggie, the older seamstress with careful fingers, yelling at everyone to leave her kitchen because she didn't trust them to chop the vegetables.

The tables were cluttered and the people were noisy, but for a time, they were the only reason why winters were bearable. After Corin left the commune, she never tried making those meals again. She wasn't someone who could offer that kind of warmth to another person. Even Elly learned that eventually.

Malicine's low hum interrupted her rumination. "So what you've said about Gyldan is true," they said. "It must be, from the way you eat like you've never eaten before."

The demon had watched them with a vigilant stare, as if Corin and Elly were specimens being studied. Then their gaze dropped to their empty goblet. Shadows passed behind their eyes, hazy memories from a time Corin could not discern.

"Tell me," they continued, "how long has it been since the princess fell asleep?"

"A hundred years," Elly answered.

Malicine formed a wry smile that didn't reach their eyes. "It feels like I came here only yesterday."

"What do you mean?"

"Time doesn't exist in dreams. Sometimes it feels like a few hours have passed. Sometimes it feels like centuries. Even now, another hundred years might have passed in the real world since you've left."

Corin and Elly exchanged confused glances. They had only jumped through the portal this morning. Or had it been evening? When Corin found Elly in the snow, had Elly been waiting for her, or was it the other way around? Corin lowered her head in her hands and strained to remember the time, but it hung like a broken string, one that she didn't remember snapping apart in the first place.

"Don't bother trying to count back. You'll only give yourself a headache," Malicine said. "Now, how did someone like you enter the princess's dreams?"

Corin squeezed her eyes shut and returned to the beginning, recalling winding tunnels, stagnant air, and rotting soil. She remembered screaming, but what had she seen? The memories were too much of a blur. Elly answered for her.

"I was traveling through the tunnels below Gyldan. There were bodies. Too many bodies left behind."

Yes, that was it. Elly had been the first to make it to the buried castle. Then Corin followed her, barely escaping from . . .

"There were three women," Corin recalled. "They looked human, but they seemed to possess magic. They were talking about opening a portal, and—"

Malicine slammed their palm on the table. Plates rattled from the sudden movement, a crack shooting along the table's iced surface like a long vein.

"You talked to three faeries?" Their tone was sharp, accusatory. "What were their names?"

"I didn't interact with them, only heard them talking to each other. There was a man with them. They called him Ezran—"

Malicine stamped the end of their staff to the ground. The table shattered as platters of food melted away. Cold water struck Corin's skin, forcing her to jump from her seat. The windows burst wide open and let in a blast of wind.

"Where did they open the portal?" Malicine demanded.

"All I remember was a hole filled with light. The portal closed after I crossed—"

"Where?"

"How am I supposed to know?" Corin snapped. "You changed the terrain."

Malicine crossed over to the balcony that overlooked snow-covered valleys. A blizzard rolled across the white land, rumbling beneath their anger. Black wings sprouted from their back as they leapt over the ledge and soared through the air. Their raven followed like a shadow. Snow dispersed from their path, and the blizzard masked their silhouettes, so that they were hidden from the rest of the world.

Corin rushed over to the windows and shut the doors. She spun around to Elly. "I have no idea what is happening, but we need to get out of here."

Elly approached the glass pane. She didn't turn away, even as ice pellets struck the window. "It's just like the story said," she murmured. "The demon who cursed the princess. The prince searching for his true love to wake her up. It's still happening, Corin."

"And it's none of our business. We need to get back to Gyldan before we're trapped here."

She snatched Elly's wrist and dragged her to the staircase. If they escaped while Malicine was distracted, they could hide until it was safe to return through the portal. She didn't know how they would find it, but if Elly was by her side, at least they would be together.

"I want to stay," Elly protested.

"I don't care. We're leaving."

Elly wrenched her hand out of Corin's grip. Their shoes slicked against the ice floor, nearly making them both fall. Corin grabbed the handrail of the staircase. The touch sent a freezing shock to her bones. The room turned unbearably cold, the warmth of her sister's hand fading away.

"I'm not going back," Elly said.

"This place isn't real, El! It's some girl's imagination fueled by demon magic!"

Corin gestured to the flowers carved underneath the ice, the white gemstones across the banister that glistened like teardrops, the cyan leaves and dewy fruits that promised a false life they could never have.

"If something's too good to be true, it isn't. It just means something worse is around the corner, waiting to catch us off guard."

Elly stared for a long moment. Her eyes, once the color of summer soil, darkened to coal. "Why do you always do this?"

"Do what?" Corin snapped.

"Anytime something good happens, you find the bad in it."

"I'm being realistic, El. It's the only reason we've survived this long."

That was the difference between Elly and Corin: Elly believed the best in things, while Corin saw the darkness for what it was. Corin had to be the one to reel them back to reality, because fairy tales were only frivolous stories for desperate people, looking to escape from the dreariness of their own lives.

Corin wouldn't be taken for a fool like the rest of them.

"No," Elly murmured. "You ruin things before they can be good."

The words cut into Corin like a knife. There it was, the open wound she tried to bury. The knot in her stomach she could never untangle. It wasn't the hazy vision of Elly's shrinking figure as she ran away, the bristles of black hair disappearing into the dead of night. It was the moment before her back turned, before her shoes pounded against the pavement, the receding footsteps of a child hurt by the only family she had.

Gray skies. Broken clay. Words Corin screamed that she could never take back. Elly's look of betrayal in the silence that followed.

The things that happened before Elly said *I hate you.*

Ice cracked beneath Corin's feet, an ugly vein beating below the surface. She imagined the floor shattering, her body drowning. She wanted cold water to fill her lungs until she blacked out. Elly's figure blurred in her vision, shrinking into darkness as Corin sank belowground. Their fingers interlaced as Elly reached out. Her mouth opened in the shape of Corin's name, but ice muffled the sound. Her sister's lips turned blue, her face a hazy blur from beneath the water.

Corin released Elly's hand and let the tide take her.

Darkness shrouded the corners of her vision like a fog. The stench of rotting flesh returned, dust and debris stinging her eyes. She drowned in memories of endless tunnels that brought her back to the familiar path of dead friends and disappointed sisters. The same dead end that came from her trying and failing anyway.

Then hands reached in the murky water and tugged her by the collar. A shadow morphed into her memory of Ezran, threatening her in the castle. His silver eyes filled with rage and power. The first, Corin always had. The second, she never could.

"You took my place in her dreams," he snarled, "and you're not even worthy of it."

Water distorted his voice, muffling the threat in her ears. "You're not real," she whispered. "Why do I see you?"

"Because you and I want the same thing."

Bubbles spewed from her mouth as the mirage gave her a hard shove. The ghosts of his fingers contorted like shadows in the shifting currents. Darkness curled in her chest, a distorted shape that remained even as his figure scattered into ripples. In the murky recesses of her mind, she recalled the words she'd overheard in the castle, how it had stoked the flames of a prince and, inadvertently, ignited something in a thief.

A gust of air filled her lungs as someone's arms pulled Corin from drowning. Malicine struck her hard in the face with their palm. She fell on top of the ice and choked until water spewed from her throat. Her lungs burned, caught between drowning and sudden air. She hadn't realized she was underwater, couldn't even tell she was sinking. But the ice returned to a smooth surface, its cracks gone, as if she was never engulfed at all.

"Stop trying to kill yourself," Malicine snapped. "You're going to ruin my floors."

Elly called her name again, her frantic voice clear as crystals this time. "What happened just now?"

Corin looked down at her drenched clothes. "I—I don't know."

Malicine sighed, as if tired of explaining rudimentary concepts. "I told you already. This is the dreamworld, where your subconscious desires come to life. You're a part of her dreams now. But those faeries and the prince you saw? They almost became part of it too. I can't let that happen."

The demon looked at the snowfall outside. The blizzard had calmed, but tension still radiated as they placed a palm on the frosted glass.

"If they come here—if *anyone* comes here—the dreamscape will collapse. The princess is not supposed to confront reality. It will destroy her, and everything else in this world."

The memory of Ezran rushed back to Corin. The fire in his silver eyes, the blade of his sword at her throat. How his determination to save the princess broiled even after all these years, never ebbing. Corin instinctively reached for her necklace, the pendant cold against her wet clothes. She understood what it was like to make a promise as well.

"What if I made a bargain with Ezran?" she asked, plans unfurling in her mind.

Malicine raised an eyebrow. "What sort of bargain?"

"He nearly killed me to protect the princess. But he mentioned a promise to protect something else. Her treasure," she said. "That's what matters most to him. If you send us back to Gyldan with that treasure, I'll offer to trade it in exchange for him leaving you alone. Hell, I'll even tell him there was nobody else here. He won't have any reason to cross over to your world."

Corin steadied herself as she met Malicine's suspicious gaze. Her clothes were already drying, the fabric rough against her chest, the necklace listening to the quick beat of her heart.

"I don't know what treasure he's talking about." Malicine paused. "But she might know."

Corin exhaled slowly to mask her relief. She didn't know if her offer would work. It seemed likelier that Malicine trapped the princess in her dreams so that they could claim the same treasure the prince sought. But the demon didn't have any idea what it might be, nor did they show interest in it.

How could that be? The mystery of the treasure intrigued Corin even more once Ezran had confirmed the rumors were true. She had heard tales of Gyldan once being rich with gold. How an ancient faerie blessed the royal family and they became the only people gilded with fortune, propelling them into ruling over a prosperous land. They had gained power, and that, ultimately, was the key to survival.

If she had that kind of wealth in her hands, she could change everything. She would wake up with a roof over her head, rolling over a soft mattress so big that Elly would have her own side. She would never need to rely on the company of loved ones for warm meals. She would move far away from Gyldan and leave behind the bad memories and dead friends she'd rather forget.

"I thought I was going to kill you to make things easier, but you've surprisingly made yourself useful," Malicine said. "I'll take you to the princess and see what she thinks."

Corin bit her bottom lip to restrain a smile. The gears of her new plan clicked together, and she finally knew a way to escape from the tunnels, the darkness she had spent so long wandering. There was a light at the end, after all, and it glinted like gold.

Malicine beckoned their raven while descending the staircase. Corin trailed behind, then stopped at the handrail when she realized Elly hadn't moved. Her sister's brows remained furrowed, a darkened expression on her face.

"You don't plan on giving the treasure back," she said. "You're going to keep it for yourself and let Ezran destroy this world."

Corin shrugged. "Not necessarily. If the treasure turns out to be an artifact or some royal heirloom, I'll sell it."

Elly's lips pressed tight. She dipped her chin to her chest, staring at her shoes. The floor reflected the icicles that dangled from the chandelier like teardrops.

"Harlow was right about you."

Corin bit her tongue to refrain from cursing at her sister. A faint taste of blood lingered in her mouth. When her lips parted, a breath of smoke came out, a tremble of air before it disappeared.

"Harlow's dead." Her voice was flat, hard. "Maybe if she had been selfish, she would've survived like we did."

A prickly silence hung between the sisters as they joined Malicine outside the castle. Corin didn't want to deal with Elly's moodiness, so they ignored each other while crossing frosted fountains and ice-coated trees. Elly ventured far enough to reach the end of the frozen lake, where the ice had pieced itself back together. Corin wished it was as easy for her to put things back in place. To no longer see the cracks of something after it broke.

She turned to Malicine, who kept an eye on Elly without saying anything. Whatever they thought of Elly or the tension between the sisters, they did not speak it out loud.

"There's something else I want to know," Corin said, breaking the silence. "If the dreamworld is supposed to collapse when people enter it, how are we still here?"

Malicine turned to her and broke into a grim smile.

"Because you and your sister are living a lie. And what are dreams, if nothing more than lies?"

CHAPTER 12

118 YEARS AGO

IT WOULD HAVE BEEN a lie to say Malicine wasn't looking forward to ruining an infant's birthday.

Though magic concealed the demon from sight, they still wore a cloak as black as their raven, the two blending as one. They floated among shadows in corridors and watched blurs of faces pour through double doors.

Crystal chandeliers spiraled from the arched ceiling of the ballroom. The floor was polished like an iced-over lake, and the room was filled with noble men and women who sparkled in shades of emerald and ruby. Between two tiers of windows were floor-to-ceiling mirrors, an infinite reflection of a room Malicine would never belong in.

They scanned the crowd to search for three faeries in the midst. The thought of seeing their sisters again shot a bolt of thrill up their spine. Four years was enough time for a family reunion. When the raven first told them about the ceremony, Malicine hardly cared about the trivial matters of a spoiled human girl. Then he revealed an even more inane tradition: inviting the entire kingdom to witness the heir's godmothers granting their gifts.

Well. It would be rude if Malicine didn't bring a gift too.

Black clouds sprawled across the sky, billowing over the moon like a flapping cloak. A low crackle of thunder rolled across the fields to rainfall. Inside the warmth of stone walls, Malicine let the muffled crackles pace their excited heart.

Tonight would be a welcome reprieve from the past few years. They had spent years searching the land for a hidden portal to the Otherworld. The raven's memories were too weathered down by time to provide helpful clues. He could not even recall his own name, so Malicine began calling him Talon. The only thing he remembered was the bloodred amulet the Demon King wore around his neck, how its color matched the edges of a circular portal before it faded as quickly as the amulet's glow. Still, they found nothing beyond the walls of foliage, the bottoms of lakes, the circle of redwood trees that created the perfect shape for a portal yet led to nothing on the other side.

After multiple failed attempts, Malicine needed a victory.

This would be a glorious one.

Guests chattered over wine and quieted to a hush when King Victor entered the room. His presence drained away every breath and conversation, the crowd stilling as he approached the throne. He wore a cardinal-red cloak that swept across his broad chest. White fox fur wrapped around the collar, a color creeping closer to his graying beard. His hair had grown like a hedgerow, his shoulders wide like a bull. A faint shadow of purple hung below his eyes, a subtle betrayal that despite his air of nobility, the morning had depleted his energy.

He refused to look at the empty seat next to him as he sat in his throne. The king gazed forward as servants brought the baby and placed her in a rocking cradle. The crowd cooed at the infant, delightful gasps that made Malicine twist their lips in scorn. These humans hardly knew the baby, yet they stared with wide-eyed wonder, like she was a miracle simply for being born. How easy it was for a girl to have the world on her side the moment she took her first breath.

"While it is a tragedy for the queen to die, we are grateful to have this blessing she left behind." King Victor's deep voice grabbed the court's attention like a fist. "I introduce to you my daughter and future heir, Princess Amelia. She may be little, but she will grow to be strong, fierce, and brave, just like her mother. For this day of birth, she will receive a special gift from each of her godmothers."

A gathering of violinists started playing from the far end of the hall. Light glimmered across the carpet. The crowd parted ways to make room for three faeries, who floated down the corridors and ended their arrival with a delicate bow.

Malicine watched through a black veil as their sisters reveled in the light. The faeries no longer possessed the scars from their last encounter. Iris had smoothed over the skin of her cheek after Malicine scratched her. Dahlia had healed the scorch marks on her face. And Clover, through pure magic, restored her vision with beautiful green eyes, the color of a forest after sunlight broke through the trees.

They were pale and lithe-limbed and beautiful, as they had always been.

"These three have faced tumultuous times and lived. That is a remarkable sign of bravery: to look tragedy in the eye and overcome it. I could not have picked a more honorable council to gift Amelia."

Hatred rose up in Malicine's belly as the crowd showered their sisters with applause. The faeries simply changed their ailments with magic, and the kingdom revered them for it. Of course. Humans were simple-minded fools who believed adversity was inspirational. That overcoming hardship was how one could be celebrated. But what about those who had no choice but to live with their flaws? What about the ones who were born doomed and could not change?

One by one, the sisters fluttered over to Amelia. Their fingertips glittered as each godmother cast a spell for the newborn.

"Sweet princess, your gift is beauty," Dahlia cooed. "Your hair will always pour sunshine, and your lips will bloom like roses."

"Tiny princess, your gift is song," Iris continued. "Your sweet serenades will bring men to your door."

Light poured onto the infant's skin like dew. She wriggled in her satin bed, babbling in ignorance. The crowd clapped in awe. Such shallow gifts for a shallow girl. Malicine wanted to rip the teeth out of their smiles.

The demon could wait no longer. Before Clover granted her final gift, Malicine tore the veil off their face. A boom of thunder rocked the castle. Doors smashed open with howling winds. Yelps erupted in the air, the cold stabbing into mortal skin like a knife. Malicine materialized before them, a tall horned figure in the center of the room with Talon on their shoulder. Their hands pushed forward, sending the circle of people around them flying against the walls. Lightning from an open door blinded everyone's eyes and made Malicine's gaze even brighter.

As the cracks in the sky faded, the crowd finally took in the demon. Malicine had grown into a lofty figure at eighteen, towering six feet tall in a midnight cloak. Time treated them as kindly as it would any malformed creature: green skin peppered with black moles, half-lidded eyes the color of greened poison, a smile as sharp as a knife. Their horns extended even larger as they grew, two gnarled hooks firmly rooted on their temples. Under the moonlight, their shadow sauntered past the carpet.

"Quite a lovely ceremony, King Victor." Their tongue flickered over their lips like they were about to taste a fresh meal. "Though I wonder, doesn't your kingdom tire of the same trivial gifts for your family?"

The godmothers huddled around the infant, covering her like a shield. King Victor stepped forward, his head held high, his back straight. The kind of posture men possessed when they confused foolishness with bravery.

"I've heard tales of you, Malicine," he rasped. "Spawned from the demon realm. Fae only by blood. A menace to humans and faeries alike."

Talon snapped his beak audibly. Malicine stroked the head of the raven as they entertained the rest of their conversation. "My invitation must have gotten lost in the mail, seeing that you, too, admit that I am Fae."

"You will never be like us," Clover snapped. Malicine needed only to flick their wrist to bend her arm backward. She screeched in pain and collapsed to her knees.

"Never be like you?" Malicine's eyes widened in mock surprise. "What a tragedy."

The king nodded to the guards, who unsheathed their swords and charged toward Malicine. The demon whipped their arms once more, sending a wave that knocked the knights against one another. Steel armor collided and restrained the soldiers to the ground. They could no longer move, like insects pinned under glass by a fine needle.

"I come with good intentions. In fact, I shall offer my own gift to the princess." Malicine waltzed across the carpet. Their arm swiped to send another ripple of air that sliced into people trying to stop them. The faeries' hands were torn from the cradle, their bodies sent flying to the walls. King Victor lunged forward but hit an invisible wall and was knocked back on his heels.

No one could cross the barrier that held together the wicked sorcerer and innocent princess. After all, Malicine needed a closer look at the baby to grant the perfect gift.

Their horns' shadows streaked across the infant's body like two jagged lines, ready to pierce into soft flesh. Amelia slept peacefully, cradled in a sea of satin blankets as soft as clouds. From the moment she was born, she was loved and accepted by everyone. Skin as white as pearls, hair as gold as sun. The beauty in her would only flourish greater with time.

These were the girls the world cared about. Girls who would grow up doted, beloved, cherished. Amelia would never understand a fraction of the pain that Malicine felt. She would dance across the gilded halls of her extravagant castle, watch men bow down at her feet and give her everything she wanted. And when she died, the world would mourn for her and drop roses beside her deathbed.

Humans and faeries yelled around them. Screams muffled behind the barrier, fists pounding against invisible glass. Still, the baby did not stir. Malicine traced a finger across Amelia's cheek, their nail curled beneath the baby's chin.

"You just love your sleep, don't you?"

Malicine was eighteen, and their life was already so different from this girl's. What about when Amelia turned eighteen? What if she had a taste of how dreadful the real world could be?

"Beauty and song are nothing more than shallow gifts. As her godmothers, you should be ashamed. Fortunately, I've thought of the perfect gift. The princess will, indeed, grow up beautiful and beloved. But when midnight strikes on her eighteenth birthday . . ."

Their eyes flickered to a spinning wheel in the corner of the room. They imagined blankets being spun, cradling the princess with comfort and safety normal for a girl like her. Their fangs flashed with a smile as sharp as the spindle they pointed toward.

"She will prick herself on the spindle of a spinning wheel and fall into eternal slumber."

The godmothers gasped, a tidal wave of shock rolling over each face as they understood the implication. Malicine had turned the crib into a casket, tainting the most sacred job the godmothers had. The faeries would be permanently disgraced by the king for failing to protect the princess. It was not just a curse on the princess, but a curse on her godmothers as well.

Fire lit Malicine's heels, and their laughter recoiled in the thick smoke until it fully engulfed their body. The cries around them faded like ash. The world turned black, and then they could breathe the autumn air of the woods once more.

Later, when Talon reported that Clover used her final gift to declare true love's kiss would break the curse, Malicine laughed so hard they wept. They imagined their sisters arguing privately after the ceremony, pointing fingers at the youngest faerie, and blaming her for wasting their last gift on something so stupid. They would have to desperately cling to the idea of true love to save face, or risk being humiliated forever.

An impossible concept, Malicine thought. They could not imagine that level of devotion to someone, the way a person could sacrifice themselves for another.

True love simply didn't exist in the real world.

CHAPTER 13

THE THINGS CORIN saw throughout their trek couldn't have existed in the real world, and it solidified her acceptance that this was, indeed, a dream. Icicle lanterns sprouted from the ground along the white woods and pulsed with soft light from each passerby. Hares vanished into snowflakes, reappearing with every gust of wind to let Elly chase them. Owls with crystal wings swooped between branches and scattered shimmering frost onto Malicine's cape. Corin learned that none of the wild animals were dangerous, yet there remained one that stopped her tracks.

The fox she'd seen earlier reappeared, as if stalking her path. He slipped between the trees like a shadow constantly shifting behind her group. Her footsteps slowed behind the others, veering toward the creature until their shadows became one under the sunlight. Seeing him again, his fur had a slick, oily texture, as if he were made of paint. She reached out to stroke his coat and confirm its familiarity. At her touch, the fox's face turned into an old tree, orange fur dissolving into charcoal. The pads of her thumbs were left stained black.

She muttered, "I don't understand how anything in this world works."

"This world isn't like yours," Malicine replied. "It's not a singular place. They're fragments of our subconscious pieced together. Unlike reality, these parts aren't finite. Cracks can form. And if someone enters, they can break apart."

Corin thought of the jagged edges in the fox's skin. Perhaps he wasn't the only thing here that was breakable. The dreamworld appeared whole, yet its parts were delicate, susceptible to collapsing. She imagined the land like her father's pottery, the way pieces shrank when they dried, creating cracks across the surface. Once, she'd knocked over his favorite bowl and shattered it by accident. She'd tried putting it back together, but there was no point. The fragile lines made her mistakes too noticeable, an ugly reminder of what she'd done.

Maybe this time, Corin would make things right. She would claim the treasure, move away from Gyldan, and start over, leaving those cracked pieces behind.

Her eyes scanned the snowy terrain in newfound determination, but the contours of the land never appeared to end. Every time they reached a new area, Corin would lose track of time, forgetting how long it took to reach their destination. She had no idea how close they were to the treasure, if it was even a linear journey to be measured at all.

"Where is the princess?" she asked, impatience growing.

Malicine simply answered, "In Springland."

"What's that?" Elly chimed in. She had continued ignoring Corin since they'd left the ice castle, only communicating with Malicine instead.

"Exactly what it sounds like. A land where only spring exists."

They held out their hand, and a snowflake landed on their fingertip. The ice melted, shifted, then re-formed into a tulip.

Red bled into its petals, bright like a stain, blooming in their hand despite the harshness of winter.

"I've forged the world with my magic and split the land into different seasons. It's easier to organize this way, otherwise we'd be floating through clusters of chaos. Obviously, this is Winterland."

Red drained from the tulip until it turned translucent like glass. The six petals folded in unison as they froze back into a snowflake, drifting away from Malicine's hand.

Corin couldn't imagine what the dreamworld would look like if Malicine hadn't enforced physics to make sense of it. Even flying across the land or shifting the terrain made her sick and disoriented, so they'd resorted to traveling by foot. Along the way, Malicine explained why the portal shouldn't have opened. Making an entryway wasn't possible without blood magic composed of the original elements Malicine had used to create Amelia's dreamworld. There needed to be a mixture of royal blood and demon blood, and the portal would close as quickly as the blood dried.

After a century of experimentation, Ezran and the godmothers had discovered the exact formula.

"What doesn't make sense is why they haven't made another attempt to cross over," Malicine said. "What is stopping them from entering again?"

The question hung in the air as the group reached a path that dipped below the glaciers. At the bottom was an open mouth filled with crystals. They headed down the slope into the ice cave, and the sight drew a stunned breath from Corin's lips. Shades of cyan coated each rock, shining like jewels. Icicles glittered like polished teeth. Ripples hung suspended over the walls, as if the ocean had nearly swallowed them whole but stopped just in time.

Their mirror selves were reflected in the crystals as they crossed inside. Malicine, with their black cape and green face, looked like sea-foam. Elly's brown skin turned a deeper shade of blue from the light breaking through. Corin was a haze of midnight, her black eyes staring back like stars.

Then a red glow emanated from one of the walls. The icy rock illuminated as burning scarlet twisted to orange, then deep purple. The glow burst into a kaleidoscope of colors before each particle came together to form a face.

The recognition of her father froze Corin in place. The crinkles of his eyes, the strong jut of his chin. His broad, flattened nose that flared whenever he laughed. He held the hand of a little girl who looked so much like Elly that it took a moment to realize she was Corin. His fingers were big and calloused, scratching against her skin in a way that comforted her. She could actually feel it.

"What is this?" Corin whispered.

"Memories." Malicine's voice echoed around the cavern walls. "Dreams take from our subconscious, which means memories show up too. This cave holds our fond memories and keeps them frozen. Unlike reality, they stay this way forever."

Visions of their lives together clung like spider silk on the ice. The low hum of her father's voice as he worked with his pottery wheel. The smell of her mother's turnip stew as she kneaded bread. Fragments of memory flitted past one by one like a whisper, until eventually, the entire cave glowed in warm orange. Corin stood inside sticky summer and sunlight, surrounded by her mother's paintings, her father's pots, her own collection of paintbrushes.

She'd been proud of her parents' work. They'd been artists by trade, just like her grandparents, who escaped to Gyldan for a better life. When they died, she didn't know how to survive other than turn to art again. Perhaps that was why the artisans took her in. The ice morphed into cracked walls and makeshift tables, old canvases and spilled paint. Maggie's hideous blanket stitched from different quilts. Rowan's wool tangling around everyone's feet. Harlow's calloused hands opening to reveal a clay figurine of a fox.

She'd laughed at Corin's mouth hanging open in shock, but Corin had never imagined seeing her father's work again. It was common for soldiers to pawn other people's belongings after raiding their homes, which meant her family's collection might as well have been destroyed. Harlow had recognized the clay figurines that once belonged to Corin's father, now upsold at the secondhand shop of Woodbine, a businessman with ties to several army generals. In one swift move, while Woodbine's eye had been distracted by another customer, Harlow had swiped the smallest piece and put it in her pocket to take back.

Now here she stood again, this precious gift in her hands, her mouth split into that cocky smile.

Corin pictured her best friend as clearly as ink spilling across the ice caverns. The rocks surrounding her bathed in shimmering yellow, and she felt as if the sun were growing in her chest. But the warmth soon turned to an unbearable heat, and the glowing tendrils that flickered across the walls turned too bright.

Her eyes started burning. She clenched her fists, refusing to take Harlow's gift.

"Stop it."

The caves continued gleaming. Corin turned away from Harlow's distorted laugh and looked back at her family. But her mother's embrace was too suffocating, and Corin couldn't stand that either. Her father's rough hands cupped a tiny clay fox, reaching out to her, as if she could touch it herself. She reared back.

"I said *stop it*!"

She thought she brushed away the memory. Instead, her fist smashed against the ice. The visions cracked and disappeared. Chunks of ice scraped her gloves and sliced the skin of her knuckles open. Her blood tingled in cold dew. Pain brought her back to reality, as it always did.

Elly ran over to her side and gasped at the blood dripping from Corin's hand. She was too frantic to remember they were supposed to be ignoring each other. "What did you see?"

Light faded from the ice, returning to blank cavern walls. Corin answered through gritted teeth. "Nothing."

Malicine's gaze lowered to the shards of ice on the floor. "Must you make a mess everywhere you go?"

"I want to get out of here," Corin said.

"Why?"

"Because there's no point. Just because it's a happy memory doesn't mean I want to revisit it."

At least with the bad memories, Corin could live in them. Like a bed she would make and lie in comfortably, knowing that at least if she stayed there, she could get used to the darkness.

Corin pushed her way past the others. She didn't realize goose bumps had prickled her flesh until she crossed her arms and shivered in the cold. As the sun emerged from the other side of the caves, whale songs faded behind them like a whistle. With each step the snow melted under her boots, dissolving into freshly sprouted grass. Dandelions sprung from soil, the wind's hum blowing seeds into the swirl of air. Her eyes followed the floating seeds, how they traced themselves in the sky like fuzzy constellations. They floated inside the caves before transforming into snowflakes on the other side.

As she stared at the opposite end of the cave, a family of foxes trekked in the snow. An icy sheen coated their fur, light bursting through crystal and turning into fragments of mauve. Milky colors floated in the distance above Winterland, ribbons of pink and violet pulsing through the darkening sky.

A single fox perched on the other side, left behind by the rest of his family. His coat had been the only one that didn't turn into ice. If Corin squinted, she could spot the cracks in his skin, the warning in his eyes.

I am breakable, his voice echoed. *But you already knew that, didn't you?*

CHAPTER 14

102 YEARS AGO

"THEY'RE DYING," AMELIA said.

She often accompanied the queen on her weekly excursions to the marketplace, and this time Lilith had bought a wreath's worth of moonflowers from a vendor. The autumn breeze carried aromas of pastries and apple cakes along the cobblestone roads of Gyldan's shopping district. Booths lined the streets, adorned with colorful strips of cloth and fallen orange leaves. Lilith had meandered inside one of the flower shops, chose a bouquet of moonflowers, and thanked the florist with a generous satchel of coins.

In the queen's hands, the flowers wilted. They were the color of bruises, their petals so wrinkled and small they could be mistaken for raisins left to bake in the sun.

"They're not dying," Lilith insisted. "They haven't gotten the chance to be alive yet."

She explained their significance: While moonflowers appeared dead most of the time, they bloomed once every century. Their petals would glow with a white sheen and unfurl into the shape of a circle, like a full moon. A sweet fragrance would emanate from their petals for a fleeting few minutes before they wilted once more. It was those rare, precious moments that made their existence worth it. That was the beauty of being alive, even if the flowers didn't have enough time in the world.

Amelia could understand why Lilith liked moonflowers. The queen's rum-dark eyes skipped past beauty to look instead for potential. She clasped hands with maids and merchants, seeing humans with futures where others saw servants. She visited brothels to offer gifts to the women so they wouldn't have to work for the rest of the day. She sought empty plots of land as fertile soil to build shelters for people displaced from Zilar. Amelia overheard Lilith discussing her intentions in hushed whispers with some of the artisans, including the one she bought moonflowers from.

"The shopkeeper said these will bloom in a year from now, exactly on your eighteenth birthday," Lilith said. "Maybe we can decorate your dress with them for good luck."

Amelia sighed, picturing a tight bodice around her chest, the carmine silk she would be forced to wear like a bleeding rose. Her godmothers were particular about the dresses she wore for her birthday ceremonies to the point where they would argue for weeks prior to the day.

"I doubt my godmothers would allow it. We can barely deal with my seventeenth coming next week."

With each passing year, her godmothers became more desperate to find a suitor who would break her curse with true love's kiss. Even if the curse couldn't be broken, King Victor still expected her to bring an heir for Gyldan. But Amelia didn't want to think about forced conversations with men and empty smiles. She only wanted to think about her time with Lilith.

She followed the queen through paths of food stalls. They trailed after smells of spices, wandered between jewelry stalls filled with diamonds and necklaces, and tossed coins at accordion players on the street, the vibrato of instruments ringing pleasantly in their ears. Amelia watched Lilith intensely, mimicking her movements and mannerisms like a child. If they were more similar, perhaps she could learn to walk through the world confidently as well.

A baker Lilith knew offered her freshly baked pies from his stall. They sat on the side of the street, their gowns bunched up at their feet and a plate balancing on top of their laps. Lilith sliced a corner of the pie with the edge of her fork. Amelia watched the tines enter Lilith's lips, then looked away so she wouldn't be caught staring. Her gaze fell to the pearls wrapped around the queen's neck. They collected themselves across her collarbone, white and smooth.

"Why do you always wear that necklace?"

She had never seen Lilith wear a different accessory since her arrival to the castle. Even at the wedding, she had kept the pearls. The question made Lilith's fingers instinctively reach for them.

"They're a gift from someone special to me."

"A lover?" Amelia asked, remembering her godmothers' gossip.

"Almost. He was going to propose when we turned eighteen." There was something soft in her half-lidded eyes, a wave of indiscernible emotions that lingered like a veil. "Naturally, he wasn't very happy when I left."

A sad smile crept onto Lilith's lips. The expression made Amelia's chest clench. Of course Lilith had cared about someone else prior to marrying her father or meeting Amelia. She had a whole life before them, one that she left behind. That was the way the world worked, wasn't it? There were too many complications for the things they wanted to become true. Lilith could not be with the boy from her past, and Amelia could not uproot the feelings she had for the woman her father married.

"You should be with someone you love." Amelia looked around, making sure no one was close enough to be in earshot, then whispered, "Not someone like my father."

Lilith placed a hand over Amelia's and gave a gentle squeeze for reassurance.

"Love comes in many forms. I don't believe it can be contained within one person." She hummed in thought. "Well, I suppose it could, but it would be quite limiting. If you live your life for only one person, that's not much of a life, is it?"

Amelia held Lilith's hand and felt the warmth spread to the rest of her body. Her grip on Lilith tightened, as if she could fuse together with the woman. It was easier to escape into another's shadow and pretend to care about tomorrow than it was to confess she wished for no tomorrows at all.

The sun dipped below the horizon when they left the marketplace. The two of them crossed leaf-covered roads, passing by carts of goat cheese, handcrafted signs, and bouquets of flowers bursting from metal buckets. It wasn't until Amelia passed by one stall that she stopped in her tracks.

The antique shop looked like it was frozen in time, filled with old hand-painted plates, mirrors with dust-coated corners, and brittle jewelry boxes with polished stone inlays. She was amused by the tiny figurines of a cat and rabbit in petticoats, as if they were on their way to a tea party. Beside them in a glass cabinet sat a row of dollhouses, delicate wooden blocks of miniature castles and manors. Their painted walls burst in rich gold-and-green trimmings, tall and pointy rooftops, and spiral staircases with flooring so smooth a marble could roll without making a sound. Each house was handmade and painstakingly crafted, every detail a delicate piece of art painted by nimble fingers.

"See something you like?" Lilith's voice trailed after her.

Amelia nodded, her gaze passing the rows of extravagant facades and narrowing on a small cottage near the back. While the surrounding miniatures were freshly painted, the cottage was so little and plain that it almost blended in with the rest of the wood casing. Only through close inspection could one see its quiet beauty. A misshapen roof crouched atop walls painted gray while its shadows created textures that mimicked stone. The rocks were mostly gray and unevenly sized, yet flashes of color faintly popped wherever her gaze lingered, like secret eyes that opened to catch a glimpse of the rest of the world they hid from.

It was as if she had dreamed this house into life. Amelia imagined herself twirling inside the cottage in a lace dress, like a dancer in a music box.

The antique collector emerged, having caught her staring. "There's more to this one than meets the eye. May I?"

The shopkeeper unlocked the glass case and held the dollhouse. She turned the cottage around to the backside. A faint gasp escaped Amelia's lips. Behind the house, where vines wrapped around the porch, a sunflower garden grew in a soil field. They were misshapen from clay and paint, their stalks bent in different directions, yet the yellow petals still looked bright.

She could see someone living here. Someone who spent warm afternoons eating cake, wearing circle skirts, watering sunflowers in her garden. A simple life in a small home. An unknown girl, forgotten by history. Exactly who she wanted to be.

LILITH BOUGHT THE dollhouse for Amelia to take home. After dinner, Amelia returned to her bedroom and found it destroyed.

Gray stones scattered on the floor, the crooked chimney broken into pieces. Shards of glass from tiny windows shone like teardrops. The rooftop had collapsed entirely. In the garden, the sunflowers were snapped in half, white cracks fracturing their seeds.

"Oh, Amelia. I'm so sorry." Dahlia was the first to notice Amelia in the doorway, while Iris and Clover stood beside the ruins. Amelia rushed over to the broken dollhouse. She fell to her knees and scooped the broken pieces. Iris flicked her wrist, causing a spark of electricity that jolted Amelia, harmless yet firm enough that she pulled her hands back instinctively.

"Don't touch, dear. We'll dispose of it."

"Why?" Amelia's voice was barely a whisper.

Clover's fingers roamed through the broken furniture inside the dollhouse. Wooden blocks representing books, clocks, and tiny bells painted in detail now had white cracks in their coating, spoiling the fantasy. She plucked a spinning wheel so small it fit into the base of her palm. The spindle looked like a toothpick in comparison to her fingers.

"The servants found this while cleaning your room. Imagine the horror if this had crossed your path!"

"I couldn't have pricked my finger on that," Amelia said. "It's made of plastic."

A low voice emerged from behind her. "It's not about the spindle, Amelia. It's about what it represents."

She turned around to her father's shadow. Under moonlight, the grays of his hair became more apparent. He nodded to the godmothers, who gestured to the broken dollhouse with glowing palms. The plastic furniture, cracked windows, and broken sunflowers shone under the light before turning to ash. A whisper of wind fluttered through the crack of Amelia's bedroom window as the debris dissolved.

"Malicine chose a spinning wheel to be your downfall for a reason," her father said. "She knows you are naive. That you are the type of girl who will let yourself be swept up in whimsical fancies and then carelessly prick your finger on a spindle."

He lowered himself to meet Amelia's gaze, clasping his hands on her shoulders in a firm grip. She wanted to avoid the icy blue of his eyes. They held the weight of judgment that made her feel unworthy and weak, like she was the dollhouse that had been torn open, every impractical decoration under scrutiny. The frills and lace, the pink wallpaper, all so feminine and trivial.

"In a few days' time, you will turn seventeen. That's too old to indulge in childish whimsies." His hands on her shoulders felt like lead, tying her down to the real world. "Do not forget your promise. You are to marry Gyldan's future king and continue our legacy. There's no time for anything else."

She squeezed her eyes shut as her breaths came out trembling. Her godmothers surrounded her, placing small hands on her back and rubbing in circles. Their soft murmurs reassured her that a prince would find her soon and save her from the curse. The two of them would spend the rest of their lives together in a real fairy tale, living in a castle even bigger than the cottage

Amelia had, and wouldn't that be so much more wonderful?

Amelia nodded, ignoring the ache in her chest. Before the godmothers left, they asked if she was all right.

"I'm fine," she answered. "Everything is fine."

CHAPTER 15

"I TOLD YOU I'M fine," Corin snapped.

"Sure, that's why you're still scowling."

Elly had given up on her silent treatment, curiosity overtaking her instead. She wanted to know what Corin had seen in the ice caves. The snow had dissolved behind their footsteps after they left the caverns, and the scenery had shifted into a new season, a few months condensed to mere minutes. Icy rivers melted into liquid light as tulips sprouted along the edge. Color filled the land in the form of blooming flowers and lengthening grass. The cuts on Corin's knuckles healed under the warmer atmosphere, as if she'd never smashed the ice at all.

She wanted to continue the land's pattern of forgetfulness, and so she ignored Elly's interrogations, instead rubbing her itching nose at the change in atmosphere. The sisters followed Malicine through alpine meadows, mirroring the rows of caterpillars that crawled down the moss. With each step, buttercups sprung from soil, unfurling their petals to greet the spring air. Fuchsia colors sprouted from low rolling peaks of mountains, a sea of flowers and blossoms that burned Corin's eyes from its brightness.

Still, Elly didn't relent. "You're hiding something."

Corin's skin prickled at the familiar words. The memory came back to her like a trickle of light intruding upon the dark veil she'd insisted on wrapping around her mind. The light grew wider, and she remembered it had been moonlight specifically, spilling through the open flap of a tent as a shadow stood before her. On the night Harlow had caught her rifling through their commune's tents, Corin had tucked the satchel behind her back. Still, Harlow always had sharp eyes.

"You're hiding something."

Corin had reared back as Harlow charged forward. Her satchel spilled open in their scuffle. Cans of vegetables cracked on the floor, the sticky preservatives staining their shoes and crumpled bills she'd swiped from their friends' coat pockets. Shame had flooded her cheeks, even though she'd already told Harlow she planned on leaving, that her years at the commune were only temporary until she found an actual home for Elly and her. She'd refused to tell anyone how she signed the lease, where the building was, and what she sacrificed to get it. She also couldn't bear the humiliation of returning and asking for supplies after she moved in and discovered the building was a broken-down hovel with four walls.

Harlow had stared in silence at the pile of perishables Corin tried to steal. The look of disappointment had made Corin cringe. She was glad that she'd waited until Elly fell asleep in their new home before sneaking to the commune to swipe essentials. She wouldn't have wanted Elly to witness this, or find out whose side her sister would have taken.

When Harlow spoke, her tone had been flat and even.

"I was wondering where you were at the last meeting, but now I understand. You were too busy stealing from friends who fed you instead of the people who took those things away from you."

Anger had flared in the pit of Corin's stomach, burning through her initial guilt. She'd stayed far away from shops where Harlow and the others met to discuss protest efforts against the war. On nights the artisans gathered in hushed whispers, Corin would usher Elly back to the river, where they struggled to fall asleep on the hard ground of their tents. As her bones ached from rocks digging into her back, Corin would stare into the darkness with quiet fury, resenting Harlow for inviting danger to their group. There were no stone walls to hide behind, no sacred space that was truly their own. Sooner or later, a soldier would catch on to their plans and follow a trail leading to where Corin and Elly slept, killing them both simply by association.

"We're a gang of vagrants, not a resistance group," Corin had replied. "Sorry for not wanting to risk my life for a pointless mission. You realize your plan won't work, don't you? People will call you violent extremists, and nothing will change. At best, a few soldiers die, while the rest execute you. It won't matter in the end."

But Harlow had shaken her head, dismissing Corin like she would a petulant child. To Corin, the reaction was worse than anger. It was pity.

"Keep choosing survival over all else," the woman who was once her friend had said, "and one day you'll look around to find loneliness surrounding you like a moat."

Countless vicious words had tugged at Corin's tongue in response. She'd swallowed down the urge and picked up her empty satchel to leave the tent. Only the guilt she'd tucked in the deep depths of her conscience had pulled her to stop beside Harlow. She hadn't met the woman's eyes, couldn't bear to see what sort of expression Harlow wore as Corin spoke to her for the last time.

"Don't go to the tunnels tomorrow." She'd tried to make it sound like a threat, not a desperate plea. "They'll kill everyone."

It had been their final exchange before the insurrection, one that Corin never took part in, yet she never felt the relief of evading death. Instead, she remembered leaving Harlow behind, her boots pounding against cobblestone, her breaths coming out as ragged gasps in the night air. Humiliation had made her heart hammer against her rib cage, as if the organ itself couldn't handle being in her own wretched body.

That night, she'd run away and reached the other side of the river that took her father. Her knees had fallen on the grass. Tears had welled in her eyes at what she'd lost, another home she could never go back to.

A bee buzzed past her ear and broke her from her reverie. Corin blinked at the grass at her feet, where wildflowers sprouted from soil. The cold night of Gyldan melted into daylight from a dream. The raging river she once remembered had shrunk into a babbling brook, where crystal-clear waters only met sunlight and not death.

That's right, she reminded herself. *It doesn't matter in the end.*

The only thing that mattered was how Corin got to the end, whether her friends were there or not. She took a deep breath, letting new purpose take priority over distant regrets.

"Where's the princess already?" she demanded. "I thought we were supposed to find her in Springland."

Corin and Elly had been following Malicine's path down the stream, and Corin was growing tired of wading through peonies and swatting away dragonflies. Malicine tossed a backward glance. "Hasty to see her, aren't you?"

Corin grunted as she ducked past a bee. "I didn't come here to smell flowers."

"Maybe you should," the demon drawled, "because your attitude stinks."

Elly snickered. "Corin wouldn't know whimsy if it hit her. She's so grouchy that I've seen her with more wrinkles on her forehead than without."

"And if I mess up your face, you'll look worse." Corin lunged for Elly, who screamed and sprinted across the meadow.

The chase didn't last long as Corin tackled her sister over a dense carpet of short grass. Elly's body rumbled with laughter, a pleasant sound to Corin's ears. She liked that conversation flowed easily between them again. Butterflies fluttered over the spikes of Elly's hair, their wings like glowing clips on her scalp. Corin brushed them away and placed a gentle hand on her sister's head. If she could make more good memories like these, perhaps she could forget the bad ones too.

Their attention shifted to a cherry blossom tree stretching over their bodies. Malicine had pulled one of the branches to an impossibly long length, pressing the wood on the ground like a set of stairs. "A better vantage point," they said.

Corin gawked at the tiny width of the branch with uncertainty. As she followed Elly's footsteps onto the branch, the tree's arm grew as wide as its own trunk and lifted them up. Pink blossoms swarmed her vision as they ascended, the smells of lilac and magnolia wafting under her nose. Malicine caught a petal in their hand and blew it into the wind. The petal drifted forward and parted the sea of blossoms, allowing them to survey the rest of the land, its rolling hills and lush meadows filled with red poppies.

Malicine's raven took flight and descended the hill to scout the area. He swooped near a massive willow tree, its draping branches nearly obscuring the garden path that wrapped behind the trunk. Corin squinted at rows of sunflowers that peeked behind a wide thatched roof. The flowers were abnormally large, swaying in the breeze as if they were waving at her.

"There she is." Malicine pointed their staff to the branch, which stretched like a bridge toward the garden path. Giant mushrooms sprouted like cobblestones paving the road. Corin and Elly hopped over the mushroom caps, which bounced beneath their shoes and gave a spring to their step. The raven waited among the branches of the willow tree that blocked the view. Once they crossed past the trunk, a cottage emerged in full sight.

The walls were made of misshapen stone, which explained why the roof crouched in an awkward position. Windows opened from each side, their pointed arches wrapped in wild plants and greenery. A soil field stretched behind the house, where sunflowers grew as tall as the roof. The place basked in sunlight, so that the moment their feet touched grass, warmth filled their bodies instantly.

Despite the surrounding land's extravagance, the cottage was smaller than Corin expected. On the porch sat a girl with chestnut hair and a satin dress embroidered with spring flowers. Shrubs grew from her sleeves, her shoulder bows and cape made of butterflies, fluttering over tulle. Daffodils wrapped around her head like a crown, while daisy petals pressed onto her eyelids and cheeks.

Corin recognized the patterns on the girl's face, the way they formed teardrops just like the pearls did. The stranger was the same person Corin had seen in Winterland. But gone were the silver hair and snowdrop flowers, the pale lace dress and snowflake lashes, the bow and arrow pointed straight to Corin's heart to kill her. This version took a different appearance. A beautiful disguise that was still a mystery.

The girl sat at a round table filled with bowls of fresh grapes and wedges of cheese that fanned out like petals on wooden boards. Slices of pie oozed lemon meringue across porcelain. Tines of tiny forks were stained in orange and cream, like paint dripping from a brush.

"You're late, Mal." Her voice was light and airy like a hummingbird. She set her teacup down and smoothed the linens on the table. Her fingers were long, slender. Their length matched the vines painted across the floral-patterned fabric.

"It would've been nice for you to show up to my tea party on time. Isn't that right, Penny?"

Across the table, a caramel-colored rabbit sat on a bentwood chair, holding a matching teacup between her paws. She wore a ruffle dress and oversized hat stacked with peacock feathers. Next to her, a gray cat continued pawing at the feathers before he sneezed on his green suit. The rabbit's nose twitched in contempt.

"Good afternoon, poorly dressed guests! I'm Penny, and this is Dime," said the rabbit. "We are Briar Rose's best friends."

"How rude. I thought I was her best friend," Malicine replied. "After all, I've known her since she was a baby."

"You mean you cursed me when I was a baby," the girl said.

Dime licked his nether regions before looking up. "Now *that* is rude."

"We had a rough start." Malicine shrugged. "Put some damn pants on, Dime."

The cat responded by pawing a teacup off the table and watching the porcelain shatter.

Corin gawked at the absurd scene. The group talked rapidly, as if acquainted from years of tea parties. They called the girl Briar Rose, though Corin could have sworn her name was supposed to be Amelia. Malicine claimed to be her best friend, which was the strangest thing that had come out of the demon's mouth the entire time Corin had been here. There was also the fact that they stood in front of talking animals who wore petticoats, but that would need to be addressed later.

Malicine's raven landed on top of a plate and pecked at a biscuit, scattering breadcrumbs across the linen. The princess looked unfazed as she plucked a lace fan from her sleeve and fluttered cool air to her face.

"What about you?" she asked Malicine. "Are you going to introduce me to your new friends too?"

"They're hardly friends," Malicine scoffed.

"Ah, yes. I forget how long it takes for you to warm up to people."

A bright shade of pink bloomed on Elly's cheeks. She wiped her palms against her trousers and stepped forward to greet the princess from the fairy tale, finally come to life.

"My name is Elly. I . . . I've been wanting to meet you for a long time."

The princess offered a gentle smile, but her lips pressed tight, as if holding a secret. "It's nice to meet you, Elly. You can call me Briar."

Elly paused before, in a sudden burst, she jumped to embrace the princess. The butterflies in Briar's cape spilled over to Elly's arms as she dug her face into the girl's shoulder.

"You're real," Elly whispered. "I always believed."

Briar ducked her head in the crook of Elly's neck, pressing the child closer so that their touch of skin would solidify the truth. The smell of strawberries and honeysuckle lingered in the air, so sweet that Corin could hear her sister inhale deeply and release a sigh of relief. But while Elly's eyes were closed, Corin watched the golden dust gleam over Briar's shoulders, how it dimmed into ordinary freckles when the sun hit a certain angle of her carefully crafted image.

"Thank you. But you must keep me a secret." Briar pressed a finger to her lips. "This place is special because not many people know of it."

"Unfortunately, that's no longer true," Malicine said. "These two stumbled upon this place by accident, but the portal was no coincidence. Your godmothers discovered a way here. And they've given Ezran immortality for his precious mission."

Briar's lips parted to break the perfect heart shape of her mouth. She let go a shaky breath, so quiet it could have been missed if Corin hadn't been watching her closely. Wind rustled through the willow tree like whispers. For a fraction of a second, Corin thought she saw the facade fade.

"Is he here?" Briar asked.

"No." Malicine lowered their voice. "But he's been looking for you."

The air grew tense as the sound of bees filled the silence. Even Penny and Dime exchanged skeptical glances with each other across the table. Corin wondered how much they knew about the prince, his steel eyes that cut through anyone who tried to disturb the princess. If Briar was as light as air, Ezran was as wild as a flame, real and solid. His passion could swallow her up.

"If they could cross whenever they wanted, they would have by now," Malicine continued. "The fact that they haven't means there's something blocking them from opening another portal."

Briar refilled her teacup. The lid rattled over the porcelain pot as her hands trembled slightly. Corin followed her gaze to the tiny white flowers swirling at the bottom of the cup. The fragrance was strong enough for the breeze to carry over, wafting under their noses, tingling her lips. A bittersweet smell.

"He's not giving up," Briar said. "He never will. Not for the one he loves."

"Yes, his devotion is ever so charming," Malicine drawled. "But Corin came from Gyldan as well. Apparently, Ezran made a promise to protect a treasure of yours. Does that sound right?"

Briar drank her tea for a long moment before lifting her lips from the cup. Quietly, she answered, "Yes, that's right."

"We'll divert him off our path, then. I'll send Corin back to Gyldan with the treasure, and she'll tell him that was the only thing she found. If a promise matters to him that much, he'll keep his word. But there's no guarantee this will work. It's up to you if we take that risk."

"Why me?"

"You're the one who married him. You know him best."

Briar folded her hands in her lap, fiddling with the daisy stems wrapped around her fingers. Corin noticed she didn't wear a wedding ring.

"That's the problem," Briar murmured. "I didn't really know him at all."

In their silence, the white petals in Briar's cup dissolved. A bee buzzed past her hair, swirling around the table as if lost. She plucked one of the daffodils from her crown and set the stem inside the centerpiece vase. The glass filled itself with water, and the bee nestled between the daffodil's petals, burrowing itself in the comfort of seeds and pollen.

Briar stood up from the table and said, "I need some time to think."

Butterflies followed her cape as she headed toward the cottage, leaving behind petals in her trail. Corin gritted her teeth and steadied her impatience. She couldn't make her motivations obvious, and so, she forced herself to remain still as the rest of the table continued their tea party.

Penny brought out a tray of desserts, a dozen buttercream cakes with lemon filling on top. Malicine swirled their hand over their teacup, turning the liquid a darker plum color, the smell of wine wafting in the air. Dime swiped the same tart that Malicine's raven pecked at, and the two creatures began squawking at each other. Elly laughed among them, because of course she would find it funny without questioning if it made sense.

Meanwhile, Corin didn't understand how anyone could behave like this was normal. Like this was *real*.

Elly turned to her, noticing Corin was the only one who hadn't joined the table. She offered Corin a plate with tarts, a gesture of reconciliation in the form of sugar and butter. Corin should have revered this opportunity. They were slowly making up for their previous argument, a rare chance to finally get along.

Instead she shook her head in response to Elly, her eyes fixed on the wooden door of the cottage. The smell of daffodils and honey drifted from inside. She pictured Briar draped over the windowsill, keeping her secrets tucked within lithe limbs and careful grace.

But Corin did not have the tolerance for feigned pleasantries. She wanted answers, even if that meant stepping up to the porch and opening that door without asking.

CHAPTER 16

101 YEARS AGO

"YOU DON'T NEED to give an answer, you know."

Amelia felt the brush of Lilith's dress as the queen gently nudged their knees together. They sat on the plush red carpet at the top of the grand staircase leading into the vacant ballroom, where empty glasses of champagne and crumb-filled plates covered the tabletops. Her tiered birthday cake, once decorated with red roses made of icing, had melted into a pile of buttercream.

The corset of her carmine gown tightened as Amelia let out a sigh. "I do. I have exactly a year left from tonight."

Now that celebrations for her seventeenth birthday were over, she needed to tell her father which man she wanted to marry. That was the true purpose of these ceremonies: not to celebrate her birthday, but to find a suitor. To King Victor, this suitor would become the father of the new heir. To her godmothers, he would be the hero who would break her curse and restore their status.

To Amelia, however, these were simply men. And she felt nothing for them.

Thunder rumbled from black clouds sprawled across the sky. Flickers of lightning created a brassy glow on the castle walls. Lilith watched the rain patter on bare trees, then laced her fingers through Amelia's. It was supposed to be a gesture of comfort, and yet, Amelia's skin tingled as if she were the one struck by lightning. When Lilith pulled away, Amelia found a bundle of wilted flowers tied together by string.

"I don't want you to throw your life away before you've even had the chance to live it," Lilith said. "You do this because you assume you will die at eighteen. You won't."

Amelia remembered Lilith claiming the moonflowers would bloom on her eighteenth birthday. Perhaps she thought if the flowers became alive, Amelia would witness her own miracle as well. How could she tell Lilith that she wasn't a flower waiting to bloom, but rest? Part of her yearned to turn eighteen and fall asleep, because that would mean not having to deal with expectations or responsibility. There would be no forced interactions with men, no wearing empty smiles, no late nights lying in bed and wondering why happiness was a feeling she could never grasp.

She had also fantasized meeting Malicine, the demon who was supposed to take her away. Instead of fleeing for safety, Amelia would walk right up to the demon and say, *Take me. I've experienced little of life, and I don't care enough to see the rest of it.*

A flash of lightning crackled the sky, as if conjured from her desperate thoughts. White streaks rippled across glass windows and revealed a raven's silhouette. The bird appeared like it had been formed by her own darkness. An invisible string pulled Amelia to her feet. She dropped the moonflower crown back in Lilith's hands and bounded to the double doors, bursting through the exit.

Another flash of lightning revealed the bare arms of trees

above her, crooked and gnarled like horns. Her heart thudded against her chest, not from fear, but a twisted version of hope that perhaps Malicine came early to collect her. Amelia ran through the woods as if she could chase after lightning and catch it in a bottle, her own version of a miracle. She heard Lilith call after her, then her godmothers, then the guards too. Thunder exploded in her ears and propelled her forward. She ran as fast as she could. The weather would aid her. No one could spot her through the pinpoint needles of rain, the darkness of trees, the way the woods curled into shadows and took her in its embrace.

Amelia chased that hope for so long that eventually her feet felt like they were on fire. She threw her heels to the side and ran barefoot in the mud. Her throat strained from shouting Malicine's name to the trees, yet still, she met no response.

Even if she saw the demon, what would she say? Would she ask why she was cursed to fall asleep? Would she want to know if, when Malicine cursed her, they had also given her the desire to be unconscious forever too?

Rain pounded against Amelia's face, turning her dress into a sopping bundle of fabric. Panic caused the world to spin as lightning blinded her eyes. She ran forward and crashed into the trunk of a tree, pain blooming across her limbs, bark biting into her skin. Her body fell backward, and she let out a cry as her ankle twisted before landing with a hard thud.

Her foot turned into an anchor, swelling at her ankle and radiating pain when she tried to move. What a hopeless fate, she thought bleakly. She closed her eyes and tried to shut out the world. Still, the world insisted on carrying her along its whims, and several moments later, she felt herself lifted in the air and into another's arms.

When she opened her eyes again, the stars swayed back and forth in the sky. Someone carried her beneath a dense tree as shield from the rain. His clothes were drenched, but Amelia could hear a slow heartbeat through his shirt, someone cold yet alive. She looked up at his jaw, a straight line that seemed carved from stone. Curls of blond hair slicked wet over sharp cheekbones. She made a sound of surprise that grabbed his attention, and suddenly a pair of eyes gazed into hers, so light blue they turned silver.

"It's all right. Let me carry you. A girl shouldn't be walking alone late at night, especially in your condition."

He offered a gentle smile, dimples forming on his cheeks. It was the kind of face that would have fluttered a girl's heart. But the blush that crept Amelia's cheeks was only from shame. She glanced down to the wilting fabric of her dress, the tears in the silk and waistband. Mud caked her bare feet, and her heels were gone. She had been too reckless running off like that. Part of her wanted to tell him to put her down and let her run so that she wouldn't have to face the consequences of returning home.

"You don't have to do this. I'd hate for my foolishness to burden you."

"Nonsense. You're as light as a feather. I could carry you forever and never be tired."

His words should have shot a thrill up her spine and made her feel special. Instead, she examined his promises with dispassion and wondered how someone could devote themselves so easily. Perhaps he was enthralled by her looks, a gift that she didn't have to even work toward. Yet when he looked at her, the silver flecks of his eyes burned with something deeper, a determination that she could not place.

He told her his name was Ezran, and that he would take her

home after the storm passed. The rain dissipated eventually, and with her ankle sprained, he carried her throughout their journey to the castle.

She was too caught up by his sturdy presence to notice the glowing tall windows as they reached her home. Lilith's voice called from the entrance, and there it was, the tingle in her skin, the ache of her heart. The way it was supposed to feel with handsome men like the one holding her.

Amelia wriggled from Ezran's grasp, embarrassed to be positioned this way in front of Lilith. It didn't matter. The queen couldn't reach them before the godmothers burst through the entryway, their shrill cries and overbearing sobs tuned like a midnight performance. They stopped when they saw the man holding her.

"Who is this handsome stranger?" Clover gasped.

He introduced himself as the prince from the kingdom of Zilar. A new energy ignited the conversation, a hum of excitement emanating from the three godmothers. A nobleman eighteen years of age, he'd originally declined the invitation to attend Amelia's birthday ceremony because he'd been traveling for diplomatic duties. The thunderstorm had scared off his horse, and as he wandered to retrieve the animal, his detour led to Amelia.

She could see the gears in her godmothers' heads turning, their smiles widening. They called this not coincidence, but destiny.

The faeries brought Amelia inside to heal her ankle and Ezran to meet the king. They crowded him with several questions and excessive compliments. There was so much buzz over the prince and their fateful encounter that Amelia barely found respite until she retreated to her own bedroom.

A hand caught her wrist. She knew it was not Ezran, because

the touch of skin sent a familiar electric current up her arm. Lilith stared at her, the flicker of candlelight in the dark hall illuminating her grave expression.

"Be careful, Amelia," she said. "I don't trust his intentions with you."

"Why?"

Lilith paused, as if deliberating her next words. "Call it intuition, I suppose."

Amelia knew she could refuse him, yet her godmothers' coos of admiration echoed in her mind, matched by her father's all-too-rare nod of respect upon meeting him. No, love did not matter here. Even in fairy tales, princesses merely existed in stories that others wanted to tell.

CHAPTER 17

BRIAR ROSE'S COTTAGE painted a scene for the story she wanted to tell: tiny bells chiming at the door, a tea kettle blowing steam on floral wallpaper, sunlight casting sideways through windows. A quaint home where the oak floors were worn and ceramic plates were piled in a sink covered with moss. As Corin crossed the living room, she noticed the books were painted wooden blocks glued to shelves. The frosted cake on the kitchen table was covered in plastic film. The wooden ladles and metal pots hanging over the stove were paper cutouts. The clock was simply a painting on the wall, a permanent image where time stood still.

Pieces of this house were carefully curated. But they were not real.

That fact unnerved Corin as she found Briar in the kitchen, bent over a basket of strawberries. The fruits had a plastic sheen, like rocks painted red. The princess twisted the sink handle and let sparkling water pour into the basket, as if she were bathing the strawberries with stars and bringing them to life.

"We've met before," Corin said, forcing Briar to look up at her. "Back in Winterland, you were going to shoot me."

Corin could match the similarities between the girl she saw in the kitchen to the girl she'd witnessed in the snow. Brown hair to silver, daisy petals to snowflakes, butterflies to nightingales. If Corin stripped those features away, who would be the real girl she'd see?

To her surprise, Briar let out a laugh. "You're right. How awkward of me."

"Why didn't you do it?"

Briar stepped closer. Her fingers grazed Corin's collarbone, shooting tingles down Corin's chest. A pendant dangled in Briar's palm.

"I was distracted by your necklace," she said. "I wondered if there was a story behind it."

Corin slapped Briar's hand away by instinct, the strike of skin ringing loud in the kitchen. Briar stepped back and knocked her hip against the table. Strawberries fell to the ground, turning back into red blocks as they clattered. Silly props, like child's play.

"That's none of your business." Corin kept her voice detached, even though the chain burned against her skin, a memory of her grandmother that she didn't want to expose. Not to a stranger like Briar, whose lace dresses and floral crowns showed she knew nothing of the dirt and blood this pendant had survived over time.

The princess took the brusque response with grace and folded her hands together in compliance. Corin tried not to think about how the girl's touch still left behind pinpricks of flesh.

"You're right. I shouldn't have touched you without asking. I'm sorry."

Corin's face burned hot. She didn't understand why she felt vulnerable, despite her efforts to remain impassive like stone. Both times she was around Briar, it felt like the girl peeled back her layers and found something to uncover. Perhaps it was the gaze in her eyes, the veiled thoughts that shone behind sea glass. But Corin was not something to be explored. She leaned against a counter, posture rigid, hands shoved in pockets, like her whole body could cave in.

Briar picked up the red blocks and washed them in the sink, as if it was her turn to play aloof as well. Corin sensed them both putting on a pretense, waiting for the other's sheen to dim just slightly before the other one.

"Tell me, Corin," Briar asked, "what did I look like out there?"

It took Corin a second to realize Briar was talking about the real world. That in her mind, the dreamscape was just like this make-believe house, small and contained and imaginary. The things they did and said only existed within this space, while the rest of the world kept turning.

"You were wearing a blue dress made of satin and a crown of moonflowers. You slept in a bed that was decorated like a garden. There must have been a hundred roses wrapped around the bed frame, and they were in full bloom. The brightest one was pinned to your chest like a brooch."

As Corin described the scene, the corners of Briar's lips turned downward. None of the descriptions impressed her. "That sounds more like a casket than a bed."

"Where I come from, people consider a casket full of roses the best thing that could happen to them when they die."

"Roses are a bit outdated, though, don't you think? I much prefer sunflowers." Briar placed the basket on a windowsill and gazed at the sunflower field outside. Under the sun, her eyes shone like false coins. "Their faces are always pointed at the sun, as if trying to reach to the skies. But they never do.

They're always tethered to their stems, forced to be rooted to the ground. Someday, I want to watch one of them reach far enough to become the sun itself."

Corin restrained herself from openly scoffing at Briar's nonsense. The girl spoke in delusions and pixie dreams. Only people like her could turn their sadness into whimsy. Corin was not interested in words spun into gold, only the real thing. She tried steering their conversation onto the right path.

"It wasn't just you I saw in the castle. I met someone else. A prince named Ezran, who said he promised to protect your treasure. He's waited a hundred years. If I returned with it, I'm sure he'd consider his job finished."

Briar turned to the frosted cake on the table and began stacking red blocks on top. They smoothed their edges into strawberries again, the plastic around the cake solidifying into white glaze. Frosting stained her fingers, and as she licked them off delicately, Corin figured the girl had to be toying with her.

"I appreciate the offer, but I'm sorry," Briar said. "I cannot give it to you."

"Why not?"

"I abandoned many things when I fell asleep. My family's treasure was one of them. It's painful to think about, so I would rather not."

Corin let out a bitter laugh. She couldn't stand the irony. "Some of us don't have the comfort of avoiding what makes us uncomfortable. You were cursed by magic. The rest of us were cursed just by being born."

"I wasn't cursed."

Corin blinked. "What?"

"A demon's curse cannot be broken unless the demon takes it

away themselves. Malicine revoked the curse before my eighteenth birthday." Briar sliced a piece of dessert, then offered the plate to Corin. "Would you like some cake?"

Corin gawked at her in disbelief. What had been the purpose of these fairy tales, then, if there wasn't a damsel in distress trapped in another world? The girl chose to be here. Left the rest of the real world behind to rot and die. When Elly traveled the tunnels and risked her life, when her sister called out for Amelia, the princess hadn't responded. She never would.

"Oh! I almost forgot."

Briar opened a drawer, rifled through its contents, and placed a cake topper on the frosting. The ceramic fox curled between buttercream and strawberries. His eyes were closed, his bushy tail a veil that hid him from the rest of the world. Recognition struck Corin like shards of clay cutting into her palm. She tried swallowing, but her throat was thick and dry like cotton. The corners of her vision blurred, only the figurine in full focus.

It was one thing to see a live fox stalking her throughout the land. It was another to see the actual figurine her father had made, the one that Harlow had given back to her, the same object that Corin would later destroy. Even the chip in the fox's tail was an exact match.

She strained to keep her voice calm. "Why do you have this?"

Briar shrugged. "Sometimes I'm not sure where the things I find here come from."

"Don't mock me. This is the same one as before."

"Before?"

Corin sucked in a shaky breath. Briar was taunting her with this carefree performance. The airy tone of her voice, the subtle tilt of her head. It didn't matter how many plants Briar tried decorating this place with. Even flowers would show their rot eventually. Corin closed her eyes to stop herself from leaping at Briar and tearing the girl apart until she found the rotten core inside. She needed to remain placid if she wanted to crack the girl open.

Her eyes opened to a plate in her hands, holding the slice of cake and fox topper. The clay figurine cracked under her touch, revealing maggots that writhed beneath the cake's frosting. They wormed through the strawberries and left red trails behind. A familiar stench of death filled her nostrils. But Corin could force Briar to remember things she would rather forget too.

"You're a liar," she said. "You, this world, everything—it's all a lie."

The plate slipped from Corin's fingers and shattered. Cracks spread over the fox figurine and dissolved like sand, spilling into the floorboards that split open. A hole caved in the middle of the room and turned the house's foundation at a slant. Trinkets fell off sliding tables, reverting to useless blocks. The armoire fell over with a violent thud and burst open its drawers, but nothing spilled out, just the hollow thud of plastic against a sinking floor.

Still Corin and Briar remained standing, as if acknowledging the catastrophe around them would mean exposing the cracks beneath their own facade.

"This place is empty, just like you," Corin continued evenly. "You think you can dress something up in flowers and tea parties and pretend to have some pretty life, but none of it is real. Here's the truth: Your name is Amelia. You've been sleeping for a hundred years. Your body has been wasting away in an empty castle buried beneath the ground. And your real home is nothing but dust and debris and ripped paintings."

Potted plants spilled soil across the floorboards. Corin's boots stomped in dirt as she backed Briar against the wall.

"Every family portrait I saw in that castle had their faces slashed out, including yours. But there was one left unscathed. The queen."

For the first time, Briar's sun-kissed complexion went pale, and she almost looked like the princess Corin saw in the real world. A vindictive part of Corin delighted in that. To turn the tables and make Briar the one uncomfortable with acknowledging the truth.

"I heard the stories about how your family lineage ended. She killed your father and nearly took your life too. Is that why you're here? You couldn't deal with reality crumbling around you, so you retreated into your dreams to hide."

"We are all running away from something," Briar replied, her voice steady. "That's why we're here. Even you."

"No, I'm the one trying to return to reality. As horrible as it is, some of us don't have the freedom to run away whenever something goes wrong. We don't get caskets full of roses, or faeries to grant us gifts, or better worlds to escape by magic. We're forced to live with the consequences of wealthy, frivolous people like you. And when we die, nobody will remember us."

Briar stared at Corin for a long moment. Veiled thoughts passed behind her eyes like shadows, as if she were examining the emotions seething behind Corin's even tone, turning them over to see every jagged edge. "You're angry," she said.

"Of course I am. It must be nice to live in dreams without any worries."

"I have plenty of worries. And regrets. And sadness," she replied. "But I bury them so I don't have to look at it anymore. You can do the same. You and Elly can be happy here."

Corin sneered. "You don't know what would make El happy."

"Do you?" Briar asked. "Do you even know what would make you happy?"

Corin's breaths turned short, as if air had just been cut from her lungs. She recalled the look on Elly's face. The way the shards of the clay figurine bit into her palm. The miserable black night when she confessed to her sister what she did.

No—there was no point looking back. They were already making up. They were supposed to be better now. Corin refocused on Briar, studying the daisy petal dripping below her eye like a teardrop. The princess could live in illusions, but she had no right to trick Corin with them, to pick at Corin's wounds while covering her own. Corin placed a finger on the petal and lifted it from Briar's cheek. The gesture was slow, almost gentle, but they both felt the sharpness of her action, the weight of her glare.

She drew her face so close that they couldn't tell their breaths apart from one another. So that, when she said these words next, they would strike Briar directly.

"What did you do to the queen?"

The daisy petal fell from Briar's cheek, revealing a permanent teardrop mark on her skin. She lifted her chin and looked directly in Corin's eyes.

"What did you do to your sister?"

I hate you.

Elly's words echoed between the walls, slipped through the stones, lingered through the water reeds of the roof. The words dissolved into the rumbles of a new sound, as if a monster was waking up. The shingles above their heads rolled like a thunderstorm. A hard crack struck the air, the windows shattering. The world shook violently in an earthquake, and glass bit into their skin as they lost balance.

Corin hit the ground first. The house's rapid shaking kept her pinned down. Rotting cake slicked over her limbs, maggots and food residue sticking to her skin. The other furniture clattered across the wood and rolled like tidal waves. Then a sharp jolt broke the roof in half.

When she looked up, the wood above collapsed. She felt a sharp stab in her stomach, a sickly cold that spread in her abdomen and told her that, no matter how solid of a fortress she tried to build, the pain would always slip through.

CHAPTER 18

101 YEARS AGO

AMELIA LIKED HIDING behind flowers, but this time, they could not protect her. Once the godmothers healed her ankle, they expected her to accompany Ezran the next morning in the greenhouse, a glass-walled enclosure situated at the end of the castle's courtyard. The room was filled with the sharp smell of living plants and fresh soil. Trailing vines ran down the enclosure, and drooping trees hung over granite benches. She liked that some flowers were big enough to cover her face, and even the bushes were tall enough to hide her figure. With Ezran by her side, however, she had to focus on making conversation with Gyldan's newest guest. Which meant she, unfortunately, needed to stay visible.

He had stayed overnight in the castle's guest chambers. It was the least the royal family could offer as thanks for rescuing Amelia last night. Her godmothers already adored him, while King Victor approved of him. Hearing Ezran's easy laughter and steady voice, it made sense. He had a casual way of moving around the world, yet a sturdy presence that commanded others to listen.

It helped, too, that he was handsome. The flecks of light in his eyes were magnetic, and the simple white shirt he borrowed was unbuttoned at his throat, highlighting his strong physique. It wasn't just the adrenaline rush of last night that could convince someone he was beautiful. He truly was. The break of morning light proved it.

"Your godmothers told me true love will break your curse," he said. "Is that true?"

Ezran watched her carefully, the sunlight gleaming so bright in his eyes it made his irises turn silver, his hair a sleek shade of white. The way he gazed at her brought warmth to Amelia's cheeks, but it was more from self-consciousness than anything deeper.

She was sure many girls would fall for him. She didn't know why she couldn't feel the same way.

"I don't put much faith in that sort of thing," she admitted.

"That's a shame," he said. "I believe it does exist."

A jewel-embedded fountain quietly spouted water at the end of the path. The sky reflected in the water's slow ripples, and as Ezran approached, the liquid glimmered with the pale moon of his face. His hand dipped in the fountain and plucked a blossom petal that had drifted from a tree.

"When I was a child, I nearly drowned in the ocean. I was dying until someone rescued me," he said. "If miracles like that can happen, who's to say you can't find true love with a stranger?"

He pressed the petal to Amelia's cheek. The cold struck her skin and made her shiver. A bead of water dripped from the petal, sliding down her face like a teardrop. Ezran's voice turned soft.

"A second chance at life isn't granted to everyone. Since then, I've kept my focus on the most important thing to me. It's not Gyldan, nor is it Zilar. Kingdoms will always rise and fall, and I have no care for petty wars and politics. Money and titles do not matter to me. The only thing I want is to build a simple life with someone I love."

A breeze whispered through the open window. She watched the petal drift from his hand and examined his slender fingers, the veins that ran down his arms. Lilith had warned her not to trust his intentions. Logically, Amelia knew Ezran had every diplomatic reason to marry into the royal family of Gyldan. The kingdom of Zilar had once been unoccupied territory before armed forces took control, resulting in native people either fleeing the land or fighting back to keep it. For centuries, Gyldan had provided military aid to Zilar, supporting their occupation in exchange for silver. If they strengthened their ties with a marriage alliance, Zilar could block their enemies from seeking asylum in Gyldan and claim even more land.

Yet Ezran's face held none of its usual masks when he told her of his priorities. His eyes met Amelia's easily, his voice softened to a lower tone.

This was the most genuine he'd been with her.

A titter of noises came from the double doors. Behind tempered glass, three faces appeared, their wide eyes roaming through the plants to locate Amelia and Ezran. He chuckled at their ogling behind the glass. "It seems your godmothers think we're a good match."

"What gave that away? When Clover kept nudging us to walk alone together? Or when Dahlia repeated the tale about my curse being broken by true love's kiss while locking eyes on you the entire time?"

Ezran let out an easy laugh, but it was polite, cordial. He knew she was embarrassed by her godmothers' overbearing behavior.

She hoped he understood that she was not as desperate as they were.

"Is that what you want, Amelia? A man to sweep you off your feet and save you?"

Amelia shook her head. "I've never wanted to be saved."

She sounded braver than she was. A noble statement that seemed to imply she would be the one saving herself. That wasn't true either. If she were to be lost in darkness, she wasn't sure she would want anyone to bring her back.

"A man to walk through gardens with you, then?" he asked.

Amelia watched the petal from before drift across cobblestone. It had already dried from its time in the fountain, the last remnant of a forgotten flower left shriveled.

She replied, "I've never wanted a man either."

Her skin prickled under the weight of Ezran's silent stare. It was her turn to be studied, but she couldn't tell what conclusion he made of her yet.

The doors opened to the sound of her godmothers' laughter. Upon their entrance, he reached for her hand and gave a gentle squeeze, one that she misinterpreted for comfort. The illusion dissolved when he pressed his lips to her ear and whispered.

"Better to fall for a man than a queen."

The shock nearly toppled her over. She stepped back and tried ripping her hand away, but Ezran gripped tight. Under his grasp, she was immobile.

"Your godmothers are watching," he murmured. "It wouldn't look good if you ran away."

"It's not what you think," she stammered. "Lilith and I, we are more like friends. I couldn't possibly—"

"I see the way you look at her. It's not normal, and it's not right."

Her stomach dropped like a heavy stone had plummeted inside, reached all the way down to her feet, and kept her rooted to the ground. The fountain sputtered water, and she wanted to drown in it. Ezran's lips grimaced in thinly veiled disgust. The expression made her want to disintegrate. She could not handle the judgment. The spiral of questions for why she was like this, wanted the wrong people, the wrong things.

"Please," she whispered, "don't tell anyone."

He took deliberate care in shifting his expression. The softness of it bristled her skin. He brushed a lock of hair behind her ear so gently it made heat spread down her neck in a horrible way.

"You are beautiful, Amelia. It would be a shame to waste your life on someone who wouldn't want you. Not the way that I do."

As she gazed into the silver flecks of his irises, she could not detect the love that he spoke about. It was a different kind of passion, frightening and carnal. Like she was a butterfly, and he was a hunter with a fine-point needle, ready to pin her down. She feared that if he stared any longer, he would find darker secrets lurking beneath her heavy heart. Something more twisted and deeply rooted than desiring another person, but the lack of desire to exist as herself.

She swallowed the lump in her throat. "I won't."

He pressed his lips to the back of her hand. Warm breath fluttered on her skin as he whispered, "Good girl."

She knew from the prickles that ran down her body what was going to happen. She saw it in slow-motion, like moments before a crash, her imminent death. His knee pressing against the grass. His free hand ripping a rose from the nearby bush. His lips parting for the sweetest of words.

"I know we've barely met, but I don't think our meeting was a coincidence. We were meant to find each other. I'd like to stay on this journey with you. Perhaps I could even show you what it means to love someone."

"Yes, yes!" her godmothers cried, drawing closer to witness the proposal. Their glowing palms clasped together, and the greenhouse transformed with flowers bursting in riotous color. Leaves and vines wrapped into an arch above their heads. Sparks flared from the tips of their fingers, a dizzying cacophony of celebration before Amelia even answered.

She wanted to say no. She should have. But if there was a voice inside her, one that spoke her innermost truths, she buried it long ago. Everything else was louder. Her godmothers shrieking. The trumpets and music blaring. Ezran revealing secrets she would have never said out loud. All the sounds drowned out her own voice, one that was too unsure of itself to begin with.

Amelia took Ezran's rose and ignored the prick of thorns cutting her fingers. The moment she answered, the room burst in cheers. Ezran swept her in an embrace, spinning her around until her vision was a blur of lights. The word stuck to her tongue like a critter struggling to crawl its way out.

Yes, because this was how fairy tales were supposed to end. Yes, because romance was how people found meaning in their lives. Yes, because maybe, if she did what everyone else did—marriage and children and family—she would finally fill the emptiness inside her, as well.

She held the rose tight, even as the thorns pierced her. When she wiped her hands on her dress, the fabric was stained with blood, and nobody noticed.

CHAPTER 19

CORIN NOTICED BRIAR'S dress was stained with blood when she crawled out of the debris. The earthquake had wrecked the cottage, the broken wood and shattered stones scattered in soil. The roof had collapsed inside the walls, breaking supporting beams and plastic furniture. Briar lay among the wreckage, her limbs strewn over the rocks, while the butterflies that once adorned her cape fluttered from her body and scattered in the air. She was too still. Corin jolted forward to reach the girl before pain spread to the side of her stomach.

She looked down to see thick splinters wedged in flesh. A patch of blood bloomed on her shirt. The pain turned clearer as the memory came back to her: The fox figurine shattering. Their thinly veiled argument. Corin's desire to attack Briar for bringing up Elly, because how dare she, when she knew Corin didn't want to think about their last fight?

Then there was Elly's face again, wide-eyed and frantic as she ran through the wreckage and yelled Corin's name. She might have asked what happened, but Corin couldn't remember, not when she gripped onto Elly so tightly as if she would vanish otherwise and asked, "Do you wish you had a different sister?"

It came as a frenzied string of words. Elly took a moment to register the question. "What?"

"If I wasn't born, or someone else had taken my place—did you ever wish for that?"

The pain blooming on the side of her stomach had reached Corin's heart, clenching the organ like a fist. She felt too raw, and perhaps that had been Briar's fault, their conversation re-surfacing the fears she tried to hide: that maybe Elly would be happier if she had been born with another sibling, someone who wasn't so resentful and bitter and cruel. Maybe the world would have been a little less miserable if it had been anyone else who took care of her.

"You definitely hit your head," Elly said, "because you're not making any sense."

She pulled Corin out of the debris with no sign of resentment, just concern. The bare simplicity of it relieved Corin, if only for now.

The air shifted with magic as stones scattered from a gust of wind and Malicine rushed to Briar's side, shouting her name. Penny and Dime appeared and helped roll the princess over to her back. A fallen beam had opened a gash in her skull. A strange patch of moss grew from the wound, trickling leaves down her temple, running vines that were supposed to be her veins. She bled flowers and greenery, her skin soft and thin like tissue paper wrapped around a bouquet. Tiny petals bloomed as her lashes fluttered open, as if she were waking up from peaceful rest.

"You're all right," Malicine sighed, placing a glowing hand over Amelia's wound. The moss shrunk as Briar's skin pieced itself back together. Aside from the gash on her head, the rest of her body remained a clean slate. She hardly looked injured, which should have been impossible. They had stood so close together, yet only Corin bore the brunt of the collapsed cottage, as if she were the target all along.

Malicine turned to Corin with a snarl. "What did you do?"

"Nothing," she replied through gritted teeth. She tried pulling the splinter from her side, but it only made the pain worse. Malicine gestured to her wound, and Corin felt the warmth of their magic, the slow release of the wooden fixture from her flesh. The splinter broke apart, and Corin's stomach pieced itself back together along with her other scratches.

"So you're telling me a natural disaster happened in a world where nothing here is natural," Malicine said. "You were alone with Briar when the cottage broke down. You must have had something to do with it."

"It's okay, Mal," Briar said. "No one was badly hurt."

Her placating tone irritated Corin, the inflection too similar to her feigned carefree demeanor inside the cottage. It didn't matter how often she played coy. Corin would remember how Briar's face had gone pale, like a bare moon unveiled in the night. The princess was hiding something. If she could choose to live in an imaginary house filled with greenery and stone, she could also choose to have the house of her dreams break down by her own will.

"You did this," Corin snapped. "You couldn't handle me interrogating your past, so you almost killed me. You'd do anything to avoid confronting the truth. Is that why you're hiding the treasure?"

"That's enough." Malicine's voice was cold, sharp. "You dare—"

"Corin is right."

Everyone turned to Briar in surprise. Penny and Dime clung to their petticoats and quieted, as if evaluating whether they would continue playing pretend.

"I abandoned Gyldan when there was no royal heir to look after the kingdom. It was my negligence that caused your suffering." Briar pressed her hands flat over her dress, calming the butterflies that swarmed her. She took a deep breath, then looked at Corin with newfound resolution. "So I've decided to help you find your treasure. But it will not go to Ezran. It will stay with you."

Corin didn't know if she heard the last part correctly until the animals gasped. Malicine blinked as a knot formed between their brows. Even Elly was surprised, as she asked, "Why?"

Briar's gaze softened. She raised a gentle hand and cupped the girl's cheek.

"Because you two have lost enough."

The words struck Corin. The sorrow seeping through. The truth in it. She should have been relieved to see Briar making amends, yet her skin prickled with a wariness that refused to leave her body. She wondered how the princess could give up the treasure so easily. Perhaps she didn't care for gold. Or perhaps she believed the certainty of being alone was better than risking any chance of loss at all.

"While it's admirable that you suddenly want to do charity work, that doesn't solve the issue of your godmothers opening another portal," Malicine said.

"We have time," Briar replied. "It will be another hundred years before they can open another one."

"How do you know?"

"Because Corin reminded me what I looked like."

The breeze scattered daisies across the debris. Briar plucked one of the petals that fell from her hair and pressed it between her fingers, crumpled and graying instead of white.

"When I fell asleep, I had just turned eighteen, exactly the time when the moonflowers bloomed. I wore them when you opened the portal, remember? That's why my godmothers couldn't follow Corin and Elly, even though they replicated the spell. Moonflowers die as quickly as they bloom. There's only a small window for them to cross over, and it opens every hundred years."

Malicine crossed their arms. "That's a long commitment. You suppose they will grow tired and simply give up?"

"No. Ezran is loyal. He will keep trying, no matter the cost."

Her words weighed on Malicine. Their shoulders sagged as they stepped carefully through the ruins, dragging their staff around the debris. They gestured to broken planks and pieced the walls together. The animals joined to help, the raven collecting plastic trinkets from the rubble, while Penny and Dime gathered stones in heaping piles. Eventually, Malicine enchanted one of the wicker chairs on the porch to stand upright. They took a seat, with their hands clasped together.

"I think this goes beyond moonflowers. We left something else behind too. Your book. That's how your godmothers learned to open portals in the first place. They put together the pages and went through the rubble for other relics. We should've been more careful instead of acting recklessly that night."

"You're right. I'm sorry," Briar said. "I hadn't given you any time to prepare."

"So let's wake up and try it again."

Corin noticed the shift in Briar immediately, a flicker of fear in her eyes. Before the princess opened her lips to protest, Malicine put up their hand.

"I don't mean right now. In the chance Ezran opens a portal and disrupts the dreamworld, I'll use my amulet to wake you up. You'll look for me again in the physical world. Then we'll start over by escaping to a new dream."

A dull ache throbbed at the side of Corin's head from listening to the conversation. "Wait," she interrupted. "How is it possible that she could wake up after hundreds of years?"

Malicine tossed Corin an impatient look, as if they were speaking a very simple concept that she was too idiotic to understand.

"Time is linear in the physical world, but it doesn't exist in the dreamworld. Here, there is no past, present, or future. That means anyone returning to the physical world would also return to their linear timeline. In Briar's case, she would wake up as soon as she'd fallen asleep hundreds of years ago."

"What about El and me? Where do we go?"

"Before she wakes up, I will send you back to the physical world with your treasure. You will awaken in your timeline—one hundred years later, as you said—and it will be as if you simply woke up from a dream. We will be gone by then, faded as quickly as your memory of this place, because I will make sure we won't leave anything behind for the godmothers and Ezran to find us again."

Corin rubbed her fingers over her temples as she pieced these plans together. She imagined Elly and herself thrown into the portal to their world once more. The new shapes of their lives once she claimed her treasure, and the glint of gold that promised them comfort that only the wealthy could afford. And in a far, distant corner of her mind, the fleeting memories of a dreamworld that never existed. The blurry shape of a demon she never truly knew, and a girl named Briar Rose, a name she may not even remember. She could not decipher how she felt about this loss when she was supposed to have had nothing to lose in the first place.

She turned to Elly. "Are you following this?"

The middle part between her sister's brows pinched in contemplation.

"If you had a second chance," she murmured, "you would take it, wouldn't you?"

A small pang struck Corin's chest. She knew the layers behind Elly's words. People like them didn't get second chances. They didn't have magic or portals or special blood. Once something was done, they couldn't take it back. Once something was lost, it couldn't be returned.

The image of a broken fox figurine entered her mind. Even if she put the pieces back, it wouldn't be the same. The cracks would always remain.

If Corin could return to a time before Elly said *I hate you*, she would.

"It's settled then. Corin gets her treasure. I'll open a new portal. Briar Rose continues sleeping. Everyone lives happily ever after," Malicine drawled.

"All right," Corin conceded, "but where am I supposed to find this treasure?"

Briar inhaled a deep breath and held it, closing her eyes. There was a subtle shift in the air as they waited, a change in the wind. The sun grew warmer, seeping through the fabric of their clothes and radiating across their skin. Familiar tingles ran down Corin's body, like fireflies chasing her at night from childhood. There were hot golden days and washed-out skies, the smell of fresh clay and new paint, vibrant colors and low hums as her father worked. A warm orange glow bloomed from the splash of sun on her mother's canvas. For a moment, Corin was taken somewhere too. A collection of memories, fractured into vignettes, so vivid it almost felt real.

Briar opened her eyes and answered, as if she could see into Corin's memories. "The treasure is in Summerland."

The skies washed back from tangerine to blue as the air turned cool again. Gone were the earthy smells of clay, replaced by the timber and debris of their current surroundings. Corin returned to the present, and the shift in time startled her. She hadn't noticed Penny and Dime digging through rubble to finish cleaning up, Malicine trekking the opposite direction, or Briar guiding Elly along for the new journey.

Corin tried catching up. Her feet balanced across a broken beam, dodging bent shingles and glass shards. She looked up to meet Briar's eyes. The weight of Briar's gaze held something she couldn't extract. There it was again, the quiet that gripped the two of them, an inexplicable prickling of her skin. She turned away to snap their tether, yet still she was left with the split ends of it, making sense of the tangled rope wrapped around them.

She thought about the kiss of the sun, the glow of fireflies, the drops of sweat that only summer brought on. How in a brief moment, she felt like she was in a memory again—and what it meant if Briar Rose felt the same as well.

CHAPTER 20

101 YEARS AGO

FOR AMELIA, DAYS repeated their tired pattern: hazy mornings bleeding into draining afternoons collapsing into listless evenings. She woke and slept, woke again and slept again, submitting to an endless routine that cut like a dull blade against her spirit.

One day, she woke up and realized she was running out of time.

It had been two months since Ezran's proposal. Their wedding had occurred the following week. Her godmothers worked overtime for the celebratory event, arguing over dresses and decorations, fighting until the last minute before the bride and groom exchanged rings beneath the arch. The ceremony took place in front of the greenhouse. Because there was a year left before Amelia turned eighteen, they had no time to waste. The wedding was so rushed that they didn't even invite most of the kingdom. Instead they promised to have a second, proper wedding in Zilar with Ezran's family after the baby was born.

The baby. Amelia didn't even want to think about that.

Moonlight cast through the window in her bedroom. Amelia

placed a hand on her flat belly and listened to her soft breathing in the darkness. She was supposed to be pregnant and give birth to a new heir before she fell asleep forever. Maybe she would still be pregnant by the time the curse worked and give birth while sleeping. She wasn't sure which would be worse.

Ezran had remained respectful, giving her time and distance since the wedding. He even let her sleep in her own bedroom rather than their shared one. Perhaps he knew she was nervous, or was waiting for her to fall in love with him first. But they were both aware of the expectations to fulfill their duty soon.

Amelia forcibly removed herself from bed, even though her skin stuck to the sheets and her heart remained in darkness. She crossed the corridor to her father's bedroom, hoping to revisit their agreement and find a sliver of chance that he might understand she wasn't ready to carry a child while allowing Lilith to stay in Gyldan. Muffled voices stopped her fist from knocking the door, and she pressed an ear to listen.

"We barely know him. How can you expect her to have a child with a stranger?"

A small gasp escaped her lips at the sound of Lilith. Since King Victor had given up on having a child with Lilith, they slept in separate chambers. The queen must have outraced Amelia in confronting him. From their conversation, it sounded like she was not there to plead, but argue.

"You didn't seem to have a problem with the arrangement when it benefited you," he replied.

"I was hoping she wouldn't follow through with it."

"You often hope for such fruitless things. A ruler without an heir. A kingdom without borders. A world without war. I should have known, before I married you, how unrealistic you were."

Amelia imagined Lilith biting her tongue so hard it bled in her mouth. There was a moment of silence, followed by a hushed tone.

"It's not unrealistic to question why you're more upset about losing a child that was never born than the child you already have."

"That's different," he snapped. "I didn't expect to lose an heir. I always expected to lose Amelia."

Amelia inhaled a sharp breath and backed away from the door. Her grip on the banister kept her from falling.

Why did the truth strike so differently when it came from her father's mouth? She remembered the times he looked at her, the way his voice rasped like sandpaper whenever they talked. Her father had always been serious, but there was a trace of vulnerability behind the blues of his eyes, a fracture in the glass barrier he put up. Sometimes the stones of his expression were so impenetrable that one would never realize it was a mask, blocking grief from ever reaching the surface.

He'd given up on her from the moment she was born. Like father, like daughter, after all.

She retreated to her chambers and dove back into bed, burying her face in pillows to stifle her gasps. Fabric suffocated her while her tears peppered the surface of her pillow. She threw the blankets over her head, hiding from the rest of the world.

A half hour passed before she heard a knock on her door, followed by Lilith's voice. "Amelia? Are you sleeping?"

She didn't reply. Ever since the proposal, she didn't know how to face Lilith. If she did, she was afraid Lilith would detect the truth in her eyes and discover the real reason she said yes to Ezran.

"We need to talk. It doesn't have to be tonight, but soon. I have something to tell you. It's important."

Amelia didn't open the door. She would rather wait for Lilith's footsteps to recede and let the mystery hang in the air. Likely, Lilith would restate that she didn't approve of their marriage. If so, Amelia didn't want to face it.

Perhaps this was what being alive meant: forcing herself through unpleasant situations because she had to, not because she wanted to. Waking up every day and dreading what was to come.

AMELIA WOKE UP in the middle of the night and remained conscious for the next hour. She resorted to wandering inside the library and reading several books to lure herself back to sleep. The room was quiet, the stillness of a space that hadn't been visited in a long time. Cherry-dark wood shelves surrounded her, and stained-glass windows shone fragments of moon as her reading light, paling pages in silver hues.

Her head leaned against the windowsill, where sunflowers she'd planted drooped over the ledge. They mourned whenever the sun disappeared and they had nothing to look for. As her vision grew blurry from boring scriptures, she mimicked the flowers with her own slouched figure. If sunflowers had emotions, she wondered if they would lose hope watching the sun rise and fall each night, never being happy in its light for long. Was staying alive worth it, she thought, when darkness was always inevitable?

She nearly nodded off to sleep before realizing the text she was staring at blankly was not a result of her blearing vision, but actual nonsense. *The Book of Samael* had a nondescript black cover, the material bumpy like scales of a snake. The tome was so old that when the royal family first discovered the relic, the pages were coated in thick layers of dust. Even after preservation, the vellum parchment felt rough like brittle autumn leaves. But the strangest part was that the writing didn't make sense. Small slashes of black ink had been drawn in odd angles, thick letters, and crooked shapes.

Despite the illegible text, the royal family had preserved the tome for generations. People believed King Samael left the book as a parting gift before he passed. Some rumored that the nonsensical text was a secret language that revealed where Oleander, his advisor, hid the last treasure of gold. Still, no one could decipher it.

Amelia didn't care for riches or gold, so the book hardly piqued her curiosity. Instead, her eyes wandered to the window, where in the moonlight, she caught the shadow of a raven.

She leapt to her feet and opened the window with a gasp.

Malicine's raven. It had to be, looking at his eyes. The stars shone bright, yet his red pupils gleamed stark in the night. He was bigger than she imagined, darker than when she last saw him at her birthday ceremony, where she chased him in such reckless fury she didn't even realize it had been her life she wanted to leave behind.

"Take me away from here," she whispered.

The raven didn't respond to her plea, merely staring back with glowing pupils. His wings spread and he took flight. She called for him, reaching a desperate hand to catch the bird, but it was too late. She only snatched the black feather he left behind.

Amelia held the quill delicately between her fingertips. Under moonlight, the feather glowed an iridescent blue. She pressed the feather into the pages and ruminated over losing the raven once again.

It took a minute before she realized the letters on the page had started moving. Crooked shapes straightened together, slashes of ink bending backward. The letters floated across the page until they formed discernible shapes, and an alphabet that she could recognize. She gawked at the text until the first sentence completed itself.

To whom this may concern:

If you are reading this, I am writing to you from the Otherworld.

Her heart thundered against her chest, a quiet storm igniting inside her body. She was wide awake, and suddenly the crinkled edges of the pages felt tinged with magic. When she pulled the quill away, the words rearranged to indiscernible text again. With the brush of the feather, the letters came back together in an alphabet, blue luminescence gleaming across the ink. Her pulse hummed. This was not a secret language, or even cryptic code. This was the result of writing from a different world.

Pages trembled in her hands as she continued reading. Her eyes fervently skimmed across the handwriting, each pen stroke illuminating long-darkened hallways. Beyond Gyldan's walls was something extraordinary, and the barriers were finally crumbling down. She assembled fragments of knowledge, piece by jagged piece, until the truth emerged:

King Samael was not dead.

He had opened a portal to somewhere else.

CHAPTER 21

CORIN SENSED THE shift in seasons as the last blossoms scattered like soft confetti along a pathway of parsley-green fields. Spring leaves deepened into lush canopies to shade her group from the warming sun. The day stretched as long as Elly's shadow, which jumped alongside the girl as she plucked ripening cherries from trees. In the golden air, Corin could hear the cicadas clicking in rhythmic patterns, their volume growing louder as her group reached a sandy terrain that curved around a jewel-blue sea. Waves crashed against black rocks foaming white. Salt-crisp air filled her lungs as she took a deep breath and turned to Briar.

"Remind me, again, why you put the treasure in Summerland?"

"I didn't," Briar replied. "You did."

Corin shielded her eyes from the sun, which reflected onto Briar's dress and turned the fabric luminescent. Butterflies had drifted away from her cape, while her sleeves shortened into layers that ebbed and flowed like ripples of water. "Is this supposed to be another cryptic message?"

"There's no fixed position in the dreamworld," Malicine explained. "The landscape changes depending on its inhabitants.

Sometimes it's our memories. Sometimes it's our wishes for better ones. Since the treasure is going to be yours, your subconscious has tucked it over there."

The demon pointed to a wildflower-studded cliff beyond a beach, where water poured from the rocky ledge and plunged into a deep pool. The rapids glimmered as if they contained stars.

"Look familiar to you?" they said.

Corin shook her head before the smell of linseed oil wafted in the breeze. The scent brought her back to paint streaked in the lines of her palms, her mother's hands guiding hers across a canvas, the sweltering sun turning both their skins a deeper brown. She'd plucked wildflowers during their hike to this cliff and learned how to draw them under the sunset. The rounded tip of her brush had glided against parchment and curved into soft petals. Her damp cloth had blurred the brushstrokes of mountains in the background. She'd been so proud of that painting, even though the work was amateur, for she never quite learned how to avoid the sharp edges her hands often made. She'd thought she would have the rest of her life to keep practicing.

"It's not familiar at all," Corin lied, but that lie became a truth as her eyes followed the waterfall cascading into a deep pool opening into an ocean. She'd never seen a body of water as large as this. Gyldan's surroundings beyond the borders were dense with trees except for the river that separated the rolling hills. When she sketched the kingdom's landscape, she'd been excited to use blue paints and draw the winding curves of the stream, not knowing that in a few years, her father would bring them there to drown in oils of teal and cobalt.

Elly took in the ocean with wide eyes, as if she did not know whether to be amazed or afraid. As an infant, her cries in Corin's ears had screamed fear. Now the girl trekked through sand and lingered near the water with the uneasiness of a distant memory. Her gaze locked on the swelling sea, and Corin could see in Elly's eyes that the girl was trying to make sense of where that fear came from, and why it lingered.

Clumps of seaweed washed ashore. Elly plucked the kelp, staring at the plant stuck to her fingers like it were a foreign object. Waves rippled gently to her feet and made her jump. She eyed the waves more tentatively, taking a few steps backward, as if they would snatch her if she got too close. Her body seemed to have remembered being taken by wild waters even if her mind had forgotten.

Briar placed a hand on Elly's shoulder like a protective raft. "Do you want to swim?"

Elly stared at the ocean, brows pinched together. "I don't know how."

"That's okay. You can learn."

Corin opened her mouth to protest, but to her surprise, Elly took Briar's hand and allowed herself to be guided to the water. Her arms wrapped around Briar's neck as they explored further. The princess lifted Elly into her arms, as if the child weighed nothing, and dipped her low enough to practice floating.

"Don't go too far," Corin warned. She watched them like a hawk, ready to dive into the currents if Elly so much as let out a gasp. But her sister's initial signs of fear soon melted into ease. Elly's face relaxed even when Briar let go, as if the princess were sending off a floating water lantern, the very same light that Corin had spent years burying for protection. It was better to snuff out a flame before others could see and claim it for their own. For the first time, Corin saw how bright this fire could last uninhibited.

Elly floated naturally on her back, her limbs wading through waves. Water droplets trailed from the slick spikes of her hair to the creases of her eyes, and she dipped her head backward, basking in the sun's warmth. The girl was a dark streak across deep blues before white lilies began to bloom in the water. The ocean transformed into clouds, a swelling mirror of the widening sky. Clouds ruffled at the edges, grazing Elly's cheeks, wrapping her limbs in puffs of silver and milk.

Corin watched in awe as her sister floated in the ocean made of skies. Not because of the acres of blues and infinite colors, but because the child looked like a speck of oil in a canvas she belonged in, like these paints were made for her alone. She would not be disturbed by the eyes of leering men and skulking shadows that took small girls. She would not be snatched by unhappy fathers or saved by hopeless sisters. Instead she existed, fully, as herself: sun on bare skin, salt on wet hair. A girl who would never be harmed.

Corin was so spellbound by the sight, she didn't realize Briar had transformed in the water as well. The shrubs of her dress melted into translucent blue, and her gown floated like pulsing jellyfish, lacy ribbons trailing her limbs as she dove below. Coral wrapped around her head like a crown as she emerged from the surface. She wiped her face with both hands, leaving behind star-shaped pearls on wet cheeks, as she swallowed the salted air.

She looked beautiful, and Corin immediately cursed herself for thinking that.

"Come in," Briar said, waving to them. "The water's perfect."

"Splash me and I'll kill you," Malicine said.

Briar laughed. "You've cursed me for less."

She continued swimming with Elly, while Malicine cast a black cloud over their head for shade. Beside them, a tiny tree sprouted from the sand, where Talon perched to also avoid the sun.

Corin tried not to pay attention to the rosy glow on Briar's bare skin and instead shifted her focus to the cliffside in the distance. She needed to remember what she came here for. Her mind fixed on a new life after claiming her treasure. She'd find a sprawling home in the borders of Gyldan, where she would be away from the noise and memories, the mistakes and loss. She didn't want to deal with people ever again. She had seen the consequences of rebels like Harlow who risked their lives for the greater good, and it was never worth it.

Malicine's voice broke her reverie. "You two had an argument, didn't you?"

The muscles in her jaw jumped. She instantly thought of Elly before realizing Malicine had meant Briar Rose.

"I figured something happened," they said. "You're extra prickly around her."

She hated that Malicine forced her to pay attention to Briar again. Cylinders of light moved across the sea and radiated across the princess's skin like glitter. Corin's mouth tightened into a grimace.

"I know I should be grateful that she's giving me the treasure. But she irritates me."

"Of course. She's a spoiled princess who's never worked a day in her life."

"Then how are you friends?"

"That's a long story." Malicine tossed their hand, as if the memory was too distant to bother grasping. "The short answer is that we both wanted an escape, and we found that with each other. She has her reasons for hiding in an imaginary world. I have mine."

Corin repeated Malicine's words from their solitary ice castle. "You don't like people?"

"I loathe them. Pathetic little parasites clawing at each other for scraps of power and praise. They dress their wars in different flags, but it will always be the same hunger underneath. I don't regret leaving your world behind. They certainly never paid me any kindness."

The demon tilted their head back. Their horns created a stark shadow over the sand, a shape of two crescent moons that no longer hid in the skies. The sun beat against their green skin, and they lacked any shame to hide it.

"Why fight to stay in a world that's not worth saving," they said, "when it's so much easier to be on our own here?"

Corin's gaze drifted toward Elly. The girl swam back to shore, her hands cupped over a collection of shells. Shades of pink and translucent blue sprinkled across her palms. They reflected light into her widened eyes, which gleamed in wonder at the novelty in her hands.

It would have been so easy for Elly to be happy, Corin thought. If she was born in the right place, the right time. The right family.

"All we've ever done is fight to survive," Corin murmured.

"Maybe your sister doesn't want to survive," Malicine said. "Maybe she just wants to live."

Corin didn't respond, because Malicine was right. Elly should know what it meant to enjoy simple pleasures. Swimming in water. Feeling the sun on her skin. Being loved. The weight of Elly's wet clothes should have dragged her down, yet she floated across the ocean as if she were light as air. This was what someone looked like when they weren't restrained by cruel soldiers or selfish sisters.

Corin let out a long exhale, shoulders sagging. Fine. She would settle inside this moment, even if it was fleeting. Elly's laughter was rowdy and obnoxious, the kind that demanded attention. Corin wanted to bottle the sound in a jar and shake it beside her ear so she could hear it even in the darkest of nights.

She took off her boots and swam in the ocean, catching up to Elly. "You learn fast," she said, then splashed water on her sister's face.

Elly kicked her feet forward. "Bet you can't catch me."

Before Corin could reply, Elly dove below. Corin followed without hesitation, puncturing clouds until they turned to white foam, deep blue-greens transforming to bursting corals, fuchsia, tangerine. She locked her arm around Elly's waist and thrust her other hand over Elly's stomach to torture the girl with tickles. Her sister's laughter came out in bubbles, and she silently flailed until they reached the surface again, gasping for air.

Corin listened to the steady beat of Elly's heart as they held each other. Sunrise turned the waves to gold, the horizon a line of silver. Waves rippled gently against their brown skin. She stared at her sister and wondered how someone could grow so fast. Despite her best efforts to hide Elly, the girl was too bright and beautiful. It scared Corin, knowing the world was cruel and often took beautiful things away from her.

As they breathed the briny air and tasted ocean salt, she wondered if this was what life would look like without fear. The lull of the ocean, the swell of the waves, her sister beside her. The feeling of being safe in an infinite world.

But this isn't real.

Salt trickled in Corin's eyes and burned. A blot of ink stained her vision. She blinked hard, yet the black spot did not disappear from the horizon. A dark patch had disrupted the silver line, so pervasive that even when birds flew toward it, dusk swallowed their silhouettes.

Thick clouds wrapped around the island in a gray halo. Among the swelling sea, the island looked dead. When had this island appeared? Or had it always been there, and she hadn't remembered? She realized too late that someone had been calling her name. The wind had drowned out Malicine's voice, barely carrying it over to her ears as she turned around and saw the demon's face had contorted to panic.

"Get out!" they yelled. "Don't go any farther!"

Corin didn't have time to react. Lightning struck the island, turning the sky white. Seaweed wrapped around her ankles and pulled her down. She lost grip of Elly as the waves pushed them apart. Elly yelled her name, but it was too late. The rope of seaweed had already dragged her below to darkness.

Her body struck a rock at the bottom of the ocean. Fish scattered and reefs disintegrated into sand. Black squid ink permeated the trenches and shrouded her legs like an ill-fitting blanket. Corin pulled her limbs and tried to scream, but there was no sound. Panic overtook her. She didn't stop thrashing, her pulse racing to burst from her skin. Her wedged foot turned blue. Bits of her flesh ripped from bone and scattered in the water.

In the corners of her vision, rocks twisted into a tunnel path filled with starved bodies and bones. Death's stench permeated her nose. Gloved hands reached for her shoulders, and she recognized the pattern of holes in the fabric, the cuts on Harlow's knuckles, every detail stained in her memory after hours of painting next to each other, foolishly believing their art could mean something just because they wanted to make it.

Strips of kelp hung from Harlow's body like flayed skin. Her fingers were like dripping strands, wrapped around Corin's throat in a chokehold. Black water streamed from the dead woman's eyes, the bullet hole in the back of her skull, even her chapped lips as they ripped open to a distorted cry.

"I trusted you, Corin. How could you?"

Corin wanted to scream, but the stench of brine and rot filled her mouth. Ghosts invaded her vision: Maggie's cracked lips, Rowan's broken nose, and a smaller, pale face with blue lips. She couldn't make out the exact arrangement of their features, nor did she want to.

Her eyes clenched shut, and her body sank deeper into an abyss, where rocks that once trapped her melted into soil, damp with blood. Pearls grew in place of budding plants. A flicker of moonlight revealed a woman draped in white, her limbs stiff, her dress stained with scarlet. They were in the woods, but the smell of death was stronger than the wilted flowers.

"How could you abandon Gyldan? Abandon her?"

A familiar voice echoed in her ears, too frail to be Harlow this time. Corin could not pinpoint the source, only a feeling of sorrow that permeated the ocean water like a distant memory. The seaweed that wrapped around her limbs turned brittle like autumn leaves. A cold wind of night air howled through her bones. She squinted at the blurred shape of the woman ahead of her, limp and pale as the pearls that scattered around their feet. Horror gripped Corin like the stake that held the woman's body.

She was dead. Corin didn't know who she was, yet the familiar voice in her ears continued sobbing. Grief from a memory not belonging to her pressed into Corin's lungs and sank her body into the ocean like an anvil. She screamed while drowning. Her vision turned black, and she was alone, and most of all, it was *her fault, her fault, her fault*. She let someone die. Someone she loved, someone whose name she could not say. The anguish was so unbearable that she could no longer breathe through her sobs. She wanted to die. She was too cowardly, too weak, to survive this life.

She threw herself forward and felt her body hitting not the ground, but the flesh of another, his touch as rough as a skinned buck. Rage broiled from the pit of her stomach and reached to her fists as they pounded against his chest. He had abandoned Gyldan and this woman, and Corin would not let him destroy more of their future. She fought against the shadow of a man until he seized her by the wrists.

"Do not defy me, Amelia," came his voice, deep and distorted.

Corin froze, like she had been caught wearing someone else's skin. The shadow twisted into a deep red, and when she looked down at her hands, so too did blood smear over her palms. Her eyes scanned the forest, where dead soldiers surrounded the soil, their helmets revealing a black abyss where their eyes should be.

Like a phantom, she felt a new presence draw closer. Another shadow swam through the darkness, an invader of her home. It lunged toward her, and she would let it kill her, if it was what she deserved for letting so many die.

Then another's arms wrapped around Corin. A soft body pressed into her skin, and a sword sliced into flesh that was not hers. Corin watched Briar open her mouth in a silent scream as the princess shielded her. Briar's hand wrapped around the blade. Instead of blood, light spilled from her fingertips. The rays poured down the weapon and to the shadow's limbs until the attacker crumbled to dust. Murky water dissipated as blinding light fractured the tides, and Corin fell through the brine.

Floating specks disappeared from her vision. She reoriented herself at the sandy bottom of the ocean, where the currents had parted and left her to dry under the beating sun. She gasped for air, something she thought she would never breathe again. Her clothes were drenched and heavy, pinning her body against coarse sand.

There was another weight on top of her. Bare skin peeked through her damp dress, pale as a dying moon. Blond hair stuck to her cracked lips. She was no longer Briar Rose, merely a girl.

"It's all my fault," the girl sobbed. Her hands covered her face, as if to keep the shame from spilling. "You weren't supposed to see this."

Grief coated Corin like sticky tree sap from a nearby forest, foreign but familiar. Her savior remained elusive, a beautiful mask covering a broken girl. Corin reached for Amelia, wanting to confirm she wasn't a dream. As her fingers grazed Amelia's cheek, her eyes traced the girl's features, searching for the truth behind the illusion.

"I see you, Amelia," she whispered.

The girl flinched and pulled away from Corin's touch. She retreated into the ocean, ignoring shouts of her real name. Corin attempted to stand, but the currents came crashing back. Water swept her into rolling waves. She mustered enough strength to swim to the surface and gasp for salted air. But no matter where she scanned beyond the ocean, from the rocky beaches to the looming island in the distance, she could no longer find Amelia.

CHAPTER 22

101 YEARS AGO

AGAINST HER BETTER judgment, Amelia started sneaking off into the woods to find the raven. The weakened chill of late winter made the night more bearable, so she had dressed in a thin cloak, where the fabric wouldn't stick to her skin but kept her disguised in the dark. She'd tucked *The Book of Samael* in the crook of her arm and headed off. Crooked trees and gnarled roots marked the area where Malicine lived. Amelia settled her bow trap and broke off two thick branches, carving large notches into them so that they could be shoveled into the ground.

She'd been practicing this ritual for weeks, improving with each attempt. Her fingers carefully tied the bowstrings to each side, then tied the trigger stick to the rear, where the bowstring would be pulled back and set behind the top. Then she set the trigger by running out the trip wire to a patch of leaves several feet away. She'd swiped grapes from dinner and sprinkled them across the wide patch. In the clear sky, moonlight shone on olive berries, hoping to catch the eyes of a hungry raven.

She had attempted and failed several times before, wasting hours and running into dead ends. But she was determined to find the raven, no matter how long her wait would be. His feather, the key to translating King Samael's book, meant demons were connected to the Otherworld.

The night she discovered his story, she didn't sleep.

A plague took over my body for months, weakening my bones and tainting my lungs. One night, Oleander informed me that I was to die in my sleep. As I retired to my chambers, he drew a magic circle around the bedposts for protection. He said this was common practice among the Fae when they aid the ill, for these circles act as a reservoir of concentrated power when ignited with fire.

Yet new suspicions plagued me that night. How did Oleander know I was to die? Do the Fae have such natural inclinations, given their immortality, or did he possess other secrets? It made little sense why I would meet death so soon. My body is sturdy as a mountain, never shaken by wind or word. The heads of wild beasts hang upon my mantel from my years of conquests. And my mind, sharper than any blades my soldiers possess, recalled weeks of his insistence to prepare my food, his overeagerness to pour liquids into my goblet, his attentive devotion that he claimed to be concern.

It came as no surprise when he completed the magic circle and lunged to set the bed ablaze. Quick-witted as I am, I kept a dagger under my pillow and expertly blocked his attack. His strikes were clumsy and desperate, no match for my sidesteps and precise swipe of my weapon. Flames spread across my chambers and caught onto my robe. Oleander was not above unscrupulous tactics and used the frenzy to knock me to the ground. I pulled him down with me, our blood mixed with dust and fire amidst combat.

Then the carpet gaped open with a blinding light, and as our blood swirled mid-air, the unthinkable happened.

We fell out of existence and into the Otherworld.

Amelia's pulse hummed as she thought about her golden blood, the same that spilled on the magic circle long ago and created a new world. The anticipation buzzed in her veins. As if on call, the raven finally appeared.

The large bird cut through the moon like an inky trail. His claws landed atop the undergrowth, crackling the coppice. He was much larger than she remembered, a big, sooty bird with a thick neck and a knife of a beak. His red eyes narrowed on the grapes she'd laid out for him. He made a two-footed hop before his claw caught on the string. The arrow shot forward and cast a wide net over his body, capturing the bird and pinning the trap to the ground.

It was exactly as planned. She'd made sure the arrow would never hit him.

Trapped inside the net, the bird scrambled across the twigs and croaked so violently she could have sworn they were expletives if she could understand his language. She rushed over to the net and held the bird down with careful hands, not wanting her fingers to be pecked to bloody pulps.

"I'm sorry," she whispered frantically. "I'm not trying to hurt you, I promise."

He shook in her grasp before spitting out a grape. The fruit rolled pathetically over the soil. He might have glared at her, if ravens could make such expressions. She stared into the red pupils of his eyes. They were just as *The Book of Samael* had described in later passages of the Otherworld. Ravens were supposed to have eyes as black as soot, but this creature possessed pupils that glinted like fresh blood, a sign that they came from a different realm.

“I’m looking for Malicine,” she said. “Will you take me to them?”

Her free hand held a grape to his beak as a peace offering. He spat it out again. She frowned. “Why did you try to eat it if you don’t like it?”

“Because he thought you left behind an eyeball.”

She jerked back. A silhouette towered over her, blacker than night, with horns that stretched like the tall, shadowed pines surrounding them. A flick of a wrist emitted a flame from the demon’s palm, a torch that illuminated Malicine’s face. Shadows danced on their grave expression, green skin and cheekbones sharp like daggers. The dark slits of their eyes narrowed.

“You’ve been looking for me for weeks. Are humans incapable of tiring themselves, or does your naivete fuel you?”

Amelia swallowed hard. She thought back to the past nights, her clumsy figure skulking in shadows, haphazardly putting together traps and flimsy arrows. All this time, Malicine had been watching her from the corners of the woods, letting her fumble in the darkness. But if she had worn off the demon’s patience for them to finally emerge, she would take advantage of this.

“My name is Amelia,” she said. “I am the girl you cursed almost eighteen years ago.”

“Your time isn’t up yet, unless you’d like me to quicken it and have you die today.”

It was a threat, but dying was never a fear for her. Even as the wind shook the branches to warn of danger, she stood her ground and let the leaves scatter. “No. I want something better than death.”

Malicine raised a brow. “You are a strange human.”

She revealed the tome hidden in her cloak. Her shaky hands untied the string to release the pages, letting them flap like the wings of a pale butterfly.

"I found a book left behind by my ancestor. The people of Gyldan believe he died, but he says he escaped death by traveling to the Otherworld—"

"Your family lore does not entertain me," Malicine interrupted. They waved toward the net that covered the raven. Sharp nails sliced open the trap, setting the bird free. "Now leave before I let Talon feed on your eyeballs after all."

She stepped forward and jutted the open book to Malicine's face. "It's true, isn't it? That there's an Otherworld beyond physical boundaries. A place we can visit through magic."

"There have been stories, but no proof. Even if another world with demons existed, the portals that bring you there are no longer active. I have searched for years."

"That's because you're not supposed to find them. Portals don't exist until the traveler creates one with magic, and they close as quickly as they open. That's how King Samael discovered the Otherworld."

The mention of portals made Malicine pause. "All right," they said, after a moment of thought. "If portals are temporary openings instead of fixed positions, how did the king discover how to create one?"

Amelia set the book on a carpet of moss and spread its yellowed pages. She explained Samael's mysterious illness, Oleander's betrayal, and the bloodshed that inadvertently created a portal. By using one of Talon's feathers, she showed how the words rearranged themselves to legibility. Malicine skimmed the text, each page deepening a new wrinkle in their forehead.

Oleander was not a faerie, but a wicked demon, envious of my power and wanting to claim my life for himself. What we did not realize during our fight was the effects of spilling blood onto his magic circle. My gilded blood, his demon blood, combined to awaken the circle and open a portal.

"Magic circles have always taken power from nature, not ourselves," Malicine murmured. "If specific ingredients are used to create a barrier from the world, perhaps using something as potent as blood could open one. But why blood, of all things? Not that I'm opposed to blood sacrifice. I suppose that would be expected for my repertoire."

"I don't think it's sacrifice. It's willingly giving a piece of yourself to birth something that's always been a part of you," Amelia said. "Every creature carries their own unique blood, and every creature originates from their own world."

Malicine stared at Amelia with a degree of skepticism, but she could tell they were considering her words. The demon crossed a wide path in the forest, brows still furrowed in contemplation. They collected twigs and connected each stick in the shape of a circle while their eyes glazed over in thought. Nails scraped across the wood like a match before fire burst to life, spreading across the arrangement in the middle of the forest.

"All right. Let's try it, then. And if it doesn't work, your life will be an early sacrifice for wasting my time."

Flames gleamed in Malicine's eyes as they looked at Amelia, a silent challenge. Amelia accepted it as she walked inside the circle. Malicine stepped forward next. The two stared at each other, flames flickering over their faces. An unspoken knowledge hung between them that in this hidden space, they would repeat history, even if they had no idea the truth of what was on the other side.

"Why do you want to go there so desperately?" Malicine asked. The contempt in their narrowed eyes fell like a cracked mask, revealing a glint of curiosity in their green irises.

“I want to know if there’s more to live for,” Amelia said.

The demon considered her answer for a long moment. “I suppose I’m the same.”

She watched Malicine straighten their posture and turn back to the circle of fire. The demon faced both palms outward, casting a spell. The flames blurred before changing to the color of sea waves. Energy pulsed in the air like electric current. The trees glowed under the light, and pure white washed over the leaves.

Amelia could feel everything beginning to change. The color of the trees, the demon by her side. Malicine slashed their palm and spilled blood over the circle. In their eyes, Amelia recognized determination. While Malicine had cursed her to fall asleep, she’d brought something inside the demon to wake in return.

She extended her palm to Malicine to cut open. The pain was sharp but small, a passing blink. Blood dripped down her hand, laced in gold and glinting under the flames. The forest lit aglow, as if sensing their energy.

The first drop hit the ground. Amelia could no longer feel the weight of herself as they fell below.

CHAPTER 23

CORIN ATTEMPTED TO swim back to Summerland, but the currents had pulled her too far. Her strength had already waned when a large shadow cast from the sky. Malicine's wings flapped rapidly as they dove toward Corin to retrieve her. It was hardly a rescue mission, since they were quick to release Corin mid-air when they reached the shore. The force rolled her body across the sand until her chest slammed into a rock. She reeled over and heaved water. Several pearls had clogged her throat and spewed into the sand. It wasn't until her retching subsided that Malicine towered over her.

"What is wrong with you?" they snapped. "I told you to get out!"

Corin looked back at the ocean. Beyond the horizon, an island loomed as a speck of gray, like a blot of ink that stained a ruined canvas. The faraway land had crept up on her without her even noticing. By the time she did, the clouds had unfurled like rotting flowers, and the bottom of the ocean had pulled her to drown. Strands of kelp had wrapped around her ankles, wrists, thighs, almost as if the island's fingers were tightening around her, claiming her for its depths.

How had it been possible that she didn't notice the island until now?

Elly's voice brought Corin back to shore. Her small figure darted across the sand, followed by Briar, who had reverted to normal in her pristine dress and sun-kissed skin. As if she hadn't been caught in the tides, wrecked with despair in her truest form mere moments ago.

Elly leapt into Corin's arms and squeezed her tight. "I thought I lost you," she sobbed.

Corin buried her face into Elly's hair, welcoming the smell of salt instead of death, her sister's warm skin instead of the corpses she had seen below. The steady drum of Elly's pulse reminded her they were both alive and safe. "I could say the same to you."

Malicine continued stewing in irritation while they healed Corin's wounds. She tested their patience anyway.

"What was that island?"

"A place I separated from the rest of the dreamworld," they growled. "Get close to Autumnland, and the island will drag you down into its abyss."

"I don't understand. You were the one who created this world. I thought this was supposed to be a perfect paradise for—"

"Just because it's a dream doesn't mean it can't turn into a nightmare," they said. "Imagine every skeleton you've kept locked in your closet. Autumnland is where they stay. And if you visit them, they will kill you."

"You mean I'll wake up," Corin said with wariness, as if this were a test.

"No. Amelia may be the one sleeping, but our bodies crossed from the physical world to the dreamworld when we entered. Which means if we die here, we will cease to exist at all."

The words raised goose bumps to the back of Corin's neck. She imagined turning into nothing, as if she'd never been real to begin with. As if she'd never even mattered.

She glanced at Briar, whose skin slowly filled with color again. The princess ran her hands over her arms, rubbing them for warmth and hiding the prickles of flesh that Corin had seen stained with blood. The strange visions in the dark depths of the ocean had revealed something real. Perhaps it was the only real thing she'd witnessed throughout the dreamworld.

I see you, Amelia.

"We should continue our journey," Briar said. "There's no need to revisit the currents again."

Corin knew Briar did not want to discuss what happened. The girl needed to avoid the pain, even if it meant severing whoever she loved before. But the agony Corin had experienced in the ocean told her it didn't matter how deep Briar tried to bury her suffering. It would always breathe back into her lungs, one way or another.

Waves crashed against the shore and retreated like a whisper. Sunlight trickled across the beach, and a group of tiny spheres glinted like stars in the sand. Corin recognized the pearls that had spewed from her throat moments ago. As they melted in sand, a small wire emerged from each gem, stringing them together into a necklace. She picked them up and inspected closer. The coating had worn off, and the glass base underneath had been what caught the light. There was a stain on several of them, so small and minuscule that they could have been constellations.

But stars were never as red as this, and blood had never looked so familiar.

THE VISIONS CONTINUED taunting the back of Corin's mind, distracting her from new senses in Summerland. Her group had left the beach to hike an upward slope in a jungle, where the air turned thick and warm, and sweat drenched the back of her shirt. Somehow, Elly had enough energy to climb thick trees and tangled vegetation. She combed her fingers through tropical flowers and jumped in mud to see how far it would splatter her clothes. Malicine even entertained her whimsies and led her below a canopy. The demon made Elly look up at the overhang until it burst with colorful birds, and she laughed in delight, climbing vines to reach them.

Corin took advantage of their distraction by seizing Briar's arm. She pulled the girl behind a thick cluster of ferns. Hanging foliage swayed behind their heads like curtains, shielding the two from view. She cornered Briar against a tree trunk, her palm pressed against the bark, her voice lowered into a whisper.

"What the hell did I see back there?" she hissed.

"It was just a nightmare," Briar replied evenly, like she had practiced this response. "It wasn't real."

"You're lying. That was a memory." Those visions had felt too real to be imagined, too painful to be a dream. Grief clung to Corin's chest long after the mirages disappeared, twisting her heart as if she, too, had experienced the worst night of her life and wanted to die. "Why are you hiding Amelia?"

A flash of pain crossed Briar's face. Her eyes lost focus, clouds from a dark night shading the once bright color of sea glass. The rosy blush in her cheeks left behind pallor and clenched teeth.

"The stories say Gyldan will prosper so long as their royalty carries golden blood. But such things never held weight. The king and queen died because of Amelia," Briar said. "It is better to be a coward. When I try to fight, it only ends in death. At least here, I can forget. I can be someone else."

"But you're not someone else," Corin argued. "You're Amelia. You saved me. Which makes everything confusing, because I'm supposed to hate you."

Sunlight filtered through the trees, fractures of light falling on Briar's face like crystal gems, yet never meeting her eyes. Their breaths were warm against each other's faces as they stared at each other. If Corin looked long enough, she could see the small crack in Briar's lips, the uneven rise and fall of her chest. If she stroked Briar's jaw, she could notice the way it clenched, the vulnerability of flaws that lingered behind a false painting. Corin had felt Briar's despair so acutely, because it lived in her bones as well.

She longed to meet Amelia and tear open her heart. She wanted to peer inside that bleeding organ and ask, *How did you know this was my pain too?*

"I saw you too," Briar said. "When we were drowning in the ocean. Your memories with your friends. What you told Elly before she ran away."

Corin took a step back, reeling in shock, as if Briar had cut her open. But of course Briar had seen it. If the ocean revealed the worst night of Amelia's life, then Corin's would have been on full display in return. In the underwater depths, their open wounds existed, gaping at one another.

"Don't," Corin said, bristling at the edge of her words. "Don't you dare judge me for that. You don't know everything."

"I would never judge you," Briar whispered, her voice so gentle it made Corin's heart crack. As if the girl sensed the fracture, she placed a hand on Corin's chest, filling it with warmth at her touch. "You and Elly can be happy here. After everything you two have been through, isn't that enough?"

Corin could no longer meet Briar's eyes. The girl saw too much, excavating her bones and unearthing her sorrows without permission. How could Briar have heard what Corin told Elly and believe she still deserved happiness? Corin glanced upward, fighting back tears, and fixated on the apricots hanging from a tree. A tiny punch of sour hit her tongue, as if she could taste the fruit. Orange paint filled her vision, a bright round orb that dripped to the bottom of a canvas, her mother's hand steadying hers over a brush.

You just made the sun, her mother had said. As if Corin really did have that kind of magic in her hands.

But she was not a girl who held magic. She was only a thief with bitter words, nothing more.

"This isn't real," she insisted, her voice close to breaking.

Briar's stare seemed to trace the curve of her face, unearthing her shame and accepting it anyway. "And what if it's not?"

She shook her head. "I can't do that to El. Or Harlow. Or anyone." Her voice trembled. "It's not fair."

Not after what I did.

Elly's shouts erupted from the other side of the foliage, her voice breaking their reverie. The sound made Corin's heart leap out of her chest and jolted her forward. Her limbs thrashed the thick grass surrounding them as she charged through tangled vines to find her sister. In the open clearing, Elly and Malicine had both turned in the same direction, gazes caught by a wild fox behind the bushes. Corin recognized the brown fur and beady eyes in the dappled sunlight. Even when the fox turned to run, she knew he had been following her.

Mud spat in the air as Elly charged after the fox's blurry tail, leaving the group behind. Panic overtook Corin's pounding heart once more.

"El, wait!"

Elly didn't listen as she disappeared into the foliage. Corin chased her through a winding path of thick trees and sliding boulders. She cut through woody vines and fallen fruit, yelling for Elly to come back. She didn't want her sister to find out.

Find out what?

She didn't know. No, not that—she didn't want to remember.

Her legs slowed down to an open area in the middle of the jungle, where clusters of trees wrapped around them like a bowl. In the center, Elly knelt in front of a limp figure, hunched over in grief. Her back looked so small. What she held, even smaller.

Corin approached them from the side, even though she already knew what was in Elly's hands. The fox had shrunk since she last saw him in Winterland. His tail drooped lifelessly over Elly's arm, his head buried in her lap. Tangled clumps of dirt matted his coat. Elly picked through his fur, as if to inspect for wounds. She only found cracks in his skin, lengthening around his face and torso, his flesh split so far open it bled in clay. Her tears stained his porcelain coat as she kept piecing him together. Each shard sliced her skin while phantom pain coursed through Corin's hands, her fists clenching to ignore it.

Fixing him was useless. Every time she fiddled with the pieces, they left cracks, evidence of it breaking apart.

"Don't you understand?" Corin said. "We can't put him back together again."

Elly placed him gently to the ground, where he separated into pieces. She turned to Corin, tears slicking the dark pools of her eyes.

"Then why did you break him?"

Elly's tears flashed in Corin's memory. She gasped on Gyldan's thick air, nearly choked on it. She didn't want the anger and desolation to return—their year in that house, walls cracked and peeling, floorboards groaning under each step, as if the building had resigned itself to ruin. Elly had hated this home. She despised its protective isolation, craving instead to return to the commune's shared tents, a place that rang with laughter and not secrets whispered through broken beams.

It didn't matter that Corin had told her sister that their friends were gone. Elly was too naïve to believe in the permanence of death. "Harlow wouldn't have been caught so easily," her sister had argued that night, fueling Corin's irritation.

Corin paced around the muddy ground of the jungle, but the dreamscape morphed to the memory as if it were happening in real time. Tall trees melted into gray walls. Tangled vines transformed to leaking pipes. Bark turned to burlap, fruit and foliage to tattered sheets and dust and mold. The familiar flare of anger coursed through her veins, where any sound her sister made would set her off like a bomb.

She was cold and tired and hungry. The lease was meant to be a new beginning, yet the decrepit house was far from the home she'd thought it would be. She'd sworn to herself that stealing from the commune would be the last time, that a steady job and clean slate would be enough, as if playing by the rules would make life fair. Soon she grew tired of tightening her wallet, rationing bites, screaming in the middle of the night from nightmares of raining bullets and dead friends. Sleep came to her only in fragments, for she refused to close her eyes and dream, terrified that she would see Harlow and the others bleeding before her every night. Her sanity was a frail thread, one that would snap under any more weight.

Still, Elly continued rambling. "Maybe their plan worked. Maybe they escaped Gyldan—"

Corin slammed a hand on the table inside their home. The ceramic fox Harlow once gave her rolled to the edge and shattered on the ground.

"They're dead, El." Her patience had worn thin, and she no longer cared about delivering the news so bluntly. "They used the tunnels to plant a bomb under a military post. The soldiers knew and wasted no time killing them. You should be grateful we never got involved."

Elly rushed to the broken fox, her knees pressed to loose floor boards, fingers pricking against the jagged edges of clay. The attempt was so useless it made Corin want to scream.

"But they planned this for so long," Elly argued. "How would they have gotten caught—"

"Because I told him, El!"

Her words spewed out in an angry rush, a dam burst open to reveal nothing but regret and self-loathing. She didn't realize the snarl at the end of her sentence until it lingered in the air, silencing them both. The leaking pipe made a small, dripping sound that matched her heartbeat, though Corin could have sworn she heard the cracks in her sister's.

"Who?" Elly whispered.

For the first time, her voice was quiet and frail, a flimsy hope that Corin would be better than this. They both knew that would be a lie. Elly believed in fairy tales, but even she couldn't believe in something as impossible as Corin being good.

Corin could not bear to say his name without wanting to vomit.

"The man who put this roof over our heads."

She had kept away from Woodbine's shop whenever she patrolled the marketplace for easy marks to pickpocket. He'd often conversed with soldiers, a business suit among steel uniforms, laughing in camaraderie as if they weren't responsible for others' suffering. The man was indistinguishable from any other landlord rubbing elbows and licking boots for approval.

She had caught his eye without stealing anything, as if her very existence had incriminated her. He'd approached her like she was a disposable body he recognized across the street, claiming she had a friend who took something of his. Even when she acted oblivious, he'd cornered her, a group of soldiers behind him in tow, ready to beat her into submission if she tried to run.

He'd claimed to see Harlow and other vagrants skulking around the shops, collecting wood pulp and sawdust and gunpowder. He knew they were the same group of people spreading protest flyers around districts. What he'd wanted to know was what they were planning.

"You'd get in a lot of trouble for stealing from me. Fortunately, I'm a generous man," he'd said. "I can tell you value the same things as I do. When there's a lucrative opportunity, we take it. That's the only way we survive in this world."

The deal had been renting one of his vacant properties for five years and only paying for one year in monthly installments. Corin had been stunned by the proposition. She hadn't allowed herself to believe it until he'd prepared the contract. A roof and four walls guaranteed by signature, even if the ink would be stained with blood.

He'd promised to send soldiers to kill her in their place if she warned the group about their conversation. On her last night at the commune, she'd told Harlow not to go to the tunnels, that they would die if they tried to execute their plan, but she could not reveal why. Did the reason matter? Her warning would have been the same even if she had not met Woodbine. They would have died regardless, with or without her.

She thought she'd made the logical choice for survival. And yet, with each night she'd screamed herself awake from nightmares, she only remembered herself as a desperate, pathetic animal that had been backed into a corner and chose to save only herself.

Elly must have thought the same, for she was still staring at Corin with disgust.

Corin had never seen her sister look at her that way before. Her skin itched with shame. She wanted to rip it off until she could no longer live inside her own wretched body.

"I warned Harlow not to go. I tried to get them to stop. But we had to leave them, El." Like an afterthought, she added, "I did it for us."

"Stop lying, Corin. You did it for yourself."

Elly stood up, her volume rising with her height. Since when had she grown so quickly? The girl used to be a wailing infant in Corin's arms. Now she stood nearly at eye level and talked back when Corin did something irreparable.

"I was happy with them, and you couldn't be. You kept wanting more."

"Of course I wanted more!" Corin shouted, a burst of fury in her chest like her heart was a star collapsing into itself. "I don't want to die a starving artist or be part of a rebellion. I don't want to sleep on the ground because every army owns the land we walk on. I don't want to hold on to little figurines and have my life be reduced to useless, sentimental trinkets just to cope with everything I've lost."

Her boots crunched against the shards of clay on the ground. The sharp edges of the fox cut into the soles. Her bare hands grabbed the pieces. She held a jagged chip, the paint already peeling off. The cuts in her palm stung as if she held that pen again, signing her fate, throwing away her friends' lives in return.

"You have no idea what I've sacrificed." The words burst from her lungs like a sob while anger shook her body. She hated the cards that life dealt her, and how, no matter which card she played, she would lose every single time.

"I didn't ask you to sacrifice for me," Elly said.

"And I didn't ask to be your sister. I never wanted any of this. I never wanted *you*."

Elly took a step back, as if Corin had taken the shard and sliced it into her sister's chest. The girl's features crumpled up on her face, the way they always did when she was about to cry.

Briefly, Corin remembered the day Elly was born. Her wrinkly face, her earsplitting wails. Slicked in blood, skin crinkled and wet in the oddest of places, her baby sister had looked disgusting. Corin had been six years old and resented losing her place as the only child. She'd hated watching their mother's gaze slip away from her to Elly, making space in her heart for a new person, a parent's love that would surely be rationed the same way food was. As Elly grew, Corin had kneaded the rolls in her sister's legs like baking dough, poked at her crooked teeth, made faces at the odd creature that inhabited her life. Elly learned to walk, but kept stumbling over her feet. Corin had never tried to catch her.

"We can't survive without each other," their mother had said. "You have to protect your little sister."

Now Elly stood, crying once more.

Corin remembered what happened next. She recalled it before the scene repeated itself in front of her. The seconds where Elly took a deep, trembling breath, before she let the words stab into Corin's chest.

"I hate you."

Elly ran into the darkness. Boots squelched in mud on Gyldan's rainy pavements as Corin chased after her. Gravel-gray skies swallowed them back inside the sun-drenched jungle of Summerland. Corin watched Elly dart between trees and reached to grab her sister until quicksand gripped her shoes. Ankles stuck, her body fell forward, hitting a fresh sheet of snow. A blizzard roared in her ears as it turned the world white. Her eyes strained to see, barely making out the black spikes of Elly's hair that ducked behind a castle formed in ice. As Corin got up, the snow melted to grass, stretching to endless meadows of green that sprouted wildflowers and camouflaged her sister. She barreled through a broken cottage, tore through stones and plastic furniture, chased after Elly through a winding maze of sunflowers.

Scenes morphed into one another. Seasons changed, the world continued turning, and still, Corin could never reach her sister.

Tears blurred her vision. It was bound to happen, ending up alone. She never understood how they always came back to this place. The cycle was the same. Talking turned to yelling. Loving turned to resenting. They didn't know any other way to be together.

She threw her head back to the sky and yelled for the world to take them back, but she didn't know where. Not to dreams or broken homes, not to any place where they had gotten along. As night descended, sunflower stalks groaned into limp postures. Their petals shriveled to brown and fell into heaps. Thick, woody vines wrapped around her ankles and pulled her deeper to the ground. She coughed out soil and rocks while her empty palms grasped for nothing. The harder she struggled, the deeper she sank. She clawed the dirt until her fingers turned raw and her nails went black.

Then a new voice emerged, one that stilled her into place.

"Don't fight it."

The sound had a familiar softness, one that brought forth a recent memory of ocean waves. From the corner of Corin's vision, a small light appeared. A lantern dangled in Briar's hand as she stepped inside the maze. The sunflowers slowly lifted, their heads tilting to one side.

Briar's voice was gentle as she knelt in front of Corin, as if Corin had simply been lost. "You don't need to run. Give in, and the sunflowers will take you where you need to go."

"It's not that easy," Corin protested.

"You're dreaming," Briar said. "In dreams, you don't need to make things harder for yourself than they already are."

She set the lantern down and watched the tiny door swivel open. Her hand reached for the flame, cupping it gently in her palm.

"In the dollhouse, you said I was retreating into my dreams to hide. But you've been running away too. Only, it's been in the opposite direction."

Corin's hands tried clawing their way out of the hole, but as she sank, she could only think about who dug this hole in the first place. Was it Briar Rose who taunted her, or had Corin been the one holding the shovel, preparing her own grave?

"I felt your memories in the ocean," Briar murmured. "I tasted you, and you were bitter. Like there was too much salt for the water to contain."

The flame burned bright in her hand, charring the tips of her fingers. Briar held it gently, not wanting to snuff the fire out, even if it hurt her. Tears welled in her eyes yet refused to spill.

"But beneath the bitterness was something else. I felt like I wanted to cry, but I couldn't. Your anger shielded me from it. I think that's what it's been doing all along."

Briar extended her palm to Corin, holding the fire close. The flame raged on, a bright burning ball that was too painful to look at. Corin wanted to turn away, but woody vines wrapped tightly around her limbs, fixing her in place. Her eyes took in the light, and there it was, the grief that she had swallowed, burning her insides. The suffocating taste of shame dried her throat like ash, curling deep into her lungs, quietly eroding her broken heart.

This kind of pain was worse than anger. It told her that she lost too many people she loved, not from the cruelty of their world, but because of her own selfishness.

As Corin continued staring into the fire, her heartbeats slowed into a dull rhythm. The pain was still there, though she became used to the sharp sting, the smoke lingering on her skin, the embers fading with each steady breath. She listened to Briar's quiet breathing while they sat in front of the light. Neither exchanged words while feeling everything beneath the flame.

Here was the truth, ugly and imperfect and a part of her: Corin was not a realist, but a coward. She'd stamped over her sister's drawings and scorned her friends' plans because they saw something she could never grasp. They had imagined a future, while she could not even believe in her own.

She understood, then, what she needed to do.

Soil eroded below her ears as she felt herself floating back to the surface. Briar placed the flame back inside the lantern before passing the torch to Corin, whose fingers grasped the handle by instinct. They watched the light spread wider, like sunlight pouring from a bottle and crashing over a field. Sunflowers rose from the soil and dove their heads into an orange sky. Their roots untangled from Corin's limbs. She shook off the vines with a strange sense of lightness in her body.

The stalks parted way for a clear path, where at the end of the field, Elly was waiting.

Corin left Briar behind and crossed the field, carrying the lantern and aching pain in her chest the entire way. Her breaths grew shaky as she drew closer to the curve of Elly's back. Her sister sat hunched over the ground, the broken shards of the fox at her feet.

At the end of the road was just the two of them. The heavy weight of silence pressed on both their sagging shoulders until, finally, Elly spoke.

"You think I'm naive for wanting to believe in things," she said. "But it's not because I'm too young to understand how life works. I know how terrible the world is, Corin. I grew up in it too. But I have to believe in something. Because if I don't, what are we even living for?"

Tears spiked Elly's lashes, gray memories flashing like nightmares. She scrubbed the tears from her cheeks and sucked in a sharp breath, like it was the first time her lungs held air.

"I hate you, Corin. I hate you for betraying our friends. I hate that you destroy things before giving them a chance. I hate how you're so afraid to be happy, like it's some kind of trap."

Corin's knuckles turned white, her fingers curling into fists. Her tongue threatened to lash out, as it often did to bury the shame. But her eyes fell upon the flame burning inside the lantern. The lamp was too heavy in her hand, yet it had guided her down the road to Elly.

If Corin was going to say the truth, as painful as it was, she needed to say it while her sister was here.

"I hate you, too, El. You piss me off constantly. You're annoying, and bratty, and never listen to what I say. When Ma was pregnant with you, I already knew you'd be a thorn in my side. The truth is that I didn't want you to be born, because you would be another burden for me to take care of."

Raw emotion tumbled out from her voice, giving way beneath the strain she'd harbored for years. She inhaled another shaky breath before sitting beside her sister. They didn't look at each other. When their shoulders touched, a brush of warmth slowly filled her body.

"Then, somehow, you ended up being the best thing that happened to me. I can't imagine life without you, El. It just—it doesn't exist."

She stared at the broken pieces of clay and felt a knot in her stomach. She would never be able to put him back together, nor would she ever be able to look away from her mistakes.

"I'm sorry I ruined everything. I thought if I always expected the worst, it would protect me. I was wrong. Harlow was a radical because she had hope. I was a coward because I couldn't even dream it. I'll always regret what I did. Every day, I think about how I should have died with them, because at least then, it wouldn't hurt anymore."

The wind whistled through the fields, rustling sunflower petals with a mourning howl. She took a deep breath, stilling herself before her confession.

"The only reason why I'm not dead is because of you. You are why I'm still here, El."

Corin knew the life raft that was her sister extended beyond her mistakes from last year. Everything she did to keep them alive, every sacrifice she resented making, those choices had been made because Elly was there. If Corin was the darkness, Elly had been her light. Her sister was the thorn in her side that she refused to pull out.

Some pain in life was too excruciating to bear. The loss of their parents. Her betrayal of their friends. The slow death of her dreams.

And then there was some pain that made it worth staying.

The wind calmed into a gentle breeze, swaying the sunflower stalks. Somewhere in the distance, wind chimes tinkled like a childhood song. Corin could hear Elly's heartbeats matching her own, a slow and steady drum. She did not expect her sister to forgive her. Some things could never be forgiven. So what was it that she was so desperate to have?

Spikes of hair grazed her cheek as Elly finally turned to look at her.

"I believe you," she whispered.

Corin blinked through the burning in her eyes. She swallowed the lump in her throat while emotions surged inside her like a storm. She placed the lantern aside and crushed Elly in an embrace, holding her sister so tight their bodies could have fused together.

In the break of dawn, the sunflowers bent from their stalks, reached for the sisters, and enveloped the two together. Petals folded over their limbs, soft and sturdy as an anchor. Corin closed her eyes. With Elly's hand in hers, the sunflowers carried them back to where they needed to go.

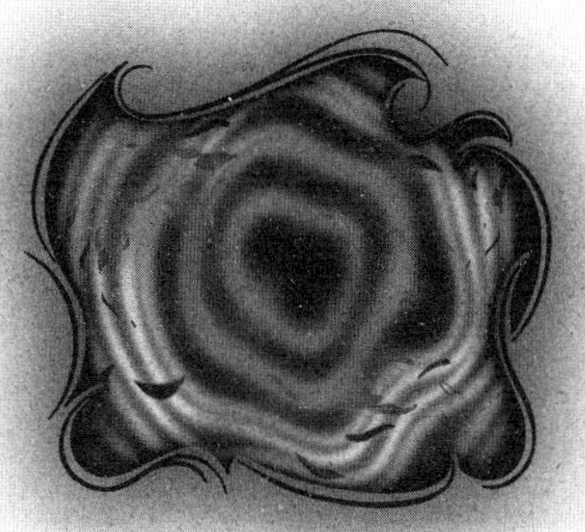

CHAPTER 24

101 YEARS AGO

AMELIA DID NOT know where she needed to go, but at some point, she felt the plunge. The descent was like hitting the first wave of an ocean, except it was a dark cloud, dense and barely breathable. The smell of blood had grown so thick that she felt like she had swallowed fistfuls of copper. Then dirt filled her mouth, and she lay face down on a hard surface. She spat out soil and let mud fill the chips of her nails as her fingers dug the ground. She hoisted herself up and inhaled her first breath, one that felt nothing like life.

She'd landed on a dusty road, rocks digging into her ribs. The air was thick with smog, filling her lungs with coal. Deep orange blanketed the hazy sky, as if a wildfire had spread across the land, except there were no flames to be seen. She'd expected roiling flames, wails of agony, even molten lava. She thought she would see horned demons fly across the sky and had mentally prepared for the scratches and fangs of predators in a new, dangerous world.

The Otherworld was nothing like she expected. Not a wall of

red, not even a secret hell living underground. Instead, it felt like she'd been encased inside a jar. A still moment in the aftermath of destruction. Reds were merely dull sepia, while everything was eerily still.

She looked down and saw her skin covered in a translucent sheen. Her body had turned to glass. Even her dress looked transparent, like water frozen in time, blue fabric melting to a river that swirled around her body. She stared at the lines of her palms like cracks in a mirror. Her hands pressed to her cheeks and felt the cool surface of glass. Her fingers fiddled with the hard crystals of her lashes. If she pressed too hard, the lashes would crack off. She wondered, if she fell over, how she might shatter entirely.

A voice called her name in the distance. A pair of horns emerged from the fog, followed by the shadow of a raven. Malicine cut through smoke and ash, then stopped when they saw her. "Why do you look like that?"

She stared at her hands, not knowing how to respond. To her surprise, the raven did.

"The Otherworld is a different counterpart from the world you know. In here, your sin becomes part of your skin."

She gawked at him. "How can I understand what you're saying?"

"Because this land is where I was born, little girl. You may call me Talon."

Malicine held up their arms and tried rubbing the green off their skin. Still the shade remained. "Looks like my sin will never go away."

"That's because you were born in sin, Malicine. It is your whole existence."

The demon swallowed a lump down their throat, their features twisting as if they had tasted something bitter, before they looked around. Amelia followed their gaze to the rust-colored sky where they had fallen from. Thick clouds rolled over the atmosphere, and between the folds, a circle glimmered in light. At first, she thought it might have been the sun. But the borders around the shape were dark like ink, and they began to crumble. Tiny flecks of gold rained from the sky like ash. She let a piece fall in her palm before the slightest movement made the scab crumble and disintegrate.

When she looked up again, the portal was gone.

"Blood opens the portal, and the portal is sealed once it dries." Malicine's eyes sharpened at Talon. "That's why you weren't able to return."

They squinted at their surroundings, but the smoke was too thick. Wings sprouted from Malicine's back as they flew in the air to find a peripheral view. As they reached higher, Amelia heard them starting to cough. A large ash chunk hurtled through the air and struck the demon's side, burning a hole in their cape. They crashed into the ground and heaved more soot from their lungs.

"What's wrong with the air?" they spat, putting out the flames with their fist.

"I do not know. It has been too long. But I am starting to remember now, life before this." Talon pecked at the crumbs littered on the ground until they dissolved in his beak. *"There used to be trees that stretched for miles in the sky. The world was a barren terrain of ice and sleet, and demons roamed everywhere. Now there is nothing but red."*

Amelia blinked at the land of ash around them. Burnt tree trunks were left as headless stumps, rotten and decayed. Everything was covered in a coat of grime, so that wherever she touched, ash smudged her brittle fingers.

They wandered around the desolate land, the oppressive heat fogging her glass skin. The air was heavy with the smell of burnt flesh, and she followed the stench of death to uncover a pile of debris, where corpses rotted in ash and dust. She recognized bent horns, broken wings, spikes and slimy black coils that had long been dried in charcoal.

"We're too late," Malicine murmured. Disappointment betrayed their stiff face. Even if there were other creatures, perhaps ones that had looked like Malicine, they were all dead.

"This can't be it," Amelia insisted. Denial fueled her to move. She raced to the shore, where waves of a dark sea creeped steadily toward them. Black water moved in a slow, rhythmic pulse. Layers of soot covered the surface in a muddy expanse. A weak gust of wind barely moved a canoe that had been stuck in the water. She tried pulling the stern, but the fixture refused to budge. Every time she pulled, the canoe groaned like it was dying, and new cracks etched her skin from straining too hard.

"You're not going anywhere," Malicine said flatly.

The shards of her fingers jammed into the rotting boat, but it refused to budge. She would never move forward. The water was too still, too solid, a semi-stagnant pool of death and decay. Frustrated, she gave up and sat inside, ruminating on yet another failure.

How quickly her hopes had disintegrated, like dreams that would never be remembered after the cruelty of waking up. She'd wanted to stay in those dreams, even for a moment, to see if she really could live somewhere.

She knew her desires were irrational for any regular person, let alone a princess. Perhaps she could at least make sense of it now. In the thick smoke, she turned to Malicine.

"Why did you curse me?"

The demon blinked, taken aback by the sudden question.

Perhaps it was the hard press of her lips and desperate eyes that made them answer in earnest.

"The curse wasn't for you. It was revenge on my sisters, who were your godmothers. I wanted to ruin their reputation."

The simplicity of the truth struck her. She was surprised, at first, to discover her godmothers were related to Malicine. Then something else burrowed beneath the initial shock. A hint of a tear crackled her cheekbone, the glass crumbling.

The curse had nothing to do with her.

For so long, she had wanted to sleep forever. Her mind was stuck in fog of perpetual apathy for life. She thought an answer would dissipate the mist and bring clarity. There had always been a shadow following her, whispering wishes for her life to end. Now she knew where these shadows came from.

"It was never you."

Her words died into a whisper as she caught a glass tear in her palm. The teardrop burst into shards so small they disappeared into her hand, becoming part of her once more, a never-ending cycle.

"There is no reason for the darkness," she murmured. "It is just who I am."

Her gaze fixed into the distance where the fog showed no future ahead of them. She was an empty glass with no reflection. Perhaps that was why she was made of it. She hadn't wanted to cross to the Otherworld because she was brave. It was not adventure she desired, but escape. Her tears continued to fall, collecting into broken shards around her feet.

A long silence passed, disrupted occasionally by her quiet weeping. She hushed when Malicine climbed into the boat with her, Talon joining their side. The demon sat in the back and placed a palm on the water's surface. Ash swirled under their skin, thick like tar. Then a white substance bubbled from the water, a sliver of air. Their fingers twirled in a circle over the water to build momentum. They extended their arm and let the energy release itself.

A gust of wind struck the boat and propelled them forward. The jet of solid wind made the ancient wood creak, nearly tipping over. Talon landed in Amelia's lap while she gripped the ledge. She readjusted her balance with him and turned back to the demon. "Thank you."

"It was only to stop your crying."

Malicine left trails in the boat's wake, a rippling chop shooting across the black sea and swelling the waves behind them. Their power was like a streak of moonlight that ripped across a dark sky. Amelia could only hope the journey wasn't aimless. That it could still lead to something on the other side. Somehow, she knew Malicine felt the same way.

She dipped her hand in the water. The murky surface broke apart under her touch. Her fingers created a trail as the boat drifted forward, the smallest ripples radiating from the tips of her skin. Ash clung onto her hand in wet layers, yet she didn't recoil back in disgust. Instead, her eyes drifted over the patterns in the water, the expanding ring over the black sea.

"Maybe you've granted me a favor with this curse," she mused. "If I live any longer, I would waste a perfectly good life."

She let out a half-hearted laugh, but Malicine didn't join her. The demon's lips turned downward into a scowl, wrinkles deepening between their brows. She had said something wrong.

Malicine stood with an abrupt swiftness that caused the boat to shake under the sudden imbalance of weight. Amelia clung onto the ledge again while the demon towered over her. Their glare was enough to make her sink lower in her seat, their eyes flashing a poisonous green, as she realized this was something deeper than annoyance. For the first time, she felt hatred radiating from them.

"We are not friends, princess. Do not expect me to feel sorry when you were born in a world that already bows to your feet. You are nothing more than a tool to me. Once I find the Demon King, you will be lucky if I choose to abandon you rather than kill you."

Their wrath simmered beneath their skin, and she fell silent. She couldn't help but notice this was the same energy that thrummed between them at their first meeting. Surely, that was the fuel that propelled them to join her in this strange place. Behind their barbed words and hardened expressions, she sensed something deeper, sadder. She thought of them being born in her world, neither human nor Fae, ostracized by a society that made no shape for them to fit inside. How alone they must have felt to live in such a place.

Talon cut the tense silence with a shrill croak. The waves turned vicious and knocked the boat against a jagged rock. Mist cloaked an unfamiliar shore as they crashed into a boulder. Amelia's weight lifted off the boat and fell into the sea stack. She hit something hard and, in the next moment, felt her body shatter.

CHAPTER 25

THE CRASHING WAVES of a waterfall rang in Corin's ears like shattered glass. The sunflowers had carried the sisters to the top of the mountain, where the higher atmosphere turned the air crisp and granted them a view of several miles of landscape. Petals unfurled over her eyes to reveal soft hues washing over the beach, its sands earthen and muted like flour on bread. She allowed the sunset to warm her skin, watching the body of brine transform into tinted sepia, the ocean into dark waves, the skies into marigold.

Briar and Malicine had also reached the summit and reunited with them. Corin stepped onto a jagged rock and let fresh air kiss her cheeks. A waterfall sprouted from the cliffside ahead. Her heart beat against the necklace resting on her chest. She thought about their new future, just within their reach, as she would finally find her treasure.

Black rocks shone around the crest of the waterfall where the stream began. A rectangular wooden box was submerged underwater, snagged by a stray branch. She hadn't spotted the box until Briar pointed out its location. Of course the treasure chest would look nondescript, hidden at the highest peak of the mountain and covered by running streams and shrubbery.

Corin's hands held two things. In her left, Elly's palm. In her right, the necklace tucked beneath her shirt. She let both go so she could approach the waterfall, careful to balance atop the pathway of rocks. Her palms scooped the box and felt the smooth wooden surface. The treasure was lighter than she expected, but her fingers started trembling, and suddenly the chest felt heavy with the knowledge that its contents would change her future.

She held more gold than she ever carried in her life. This was the sort of wealth people fought wars and betrayed lovers for. Her eyes stole a glance at the others waiting near the plateau. She could not read the expressions on Briar and Malicine, but Elly, she could always recognize. The pinch between her brows, the worried teeth mark on her bottom lip. Corin wanted to reassure her that she didn't need to be nervous. For the first time, they were going to be okay. Corin would be the one to prove it.

Her fingers pried open the hinge, a slow yawning of the box for the grand reveal. Yet contained inside velvet lining was not a necklace glittering in gold, a long-lost crown jewel made of hundreds of carats, or any item belonging to royalty at all.

Instead there was a canvas, flat and old and barely bigger than her hand. Splatters of paint created a familiar scene: tangerine skies, puffy clouds, rolling green hills separated by a river. This painting looked like Summerland, except she recognized in the picture the rows of rooftops from Gyldan, the chimney smoke wafting in the air, the bundle of wildflowers in the foreground. She remembered how shaky her hand had become from painting every tiny petal. How the sunset looked beautiful as she'd followed her mother down the cliff, their skin turning a darker shade of brown.

How much she had loved that ordinary day.

"What is it?" Elly asked, trying to peer over Corin's shoulder. Corin couldn't respond. The box collapsed to the ground, and the waterfall seized it in roaring waves. She held the painting in shaking hands, but she couldn't see it anymore, only a curtain of red rage.

The painting shouldn't have existed. Not anymore. A soldier had smashed his foot through the canvas during one of their invasions. She remembered thinking she should have sold the art and at least gotten a few coins, rather than cling onto it in foolish sentimentality.

Why was it in her hands now? With her dreams gone, what use could she possibly have for it anymore?

"Whatever appears inside the box is your treasure," Briar said. "You used to paint, didn't you? It's—"

Corin spun around, nearly snapping the canvas in half. "You promised you'd give me your family's treasure. The one that Ezran waited a hundred years for. The one that *you* abandoned."

"Briar didn't promise that," Malicine interrupted. "She said she would help find your treasure. The one that belongs to you."

Corin couldn't believe it. She let out a bitter laugh. What was art but just a rich man's dream? It would never provide for her, put food in her stomach, or help her feel safe at night. She didn't have the capacity to create beautiful things. She had no energy left for dreaming.

"Is this some kind of joke? You get my hopes up, string me along, just to give me something worthless and say that's all I ever wanted?"

The sunset softened Briar's sad expression. She spoke more gently, and that infuriated Corin even more. "If it matters to you, it's not worthless."

Something snapped in Corin. The frivolity of Briar's words, the useless emotions behind them. If she was trying to teach Corin a lesson, she picked the wrong person. Rage broke the canvas into pieces, splintering the frames, cracking the varnish. Corin hurled the painting over the waterfall, where the waves would swallow it whole, bleeding the paints together until the scenery became soaked in sludge.

Elly yelled, her hand reaching in useless grasps. She jumped over the rocks and tried catching the broken pieces, but it was too late. The sight reminded Corin of her sister picking up the fox's shattered parts once more. Her knees were on the ground again, her fingers picking apart the pieces left behind by her older sister's rage. Things returned to the way they were so easily.

Corin shoved regret in the back of her mind, as easy as fitting her hand into a glove, and turned to Briar.

"Just because you were miserable with your life doesn't give you the right to decide what's best for mine."

Elly returned from the rocks. "Corin, stop—"

"Shut up, El." She saw the flash of hurt in her sister's eyes, but she couldn't stop herself. She was too angry to care. "There's a reason why you're hiding the real treasure, isn't there? You're ashamed of what it means. You can't bear facing the truth."

Briar didn't flinch, even as Corin raised her voice. Malicine stepped forward and said, "That's enough."

"No. I'm not listening to either of you anymore."

Her anger returned like a bright, burning ball. The waterfall roiled in her ears, a bitter sound that sloshed over rocks and crashed into the pool below. The figures surrounding her blurred in her shaky vision. She refused to see them with clarity. Her legs moved before she thought twice, closer to the roaring water. A rumble of thunder breathed in the distance as an island revealed itself on the horizon.

She stared at the patch of gray spreading in the sky. Thick clouds turned black as they choked out the sun. The darkness had an alluring quality, calling her name. She knew unspeakable things were buried in Autumnland and had only a taste of them when she drowned in the ocean. What other painful things had Briar buried during the last autumn of her life? And what would happen if Corin fully uncovered the truth?

She stepped to the edge of the cliff, where the waterfall sputtered into the ocean. The threat of leaping made Briar and the others move. Their arms reached forward to stop her, but it was too late. She had already jumped and let the water take her.

As her body descended into the rapids, she felt Malicine's magic grasping for her, a force of energy that curled around her ankles. The presence weakened within seconds. She'd descended too quickly for them to catch up.

Crashing into the ocean felt like hitting concrete. Her body fractured into pieces before the waves washed the shards back together. Even in the black trenches of the sea, she knew where the currents would take her next.

The tides carried her along the ebbs and flows of time, following her rage like a moon that pulled the waves. Sunset colors shifted in the water, gold bleeding into silver, silver into dusk. The stars reflecting in the water pricked her skin until, eventually, she washed ashore in a new body, one hardened by resentment. The ocean salt tasted bitter on her lips.

On the island, the air whistled through her stringy hair, a kind of cold that nibbled beneath her skin and scraped her bones. She squeezed water from the ends of her shirt and pants so that the wet fabric wouldn't weigh her down. Her eyes scanned the island's outskirts, where the trees looked like skeletons and piles of mulch covered the forest floor. Dead leaves wilted from branches, crumbling to dust as they scattered from the wind. The bark looked brittle, like it would disintegrate under a single touch. That was what happened when winds stripped leaves from trees, once tall and grand. They revealed how small and vulnerable things were underneath the facade.

Behind her, the ocean was barely visible from the fog. She would not be seen by Briar, Malicine, or Elly if they looked for her. If she became lost, perhaps they would never find her body.

"They betrayed you. You can't return now," a voice whispered. "Not until you get answers first."

She turned to the shadow standing in the mist. Ezran's form blurred in the shifting currents of the wind, yet she could feel vitriol radiating from his mirage, for it had been shared by her as well.

"Briar Rose forced you to bare your vulnerabilities. She made you slice yourself open just to be hung dry," he hissed. "But if you do the same to her, you can prove she is worse."

Her fingers wrapped into a tight fist. She stared at the endless pathway of dead trees and blackened leaves. Swathed in a silvery fog, she had no idea what would lie inside. Still, she took a deep breath and walked forward into the darkness.

NONEXISTENT HOURS CREPT by like the scatter of dead leaves from a weakening wind throughout Corin's trek. Nightfall came by the time blisters oozed between her toes and she slowed her pace. If

Malicine were here, she'd tell the demon that they had exaggerated the terrors of the island. The truth was that the forest was mostly uneventful, more a monotonous slog than a nightmare.

There had been expected sights, of course. Trees with screaming faces carved into bark, spiders the size of her head hanging from branches in silky trails. The bark stretched into arms and swayed back and forth. They looked like creatures stalking her in the night, yet as they breathed down her neck, she was not afraid. She had witnessed more terrifying things in the real world.

This couldn't be it, she thought. She was supposed to uncover secrets, monsters that people kept hidden in the dark, skeletons that would be unearthed. She expected to find clues for what Briar was hiding, perhaps even signs that would lead to the real treasure. These visions gave her nothing in return.

"You're lost," the wind hissed.

Shadows lengthened into Ezran's tall figure between the trees. He slinked between twisted branches, his face as hollowed as the creatures around her. A scowl marred his lips.

"I wouldn't have hunted her for a hundred years just to wander here listlessly," he said. "You know she's hiding something. Hurry up and find it."

Her knee crushed dirt as she bent down to make a torch to see better in the dark. A few minutes spent rubbing together sticks created a decent flame, one that melted away Ezran's shadow and made room for something else glistening in the light. She followed the shining object and found small white orbs half buried in soil. Her fingers carefully picked up one of the tiny spheres and scrutinized the object. Pearls.

There were several of them, lined over the ground as a trail, leading deeper inside the forest. The familiarity of the object gave her a flicker of hope. She followed the trail, picking up the pearls one by one, collecting them in her fist. As she traveled farther into the woods, the ground turned softer, a muddy expanse that clung to her boots. Her feet took extra effort pulling her forward so she wouldn't sink.

Then she heard a low groan.

The sound rose above the whistle of wind and creaking of branches. A long and brutal moan, like an animal dying. She held the torch in the air and scanned the leaves.

"Who's there?"

The groaning continued, horrible and pleading. She followed the sound, feet moving as fast as her pounding heart. Her chest slammed against a wall of dead ivy and she fell to the ground. A hard blink, and she realized it hadn't been a wall at all.

The man turned around, slowly, torturously, like a creaking door about to rip open its hinges. Antlers protruded from his head like a gnarled crown, exposing muscle and oozing blood where the tusks had been jammed in his skull. Matted fur covered his cape, mangy and rotten with fleas. He looked like a skinned animal hanging from a mantel. Her skin crawled like the flies latched onto his graying skin.

"Do not defy me, Amelia."

His mouth gaped wide open in a continuous groan, deep as grit and gravel. She swallowed down her vomit and dared to speak.

"What happened when she defied you?"

Fear sparked in his hollowed eyes, and he lunged forward. The stench of blood and rot and death was so foul she jumped back. She thrashed the torch in his face, but couldn't deter his arms from reaching out and shoving her. They both fell to the ground. His weight pressed on top of her like a colossal animal. She couldn't breathe through crushed ribs. The flame of her torch was too weak and died instantly.

She struggled to fight back, grasping his neck to strangle him, but brittle leaves covered his throat like a dying tree. Her fingers dug into black crumbs and foliage. Rotten berries spewed from his mouth and drenched her face. She thought she would drown in sludge, choking on both of their bile.

A blade swung in the air and struck him. His weight stiffened on top of her, allowing a sliver of time to kick him off. She heard the pierce of flesh as he rolled over, a sword wedged deep through his heart.

Corin bit back a scream. The man dissolved into leaves, yet as she backed away from his body, she felt the graze of another one. A litter of dead soldiers had been strewn around the woods, as if she'd been caught in the aftermath of a bloody battle. Her trembling hands shook their bodies and met the clanking sound of empty armor. She ripped off their helmets. Where their heads should be was nothing but a black void.

Her breaths turned quick and panicked. She raced across the forest, but the trees twisted into columns, the damp soil solidifying to hard marble. Faces in the bark turned real, blurry men and women and faeries that chattered around her without making a coherent sound. She wanted to shout that the antler king was dead, and it had been *her fault, her fault, her fault.*

She continued fleeing through the woods, for the thing Amelia knew best was running away.

What? No—this was Corin.

The thing Corin knew best was running away.

Her foot hit something hard and she fell forward. She looked over her shoulder and sucked in a sharp breath at the body writhing behind her. Dead foliage stuck to the person's skin like a suffocating suit. The woman's lips moved soundlessly, a cry for help, yet no sound escaped her mouth. Hollow, vacant eyes stared from behind a mask of twisted branches and decay. The white pupils reminded Corin of pearls.

The body began to sink as a hole opened in the ground like a stretching mouth. Panicked, Corin jumped forward to grab her. She didn't understand why desperation compelled her to cling onto this woman. Regret settled in as branches twisted around her arms and pulled her down below. Dirt filled her lungs and muffled her screams. Twigs and sharp leaves cut her skin as she descended into the rotten core of the island.

Her body struck hard rock. She gasped in familiar pain. Darkness carried her to a familiar place with stagnant air and winding paths, where the trapped woman was nowhere to be found. Sharp gravel stabbed her back as she rolled over dirt and coughed out dust. When she got up, she stared into an abyss. Her hands blindly reached for the walls, now solid rock instead of debris. A stench of rotten eggs wafted under her nose, and she wanted to gag.

A voice echoed down the passageway. Not the woman who had been trapped in foliage, but someone she recognized. Elly was calling her name.

"El?" Corin shouted, terror overtaking her shaking breath. Elly wasn't supposed to follow her. Her sister would not survive the island. Her hands slammed against the walls until rocks scraped her skin raw. "El! Get out of here! Run!"

She couldn't tell if Elly responded or if the sound was too far away. Maybe the girl couldn't even hear her. Corin ran through the tunnels, yelling until her throat turned hoarse, slamming her shoulders against boulders until her body felt like it would break apart from fear and desperation. She couldn't lose her sister. Not when they had been through so much together. Not when they were finally repairing the closest thing they had to family.

The exertion made the rocks spin around her. Corin knelt over to heave, but nothing came out of her parched throat. She hadn't eaten or drank in the several hours she wandered through these tunnels. Or had it been days? She couldn't remember. Time slipped through her fingers. The walls were shrinking. The stench of death became suffocating. Bodies grew from soil, sprouting from the seeds of her mind. She saw Harlow's cracked skull, the pale sheet of Maggie's cheek, Rowan's twisted limbs. Her friends buried in the dirt with the rest of their forgotten dreams. There were the other corpses, strewn around the passages, time eroding their skin until they were nothing but bone. How many people had died in these tunnels, searching for the princess?

She stopped as she saw one of them.

The girl's body was small and sunken in, like hunger had overtaken her body and hollowed her whole. Maggots buried themselves in the flesh of her back. Her dark skin had turned pale gray, like a withered flower that never saw the sun. Her lips were blue, and her hair was cut in such a way where it curled behind her ears, just as Corin had recalled.

"No," she whispered. "This is a dream. This isn't real."

But she remembered everything about her sister. The shape of her body, the jut of her bones, the fabric of her clothes. She remembered looking for Elly in the tunnels. She remembered finding bodies in a winding path. She remembered a smaller body left behind, one of a girl who had died alone.

Corin screamed, because this wasn't a nightmare.

This was the truth.

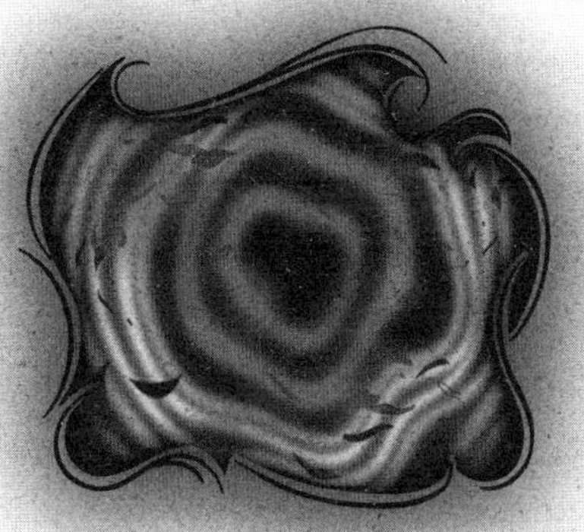

CHAPTER 26

101 YEARS AGO

THE TRUTH WAS that Malicine wasn't terrified of being alone. They were terrified of having no choice but to be.

Either way, it didn't matter. They couldn't contemplate this for long with Talon pecking their face.

"Get up. We're here."

They swatted his beak away. Dull pain settled in their bones, a memory of crashing into an unfamiliar shore. They looked around and pieced the scenery together. The limestone pavement was a muddy ooze, while coral fossils speckled the area like whiteflies. They were the closest thing to color. Everything else on the island was gray melted together: the sky, the water, the rocks.

The smoke dissipated, so that when Malicine stood up, they could see the dented boat they fell from. Amelia's glass body had strewn over the rocks a few feet away, motionless. Fractures cracked her skin like spiderwebs, but there was no blood, only shards that had been chipped away from her joints. Her chest moved up and down in shallow breaths. She was so weak, Malicine thought, that any little hardship could easily break her. This was the kind of girl who could not survive anything.

"She is still breathing. I checked." Talon stepped on the small groove of her back. *"If she does not wake up, I will eat her eyes."*

Malicine could still taste the bitterness from the words they threw to Amelia before the boat crashed. Hatred had boiled in their belly during the princess's self-pitying charade. Even sadness dressed itself as a beautiful gown upon her, with sparkling tears and downturned doe eyes. She would never understand how wretched misery could be, a pain so inconsolably ugly it would never experience sympathy. She only reminded Malicine how different they were.

"Leave her," they said. "We have better things to do."

Malicine's wings splayed open as they leapt into flight. With the smoke gone, they surveyed the land with new clarity. Among the black sand were enormous columns of basalt, the rocks separated by joints like a broken skeleton. They stretched into cliffs hundreds of feet into the air, so tall the demon would have missed the tower looping at the top. Their heart thudded against their chest, an instinctual knowledge that somewhere, up there, could be the Demon King. Their father.

This was what they needed to focus on: answers to a lineage they finally belonged to, rather than the woes of humans who alienated them further from the world. The truth of why Malicine was born, and maybe, why they mattered.

Talon's croaks rippled across the black sky as the raven followed Malicine's flight. They drew closer to the tower in the distance, where columns of rock draped like a waterfall, twisting like gnarled fingers that pointed to a bloodred moon. The fortress drifted through the air like a massive, floating rock. The architecture was physically impossible: crown spires barely balanced atop needles, pointed arches spiked in different directions. Yet as they approached the entrance and watched its double doors open on their own, they knew this place had been calling for them.

Footsteps on cold marble. Cold air grazing their cheek. Their raven on their shoulder. A deep breath. Every sensation they savored, culminating to this moment.

They stormed the entrance, letting the cold envelop their body like a well-worn cloak. Grand-vaulted ceilings sharpened their corners, their ribs cascading down the roof. Clustered columns led them across the short hall, where stone bars divided a row of windows. They marched and marched until—

An empty throne sat at the end of the room.

Malicine stared at it, struck by the hollowness. The tower suddenly seemed too small. They had already reached the end, and the four walls began closing in.

"You said he'd be here," they snapped to Talon. The massive chair contained the Demon King's absence, boasting a deep hard-carved back and legs, chalky white to contrast with the deep blackness of the walls. A piece of work only a carver with centuries of time could afford to assemble. The sight of it irritated Malicine. He was here, yet he wasn't. So close, and still impossible to reach.

And not once had he reached out for Malicine.

They swiftly kicked a foot through the chair. The throne slumped forward. They gawked at the chair's crooked legs, noticing that the nubs at the bottom curved in different directions. Their foot was now covered with a grainy texture, like dust. The subtle hue of gold that covered the surface wasn't old ceramic like they assumed. Instead, it was—

"Bones are much more fragile than you think. Then again, most people do not visit to break my furniture."

The baritone of his voice reverberated through the room. Malicine spun around. The hallway was empty, but his voice had been too solid to be a figment of their imagination. Their eyes spiraled around the room before turning to one of the vaulted ceilings. A light swirled from a hole inside the stone arch. The portal widened for someone to emerge. First his horns, then his wings, and then the rest of him.

The hairs at the back of Malicine's neck stood up. His skin was green, just like theirs.

The demon was a colossal figure over seven feet tall. His limbs were abnormally long, more a skulking shadow than man. Massive horns protruded from his temples and curved like an ox. A black mantle hung loosely over his broad chest, revealing pangolin-like scales. The brightest thing about him was the amulet he wore around his neck, where a red light glowed just like the portal once did. The light that came from the opening had faded, the blood dried into a crusted border, until scabs peeled off limestone and withered to dust.

Talon flew over and landed at the demon's feet. Head bowed, the raven croaked, *"It has been too long, Master. I come with your descendent, who hails from the human world."*

"I know who they are."

His eyes were beady and black, and Malicine was taken aback by the starkness of it, the void of color. There were subtle differences between them, yet when Malicine gazed at his horns and skin, there was no denying it. The two of them were each other's spitting image.

"Never did I think, in the centuries I've lived, that I would see another of my own flesh and bone."

He stepped forward and lifted a sharp claw to Malicine's cheek. They shot a hand up to block his.

"You left me." Their voice hardened, a rock that refused to be smoothed over by the river of his words. "Thirty and five years ago, I was born in the woods and killed my mother out of the womb. No one knew who I was. Not even me. You never looked for me."

"You are wrong. I always searched for you, my child. You have no idea how many times I returned, trying to get you back here." His gruff voice penetrated the walls, a crack of desperation that muffled somewhere deep in his throat. Malicine could feel their shield slowly slipping. Their fingers curled into fists, grasping to maintain an impenetrable facade.

"Do you even know my name?"

"You are my flesh and blood. I do not need to give you a name to know that you belong to me."

"I don't belong to anybody," they said. "People call me Malicine. A wicked name to match the monster they saw in me. You do not know what it was like for me to be trapped there, surrounded by faeries who wanted me dead."

His black eyes glittered in amusement. He pulled his head back and laughed, the sound rumbling the walls like an earthquake. His leather wings flapped from the jostling, and when he looked back at them, his mouth stretched wider. "They are fools for thinking you are not like them. We are the most powerful Fae who will ever live."

"But I am only half. You were the one who intruded into my world, impregnated my mother, and—"

"The Fae are demons. Wicked spirits born with powers, capable of healing just as much as destroying. The only difference is whether we delude ourselves into thinking we're pure and good, like many of the fair folk do, or admit to the wicked nature of ourselves as demons."

Malicine cast a doubtful look at him. If this was a joke, they couldn't decipher its humor. Comparing the two seemed ludicrous. Demons and Fae had always been divided. They were like day and night, light and dark.

Then Malicine thought about Iris, Dahlia, and Clover. They remembered the wicked spells, the lashes against their skin, the years of torture and laughter at their pain. To the rest of the world, their sisters were godmothers to royalty, a noble elite of society revered in magic and purity. But they were not kind or virtuous. No, they were wretched creatures who had harmed their own family.

"When we first crossed to the mortal world, we had enchanted ourselves to be beautiful to the human eye, so much so that they romanticized us and called us Fae. Over generations, the Fae in the mortal realm remained beautiful, as we became acclimated to their world and less to our original one. I, too, believed I could be special there. Until I realized humans were traitors, and that it was better for me to stay here and revert to the form I was intended to be."

A cold breeze wafted through the window, prickling Malicine's skin. They had not considered they could become different versions of themselves in different worlds. How someone could be a hero in one realm, and a monster in another.

The Demon King stretched an arm toward the end of the hallway. A black aura radiated from his palm. In response, a large chunk of stone broke off the wall and slid across the floor.

"We have a lot to catch up on," he said, "so have a seat."

CHAPTER 27

THERE WAS NO monster hiding in the dark. Instead, there was a body that Corin once buried.

Long ago, in the depths of a cave, in the depths of her mind, she had found a body and pretended it never existed. Elly simply floated away into a dream, where she shared teacups with talking animals and swam star-filled oceans with princesses. Elly was beside her, and they argued and fought and laughed, the way sisters could.

But the truth was that Elly was dead.

So Corin might as well have been too.

Thunder rumbled across the island. Corin couldn't hear the raindrops anymore, only soft pelts against numb skin. She held Elly for what felt like eternity, thumbpads brushing against wounds that were split open like overripe fruit. Each sob scratched against Corin's throat, her chest hollowing with every breath until she feared collapse.

She never told Elly she was sorry.

Everything began to sink. The surrounding walls, the starved bodies, the bones, the sisters. The tunnels or the island or wherever they were. In the darkness, it didn't matter. As mud sloshed inside her ears and worms crawled beneath her skin, Corin curled into a ball beside Elly. Even with their bones pressed together, Corin still felt her sister's absence, an empty and hollow thing.

The darkness whispered back to her.

Your fault.

Everything has always been your fault.

You're too angry, too mean, too selfish, too resentful. Look where it brought you. You don't know how to care for someone, and you don't even know how to love.

It should have been you who died.

Roots twisted around Corin's limbs, dragging her deeper into the dark abyss. She understood, then, the desire she harbored to be pulled down all along. By ice in Winterland. By broken houses in Springland. By oceans in Summerland. By sinkholes in Autumnland. To here and now, where she belonged in the dirt with Elly.

It had never been Briar Rose who planned her downfall. It had only been Corin, pushing herself to the comforting arms of death, a deserving punishment for her horrible mistakes.

Thousands of black flies swarmed their graves. They feasted on her stench and despair. Their drones turned into muffled noise as soil buried Corin deeper until she could feel nothing, not even the weight of her sad existence.

Then a new sound drilled her mind, sharp yet muffled. The noise grew louder alongside pounding footsteps and smashing fists. A rush of cold air struck her body. Soil slipped from her grave as nails pierced into the flesh of her arms. The sound turned strikingly clear. A harsh voice—

"Get up!"

Malicine lifted her from the ground and tossed her out of the sinking grave. Corin's body rolled across the dirt, then lay limp. Her cheek pressed into the soil as raindrops pelted her skull like tiny bullets. She wanted to tell Malicine to leave her alone and let her die, but she was too tired to speak. She tried to slip back into unconsciousness, yet Malicine persisted in shaking her awake.

"Snap out of it! None of this is real."

A flash of anger sparked Corin to finally look at the demon. "But it is real." As soon as anger came, it broke under the weight of defeat. Her voice cracked as she said, "It's the only real thing in this world."

If anything had been a lie, it was the rest of the dreamworld. With cruel kindness, these dreams told her she had more seasons with Elly. They had time to grow old together. If they argued, they could make up. If Corin did something horrible, she could still say she was sorry.

But the reality was this: There were no second chances.

Corin said she never wanted Elly, and Elly died believing it.

Corin reached for her sister, but Elly's cold flesh slipped through her fingers, the bones dissolving to gray ash. The storm carried the girl away, scattering her into the air to leave Corin clutching nothing. She tucked herself into a ball once more and let the roots curl around her limbs. They squeezed tight, the thickest around her throat, until she could no longer breathe.

Before darkness filled her vision, a light burst through the air, slicing branches and scattering its pieces to the ground. She felt a gust of air enter her lungs as she breathed, even though she wanted so desperately to never do so again.

"I'm not going to tell you it gets better, because that would be a lie." There was a forced solidness to Malicine's voice, a striking contrast to the haziness of Corin's mind. "But if you die, you're not going to wake up. Ever. So you can't make a permanent decision like that here. Not right now, not in this place. You need to get out of the darkness before it swallows you whole."

Another branch shot toward them like the tongue of a snake. Malicine spun around and sliced it with their staff. They grabbed Corin's arm to hoist her up. Her legs wobbled like a broken puppet, stumbling over roots as the demon pulled her forward.

"Stop dragging your feet and move!"

"I can't."

Corin's words barely came out a whisper. Malicine's eyes fell to her blood-soaked shoes and oozing blisters. They pulled her arms over their shoulders, draping her on their back, and splayed their wings open. Before they could take flight, a swarm of thorns stretched across the sky and trapped them inside. Malicine pointed their staff and sent another beam of light to cut the thorns. As quickly as they shot a path, the thorns regrew, enveloping them in darkness once more.

They cursed under their breath. "I hate this place."

They hauled Corin down a winding path, trying to make sense of the overhanging limbs that stretched like bony fingers, the dark trees with screaming faces carved into their trunks. Branches thrashed at them in the storm. Icy drops of rain stung their skin like pellets. Even in Corin's haze, she could tell they were going nowhere. The woods were sheathed in shadow. Too many rotting leaves covered each path, blending them together.

Malicine let out a strained yell as a sharpened branch cut through their sleeves and into flesh. The wind screamed to push them back. Corin felt them pull their full body weight forward along with hers. She wondered, watching them struggle, why anyone would fight so hard to live.

They managed to find a stream past the woods, where water turned into a muddy sludge that sloshed against a trail of rocks. Malicine attempted to cross, even though Corin's weight on their back barely allowed them to keep balance. The smell of rotten eggs from the water hit her nose as she strained to hold her breath.

They had just stepped on the last rock when a blast of wind hit them. Both Malicine and Corin fell forward, crashing into water. Corin let the tides wrap around her limbs and pull her down. If Malicine yelled for her, she wouldn't have heard. But a red light kept blinking, no matter how tightly she clenched her eyes shut. She opened them to a blur of dark river and a red orb turning smaller, like a light close to extinguishing.

She grasped for a rock and pulled her head from the surface in time to hear Malicine.

"Don't let it get away!"

Their empty hand pointed at the staff floating down the river. The gem flickered in dying red. Corin swam in the tide's direction and reached for the stick, but the end of its crooked shape melted to mud, and her hand was covered in leeches. They sank their teeth into her arm. She shook away their wriggling bodies, watching them drop like pebbles into the river and get sucked down the end of nowhere, where the staff and its amulet were gone forever.

Panic raced through her mind. The gemstone was important, but she didn't know why. She could only remember the way clouds of blood swirled inside the stone whenever Malicine cast their magic. How the staff only reacted that way whenever the demon changed the land around them. What it would mean if the amulet never returned.

She turned to Malicine, but their face had paled into a sickly shade of green. In their eyes she saw pupils so wide they shrank color. Two pits of black for what should have been life.

As if the island sensed their fear, the wind picked up with a howling storm. Waves crashed around them, and Corin felt the strangle on their bodies, pushing both of them to the bottom to drown.

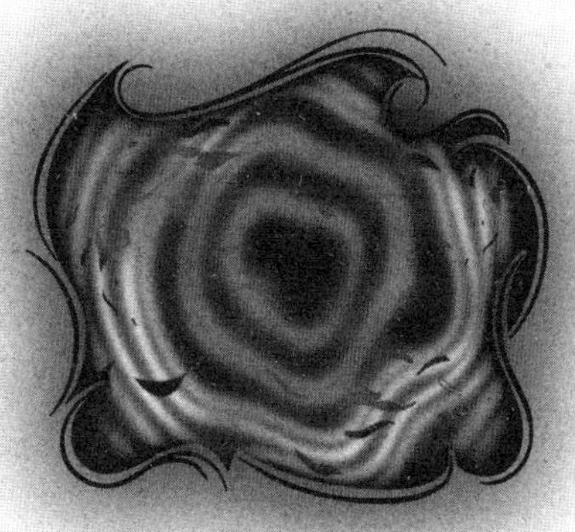

CHAPTER 28

101 YEARS AGO

MALICINE WAS DROWNING in new smells and lavish decor. Slabs of meat filled the trays, cooked to warm brown tones, dripping in golden oils. A large bird had been finely sliced with pink hues glistening on each tender side. Goblets sprouted from the stone and filled themselves with wine, rich in maroon with the sweet smell of cherries. At the center sat a bowl filled with grapes for Talon to peck and chew noisily.

A second ago, the food and wine had been dust particles. The Demon King needed only to hover his hand across the table before conjuring them into shapes on silver plates.

"You say we should talk, but it looks like you just wanted to show off," Malicine said.

He smiled. "Can't your father do both?"

Malicine took the first buttery bite of a meat slice and let the flavors burst in their mouth. For the first time, they understood what it meant to savor power. Cherries from the wine goblet swirled in their mouth next, bitter and sweet at the same time. Still, questions remained hanging on their tongue.

"What happened out there?" Malicine's gaze flickered to the circular window. A bloodred moon hung over the smoke and ashes that permeated outside the tower's fortress. They remembered first entering the Otherworld, the way ash rained from the sky and smoke clogged their throat. Despite the safety of the tower, they could not ignore the forces outside.

"A wildfire spread while I had been traveling to the human realm. I could not stop it," he answered. "The fires swept across the land and killed everyone. This fortress is the only place left for me to protect."

Malicine recalled the smell of burnt flesh, the array of bent horns and broken wings that were left abandoned in charcoal. How utterly alone they felt knowing they were too late.

"A terrible way to die," they murmured. "I would have wanted to meet the others."

Their father made an impassive shrug, but Malicine could tell from the way his shoulders tightened that the incident bothered him more than he let on. "One can get used to being alone, as I'm sure you have."

"Not by choice."

It was one thing to view humans and Fae with disdain, but another to know, deep down, that ostracization only happened from being repulsive in the first place. Malicine filled the silence by taking another sip of wine. The Demon King sat back in his throne. He didn't touch any the plates, choosing instead to watch Malicine.

"You and I are similar in ways beyond blood, my child. I was trapped in the prisons of your world's rules. A world where humans are in power, and Fae are merely their slaves, expected to dedicate our entire lives to their bidding. I wasted so many years tending to his side, harvesting my magic only to fulfill a greedy human's desires."

"You mean King Samael."

Sharp points of his teeth jutted over his lips. "You know of Gyldan history."

"Enough of it, yes. I know there was an orphaned faerie who swore loyalty to the king of Gyldan after he took him in, only to betray him later by attempting murder. In their fight, they shed blood, and with his magic, created a portal to the underworld."

Malicine set the goblet down on the table and stared into the black pits of his eyes. Talon stopped eating as well. The question hung in the air, unvoiced until now.

"You are Oleander, aren't you?"

Malicine could hear the hum in both their pulses, syncing like two creatures of the same blood. They had put the pieces together the moment he revealed he had been a Fae in their world, only to morph into a demon here. It made sense, then, how he came here in the first place, and why his skin had turned green from the wicked envy he held against Samael.

"You found Samael's book," Oleander said.

"I assume you hid it from the humans because it didn't paint you in a good light."

His nostrils flared in indignation. "No. Samael wrote that I tried to kill him. But the truth is he was a coward who could not bear the thought of letting others know he was growing old and weak."

Platters of food shook across the table and scattered apart. Stone faded away into darkness, shrouded by black smoke that entered the corners of Malicine's vision. A red light filtered through the fog and drew a scene. Red curtains, candlelit walls. A man with bones protruding from sickly pale skin, begging on his knees. Standing in front of him was a younger man—no, not younger. He only appeared that way. In those familiar black eyes, Malicine could recognize their father. He looked strangely normal as a faerie: spider-spun wings, pale skin, sharp ears instead of horns.

Malicine watched King Samael beg Oleander to extend his life. He couldn't handle the pain that came with a deteriorating body of old age. Oleander rejected his pleas, for granting humans immortality was forbidden among faeries. They reached a compromise where he would let the king pass peacefully instead. He began setting candles around the chambers, each flame a delicate piece of the magic circle he would cast.

Then King Samael attacked.

It happened before Oleander turned around, before Malicine could even blink. The knife flashed underneath his robe and pierced through Oleander's skull. A squelch of flesh, an eruption of blood. The blade went through his head, two holes for him to bleed from.

Malicine tried blinking away the bloodshed. They gripped onto the edge of the table to anchor them to reality, not the flashbacks and anguished sounds of pain. "It was Samael who struck first," they breathed. "Not you."

Their vision crystallized from one Oleander to another. Where two holes gaped in his skull, black horns sprouted. The look of betrayal melted into a jaw clenched with resignation.

"Stories are written by the rulers of the world," he spoke, "which means not every story is true."

He evaporated back to his old self, a frail creature bleeding across marble floor. King Samael towered over him, but the sight looked pathetic to Malicine. It was not a fair battle. The king breathed heavily, weak and old, a coward who needed to bring another creature to his knees to put them on the same level. Before he struck again, Oleander grabbed one of the candles and set Samael's cape ablaze. The king stumbled backward to put the fire out. Oleander lunged forward and tackled him to the ground.

In the flames, they fought for their lives. Blood spilled, red mingling with gold. Blinding light traced around the magic circle and lit the entire room. Malicine covered their eyes from the searing brightness. Between their fingers, they saw the floor open. The portal gaped wide as the men fell below.

Wind rushed past Malicine before gravity inverted. Floating boulders nearly knocked them over as they flew across sprawling mountains. They grabbed one of the tendrils of a climbing plant and clung onto it for balance. Strange spores entered their lungs as they breathed heavily, turning to watch the scene below.

"Samael got his wish, after all," Oleander's voice echoed. "He found a way to escape mortality and never age."

Through the fog, something picked up under the light. Malicine strained their eyes to make out the figure sprawled in the sand. His skin had thickened into a garish shade between yellow and orange. Samael's graying hair had melted into his crown. As he stood, his body looked limber, his bones solid and sturdy. He moved like a new man. But unlike any other man, his stature was drenched in gold. He stared at his hands with a sense of awe. He would never rust or tarnish, let alone depreciate the way that regular humans would.

Malicine remembered one of Talon's first words upon entering the Otherworld. *In here, your sin becomes part of your skin.*

If Samael's greed took over him, then surely, Oleander's envy had turned his skin green. Malicine caught the flash of vitriol in their father's eyes as he stared at his gold-drenched king. Horns sprouted from where his wounds once were, then twisted themselves into gnarled hooks. His expression softened once the king returned his gaze, yet resentment radiated from him in waves that Malicine could sense too well in its familiarity.

"Samael wanted to rule this world and start a new life here," Oleander said. "We called for a truce so that we could build a new beginning."

Malicine sneered. "What a foolish thing you did for a human who betrayed you."

"I dismissed it as an act of desperation, one that would no longer happen now that he could live. I couldn't imagine abandoning him after he took me in when no one else did. You must understand: I had no family. My parents were dead. He was the one who found and raised me."

Oleander gripped the chalice tight, regret twisting his lips to a downward curve.

"One day, he ordered me to deliver a book he wrote to Gyldan so that his family would learn about what happened and cross to the Otherworld. I forged my magic and our blood into this amulet so I could travel between worlds easily. It would have been a simple task. Yet suspicion kept gnawing my mind. I knew he must have written about me."

Across the dining table, his amulet glowed in burning red. Darkness shrouded Malicine's vision once more, the clouds dissipating once they stood in the middle of a library. The polished oak shelves and stained-glass windows indicated they were inside the Gyldan castle. A door cracked open to a hidden alcove. Malicine peered inside to see their father hunched over Samael's book. His body trembled as text melded together onto the pages.

Malicine turned away. They didn't need to see more when they had already read it themselves. They remembered the night Amelia opened the book and they read the last page of his story. Out of all the lies Samael wrote, there had been a grain of truth in the end.

These unusual spirits aren't innocent faeries, but demons. They are wicked creatures, but they can be tamed. That is what I have done with Oleander. My instincts had been correct when I killed his parents.

There is no such thing as a good monster, after all.

For how many years did Oleander think Samael had saved him in the wild forests? Perhaps at one point he even considered the king to be his own father, Malicine thought bleakly.

"What did you do?" they asked.

"You already know the answer to that."

Even though Malicine had kicked down his throne moments ago, he'd already pieced it back together, tapping his fingers across the ribbed armrests. The bones were chalky white and jagged, carved so that they could fit Oleander's arms like a sleeve.

Malicine couldn't help but smile. "No wonder he was so satisfying to kick."

"These fairy tales are merely lies humans tell themselves to feel important. I shall write an even better story. A story about how a demon discovered his true worth, left behind a false book, and came back to kill the one who betrayed him. I am the king now, and this world is only the first of many."

He stood up from his seat, his goblet untouched, and crossed toward the rows of windows. Something pulled Malicine to follow him, the way a child would a father. They moved like someone who was starting to believe that things could be better.

"Let me join you," Malicine said, "and we'll repair this world to be ours again."

They looked up at the sky. Thick smoke permeated outside the fortress, the smog so dense they could hardly see beyond the barrier. Malicine wondered if it would have been possible to hear the cries of anguish within their bubble, the screams of demons burning within the flames in the forest across the sea. The sky must have lit up in orange. Perhaps one day they could paint it blue again.

Light flickered in his eyes as Oleander looked at them. "You'll help me create a new world."

Power hummed through Malicine's veins. Oleander's amulet glowed brighter, responding to kindred blood. In the fractures of light, something else caught their eye. Below the tower, amid columned rocks and fog, the glass sheen of Amelia's skin reflected.

Malicine grabbed the window ledge and gaped at the girl. Wider cracks had formed across her limbs. Her footsteps were uneven on the choppy rocks. She roamed aimlessly around the terrain, scanning the columns and calling Malicine's name in a voice so frail the demon could barely hear her.

They didn't know whether to laugh or scream. How could she be so stupid? They'd left her behind, and here she was, still searching for them as if her body wasn't falling apart.

"She is like the king she descends from." Disgust tinged Oleander's voice. "She wants to use you and keep you as her little pet, as Samael did with me. But do not worry. I have other plans for her."

His gnarled finger pointed ahead where Amelia walked. Streaks of red light radiated from his amulet. Dead leaves swirled around the princess, trapping her in place. Sticks rose in the air and curved into the shape of a circle as large as her body. The circle's surface turned opaque, an oily iridescent sheen that contained light. Once she saw whatever was inside, her eyes turned glossy, her mouth parting in awe. She stretched an arm toward the portal and walked like someone under hypnosis.

“Where is she going?” Malicine asked, trying to contain the alarm in their voice.

“Nowhere. She thinks she sees an ideal world, but she will be trapped in nothingness.”

Malicine’s heartbeats slowed as they watched Amelia place her hands at the edge of the portal, peering inside with wonder. Light shimmered through her glass silhouette, as if she would disappear into the stars.

But wasn’t that what Amelia wanted, after all, to no longer exist? If anything invited disaster, she’d already willingly accepted it. Malicine didn’t need to stop her. Yet a heavy anchor brought them forward and made them grip the window. Their movements were slow, as if they were drowning. A bitter aftertaste lingered on their tongue, the familiar scent of wine.

“Wait,” they said, but it came out as a whisper.

The light from the portal dimmed, only for Malicine to realize it was their own vision, dark blotches blooming in the corners of their sight. Amelia became a blur, and when they turned to their father, they could barely see his face. They sought out Talon for help, yet the raven was limp and motionless on the dining table, half eaten grapes rolled aside their beak.

Something was wrong. Malicine’s eyelids were too heavy, their mouth too dry. The edges of the vaulted ceiling pulled in. The room spun, and they couldn’t stop it. The last thing they felt was the hard crack of their skull against the floor before their body turned limp, their limbs in a fixed position, unable to move. Their eyes caught the glint of Oleander’s fangs as he stared at her, smiling, the both of them knowing that Malicine could do absolutely nothing to escape.

CHAPTER 29

CORIN GASPED FOR air, limbs thrashing to hold on to the rocks at the river's edge. She crawled a few steps onto solid ground before heaving water. Her throat burned, but as she wrapped her necklace around it, the pendant pressed against her chest and slowed her heartbeats.

She lay on the ground of rotting leaves and bumpy roots. There was a tree next to where she'd rolled over, so she pressed her face against the bark and let the ridges bite into her cheeks. She needed everything to slow down, to stop feeling the motions of the river carrying her to her own death. She needed, for a moment, to let it sink in that she was still alive. Even though she didn't want to be.

All because Malicine had saved her.

The demon was nowhere to be seen. The tides had separated them after Malicine lost their staff, and Corin was stranded in some indiscernible part of the woods. She shouted for Malicine, only to be met with the howl of wind through the oaks.

Logically, she knew she was still trapped in Autumnland. Yet as snow poured from the sky and the air turned cold enough to bite into her bones, Corin felt like she had been transported somewhere else. She shivered in the moonlit dark, then forced her chattering teeth to stop when she heard whispers. A crowd of them, each one speaking over the other, but none whose words she could distinguish.

Then the sound of a woman wailing split the air.

Her moans sounded so pained that Corin moved instantly, following the source. She winded through trees, panic pushing her forward as the woman continued crying. No matter how quickly she ran, she couldn't find the woman. The snow blinded her, a world of black and white. The sky only turned red when the woman let out a dying screech. Corin jumped as the crowd of whispers turned into a chorus of screams. Several winged creatures appeared through the trees and ran toward her. She tried jumping out of the way, but they flitted through her like ghosts. A baby wailed in the distance, the sound deep and guttural, teeth scraping against flesh. It struck fear in all the creatures. Part of Corin was scared, while another part her recognized the voice.

She ran forward, calling for Malicine. Stars bled from the sky while snow turned to ash. Three figures appeared from the trees, and something wet struck her, burning her skin. She screamed and fell to the ground. Blisters formed over her arms and face as she writhed on a stone floor. The three women surrounded her like a cage. One of them held the bucket, dripping with bleach.

"Monster! Demon! Freak!"

Their voices drilled into Corin's ears even as she clamped them shut. Her body drowned in a lake of acid, melting her atom by atom until nothing remained. A terrible feeling overcame her: She was alone, and always would be. A creature abandoned by their world since birth. They might as well listen to the voices and die too.

Where did this despair come from? Had it taken root in Corin's heart, or had she intertwined with another? She could not tell. Whispers grew louder, urging her to follow death's path, while she resisted by clinging to a different memory, another pattern, a sense of recognition.

Whenever Corin drowned, it was always Malicine who came after her.

Different voices clawed at Corin, reminding her the kind of person she was. She had once abandoned allies, fled toward safety while bridges burned behind her, leaving others for dead. Regret twisted in her stomach and lived in her bones every day since she lost Harlow, her friends, her Elly. She did not save them.

Maybe this time, she could save someone.

Her eyes burned as she forced them open. Bleeding stars painted the sky red, silhouettes of gnarled branches twisting around her vision. Some of their shapes looked like horns. In one of the branches, a warning signal came from a raven. Corin pulled herself from the ground, hand desperately reaching for the bird.

"Talon!" Her voice echoed Malicine's. The raven flapped his wings, ready to take flight. Strangled noises came from his throat. Poison spewed from his beak. Talon fell from the branch and into an open cage, where the iron bars grew smaller until they crushed his bones. Corin cried out, but the tears weren't only hers. She could feel Malicine somewhere. The demon's nightmares had imprisoned them all, but these scenes, this anguish, were too detailed to exist in mere imagination.

Corin knew how Autumnland tortured people within. The island used the truth.

"You gave the creature a name. How quaint." A deep, distorted voice echoed in the darkness. The island sucked away every tree until they turned to stone columns. Corin blinked at vaulted ceilings, a slab of a stone table, an overturned goblet where poison dripped from the rim. Talon lay limp in his cage.

"I was the one who created him. Yet someone like you gives him a simple little name, and he follows you around like a dog."

Corin turned to the baritone voice that reverberated through her bones and hollowed out her body. A skulking shadow of long limbs and gnarled horns emerged. Scales of green skin, thin like paper, had cracks over protruding bones. Every nick and notch from centuries of treachery sank into his face. He was immortal, yet dead in every way, an emaciated corpse who refused to pass. Draped over his scaled chest was an amulet, one with a shape and hue just like the one embedded in Malicine's staff.

"I've reigned over this world for as long as you can imagine. After a while, one grows tired. It doesn't change the fact that the world you left behind is rotten, that the people who wronged you are still prosperous."

He paced around, leaving ash in his footsteps. The circle of soot contained perpendicular lines, drawing a symmetrical pattern that looked too complex for Corin to discern. She heard the rattling sound of iron chains somewhere nearby.

"I realized it's not enough that I go back to your world and cause destruction. That doesn't make things even. I need to change the tides altogether."

Corin realized he wasn't talking to her. She looked around the darkness for Malicine as the sound of scraping chains grew louder. In her hazy vision, she finally made them out. A bruise had formed on the back of their head. Their limbs twitched with unnatural movements, like they were fighting to regain mobility. Even their attempt to lunge for him proved useless. Iron chains violently tugged their body back to the chair, their head knocking against the curved bones of the throne.

"You're not real, Oleander," they hissed. "And I'm not interested in revisiting this memory."

Malicine was here. Not part of a mirage, like the other demon was, but here. Corin banged her fists against an invisible barrier and shouted for them, but Malicine was too far away, trapped inside their own nightmare.

"You said you'd help me rebuild this world. I'm simply accepting your offer," Oleander said. "The problem is you won't make it out alive."

Chains rubbed against Malicine's skin and tore open a wound. A drop of blood landed on the ground. The single splatter lit the ash in a tiny flame, and Oleander's amulet glowed once more. Malicine stared at the glimmer of the light, how the gem hungered for a taste of them.

"You were only looking for me because you wanted my blood." Corin felt the cracks in the stone of their voice, the resignation of their new reality. She grasped for a way to get through the barricade and reach them, but realized her hands had disappeared with the rest of her body. She had been dissolved, ceased to exist within Malicine's memory from a time long ago.

"You should be flattered. I've sacrificed many demons to make my magic stronger, ended so many lives to tailor energy potent enough to create a new portal. None of them were right," Oleander said. "Then I realized that energy could never come from any demon born in one time. The type of blood affects the type of portal created, after all. It must come from someone whose blood is so special, it comes from multiple places. A creature whose mother belongs in one time, and whose father in another. Someone who could never belong anywhere, in any time. Someone like you."

His hand stroked Malicine's cheek, the tip of his nails scraping their skin. They spat in his face. Dribble slicked down his chin, and he wiped it with the back of his hand. The corner of his lips twisted in disgust. It didn't compare to the glare that Malicine bore into him.

"You killed them all." Corin watched flashes of burnt bodies and blackened bones pass through Malicine's memory and flicker into her own vision. "That fire wasn't an accident."

"I never said it was. They set it upon themselves, thinking it would be better to die than to aid my cause. Quite poor timing for them to think a mass suicide was the only solution, when I had just learned I no longer needed them."

Corin stared at the floor beneath Malicine, where ash had scattered to form the shape of a circle. She imagined the lines turning from gray to red, their blood filling the gaps like spilled ink. This was no simple cut, not a trim of the skin like it had been whenever she heard about creating portals. The Demon King was preparing a bloodbath.

"Don't be so petulant," he chided. "Without me, you would have never existed. Neither would all the other demons that found refuge here. I have the right to do what I want with your lives, because I already owned them from the beginning."

"Nobody has the right to own another life."

"Are you certain about that? History would beg to differ. Faeries have served humans, and even humans themselves have owned each other. When people fear others, they seek differences and find ways to demonize them. Something as arbitrary as your skin, pedigree, the way you speak—all rules made up so that certain people can stay in power. A world cannot exist without such a system. But when I create a new world, there will be new rules. And then I will show them what true power looks like."

Malicine tried to laugh, but the sound died on their lips.

"Does something amuse you?" he said.

"You don't care about making things right. You just want to be in their place. The ruler instead of the ruled."

For a moment, Oleander turned silent. Then he knelt and pressed a palm flat on the ground. An orange glow emanated from his fingers. The stones beneath melded into a blade. He pulled an obsidian knife from the floor and pressed it against Malicine's neck. The edges brimmed with volcanic red. A trickle of blood flowed down their throat as half-moons burned into their skin. Oleander's amulet gleamed in response, as if it knew the artery in their neck would feed it the most blood once cut.

Panic surged inside Corin. She needed to do something, even if she no longer existed in Malicine's nightmare. She pressed figments of herself against the stone walls of the tower and tried to feel her way around the scene. Her non-body slipped through the cracks as Oleander spoke.

"Our skin may be the same, but don't make the mistake of comparing yourself to me."

A pained gasp. A trickle of blood from a blade piercing deep. His voice boomed again, a toneless sound that drilled inside their ears and infected their mind.

"I am more powerful than you will ever be."

Malicine, Corin wanted to scream.

"You are only half of me and what I can do."

I'm here, Malicine—

"You are too broken to be the whole of anything."

—and I'm not going to leave you behind.

Corin felt the dagger crystallize in her palm as she plunged it in his back.

She didn't know how it happened. She had materialized into something solid, a translucent force that moved with only one goal in mind. But she barely made a difference. The Demon King had hardly been wounded. Instead, he turned around, black eyes narrowing at Corin.

No, that wasn't right. His eyes were looking through her.

A scream ripped out of Malicine's throat. "Amelia—!"

Corin didn't have time to react. Oleander's arm swung at her, and the impact made her entire being shatter. Pain bloomed her whole body, then tore it into pieces. She broke apart until fragments of herself were left on the floor.

Darkness returned to the edges of her vision. A blinding, searing ache that made its way through her bones into tingling numbness. She felt herself losing shape and sensation. Then heat warmed her skin, reminding her the edges of her body. The room turned hot, and the walls around them shook like an earthquake. The scream that once echoed from Malicine transformed into something deep, guttural. Their presence shifted into a bigger force than the tower could contain. The roof split apart, and the ground caved in.

As Corin slid inside the rocky debris, flames trickled between the gaps, a wall of vermillion that shone through the darkness. For a moment, she forgot about the pain and cracked an impossible smile. She could see the dragon rising from the ashes. The creature tore through the sky, terrifying and magnificent at the same time. She knew the dragon would save her and get them out of this island. This was Malicine, after all, and they were more powerful than anything in this world.

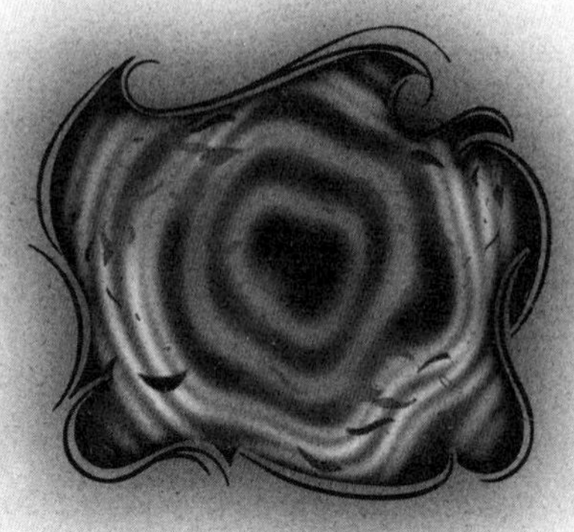

CHAPTER 30

101 YEARS AGO

MALICINE WAS SUPPOSED to die alone by their own father's hands. Sacrificed to make some impossible wish come true, all so that Oleander could create a new world from his own flesh and blood. He didn't care if that meant killing his own child. The dagger would slash Malicine's throat open, the blade already pressed into their neck.

Instead, the knife retracted, and the pain was gone.

There was the sound of something piercing flesh, but it wasn't Malicine's. They opened their eyes and saw a glass dagger punctured through Oleander's chest. The blade looked hastily carved, yet sharp enough to wound him. A shudder of breath, and Malicine noticed it came from a new person, one whose silhouette was made of glass.

Amelia pulled out the dagger and stumbled backward. Her body toppled to the ground, slicked in blood and stone. There was a crack in her ribs, translucent bones protruding from paper-thin skin. She struggled to push herself up, and Malicine realized it hadn't been a dagger she carried, but the sharp end of a broken hand.

Questions spun in Malicine's mind. How long had Amelia been wandering to find Malicine? How could she break so easily and still be here?

And why, *why* didn't she leave Malicine behind?

The stab wasn't enough to kill Oleander. If anything, it only resulted in a minor wound. A temporary distraction that would result in another death, one that didn't even need to happen if Amelia hadn't been foolish enough to return. She backed away as he turned around, trembling under his shadow. Sharp talons flashed. A blur of claws swiped the air. A guttural scream ripped from Malicine's throat before they could make sense of why they cared.

"Amelia—!"

She shattered before them, a burst of glass and silent cries. She didn't even make a sound as she broke apart. The shards split in different directions across the floor, pieces of her scattering near Malicine's feet.

They stared at the fragments of the only person who looked for them. In their reflection, they shed tears. Amelia had been falling apart, and yet she came back for Malicine.

The world turned still, only the sound of their shaky breaths betraying their body to tremble. Outside, the sky rumbled through the smoke. If there were stars, they'd bleed the world red. The black rocks looked like expressionless figures, but if Malicine concentrated hard enough, their pulse beat alongside the trees beyond. There used to be life in this world, and perhaps it still existed, something innate and covered. Like lava that once flowed through the forest, incinerating tree trunks to form the hollow cylinders around Malicine. A flame that broiled inside them, as well.

Oleander turned to them with a wicked smile, assuming they trembled from fear, not anger. He had said that Malicine was broken. He was wrong. Broken people didn't feel the sort of rage that made them alive. Broken people didn't have ravens who followed their side or lost princesses who chose them over anywhere else.

If anyone was broken and alone, it was him. It was why he sought them. Because the core of Malicine's existence, their blood, their soul, held more multitudes than he could ever dream.

Popping noises rang from the sky. Cracks appeared in the fortress, running down the invisible barrier in the jagged shape of veins. It allowed for black smoke to trickle inside the tower, the red sky to bleed through the fissures. Oleander spun around, watching his world fall apart. But it wasn't breaking down at all. It was only becoming alive for Malicine.

Rage exploded from within. Their mouth expelled a whorl of fire and blasted Oleander to the other side of the tower. He broke through the window, a ball of flames that barely had time to react. Chains broke from Malicine's limbs as they grew bigger, taller, crashing through the vaulted ceiling and rising higher than any spire. Walls crumbled, and from the debris and ash, they rose as a dragon.

Their tail swung at the columns in Oleander's direction. He moved quickly, arms raised to block the rocks. Black scales crackled across his skin as his horns spiraled into the sky. Laughter rumbled from his extending throat, his neck twisting around the trees, sharp teeth gleaming between the branches. The amulet glowed from his scales, and in his reddened eyes, Malicine saw blood.

"You are too inept to be acting stubborn." When he spoke as a dragon, his voice was toneless, guttural. It echoed through every tree and shook the ground. "Don't you understand, child? In every world, you are the same."

Oleander's mouth gaped open, a large void with teeth sharp enough to tear Malicine to shreds. Gusts of violent wind blew as he charged forward. Malicine didn't retreat. Instead, they faced their father directly, green eyes locked onto the amulet at his throat. The gem radiated light through the void, as if sensing Malicine's blood and ready to consume them.

They soared toward Oleander and swung for the gem. Their claws pierced his scales, digging into flesh until they could rip the amulet from his body. They let out a guttural snarl as his teeth clamped over their limbs. Blood spurted from both dragons as they tore into each other. Pain blossomed through Malicine's body with each scratch. A blinding light split the sky open. The amulet pulsed like a beating heart, slicked with both their blood. Oleander's laugh was monstrous as he grabbed the gem, keen to take the newfound power. But it burned under his touch, and he let out a howl as holes burned into his scales.

"You're wrong, Oleander." Malicine spat his name like they were cleansing themselves from poison. Their voice boomed through the black smoke that surrounded them. The amulet floated toward their body like it was returning not to its past, but a new home. Their scales latched onto the gem and they felt their heart beating as one with it.

For centuries, Oleander thought magic meant taking power from others. But Malicine was the one who could open worlds and change the tides of time. They only needed power from themselves, for they were not a curse, but a miracle.

Energy roiled inside them like a flame. Blood pulsed against their skin, pounding to the breath of every generation that came before them, every source of life merging for a new future in Malicine's hands.

"I am neither human nor Fae, man nor woman, good nor evil."

Malicine leapt to the sky, covering the red moon until they shaded the entire land into darkness.

"I am Malicine, and I cannot be contained."

They let out a deafening screech that shook the world. The fire was electric blue, spreading across the land like lightning. The ground crumbled into molten rock and erupted where Oleander stood. Magma swallowed him whole, the flow of lava drowning him until his blackened bones withered to dust. The fortress surrounding them shattered. Black clouds tore apart like a rip in the seams of the sky.

Pure white light washed across the atmosphere. The moon waxed into a pearl, reflecting the remnants of fire and oceans into an iridescent hue.

For the first time, the sky turned clear.

DRAFTS OF WIND cooled down the fires like a whisper. In the dead woods, an amulet sat still in Malicine's palm. The root of a broken tree stretched toward them, curling around their fingers like a serpent finding its home. Malicine let the root grow in their hands until it was thick enough to hold as a staff. At the top of the scepter, they stared at their own reflection, mirrored within the scarlet clouds that swirled inside the amulet.

Magic coursed through their veins and radiated to the staff. They waved the stick over the pile of debris where the tower had fallen. Rocks dispersed in the air, shifting like puzzle pieces until the rubble revealed Talon's body. The feathers on his tail had burnt to crisps, uncovering part of his raw, pink flesh. Gingerly, Malicine placed a hand on his wound. The warmth of their palm pieced his feathers back together. His eyes opened once more.

As he took in the scene, he let out a mournful croak. *"We should have never come here. I . . . am deeply sorry."*

Malicine shook their head. "You wanted to remember what he was like. I wanted to know the truth. We got what we came here for."

They scanned their surroundings, where clear skies shed light across indistinct columns and barren caves. Rocks contracted back into basalt pillars, cooling down from lava. Stones froze in the shape of jagged teeth like a silent scream that already passed.

Malicine looked at the ground where glass shards scattered over the dirt. Under the light, the glass glinted like teardrops. They dug the end of the staff into the debris. Power pulsed from the wooden stick, trickled down to the root, and crept through the rubble. Shards of glass floated to the same spot until they coalesced, forming the silhouette of a woman. The last pieces of an eyelash stuck together before Amelia fluttered her eyes open.

She sat up with a gasp, readjusting to the air around them, the bright sky, and the fact that moments ago, she had been smashed into pieces. Translucent hair fell over her shoulders like a waterfall, and she stared at the palms of her transparent hands, wondering how she'd come to life again.

Malicine reached a hand out to the girl. She stared back at the demon, stunned, before taking Malicine's palm and pulling herself up.

"Why did you come back for me?" Malicine stilled the anger from seeping into their voice. Part of them wanted to yell at the girl for her stupidity, her willingness to turn back and run into danger, even if that meant getting killed. But the demon was tired of anger, how it clung onto them like a mask, hiding something sadder beneath.

Amelia looked at them as if she had already taken off that mask.

"I saw a portal with a hidden world on the other side. It was magical, and beautiful, and perfect," she said. "It looked just like a dollhouse I once had. There was a maze of sunflowers, a cottage with a balcony, and green fields that stretched for miles. When I saw it, I thought this must be the closest thing to happiness. Something close to perfection, yet it could never be real. My secret, imaginary world."

A hopeful look washed over her sea glass eyes, an endless ocean that feared no limits.

"I realized that if I crossed over, you needed to come with me too."

"Why would I go with you?"

"Because you wouldn't have agreed to leave our world," she said, "if you weren't unhappy living in it."

The revelation hit Malicine like a strike in the gut. It was a different type of affliction, one that bit beneath their skin and chewed them raw. For all the snarled lips and cruel words they could utter, Amelia still saw past their skin, staring at the deep unhappiness they harbored inside. They turned away from the girl, as if their back could shield the rest of their vulnerability she hadn't already seen.

"You should go home," they said.

Amelia stepped closer to them. "Malicine, what if we—"

They spun around and placed a hand in front of her face. Magic glowed from their palm, silencing the words from Amelia's lips. Her glass eyes turned blank as shadows spewed from her open mouth, floating into the air and disappearing like mist. A few seconds passed before she blinked herself back to recognition.

"We're even," Malicine said. "I revoked the curse. You will no longer sleep for eternity when you turn eighteen."

Amelia gaped at the demon, mouth hanging open as she processed what this meant. "Why would you do that?"

They ignored her question and focused on the amulet embedded in their staff. The gem sensed the magic pulsing in their veins and reacted with light. The air shifted, the smell of iron and magic swirling with the wind as a portal gaped open behind Amelia. She stared at the entrance, surprised by how quickly it opened, while Malicine knew they no longer needed to cast magic circles or even spill blood. With the amulet forged from different lives across different times, they could open portals with magic alone.

"You belong in your world, Amelia." Malicine knew that humans could not exist any other way. Lore would claim Gyldan was prosperous because of gold. People would fight wars and kill each other over it, refusing to see that such trivial minerals would never save them. These were the stories the victors would tell, a romanticized history to mask their own greed as they destroyed the world for it.

Malicine flicked their staff and sent a gust of wind, knocking Amelia on her heels. She reached a hand toward the demon, mouth open to protest, before the portal swallowed her whole and she disappeared.

In the human world, she would return to her regular body. But when Malicine returned, they would remain the same.

They stepped away from the portal and stared at the rest of the Otherworld. A deafening silence hung across empty land, where only death and ash existed. Malicine spent the next few minutes wandering across rubble, searching for the charred remains of their father, but he was truly gone. They walked until they reached the black sea, where thick waves slowly rolled to shore, and their wet footprints left soot wherever they went.

Talon hopped on a boulder overlooking the water. There was nothing beyond the darkness.

"We will have to return eventually," he croaked. *"There is nothing left for us here."*

Malicine sat next to him on the boulder. If they strained hard enough, they could make out their reflection in the sludge from the ocean, the way even tar could arrange together their features that they tried so hard to escape.

They had refused to hear what Amelia had to say, because it didn't matter if she wanted to seek another world with Malicine. No matter where they went, there would never be a place where Malicine would find home. They would return to the human world, and the two of them would lead separate lives: Amelia becoming the next queen of Gyldan, and Malicine remaining in shadows.

Behind them, the portal was still open, waiting for their entrance.

"We will return," they told Talon. "I just couldn't say goodbye to her."

CHAPTER 31

FLAMES LICKED HER heels as Corin climbed on Malicine's back. The demon's wings flapped hard, sending a gust of wind so fierce it allowed them to puncture through fog. Corin gasped for fresh air as they soared into the sky. Below them, Autumnland turned into blazing trees and crimson mountains.

Her heart still hammered against her chest as she clung onto Malicine's scales. She had watched them transform into a dragon and kill the monster that tormented them with a fiery tidal wave. Relief filled her body as parts of her pieced back together, rematerializing once the demon burned down their nightmares.

But Corin looked back at the island and felt her heart drop once again. It took only a breeze to cool the fires down. Tree stumps grew back to where they once were, skeletal arms and withered leaves that haunted her moments ago. Thick clouds wrapped around the island like a cocoon. Through the fog, a monster's growl echoed, the faint roars of thunder muffled behind an invisible fortress. Restored to its original form, the island told Corin that she may have left, but the land would always remain. A secret stored in the back of her conscience that she would never truly erase.

She had doubled over with nausea by the time they reached Summerland, despite the salt air and jewel-blue ocean welcoming them. Talon's familiar croak greeted Malicine at the shore while Corin tumbled on her hands and knees. Her palm squeezed fistfuls of sand, the sun's warmth trickling between her fingers, a sensation she never thought she would feel again. She focused on the gentle waves of the ocean and the birds cawing in the sky. The sounds, the touch, all the reminders she needed that they were safe now.

Except none of this was real either.

Grief crashed back into Corin as she remembered her sister's blue lips and cold skin. Her ragged fingernails with dirt packed beneath. The way her body sagged in Corin's hands. Corin rolled over in the sand and threw up. The sickness didn't stop, even as Malicine transformed back to their original form, knelt beside her, and healed her wounds. Her flesh may have reassembled whole, but pain ate at her heart until she felt like there was only a gaping hole left inside her chest. What had once filled its place, a little girl who never grew up to be cherished.

What future could they ever have together but an imagined one?

Corin did not know how long she cried. Time stretched and warped, the sound of waves crashing to the shore along with her sobs, then returning to the ocean, leaving her behind. Her cheek had stuck to the sand, the sideways clouds she watched crawling for miles across blue. She didn't get up. Neither did Malicine or Talon, who sat quietly by her side the entire time.

Across the ocean, the island rumbled. Waves left behind clumps of seaweed that glittered under the light. Black kelp crawled across the sand like snails, slowly inching their way toward Corin's body. Their slimy arms wrapped around her ankles, and she was ready for its pull, wanted it to bring her down to the depths of the ocean where darkness would drown her.

"You're doing it again." Malicine's voice cut through the seaweed. Corin felt magic tingling her skin as the kelp unwrapped itself from her ankles and retreated to the ocean.

"Doing what?" she muttered.

"Punishing yourself."

Corin watched the water swallow the seaweed until it disintegrated, leaving black residue even where light refracted. It was guilt that once made her nearly drown, the truth in the back of her mind when she had swam with Elly and knew it wasn't real. Corin didn't know any other way to continue existing without harming herself. She didn't know how it was possible to keep living without suffering too.

She wanted to ask Malicine who else she could be angry with, but the question died on her tongue, the answer coming to her first. There had been a person who tried saving her from drowning, reaching out with gentle arms and telling Corin not to fight her grief. In the end, her kindness had been deception. This person should have known it was crueler to let Corin believe in the light refracting in the water rather than the darkness below.

At last, Corin sat up. Grains of sand trickled down her cheek, following where her tears had dried. Her eyes narrowed in resolve, staring at the sun that burned so bright she wanted to stab into the star and watch it sink, so that she would never see the light again.

Her voice willed itself to stay calm as she turned to Malicine and said, "Take me to Briar Rose."

CORIN WATCHED MALICINE and Talon cut through dense undergrowth to reach the center of the jungle. She kicked rough vines blocking the path, stomping wet ground in a silent scowl. She no longer believed in the sun's warmth or the smell of clay wafting through trees. They were nostalgia steeped in lies, a web of fake memories spun by a princess who wanted to forget her own.

They reached the base of the waterfall, where Corin had first plunged before the tides swept her away. The water rippled calmly with no hint of the turmoil from earlier. Instead the stream burbled quietly, spitting on rocks with the same contained anger she had reserved for one person.

Briar sat on one of the boulders, her arms crossed around her knees, the bottom of her dress cascading in water so one couldn't tell where fabric ended and liquid began. Stray sunflowers floated around her bare feet, wilting like her posture of grief. Corin tried to still herself, curling her fingers to fists at her side. She refused to shake in anger, even though she wanted to thrash the trees around them, yell at the chirping birds to quiet down, tear the peaceful scenery apart so they would stop pretending any of this was real. She wanted to destroy something beautiful, and the most beautiful thing was the girl in front of her.

Briar sensed their presence and looked up. Hopeful light shone in her widened eyes. She leapt off the boulder and wrapped her arms around Malicine.

"You made it," she gasped, a sob of relief muffled in their chest.

"Barely. But we have a problem. I lost the amulet."

Briar pulled away to examine Malicine, whose hands were empty without their staff. A faint worry etched her forehead. The silence made Corin's stomach coil with guilt. It had been her fault that Malicine chased her into the island. She risked both their lives and lost the demon's amulet in the process. Without the gem, Malicine could no longer open a portal. Their plan for stopping Prince Ezran and the godmothers from following their tracks would not work. Corin had no way of returning to Gyldan anymore either.

A new, terrifying thought trickled to the back of her mind. Without Elly, there was no reason for Corin to return to Gyldan. She had nowhere to go. No reason to continue living.

"We will figure it out," Briar reassured. "The important thing is that both of you made it back safe."

The softness of her voice made Corin's anger flare once again. How could this girl be so insistent on suppressing the guilt and pain? They could have died. Now they were trapped forever. She acted like things could easily go back to normal. Sunsets, afternoon tea, parties and pretty dresses. Trivial props to play pretend for the entirety of her sad existence.

Corin couldn't bring herself to look at Briar, so she walked toward the waterfall. Her pants soaked from the stream as she jumped over the rocks. She stopped at the cascade, where beyond the white foam, her reflection stared back at her. Dark skin, cracked lips, bloodshot eyes. A broken person who could never be put back together.

"Are you all right, Corin?"

She watched Briar drawing nearer behind her. White foam blurred the princess's expression, but Corin could already imagine the mock concern, the furrow of her brows, the bite of her lower lip.

"Malicine said that in the dreamworld, your subconscious thoughts come to life," Corin said. "That means, if I want something, I can make it appear in my own hands."

She reached inside the waterfall, feeling the cool river wash over her skin and drizzle between her empty fingers. They curled into a fist until something solid filled her palm like a block of ice. It was the same feeling she had when she first pulled out a sword in Winterland. She had wanted to protect Elly.

"I know what I want now."

Now she would protect herself.

Corin unsheathed the dagger from the water and leapt at Briar's throat. The force knocked her over, and they were both on the ground, Corin's knees locked around Briar's waist, the make-shift weapon at her neck. Boulders rose to the sky, jagged slabs of rock surrounding them as walls to muffle Malicine's yells from outside. The waterfall roared above their heads, drenching them both until Corin could feel her own skin against Briar's between wet fabric. Corin breathed heavily, heart pounding against her chest, the violent urge to tear into Briar and expose every part of her.

The girl's voice cut through the noise like a lacy embrace.

"It's okay, Mal. Let her do it."

Briar tilted her head back, exposing the gold-tinted veins that ran down her throat where Corin's dagger touched. Corin could hear the flutter of breath, the swirl of emotions that rocked her body on top of Briar.

"You have that little regard for your life?" she hissed.

Her hand pressed the blade harder to Briar's throat like a challenge. She could feel the princess suck in a breath and let it go, the slow rise and fall of her chest beneath her damp dress. She wanted to cut the girl open and demand answers from the wretched, beating heart that gave her foolish hope. Somewhere, between the crooks of Briar's limbs and paths of her veins, Corin searched for the truth.

Yet when Briar replied, her voice carried a lightness. Like she could float away at any moment, even as Corin pinned her body to the ground.

"Why not? Death means no uncertainty. No pain. No sadness. Why, it's almost like being in a dream."

The shock of Briar's calmness spread through Corin's body. She didn't know why it felt like she was the one being cut. She needed to patch the wound the only way she knew how: with rage. She wanted Briar to show she was afraid. That the girl wasn't so resigned to toss away her life like it meant nothing.

Corin raised her weapon in the air and plunged it down.

The blade hit the rock beside Briar's head with a hard crack. The dagger shattered like ice, and the waterfall split into opposite directions, a flood that rolled across stones and emptied the pool. Without water, the sleeves of Briar's dress looked deflated, her hair slicked wet against her face, eyes closed and waiting. But Corin was still on her knees, staring at the flutter of her lashes, watching her cheeks gleam as a single drop of water hit her face.

Briar's eyes fluttered open. Disbelief flickered across her face as she realized Corin was crying.

"I looked for you," Corin whispered. "In the tunnels, in Gyldan—I looked for you."

Then a new flood came, one of her own doing. She thought she couldn't cry anymore, but her broken heart was an endless pool, and Briar was going to drown in it.

"I cried out for you when I found El. I called your name. I prayed and begged to a god, any god, that somewhere, out there, you would wake up and make things better. But you never came."

The memories came rushing back. Elly's body cradled to her chest. Her throat turning raw from screaming. The name of a sleeping princess echoing through the tunnels. The deafening silence that told her nobody was going to help them.

For so long, she had told Elly not to get her hopes up with magic and fairy tales. She had dismissed the stories as desperate imagination for fools who had nothing else to live for. Yet even after discovering Elly's body starved to death with the other lost souls, Corin had continued wandering through the tunnels in search for the castle ruins. She had done it because, more than anything, it was Corin who wanted to believe the fairy tale was real.

In the end, she had been the fool who dreamed.

Briar recognized this truth as well, because her face crumpled under the weight of it. She let go a shuddering breath as if she were in pain, even though Corin no longer pinned her to the ground. Something heavier pressed against Briar's chest, forcing tears to spring to her eyes, a broken sob to crawl out of her throat.

"I'm sorry," Briar said. "But there would be no difference in the world if I was in it. In fact, the world would be better off without me."

"Why?" The question sounded more like a beg. Corin saw the image of the perfect princess crumbling before her, an ethereal vision cracked into glass shards. Briar's flowers washed away in the river, her skin turning pale like the sleeping princess Corin had seen in Gyldan. Blond, limp hair slicked her real face.

"Because I am a coward," Amelia answered, "and cowards do not change lives."

Corin stared at her, remembering every clue of Amelia's life she had witnessed, every wound the princess tried to hide. Broken crowns, dented chain mail, rows of pearls with specks of blood. An act of defiance ending with a dead king's blood crusted beneath her nails. They came in flashes, the memories diluted from suppression, like watching something submerged underwater. Corin had only seen pieces in Autumnland, yet she felt the weight of Amelia's pain, the way it suffocated her. It was the same sinking feeling Corin possessed when she held Elly's body to her sobbing chest, knowing that even when her sister was alive, Corin couldn't have given her a better life anyway.

She had been suspicious of Briar Rose, not because of her unfamiliarity, but her uncomfortable likeness. Beneath Briar's facade, Corin had seen the very thing she hated within herself.

The realization washed over her like the last wave of an ocean. The sun broke through the sky in fractured light, shining through the waterfall that streamed over the cliffside again. What once were walls surrounding them shrank back to rocks. Malicine and Talon stood from the other side, watching in stunned silence.

Corin could not stand up or apologize. Instead, she broke down in Briar's arms.

The stream trickled past their skin and tried to wash away their pain, but the sounds Corin made were too loud and horrid, disrupting what should have been serene. She cried like someone who felt the whole truth: that sometimes people died and the world was cruel and there was nothing left to do but feel every loss.

Briar held her for what felt like an eternity. She didn't let go, even as Corin gripped her arms and wailed. They curled inside the pool, floating between each other's limbs. This was different from drowning herself in the darkest depths of the ocean or burying herself in soil like a grave. Corin could no longer sink into oblivion and self-hatred, because this time, Briar Rose carried her.

CHAPTER 32

NEARLY 100 YEARS AGO

LILITH DID NOT remember dreams, but she remembered this one like a memory bubbling to her subconscious. The swell of the ocean, the burning light of sun. How the earth carried to shore a dying boy. At twelve years old, she'd already had lungs powerful enough to scream for help. She'd already lost her mother. The thought of losing another person, even if it was a stranger, was earth-shattering.

Her arms had hooked underneath his armpits as she'd dragged him away from water and dropped him into sand. He was skinny and pale, and appeared almost the same age as her, perhaps younger. She'd brushed wet, blond locks of hair from his face and crushed her lips against his. He'd tasted like the salt of the ocean and her tears.

She'd switched between pressing her palms hard against his chest and blowing air into his mouth. In those frantic minutes, she'd pleaded for him to open his eyes, waited for air to expel from his lips. A single breath to let her know he was alive.

Please, please, please.

Breathe.

Lilith woke up with his cold breath against her ear.

Moonlight slanted into her bedroom, casting rippling shadows on patterned wallpaper. Satin drapes were left open to reveal a full moon hanging bare in the sky. Parts of Lilith's room brought her back to reality: red upholstered furniture, malachite candelabras, the cabinet that doubled as a mirror, reflecting her body entwined with another in bed.

She turned to look at the boy from the ocean, grown into a man a decade later. His jaw had become more defined, sharp as the slice of light that fell through the windows. His hair's white-blond locks were tousled like the blankets. Long lashes swept over pale cheeks, and the gentle breath of his lips fluttered over her face.

He looked so innocent whenever he slept. Soft and ethereal, the light of the moon gently caressing his cheek. For a moment, his expression was the exact replica of the time she'd pulled him from the ocean in Zilar. A moment of peaceful unconsciousness before she'd breathed air back into his lungs.

Lilith untangled herself from his arms and sat up from the bed. The movement made him stir awake. When she was certain he was fully conscious, she said, "I told you not to come here anymore."

She thought she had locked the door. Maybe she hadn't. Maybe some part of her pretended to forget. When Amelia accepted Ezran's marriage proposal, Lilith had been horrified by the news. He'd intruded upon their lives and fooled the kingdom into letting him stay by proposing to the princess. All so that he could be in Lilith's life again.

Ezran crawled toward her on the mattress and wrapped his arm around her waist, burying his face into her back like a lost child.

She fought the urge to take his embrace, but didn't push him away either.

"I can't keep acting like you're a stranger, Lilith. It doesn't come as easily to me as it does to you." His voice was husky and low, muffled by the fabric of her nightgown.

Guilt panged her chest. She whispered, "It's not easy."

Acting like she didn't know the man who arrived at the castle was an act of willpower, a conscious gesture for her to maintain composure and avoid letting too much blood drain from her face. Still, when she warned Victor and Amelia to stay away from him, that he did not have the right intentions in coming here, an edge in her voice had slipped. Like a hidden dagger falling out of her sleeve.

They didn't listen. She couldn't give them a good reason to.

No, it wasn't that. She just didn't. Perhaps, deep down, she felt relief in having someone she knew and loved close to her again.

Their friendship had bloomed the day she saved him from the ocean. The king and queen of Zilar had thanked her for rescuing their only child and welcomed her inside their castle. Her childhood, once lonely after her mother's passing and father's abandonment, brightened with new memories of running down banquet halls, sharing pastries in the kitchens, and feeding carrots to the horse in the stables. She became close to the servants and cooks in the castle, kind-hearted folks who were native to Zilar just like her mother was, and learned about their dreams to move to Gyldan. They'd echoed the sentiments her mother once told her: that this land, once nothing more than barren desert, could be turned into anything. Even a home.

When her father returned to her life with a proposition for her to marry the king of Gyldan, she knew it was only to restore his social standing. After she'd accepted the union, Ezran had argued, "If it's a life of easy wealth you want, I can give you that." He couldn't understand her reasonings because he always had a home, one that was stolen from people like her mother and his servants.

On the day of their tearful goodbye, Ezran had said he would never forget her.

Of course, he was always true to his promises.

Lilith lit the candle on her nightstand, illuminating the bedroom with a warm glow. Her shadow loomed against the patterned wallpaper, and she remembered staring at that same silhouette on a closed door the night she had visited Amelia's bedroom. She wanted to tell the princess the truth. If Amelia hadn't been sleeping, if Lilith had only come to her sooner, she wondered if things could have changed.

"I can't stop thinking about Amelia," she said.

Nine months had passed since Amelia disappeared. The castle fell into a state of disarray over the missing princess, uncertainty and rumors spreading across servants and faeries like wildfire. Her godmothers worried that Malicine had lured her into the woods to ensure she would die at eighteen. But as Lilith organized search parties, neither Malicine nor Amelia could be found throughout the kingdom.

Autumn rolled in, and they had only a week before Amelia's eighteenth birthday. There was no heir to the throne, no princess to even save from a spinning wheel. Lilith felt pressured to expand her search beyond the country, but Victor limited the expedition with his own journey to neighboring kingdoms. He'd left a month ago to seek women who would give him another heir, insisting that he needed to travel far away from Gyldan so that people would not discover how fragile their monarchy was. As a result, he took away the resources Lilith needed by bringing guards and servants with him.

Frustration twisted in Lilith's stomach at his decision to find a new heir rather than stay to find Amelia. It was a gamble for Gyldan's future, and he'd placed the wrong bet.

"She's not coming back," Ezran replied.

The affirmation made Lilith's skin bristle. "She will."

"She's not the type of person who can do anything for herself. The pre-wedding jitters, her moodiness, the pressure of either ruling a kingdom or dying from a spindle . . . she probably couldn't handle any of it and ran away. Weak-minded girls like her are far too common. They aren't like you, Lilith. They crumble at any sign of hardship."

"Amelia is not weak," Lilith replied fiercely. "If you think dismissing other women is a compliment to me, it's not."

Lilith knew Amelia had a tendency to run away, an instinct as natural for her as breathing, but what mattered more was that she came back. She would show up and confront the darkness anyway, even when it felt too consuming. Amelia was capable of that strength, even if the princess herself didn't know that yet.

Ezran grabbed Lilith's hand and pressed his lips to the curve of her fingers. "Forgive me." His voice turned soft, coaxing, an attempt to appease her. "You're right. She'll come back, and we'll figure out the rest from there."

Lilith yanked her hand away from his lips, still angry. She stood up from the bed and let her distracted thoughts lift her away from Ezran. She approached the dressing table and sank into the cushioned stool. Absent-minded fingers danced over vials of perfume, clouds of powder puffs, porcelain cups of cream. An armoire cabinet made of solid wood sat behind a bowl of ivory hairpins, displaying assortments of jewelry that glinted under moonlight. The tangible objects grounded her back to reality. She didn't care for such luxuries, but these gifts reminded her the duty of being queen and the responsibilities she had for Gyldan.

Then there was Ezran again, a shadow approaching from behind. His arms wrapped around her, the warmth of his skin luring fond memories like soft waves against a shore. He held her as gently as he did when they were caught in summer storms as children or reading old stories by candlelight past their bedtimes. He would smuggle lost history books from every trip because she'd wanted to read stories before they were rewritten by Zilar. He never cared that those archives were banned in his kingdom. That was something she'd always admired about him: He held no loyalty to any country or crown. His priority had always been the people he cared about.

She could feel her initial anger at him melting away under his embrace. Ezran was an arrogant fool, but she had seen the goodness in him throughout their childhoods, had tasted his potential in the very first breath they shared.

Their silent embrace was interrupted by the hitch of his breath. The table groaned as he leaned over the surface, fingers running through velvet cushions until he grasped what he'd seen.

"You kept the pearls."

They were the only necklace that had not been arranged neatly inside its case because of how often she wore them. Ezran had gifted the pearls on her eighteenth birthday, a reminder of the ocean where he owed her his breath. As she came to know him, she understood how the tides favored a wrathful boy. But there were the rare glimpses of gentleness she would see, his delicate heart soft as sea-foam.

"They're my favorite," she confessed. "I wear them every day."

She knew a world didn't exist where she could tell Ezran goodbye forever while keeping a piece of him wherever she went. The truth of it was that no matter how her life could change, he would always be the boy who loved her when no one else did.

He gently took the pearls and wrapped them around her neck, leaving a trail of kisses down her nape. Her skin tingled from the touch. She allowed a reckless thought that, perhaps, this kind of love was enough for her to be happy. Maybe something like this could be more than enough.

Like an answer, a flash of lightning tore the sky. Lilith jumped from her seat, toppling her chair over. The sky had been clear, with not a cloud in sight that would have signaled a thunderstorm. Yet the air howled something fierce, the leaves of every tree rustling. Light radiated from the forest surrounding the castle. A hole opened in the sky, and though she couldn't make sense of the sight, her gut told her this was Amelia.

Ezran called her name as Lilith bounded for the door, ran across the hall, and rushed down the staircase. The doors burst open to pouring rain. When she scanned the sky, the clouds were still and unchanging. No, that couldn't be. What she'd seen could not have been simply her imagination.

Lilith ran deeper into the woods, even as her slippers splashed in puddles and dirt kicked up her skirt. Her throat turned sore from yelling Amelia's name, hoping her plea would echo far enough through the branches. She circled around looming trees and pushed through foliage, straining to find the princess in heavy rain. The weather turned unforgiving, the undergrowth crackling beneath her shoes. A rush of footsteps came from behind. She spun around and ran into Ezran's chest. He steadied her by the shoulders as she gasped for breath.

"Slow down," he said. "Are you sure it wasn't a trick of the light?"

"It's Amelia. I'm certain of it!"

Despite her insistence, Ezran led her beneath a canopy to shield them from the rain. He draped his coat over her head so that the water from the leaves would not drip on her. He was always like this, putting her first and center in his world. She counted her breaths to pace herself, but frustration seeped from her dry throat as she said, "I just wish she knew she didn't need to run away."

Rain dripped from Ezran's temple, and his damp cheeks took on a sheen under the moonlight. His silver eyes stewed in thought.

"Maybe she's right for running away," he said.

"What do you mean?"

They stared at each other in weighted silence until he stepped close enough for her to feel his breath. His palm cupped her cheek, and he looked at her tenderly like she was the most important thing in the world.

"We could do it too. Abandon it all," he murmured. "We'd finally be together. There wouldn't be a need for me to take over as king or marry Amelia. I don't care about ruling any kingdom, as long as I'm with you."

He steadied his hand over hers, but she could still feel the squeeze of his fingers, the pressure of his skin on hers. She knew he meant every word. Ezran would have done anything for her. It was the kind of hopeless devotion that any lucky woman would dream of. But the declaration also came from desperation. He had no other option than to run away with her. If Amelia didn't show up, there would be no heir. If Amelia did appear, he would have to stay married to her. There were no other circumstances where Ezran and Lilith could be together.

She took off his coat, drenched from the rain, and handed it back to Ezran. "We can't."

"We can."

"Let me correct myself. We can. But I won't." She tightened her grip on his hands and stared deep into his eyes for the truth. "I want to make a difference in the world. Don't you?"

There was a hitch in his throat. "No," he rasped. "I only want you."

Lilith let go of his hands. The weight of his hold lifted everything away.

"I'm sorry, Ezran," she said. "That's not good enough for me."

He stared at her with a pain-stricken face, like she had just ripped his heart out and he didn't understand why. It was the same expression he wore the day she had told him goodbye and married Victor. Lilith clenched her eyes shut, if only to block out the pained look of the broken boy, or else risk hearing her heart crack in two. She needed to stay firmly rooted into the ground, not let her feelings be easily swayed by the turns of the wind. There was a reason why dreams were only for sleeping. Why they only met at the thick of night, between the sleepy haze of reverie and wishful thinking.

"You should go," she said, departing from the canopy's shade. She wanted to return to the castle and alert the guards that she'd seen Amelia. Perhaps they would find the princess if Lilith recruited another search party tonight. She barely made it past the tree when Ezran grabbed her by the wrist. He pulled her back, demanding her to face him again.

"Kiss me," he said. "Even if it's the last time. Please. Before you say goodbye."

Lilith held her breath, afraid that any exhale would push her forward into his arms and let her sink into his embrace. Water trailed down his cheeks, and this time, it wasn't the rain. His mouth twisted in anguish. The wait looked like it was killing him.

She placed a gentle hand on his cheek, where his tears slicked the tip of her thumb. Their noses brushed against each other, and their faces finally met in the rain. He tasted like air at night, heavy with the weight of autumn storm. Salt tinged their lips, a mixture of rain and tears, his kiss like a flame that wanted to swallow her whole. He tasted just like the boy in her dreams.

But that was all they were: dreams.

A shriek pierced the air, pulling Lilith away. Behind Ezran, at the entrance of the forest, stood Amelia's godmothers, silhouetted by candlelight.

"Run," Lilith urged. "I'll stay so they won't catch you."

Ezran shook his head. "I'm not leaving you—"

"Someone needs to find Amelia," she whispered fiercely. "If you don't leave now, I'll never forgive us for losing her."

She didn't promise they'd see each other again, because there was no guarantee. But he must have believed it from the flicker of hope in his eyes. His lips twisted in regret, while his feet staggered backward. A mental battle raged inside his mind. She shoved him back, forcing him to commit to their plan.

"Protect my treasure." This wasn't a plea, but a demand. "Find Amelia. It's always belonged to her."

CHAPTER 33

THE SUNSET HURT to watch. Corin's eyes remained swollen long after crying, and the light didn't help.

She'd gone through the trouble of climbing on top of the overlook in Summerland to be alone. Miles of landscape stretched endlessly, the sands turning gold under the sun, the ocean gleaming under marigold skies. She tried to replicate the colors on a canvas, but the paint didn't mix quite right, and the shapes were all wrong. The brush felt stiff in her palm, the bristles prickly against her skin.

A frustrated groan hissed from her lips. She threw black paint across the canvas and smeared the dark oils until no other colors were left. The sunset, as if sensing her derision, melted below the ocean. The sky turned black in response, and the world enveloped itself in the night. She stared into the darkness and watched ocean waves turn so black it blended with her ruined painting, as if it were a colorless void.

The night was quiet except for crickets and a quiet stream of waterfall from the cliffside. If she listened closely enough, she could hear howling in the distance, the tides of wind that swirled around Autumnland and threatened to pull her legs down the cliff-side. Perhaps that was why the island kept calling. No matter how terrifying the nightmares were, that pain was still the most familiar thing to her. At least in the darkness, she knew she would get hurt. Better the comfort of familiarity than the possibility of loss.

"Our minds are such messy things."

Corin pulled away from the cliffside, attention snapped to the figure approaching. Malicine emerged from the jungle's foliage. Their fingers flexed in the awkward absence of their staff as they sat beside her at the cliffside and observed the island in the distance.

The clouds surrounding Autumnland rumbled. Corin thought of the beast that ripped through the bloodred moon with his horns, the echoes of laughter as he'd taunted Malicine with lies that they would never belong in any world. He'd been the darkness within them that kept everyone tied to the island. Corin had pushed the darkness at bay, but it never truly left.

"She's a good kid," Malicine said. Corin didn't need to ask who they were talking about. "I like her. And I don't like most people."

Corin shook her head. "You've never even met her."

"I met your memories of her. She lives there too."

But memories weren't enough. They couldn't change the reality that Elly was gone. Corin refused to see Elly in her dreams now that she acknowledged the aching truth of her sister's absence. How could someone escape from shame and sustain themselves with imagination? How could she do that with the knowledge that none of this was real?

"I don't understand how we're expected to just move on," she said.

Malicine let out a bitter laugh. "You think the pain goes away? It doesn't. We just make a bigger space to contain it."

"I don't know if I can," she murmured, "or deserve to."

Her gaze dipped below the waterfall, watching the stream make its way to the rest of the ocean. Dark waves rolled gently across the surface. They glittered underneath stars and buzzed in dormant strength. But there had been nights when the waves were wilder, when tides grasped her ankles and tried to pull her down to the bottom.

"I told her I never wanted her," she whispered. "It was the most horrible thing I said to her, because it was true."

That was it, the very thing that kept her from embracing forgiveness. Maybe she could have fooled herself into believing Elly's death was unpreventable, but she couldn't deny this. She wasn't meant to be a parent, let alone a sister. There were too many tireless days she worked to feed two mouths, too many sleepless nights where she came home to a crying child, and she couldn't stand dealing with that burden.

She hated Elly, and yet, she loved her. Corin loved her so much more than dreams could ever make of her.

"She died thinking I didn't love her." Corin let out a sob, then covered her mouth, biting into the skin of her palm. It wasn't fair for her to cry.

"She knows," said Malicine.

"No, she doesn't. I never told her."

"You did."

Malicine gripped Corin's shoulder, forcing her to look at them and listen.

"You tell her every time you warn her to be careful or ask if she's eaten. You tell her every time you hold on to her the second there's danger. You tell her every time you look at her when something amazing happens, because you want her to be there. I know what lack of love from sisters feels like, Corin. And it is not you."

Malicine's gaze dipped below to the shores of the beach, where a girl had been walking across the sand. Briar was a speck in the distance, yet her skin illuminated from the stars sewn in her dress. Her toes balanced across rocks as Talon circled around her. He perched on her fingers, and she talked to the raven in a secret language, like they were friends.

"Humans speak about love all the time as if they have something to prove," Malicine said. "But love isn't always obvious, and you don't need to state it to be true."

Stars emerged from the sky like tiny lights. Constellations danced across a dark canvas, glittering into delicate lines and shapes. Corin pictured Elly's fingers tracing each spot. In the abandoned building they slept in, Elly had often positioned herself beneath the hole in the roof to see the stars. Corin used to yell at her to stop or she would get sick.

In the dreamworld, a shooting star leapt across the sky. The motion was so sudden that Corin blinked and nearly missed it. The star descended to the shore and drifted toward Briar. She caught the light in her palms and cupped it like a firefly. The rock shimmered on her skin, a moment of life before it disintegrated into colorful dust. She looked up at Corin, realizing who was watching. When Briar waved, her hand glimmered in the darkness.

Corin held her breath, watching stars twinkle between Briar's fingers, remembering Elly's own hand stretched to the sky. This was the fairy tale Elly had been talking about. She hadn't searched for gold or some grander power to rule over a kingdom. She had been looking for the magic of ordinary things, seen the possibility of an infinite night sky.

A new dawn broke through the atmosphere. Fractures of

sunlight whisked away clouds until a crown shone over the ocean. An itch to capture everything in memory compelled Corin to grab the black canvas and return to work. Careful strokes painted golds that hit the peak of the mountains. Green shimmered over moss-covered rocks, while specks of white dotted the pale sky to show the remaining stars.

She was so absorbed in painting this scene that she didn't realize Malicine had spoken.

"Don't get into any more trouble while I'm gone."

Corin jerked her head up, but the demon had already stood to walk away. "Where are you going?"

"I'm getting my amulet back." Their silhouette disappeared inside the jungle. Corin followed the flicker of their cape, bounding past the foliage until she could reach them. Her boots pressed heavy into the soil as she blocked their path.

"I'll go with you," she said. "It was my fault you lost the amulet in the first place."

"No. It's too dangerous, and you'll only cause more trouble. The more people who venture inside the island, the more chaos unfolds."

Corin swallowed hard, remembering how Malicine had to carry her through the island. Terrors in all figments had swarmed them both. The two of them had barely made it out. If she joined Malicine, she couldn't guarantee she would prevent the nightmares from taking her again.

The demon brushed the woody vines from their view to catch a glimpse of the rumbling island across the ocean. Their eyes turned distant, a veil of thoughts that Corin couldn't discern.

"It's strange. I always thought abandonment would be all I'd ever know. Yet somehow, the most unexpected of people have come back for me. First Amelia, now you." A chuckle escaped Malicine's lips as they shook their head, finding humor in the irony. "I wonder how many people in the real world share your foolish hearts."

Corin followed the demon's descent down the mountains. Sunlight brought warm air to the jungle as bees buzzed around orchids and giant water lilies. Sweat slicked the side of her temple, but instead of humidity, it came from frantic thoughts racing through her head. There was no way Malicine could escape Autumnland unscathed. She tried not to listen to crackling branches as they moved, or else she would continue to imagine them trapped in the island forever.

A path of rubber trees parted for the beach's sandy opening. The sun fully emerged above the ocean as Briar waved them over. Before Malicine took another step, they turned to Corin.

"If I don't make it back, tell Briar that I . . ."

The words drifted away like salt in the air. They paused, lost in thought.

"Tell her what?" Corin asked.

"It's fine. I don't have to say it for her to know."

Briar stopped when she saw the expression on Malicine's face. Her arms fell to her sides, like a sunflower drooping once it sensed the light would not stay forever.

"You're leaving." She said it not as a question but a sad truth, one of many she had been accustomed to in a previous life. Malicine nodded, and Briar's face fell, as if she already knew she wouldn't be able to change the demon's mind. She balled her hands into fists for a long moment. Her fingers eventually flexed free as she threw herself to Malicine in a tight embrace.

"When you come back, we'll have a tea party," she said. "There will be pastries, and scones, and even those ugly floppy hats you hate. That's why you must come back, Mal."

Malicine ran their nails through Briar's hair. Corin witnessed a flicker of sadness pass their eyes, an unspoken truth that settled on their lips. They didn't reply, because they couldn't promise anything. Instead, they pressed a kiss at Briar's temple. It was the most tender Corin had ever seen Malicine, and that was how she knew the demon did not expect to return.

Malicine and their raven spread their wings and soared toward Autumnland, their figures swallowed whole by gray clouds. Briar watched with a quiet intensity that Corin recognized in fleeting moments. The girl's eyes were the color of sea glass, filled with endless water and light. They knew more than she let on, and more than Corin had understood before. She was not a naive princess cursed against her will, and Malicine was not a villain. They were simply people who wanted to escape.

This world wasn't real, but its inhabitants were. Like a secret, Corin wanted to protect it.

"You should paint again," Briar spoke while staring into the ocean. "That way, when Mal and Talon return, you'll have something to show them."

Saliva dried in Corin's mouth. "I can't—" She cleared her throat. "I don't know how to do this."

"You don't know how to paint? I don't believe that."

"No. I don't know how to do any of this."

Corin gestured to their surroundings, the waves washing over rocks, the sunlight filtering through clouds. Beautiful colors, whimsical shapes, a sense of peace that could never be possible in the real world. These had always belonged in paintings, not reality. But Briar placed a hand on Corin's cheek, and somehow, her touch didn't feel like a lie. As their skin warmed against each other, Corin realized she was trembling, and that Briar had tried to keep her still.

“You’ve always shielded yourself with anger, but that doesn’t have to be the only way to deal with the pain,” Briar said. “Maybe you can’t forgive yourself out there, but you can here.”

Corin wanted to hope this was true. That all she needed to do was remember she loved Elly, and that would be enough. Perhaps, in this world, she could think of impossible things and make them possible. She closed her eyes as her heart ached with a strange, sweet throbbing. Her fingers wrapped around Briar’s hand and squeezed it so she could feel the warmth of the Briar’s skin, the pulse in her veins, that truth in her voice.

Waves rippled gently against her feet. A burst of seagulls chimed in the sky at the arrival of a new presence.

Corin opened her eyes to see the water swell. The sea gave birth to familiar life. She ran to the ocean and caught the girl in her arms. The girl wasn’t limp and cold, like the infant Corin once saved in the river, but full and warm. Her face slicked wet like a newborn, her spiky hair peppered by the salt of sea. Water dripped down her long lashes, and Corin’s thumbs rubbed over her cheeks to wipe them away, cupping her small face until the girl finally took a breath. Brown eyes opened, round and full of light from a sun that kissed her skin and brought her to life.

Corin stared at her for a long time, memorizing every detail of her beautiful sister’s dark skin, her pattern of freckles, her crooked tooth. Elly was here, and at the same time, Corin knew she was not.

“I wish you were real,” she whispered. “There were so many things I should have done for you.”

Elly blinked, as if processing Corin’s words and the truth of her existence. Her chin slowly rose as she stared at the sky. A bird’s whistle cracked through the dawn. In the pale blues, there were still glimmers of white dots for her to reach.

"We could try again," said Elly. "Maybe we can start by watching the stars together."

Corin raised her head at the constellations. The stars were difficult to spot in the morning light, yet she waited patiently, watching her sister's fingers trace each one.

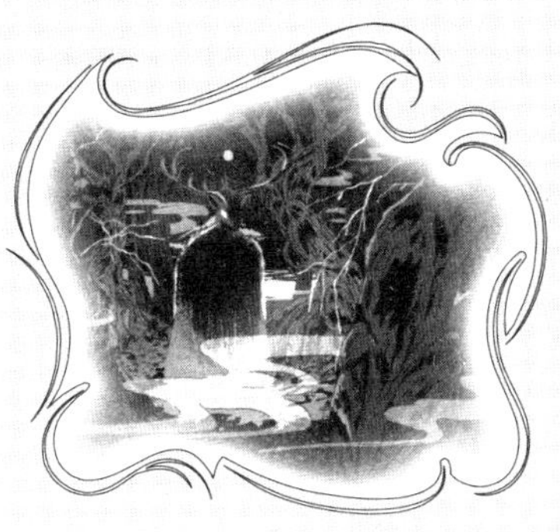

CHAPTER 34

ALMOST 100 YEARS AGO

AMELIA WOKE UP to her body tossed to the ground, the strike of skin and bone against a tree trunk. It took her a moment to realize she hadn't shattered like glass, then another moment to realize who had thrown her to the dirt.

Shadows cut sharp across Ezran's face in the harsh contrast of moonlight. "Wake up, you useless girl."

She flinched at the sudden shift in his demeanor. His voice had a tired rasp, and bags hung below his red eyes, as if he had been crying. But it wasn't shock she felt from Ezran behaving this way. She was surprised he let his mask slip at all.

Amelia scanned the woods frantically, mind already set on running. Yet between every tree was another one, an endless tunnel of foliage that nestled them in hidden corners. A familiar snap of branches jolted a memory of searching for Malicine. She'd found the demon, and they'd explored a new world together. Then Malicine sent her back to reality, and somehow, that felt even worse than hell.

"We're several miles away from your castle," Ezran said. "Which means I could kill you this instant and dispose of your body here, and nobody would ever know. Luckily for you, I won't."

She would have been eaten alive by wild animals if Ezran hadn't rescued her. He always played the part well, being her hero, yet never truly showing his cards. Until now. "Why do you want to kill me?"

"Because you ruined everything."

"Why *won't* you kill me, then?"

"Because I made a promise."

Her heart sank to the pit of her stomach as he retold what she'd missed. She discovered Ezran was from Lilith's past, left behind when she chose the life of a royal in Gyldan. When Amelia heard that her godmothers had witnessed their affair, her heart split in half. She pictured the couple's faces shrouded in shadows, brushed lips, whispered messages. A part of Lilith that she never knew. A secret she hadn't been trusted to keep.

Or maybe Lilith was going to tell her, if Amelia had listened. There had been a night the queen approached her door and asked to talk, only to be met with silence as Amelia chose sleep over confrontation. If she hadn't run away, perhaps she could have changed things. Maybe then, Lilith wouldn't be imprisoned by the godmothers.

"We were supposed to run away together," Ezran said. "But she urged me to go, while she'd stay. I shouldn't have listened."

He shook his head, as if it didn't make sense why Lilith chose to stay behind. Meanwhile, Amelia could picture the queen walking alone, facing her own fate. That was what queens did. She chose to do things, then face the consequences of those things. Amelia couldn't decide on anything, nor did she have the strength to deal with the repercussions.

"Before I left, she made me promise to protect her treasure," he said. “That’s the only reason why I haven’t killed you. Show me where it is.”

Amelia furrowed her brows, straining for an answer in the murky depths of her mind. They had never talked about treasures before. Was this another secret Lilith didn’t tell her? “I don’t know what you mean.”

Ezran looked close to killing her, but redirected his anger to the tree beside him. She jumped as his fist cracked against the trunk, splinters wedged in his knuckles.

“You truly are useless,” he hissed. “If only you’d stayed where you came from.”

But that was what Amelia had tried to do. She never wanted to return to reality. Malicine forced her, even though her existence only made things worse for others. Lilith and Ezran had followed her and gotten caught. She had put Lilith in danger. If she was forced to be here, she couldn’t bear to live in a world without the person who’d brought light into it.

“We need to get Lilith out of the castle,” she urged. “I’m afraid of what my father may do to her—”

“You think I haven’t already planned that?” Ezran snapped. “She is mine, not yours.”

His words stung, laced with hatred but also truth. Since the history of time, there had always been a king and his queen, a prince and his princess, Ezran and his Lilith. Amelia merely stood at the fringe of stories, present by technicality of her blood, never truly residing in anyone’s heart.

Yet Lilith had done so much for her. Even if Amelia could never be part of the queen’s past, she could at least salvage something for the future.

“I’ll help her escape with you,” she said. “You can have a better life together, just like you wanted. I want that for her too."

Ezran brushed the splinters from his knuckles as he paced around, stewing in thought. A rough palm rubbed his face, as if it could wash away the tired lines and weariness. The clouds fully shrouded the moon in darkness when an idea struck him.

"When do you turn eighteen?"

IN THE OTHERWORLD, it had only felt like a day. In this world, Amelia had missed seasons of leaves changing, snow falling, babies crying, the elders dying. Nine months had escaped her like dandelion seeds from her fingertips with the change of the wind's direction.

Tonight, midnight would mark her eighteenth year.

Even as she appeared at the castle's doorsteps that morning, shivering and coated in mud, her godmothers moved quickly to fix her into someone appropriately part of this world. The faeries swarmed around her, both efficient and hysterical, hurrying her inside the castle. They washed her hair, changed her clothes, drew her baths, scrubbed her skin raw. They sanitized her as if they could cleanse any ugly darkness she'd been a part of, covering it instead with pretty bows and sweet perfume.

The godmothers fretted over Ezran, too, but there was an innate understanding that he was a prince who could take care of himself, while Amelia was fragile glass. They were right. Even though Amelia and Ezran agreed upon a fabricated story beforehand, he maintained a straight face as the prince who rescued Amelia from Malicine. Meanwhile, her nerves made it easy to believe she was too traumatized to recall specific details or speak more about the torture she went through.

I'm sorry, Malicine. The apologies repeated in her mind. Casting blame on the demon felt like a betrayal, as if Malicine had been right about her all along. But she glanced at Ezran's whitened knuckles every time the godmothers spoke ill about Lilith and knew that he, too, restrained himself for the greater good of their plan. The godmothers needed to believe Ezran hadn't reciprocated Lilith's attempts to seduce him and remained loyal to Amelia. Ezran needed to return to the castle and help Lilith escape without suspicion of collusion.

As Ezran predicted, the godmothers filled the gaps in their stories with what they wanted to believe. Lilith was a wicked woman who sought power and seduced men, just like the women she helped in the brothels, while Malicine was a demon who kidnapped innocent girls. Of course Amelia and Ezran had nothing to do with this. Handsome men and beautiful girls were always innocent. How unfair it was, Amelia thought, for something as arbitrary as looks to allow someone good faith.

In the dressing room, she drowned in silk and tulle, choked in corsets and ruffles. Her gown spun in changing colors as her godmothers argued over the perfect attire for her eighteenth birthday. Her insistence on having a celebration excited them into nonstop chatter, a background noise she realized people only made to distract from sadder topics.

Several hours later, they transformed the ballroom into a gallery of beautiful people and decadent food. Her birthday cake, painted with buttercream and handcrafted flowers, floated on a glass pedestal as the centerpiece of the crowded ballroom, its opulence matching Amelia's champagne-hued dress. Both existed to be observed, never cut open to see the messy insides.

While the castle attended her celebration and heavily guarded the event, Ezran used the distraction to slip into the dungeons, where he would help Lilith escape. Amelia simply needed to sit and look pretty, like any other useless thing. As she stared at the empty space where Ezran had vanished, an older nobleman talked to her.

"We were worried sick for you," the guest said, even though they'd never met. "Thank goodness you're safe."

She smiled at false platitudes and brushed the moonflower crown weaved around her hair. It was the only accessory she chose without her godmothers' input. The touch of its wrinkled petals, yet to bloom, reminded her why she needed to endure this. Lilith told her of real miracles, like kingdoms that could rebuild themselves from sand, and flowers that bloomed every hundred years.

Then a petal disintegrated between her fingers, and as Amelia stared at the crumbly bits in her palm, she remembered that if Ezran's plan had worked, she would never see Lilith again. The queen would never witness the flowers she gifted become alive after Amelia's birthday.

Amelia wasn't even supposed to live after her birthday.

The realization hit her like a stab in the gut now that her curse had been revoked. She had never pictured a future for herself beyond eighteen. Without the curse, her life expanded in decades. How could life be a miracle if it sounded so terrifying? The thought made her knees buckle, and the godmothers rushed to her side to catch her.

"What's wrong?" Clover cried.

Her breaths shortened as quickly as her mouth dried. She felt like she was choking, but it was her pounding heart, reaching up her throat, demanding to be spat out. Goose bumps rose against her skin like needles. They didn't stop forming, even though her godmothers' hands were so warm they burned against her shivers.

“I don’t want to do this,” she whispered.

“But this is your party,” Iris said, “and you’re having a wonderful time!”

Amelia shook her head but couldn’t get the words out. She couldn’t explain how it wasn’t the party she was talking about. She didn’t want to do this. She didn’t want to live.

Because this was what life was: Waking up and enduring. Sleeping and escaping. Waking up and enduring all over again. She was so tired of feeling this way whenever she was conscious, exhausted from pretending she could be happy. Perhaps for another girl, these parties would be enough to fill the emptiness. But nothing would be enough for Amelia. She’d always keep wishing for another world, another life, another way to fill the void.

The corners of the ballroom spun as the godmothers tried holding her up. They wanted to piece her back together, but she was born broken. It had never been the curse that created the cracks within her. That had been all her doing. More empty platitudes scraped her ears, and she wondered how it was possible that a room could be filled with so many people, while she felt utterly alone.

She had barely steadied herself by the time the doors opened. Murmurs died to a quiet hush. The sea of people parted ways as a familiar face emerged from the crowd. It should have comforted her, seeing her family again. Her father had returned to Gyldan from his trip. Yet, even standing in his own castle, he felt like a stranger.

“I’m glad you’re back, Amelia.” King Victor spoke as if they were the only two in the ballroom. The crowd fell silent in his presence. “We have a lot to catch up on.”

CHAPTER 35

WHILE THE REAL world burned, they dreamed.

Corin learned that this was what dreaming meant: Basking in the softness of grass without worrying about running when dusk came. Letting go of the heaviness of holding everything up. Never having to be resilient again.

She spent her days with Elly making snowballs in winter, picking flowers in spring, tasting new fruits in summer. An excess of activities she once deemed too frivolous to endure the passage of time, now given to her as a second chance. The sun saw them collect wildflower bouquets while meandering along streams, and the moon watched them huddle around crackling fire and wrap themselves in thick, soft blankets.

Corin brushed her fingers through Elly's hair, which had grown long and thick, curling past her shoulders and tied with daisy stems. The girl looked just like their mother. For so long, Corin had been afraid of their similarities, a paralyzing fear that fate would take Elly away the same way it did their mother. But they were surrounded by parsley-green fields instead of concrete and grime, sunflowers and bees instead of shadows and leering eyes.

She helped press flower petals into Elly's hair, watching the buds painted on her sister's nails bloom. For all the wasted moments they lost, Corin could make up for them now.

Yet a darkness loomed in the back of her mind, manifesting into an island she watched whenever she stared past the ocean. A lingering fear told her that, if Malicine didn't return, it would be Corin's fault. She had been the reason they chased her into Autumnland and lost their amulet, endangering everyone if intruders came into the world.

She wanted to enjoy this second chance, but couldn't forget the real person she left in peril.

"This doesn't feel right."

Her words came out as harsh as the clatter of teacup on porcelain. They had gathered on the porch with Briar, Penny, and Dime, sitting around a circular table set with pastries and teapots. The attempt at normalcy seemed ridiculous in front of Briar's collapsed cottage. Broken pieces of wood scattered the grass, while some of the stones had stacked together into a smaller house fit for animals. A lace parasol replaced the collapsed roof, trickling small rays of light for Dime to sunbathe in. Without Malicine's amulet, they couldn't restore parts of the dreamscape back to pristine condition.

Elly's brows pinched together. "You still aren't used to me here. Pretending I'm alive."

"No! That's not—" Corin stopped. It was true that Elly's presence didn't feel whole yet. Every time Corin wrapped her sister in her arms and felt a beating heart against hers, the gesture seemed incomplete. The sense of peace remained foreign, yet still, she wanted to become familiar with it.

"I need you here, El." Her hand wrapped around Elly's fingers and squeezed them, as if her sister were a mirage that could disappear if Corin didn't hold tightly enough. "But I keep wondering when Malicine will return. Sometimes it feels like they've been gone for weeks. Then it's as if they only left a few hours ago. Time warps itself here."

Corin's gaze stretched to the empty chair at the end of the table. Their absence carved a blank space between the others. All the questions without answers, the stories without endings, hovered in the chasm. Briar must have known this, because she stood from the table and walked toward the red poppies sprawled in the field. She held her breath, as if measuring her words next.

"I want to leave and find Malicine."

Her confession made the animals gasp around the table. "It's dangerous out there," Penny protested. "Wouldn't you rather stay here with us? We can pick chamomile flowers for the lemon cake. I promise Dime won't eat the flowers this time."

"I don't promise that," Dime said, earning a beady-eyed glare from his rabbit companion. Penny jumped to kick sugar cubes at the cat's face. The table dissolved into yowling and thrashing paws until Briar broke the playfighting and pulled Dime away by his arms. She laughed as she cradled the cat to her chest, her fingers combing gently through his fur.

"It's odd. My imaginations have been such a familiar comfort. But the best part about this world was being with people who didn't come from my imagination." She looked up to meet eyes with Corin. A breeze carried petals over to her chiffon gown and tugged at the ribbons in her hair until the lace unfurled. "And now, I'm afraid of losing what's real."

The lace drifted in Corin's direction. She snatched the ribbons and watched the string tangle into webs between her fingers. She thought of fleeting conversations, accidental meetings, the unexpected threads of people that traced throughout her life. She should have never met Briar Rose or Malicine. Somehow, in the hazy, watercolor edges that bled into their shared dreams, they found each other in crystal clarity.

"I don't want to wait anymore either." Corin's lips pressed together in a determined line. "Let's bring Malicine back."

PERHAPS IT WAS a reckless decision to go together, Corin thought. Malicine surely would have said so. She stood at the shores of Summerland, watching thunder rumble the island across the ocean like a slumbering beast. Veils of mist clung to the jagged cliffs and obscured any glimpse of the nightmares that lay beyond the desolate landscape. Beside her, she could feel the subtle trembles in Briar's body, watching the island that manifested everything the princess had been running away from. Corin would have mirrored Briar's tremors had she not kept her grip on Elly's shoulder, the only force who could keep herself still.

Her arms pulled Elly into an embrace. She pressed her lips against her sister's temple and murmured, "I'll come back."

"You promise?" Elly's voice was strained, as if she held back from crying.

Corin said yes, because she wanted it to be true. They needed to be together: Briar Rose, Malicine, Elly, the animals, and Corin. They would retrieve Malicine, and Malicine would open another portal for a new dream. They would keep running and hiding, as long as they could stay together.

A boat pulled ashore as Corin and Briar said goodbye to Elly.

They grabbed a pair of oars and started rowing. Corin kept her gaze fixed on her sister instead of looking back at the island. She told herself this wouldn't be the last time they'd see each other. As Elly's figure turned into a speck in the distance, Corin found a steady rhythm in the waves carrying them to the island, the back-and-forth motion of her oars dipping into the water. Though she wished they had Malicine's magic to transport to the island faster, she would savor this sense of calm before the inevitable storm at their destination.

Beside her, Briar had also adopted the steady motion of guiding the oars along the water. Corin watched the careful purse of her lips, the small knot on her forehead. The girl was frightened, yet she was willing to travel to the island anyway. As the princess leaned forward, Corin noticed the bow and quiver of arrows strapped to Briar's back.

A memory of their first meeting floated in her mind, when the girl was hidden in trees and covered in snow. Corin could picture it clearly, the bow in her hands, the bow of her lips. Briar had held a penetrating stare that burrowed under Corin's skin and lingered like a kiss. Corin had thought Briar would shoot her. She knew now that the girl had only been practicing for another intruder.

"If Ezran arrives," Corin murmured, "will he hurt you?"

A stinging pain from crescent shaped wounds bloomed in her palms. She'd stopped rowing and let her nails dig into her hands. At first, her hatred of Ezran stemmed from survival instincts. Now it had transformed into something deeper, knowing Ezran would hurt Briar.

And Corin cared about Briar Rose. More than she'd like to admit.

"I don't know," Briar said. "A foolish part of me hopes that, maybe, I could convince him to be on my side. Perhaps the real world wouldn't be so frightening if we worked together."

Corin's posture stiffened. She tried to ignore it as she leaned back and continued rowing, though she couldn't hide the bristle in her voice. "You realize that waking up would mean risking everything, don't you? I told you about the state of the world. Nothing worthwhile exists out there."

"You existed out there," Briar said. "You deserved to live a better life, and it was my fault you didn't. Every time I think about how much I care about you, I think about everyone else who exists on the other side too. Maybe what's scarier is not what's real, but never finding out what could be real."

Corin's mouth cracked open to release a wry laugh, but her throat was too dry, and the noise turned strangled. "Don't use me as an example that the world can be a better place. Everything I touch always breaks."

The boat cut through the endless expanse of ocean, where sliced water reflected fragmented faces that she ignored. It was easier to leave regrets in the past rather than conjure them in full flesh. Corin could bear the contortions of her half memories, like the ripples of water that drew Harlow's face. The whispers of trees that sounded like her mother's voice. The shadows lurking at the bottom of the ocean that made the vague silhouette of her father's body, drowned and waiting for her next. Small distortions in their environment that could easily be dismissed as nothing more than the sway of the boat or the ebb of the tide. Because if her gaze lingered over these reflections in the water for too long, she would see the truth: that she spent her entire life justifying her selfishness for survival and lost everyone because of it.

She didn't realize her knuckles had whitened until Briar

reached for her. The girl's fingers tightened around her own.

"I've seen the things you make," Briar murmured, "and your hands are gentler than you think."

Corin's ears grew hot as she recalled painting around the dreamworld. It had been a way to pass the time once she accepted living here, but she hadn't considered Briar's eyes watching her brushstrokes. Self-conscious, she looked down at her palms, the discolored patches of skin from old scars. Her hands had always been rough like sandpaper. But maybe she could make something soft and beautiful, like a world where even gentleness could survive.

Would it be foolish, she wondered, to dream of such a thing?

Night descended into a shifting sky of milky colors. Their boat passed Winterland, or perhaps the land shifted itself upon the memory of their first meeting. In the distance, glass deer glistened like crystals. Ice-coated fur reflected ribbons of pink and violet pulsing in the air. The aurora wrapped around the darkening sky above their heads, so that when Briar looked up, her eyes shone like magic. Corin would remember her like a painting, with every trace of sadness and joy that flickered in the lights across her face.

"Beautiful, isn't it?" Briar whispered, looking at the sky.

"Yes," Corin replied, looking at her.

They watched the aurora dance across stars and ripple through trees. Briar set aside her bow and stood up. Her arm stretched to the sky, fingers splaying to touch the lights. She reached too far, and her weight toppled over the boat.

Corin jumped to grab her. They fell over the ledge and plunged into water. In the crystal blue, their limbs moved in slow motion, their fingers still grasped between one another. Briar's gown swelled like a balloon, the fabric enveloping them both in silk.

Bubbles spewed from the girl's lips with silent laughter. Corin's skin tingled as she felt the brush of Briar's hands wrap around her body and lift them both to the surface.

They gasped for air, and this time, Corin could hear the chime in Briar's laughter. Her eyes lingered on the salt stuck to Briar's cheeks. She wanted to brush her thumb over it and leave her hand there. She would have, if Briar's touch hadn't made her jolt first.

Warm skin brushed against her collarbone, fingers hovering inches away from the chain around Corin's neck. Briar left her hand on Corin's pulse, too fixated on the necklace to notice the tiny drum beating against her.

"I won't touch it," Briar murmured. "I know it's important to you."

Instinctively, Corin placed a hand over her chest where the pendant hid beneath her shirt. She felt the weight of it in her palm where every heartbeat thrummed beside it. They climbed back into the boat and attempted to wring water from their clothes. She could still taste the salt on her lips. The air turned quiet, and she waited for her heart to still before deciding to open it.

"It belonged to my grandmother."

Aurora lights shifted gently in the sky like softly blowing curtains. Beyond it, an endless expanse of stars stretched beyond Corin's imagination. She thought about how there were miracles that existed in ways she would never comprehend.

"When she was younger, she tried to kill herself. A fortune teller stopped her just in time. She had no idea who this stranger was. The woman was elderly and didn't appear to have family either. She had insisted my grandmother needed to survive and see a better future ahead. I don't know if it was a fortune, or a plea. But she saved my grandmother's life that night and left behind this necklace."

Corin untucked the chain from her shirt and held the necklace to the sky. Under any other light, it looked incomplete, the pendant's shape a hollowed ring that didn't hold gold or any sparkling gem. Yet the aurora's light glimmered streaks of green and blue around the ring's edges, so that for a moment, Corin could almost believe she held magic.

Perhaps the fortune teller truly saw the future, or perhaps she made a lucky guess. Corin's grandmother had lived to have children and buy a farm in Gyldan. She had rescued stray animals, discovered favorite foods, witnessed dozens of sunsets. She'd given the necklace to her daughter, who dreamed of painting the same sunsets that had moved her mother to tears. That daughter met a man whose rough hands made beautiful things, clay pots to hold flowers, misshaped dishes to hold soap that smelled like honey and goat milk. She eventually passed the necklace to her first daughter, an angry girl who wanted to throw it away so many times because she thought the fortune teller was wrong.

So why couldn't Corin let it go?

"We can't survive without each other," Briar said, as if recalling a memory.

The familiarity of the words struck Corin. "Do you really think so?"

"That's what my stepmother said. She dedicated her life to housing people who were fleeing from war, even if it was dangerous to do so. There's so much cruelty in the world, perhaps the only thing that made sense to her was helping people in ways she wished she had been helped too."

Their boat passed by icy rocks that were chipped into familiar pieces, a flicker of Harlow's burning gaze. Corin shook her head to ward off the presence. "That's a noble cause, but it's not how reality works. We only survive by helping ourselves."

“Maybe you’re right.” There was a long pause. When Briar spoke again, her voice shook. “Lilith was the most selfless person I knew, and she died because of it. When I tried to help, my father died next.”

Tears spiked her lashes. She pressed a palm over her face and began to cry quietly. The stars blinked into dying lights. The aurora dimmed into silver before vanishing into wisps. Darkness descended on them like a blanket. Corin reached for Briar’s free hand. She focused on the gentle rocking of the boat beneath their bodies as proof that they were still here, and not disappearing as well.

“I keep wondering, does anything we do matter? Am I foolish to wish that it does? When I think about the people that Lilith brought to Gyldan, surely, their lives have changed. There are generations that exist, mothers and daughters, fathers and sons, who live and dream and experience wonderful things because someone once helped.”

Briar inhaled deeply, letting the tears subside. A quiet conviction overtook her voice.

“That’s why you keep your necklace, isn’t it? Without a stranger’s kindness, you wouldn’t have existed. And what a terrible world that would have been.”

Corin thought about what would happen if she were to wake up and return to Gyldan, existing once more in reality. Would the time she experienced here no longer matter? She hardly remembered her dreams after waking up. Memories often turned abstract and blurry, disintegrating into wisps. She fixed her sight onto the snowflakes that fell on Briar’s lashes. She counted each one so that if she forgot, she could still piece together the details of the girl before her. The slope of her ear, the freckles on her cheeks. The truth was that Corin didn’t plan on waking up at all. Not if it meant saying goodbye to Elly, or never seeing Malicine return, or losing her only connection to Briar Rose.

"The only way I can exist is by being here," Corin said. "If you wake up, I'll disappear. And for the first time in my life, you make me not want to."

Corin would rather believe in the existence of forever, where time could freeze in place for love to remain. If she were to wake up in the real world, she wouldn't survive it. She was sure Briar felt the same way, or their grief wouldn't have mixed together as one when they'd drowned in the ocean. They didn't want change. Corin wanted stability, Briar wanted escape. If they were together, they could cling onto that hope.

"Let's sleep forever," Corin said. "We'll never wake up, and we'll never say goodbye."

She knew she was being selfish. But in their dreams, it was okay to be, wasn't it?

Briar's shoulders lowered with relief, because they both knew it was easier to give in. Better to live in the calm after the storm than turn back and face it again.

A shrill croak erupted their reverie. Their heads snapped to the sky, where a row of stars parted for a flapping shadow. One wing drooped as if it were stuck in the wrong position, while the other wing fought to keep the rest of his body midair. Corin lunged forward and caught Talon before he could plunge in water. His feathers smelled like ash, and when she touched the drooping wing, he screeched in pain.

An item fell from his beak and onto the boat. Briar picked up the cloth, small and torn, barely the size of her palm. Corin held on to the raven, hoping he would stay with them, but his body already turned limp and cold. He had used the last of his remaining strength to carry the torn cloth.

Fear struck Corin at the same time Briar recognized where the fabric came from. The cloth was dark, but under the stars, they still recognized Malicine's blood.

They were close to reaching Autumnland when a deafening rumble shattered the island and rippled across the ocean. The waves beneath the boat shook violently, as if the sea itself convulsed in agony. Corin held on to Briar as they watched rocks tumble down cliffsides and light shoot through the fog. She imagined a fissure splitting the earth, but knew the sudden earthquake was not an isolated incident.

"We're too late," Briar whispered. "He's here. I can feel him."

She knelt over, hands wrapped around her skull as a pounding headache took over. Her body trembled, matching the aftershocks ripping through the ocean. Corin seized her by the shoulders.

"You need to go back and hide. Now."

"But—"

"He will kill you." Corin remembered the rage in Ezran's eyes, the trickle of blood from his blade at her throat. He was someone accustomed to violence, readily wielding it in his hands. "I'll find Malicine and bring the amulet so we can escape. Together. I can't—I don't want to live a life without you, Briar Rose."

Tears sprung from Briar's eyes as she nodded and grabbed her bow and arrows. Corin handed her the oars and stepped onto the ledge. Ocean waves churned below them like snapping piranhas. As Corin jumped, memories triggered her mind to long unanswered questions. What thoughts had raced in her father's mind during his own fatal plunge? Did regret course through him in that last breath before the water claimed him?

And had he realized, in that final split second, that he had wanted to live, after all?

CHAPTER 36

ALMOST 100 YEARS AGO

AMELIA PROMISED HER godmothers she and her father would return before midnight so they could celebrate her eighteenth birthday and watch the moonflowers bloom. In truth, she had no idea how long her father's excursion would take. She followed him through the forest, their shoes crackling dead leaves on damp earth. Autumn proved itself foggy at night. Even with three soldiers trailing after them, she could hardly decipher chain mail from gray clouds.

"How could you abandon Gyldan? Abandon *her*?" Amelia cried. She could not tolerate any small talk about her father's trip, even though the flat mouth of his expression indicated his search for an heir was unsuccessful. His journey had been interrupted by news of Lilith's affair, yet nothing could justify throwing her to the dungeons.

"I do not need insolence from my child for doing the very same thing," Victor replied. He took a sharp turn down a hidden path, barely discernible amidst undergrowth, where the trees looked like carved faces.

“What are you talking about?”

“Do you expect me to believe a demon abducted you for almost a year? Your godmothers may be easily fooled, but not me.” He shook his head. Weariness made the bags under his eyes sag further. “Where were you, Amelia?”

She swallowed the lump down her throat. “I will tell you if you release Lilith,” she lied. “I know the godmothers told you Lilith seduced the prince, but that’s their version of the story—”

“She’s already been released.”

Amelia pictured Ezran sneaking to the dungeons, only to be met with empty cells. “Where is she?”

Moonlight filtered through a thinning canopy and illuminated the narrow trail. Familiarity prickled her skin as she recognized the area. Her father had taken her down this same path years ago when he tried teaching her how to hunt. She recalled the faint scent of decay and damp earth, the tightening of her throat as she cried, the arrow that missed the deer she could never kill.

“Do you know why I wanted to bring you to the woods long ago?” he said. “It’s because I knew you’d learn more here than any of those idyllic days you spent with Lilith in the library.”

With a steady hand and focused gaze, he reached for the sling that carried his bow and arrows. The pointed weapon looked sharp enough to cut into cloth and pierce skin.

“I was pleased to find, during my visit to Zilar, that their king enjoyed hunting as well. A conqueror in nature as much as a conqueror in his kingdom. He took his son on trips and made Ezran keep a hunting journal. I was impressed, flipping through the pages, by how he recorded deer movement and behavior. He took great interest in tracking animals near Gyldan. So much so, that I started to wonder if they were truly animals at all.”

The air around Amelia thickened with something sharp and metallic, as if she'd bitten her lip and tasted the blood spilling down her throat. She couldn't breathe as they reached the end of a narrow path, where thick trees blocked the clearing. No one from afar would have spotted two bodies hanging from their stakes.

"I knew I needed to return home and find my answer," Victor said, gaze fixed on the man bound by rope. "Who is the hunter, and who will be the hunted?"

Fresh bruises marred Ezran's cheeks, evidence of his failed venture into the dungeons that led to his altercation. While he made noise through the rag stuffed in his mouth, far from his reach was a limp body that no longer moved. Amelia gasped, vision swimming with tears before her mind could process the sight. Lilith's eyes were shut, her limbs tied by rope around the stake. Her skin, once golden, was as white as the pearls scattered near her feet. Splotches of red dried in the dead patch of grass where she hung. Ezran had only recently been caught, while it had been hours since they tied Lilith there.

Amelia lunged forward, but the rough arm of a soldier restrained her. A scream tore from her throat, so primal she couldn't recognize the wail was her own. She clawed at chain mail as if she'd gone mad.

"They are traitors," her father said. "Our blood and gold are so valued that we cannot trust those beyond borders and at home. I brought you here to understand the consequences of deception. It's why we hunt: to show who has power and who is merely prey."

Ezran continued thrashing against the rope, his yells muffled behind the rag stuffed in his mouth. The bruises on his face welled up, shiny and purple. No matter how severe his injuries were, he didn't tire of resisting. A soldier removed the cloth from Lilith's mouth, then Ezran's. Lilith remained still while Ezran spat blood in front of their feet.

"I had higher expectations for you to at least commit to a public execution. But I suppose that would start a war with my father, and Gyldan's not as powerful of a kingdom as you'd like to portray," he snarled, teeth gleaming red. "The only people who know of tonight are three of your most trusted soldiers, while you let the rest of the kingdom fill in the stories for themselves. So who shall take the blame in this story? A wicked queen, deemed at fault by status of being a common woman, while their king hides in cowardice?"

The muscles in Victor's jaw tightened, yet he paid Ezran no response. Instead, he drew his bowstring taut. Ezran continued fighting his restraints, pushing his chest forward to put pressure on the bindings. Welts formed over his limbs from the friction of skin against rope. But brute strength wasn't enough. Victor's arrow already pointed directly at Ezran's head.

It happened in a single breath. The exhale from Victor's lips, the release of his fingers from the bow. Amelia leapt forward and shoved her father with her full body weight. The arrow took flight, direction askew, and hit Ezran's arm. Rope splintered as his limbs pulled forward to break free. He tore the arrow from his flesh and stabbed the guard beside him in the eyes. The soldier reared backward, screaming in pain, as Ezran took his sword and thrust the blade into the soldier's abdomen.

Amelia was on top of her father, his back flat on the ground. Her fists pounded against his chest. "I won't let you kill them," she cried. "Lilith wanted nothing but a better future for us. For Gyldan—"

Victor seized her by the wrists. "Do not defy me, Amelia. She betrayed Gyldan."

Her tears blurred the sharpness of his face. He looked nothing more than a shadow to her, a vague entity, a monster.

"No. She betrayed you. But you do not represent Gyldan."

She ripped herself away from his grip. Her heartbeats pounded like thunder. They ricochet across her veins. She burned hot, like she was on fire. It wasn't panic that had overtaken her body. It was rage.

"Our bloodline is not why Gyldan prospers. It's the hard work of people like Lilith who wanted to make it a better place. You never worked for anyone but yourself. There will be no heir to the throne, Father, because that ends with—!"

The force of Victor's hands shoving her cut the air from her lungs. She landed on the ground before a sword sliced her vision, blade sinking into flesh. Her father's agonized cry pierced the air. Blood spread from his chest and soaked his shirt. Ezran drew his sword back, leaving a gaping wound where the king's heart stopped beating.

Ezran retreated to unbind Lilith from the stake, while Amelia remained frozen, staring at the bleeding body before her. Her father had pushed her away from death, only to meet it himself.

There was something petrifying about seeing someone in death. She noticed details she hadn't before. The grays of his hair, how he hadn't trimmed his beard for so long that they overtook his face. The sagging skin beneath his eyes. The dimming blues of his irises, ready to erode. He was no longer a king. Only a father who protected his daughter.

She placed shaking hands over his wound, as if her palms could stop the soul from leaving his body. Blood soaked into the fabric of her dress and watered the soil beneath them, thick and foul with the smell of iron. She listened to his fading breaths before his eyes turned to glass. Once he was still, she scanned their surroundings and took in three more bodies splayed on the ground. The two guards that had accompanied them were dead. The third one had an arrow stuck to his eye and a deep slash in his abdomen. She vaguely recalled the sounds of fighting in the background, but the world had tilted its axis the moment she'd tackled her father and let rage blind her. Now it was grief that turned her vision blurry, tears that clogged her throat and kept her from sobbing.

Ezran was on his knees with Lilith in a chokehold of an embrace. Pieces of rope scattered around them, limp as her pale arms draped on the ground. Blood had long left her body from hours spent hanging at the stake. Ezran continued shaking her anyway, screaming her name until his voice turned hoarse and broken.

The sound rang hollow in Amelia's ears like she was an empty shell. She could not believe the woman in front of them was dead. Lilith looked too cold, like the family portrait hung on the castle walls. Not the queen made of sunlight, whose skin smelled like old books and hands were always smeared with ink. Not her Lilith.

But it was Ezran who held her, not Amelia. It was Ezran who pressed a kiss to her lips, and when he pulled away, left her face damp with his tears. He rolled his head back and released a guttural scream to the sky. The sound was like thunder, raising bumps in Amelia's flesh in its reverberating anguish. Grief mutated into rage, all-consuming, as he slowly turned to her. His eyes changed first, pupils dilating. A transformation from prince to madman.

Her blood ran cold as his grip twisted around the hilt of his sword. She scrambled to her feet before he lunged for her.

Perhaps it was her distance from him already, or perhaps it was quick thinking that helped her escape into the shadows of the woods. Amelia knew neither was true. She had only done what she knew best: running away.

CHAPTER 37

A FALLING STAR LANDED on the coast of Autumnland when Corin arrived. Her limbs had grown weak and tired from swimming, her lungs taking in desperate gasps of air as she crawled over the shore. The earthquake had spewed plumes of dust and debris into the air. She coughed violently, forcing her body forward. The woods swallowed her whole as she trudged through the path of trees and shouted for Malicine.

Her voice echoed through hollow trees and winding roads. Whispers of imagined voices scraped the leaves, urging for distraction, a lure to an offbeat path. Her skin prickled from the bitter cold, a familiar sensation. She remembered what she had seen the last time she was here: bloodstained pearl earrings, a dead king with antlers, trails of ants that crawled over Elly's sunken face. A voice that said Briar, or Amelia, or maybe even Corin herself, would never be forgiven.

Surrounding trees morphed into screaming faces. The arrangement of bark twisted into familiar features belonging to Harlow, Maggie, Rowan, everyone she had lost. Cold breezes dissolved to whispers like their voices, pleading for her to look at them, remember the taste of death and regret. She shook her head, trying to ward off the memories. This wasn't real, she kept telling herself. The island used her subconscious for tricks, reflecting the darkest of thoughts the deeper she crossed. As long as she remembered light existed too, she could escape the island with Malicine, both their minds intact.

She cupped her hands over her mouth and continued shouting the demon's name until it strained her throat. The darkness was so vast that she couldn't tell where they were or if they even heard her. Dead trees remained still, as if nothing changed. The wind howled mockingly, drowning her voice.

She took another step before the ground rumbled once again. Branches rattled like bones before the sound of splitting wood tore the sky. Violent tremors pushed rocks off a mountainside. She dodged the boulders, but mud gripped her ankles and pulled her down the landslide. The sudden descent was too familiar. It terrified her as the ground swallowed her whole.

Debris and snapped branches collapsed on her body, pinning her down the bottom of a hole. Mud slicked her clothes as cold air breathed into reopened wounds. There came the pain again, one she knew too well. It bloomed in the pit of her stomach and rolled waves of nausea across her skin.

Malicine was right when they said she couldn't truly escape her nightmares. The harder she tried not to think of something, the more she did.

Even if she closed her eyes, she knew who would speak next.

"You should have been there for me."

She turned to the body draped over the landslide. A white film had washed over Elly's eyes like clouds. Corin's silhouette looked too big, too monstrous in the reflection.

"You're not real." She repeated the words like a mantra and clamped her hands over her ears, but there was no point. Her sister's voice rang clear between muddy walls.

"It doesn't matter whether or not I'm real," Elly said. "In the end, I'm still dead. Don't you understand?"

Elly didn't blink. Ants crawled between the gaps in her teeth as her cracked lips parted. Collarbones protruded from her dirty shirt like a jagged tooth. Tears burned Corin's eyes. Her hands fell to her sides, no longer blocking the truth. She could pretend to believe in two versions of her sister: the one covered in wildflowers, waiting for her safe return, or the one covered in dirt, cursing her for her abandonment. But as long as both versions continued breathing, neither was truly real.

"I'm sorry, El," she pleaded. "I'll never forgive my—"

"Being sorry doesn't change what happened."

The words settled into Corin's skin. A hard lump in her throat burned as if it had caught on fire. Her feet sank into the soil, the roots twisting around her limbs and pulling deeper. It was happening again. She was supposed to make it through the island. She thought she was stronger than this. But maybe that had been a lie too, one of the hundreds she had told herself.

Why had she come here in the first place? Her willpower dulled, as if she were observing herself in a dream. No, she needed to remember. She came here for someone, and she needed to return into the arms of another someone too. Yet she couldn't forget the little girl she came for in the first place, long ago in the tunnels.

Maybe it didn't matter, the difference between real or fake, living or dead. There would always be a girl etched permanently in Corin's mind, one that her sad little heart could never erase. The complicated feelings she had for that girl were real. They had made her wretched life worth living too.

She willed herself not to turn away. Instead, she strained in the howling wind to remember this girl. If she listened closely enough, the wind would remind her of a wailing baby that once squirmed in her arms. The wet dirt would feel like sticky palms she'd held on to whenever they crossed the street. The feeling of wanting to curl in bed would be accompanied by a familiar body next to hers, breathing down her chest, arms wrapped around her stomach like an anchor that brought her home.

She let that familiarity guide her, even though she knew the words she would hear next.

"I hate you," Elly said.

Corin opened her eyes and faced the mirage of her sister. "No, you don't."

Elly blinked slowly. The clouds in her eyes flickered, as if uncertain of whether a storm would arrive. Corin pulled her legs out of the sinking soil and trudged over to her sister. Muddy walls framed Elly's body like a painting. The girl only existed because Corin had twisted her memories this way, letting grief and shame sculpt the creature before her. Maybe, if she remembered other truths, she could look at this scene again in a different light.

"I know you don't hate me, because when you were five, you held my hand every time we crossed the street and wouldn't let go. When you were seven, you collected rocks so I could paint again, thinking they were the same thing as charcoal. When you were nine, you got in trouble for stealing a peach from the marketplace because you were worried I'd go hungry. And when I yelled at you in front of the shopkeeper, you saw I pocketed the rest of the peaches behind his back, and we laughed while eating them on our way home."

Corin's hand stretched to Elly's cropped hair, fingers threading through rough spikes with all the gentleness she could hold.

"The truth is you always loved me, El," she whispered, "and that's better than anything I could have ever dreamed."

Clouds dispersed from Elly's eyes, leaving behind a pool of black that reflected Corin's own face. She saw the projection of what she told herself through her sister, the nightmares that tormented her conscience with reminders of their past. But accepting the pain of losing Elly meant accepting that they had loved each other too.

Corin couldn't punish herself anymore. Not when they needed a better future.

"Come with me," she said. "We can't be together in the real world, but I promise we will be in this one."

Ants dispersed from Elly's face, the white clouds in her eyes parting in new clarity. Color restored to her skin, deep brown like fresh summer soil. Light gleamed in the dark pools of her irises as she grasped Corin's hand. Their fingers interlocked in a tight squeeze, and Corin vowed to never let her go, even if her sister was only a memory.

A deep rumbling echoed over their heads, followed by screeches of a familiar voice. Panic struck her chest. She climbed over the landslide and helped Elly up. When they reached the top, the smell of burning wood struck her nose. Wildfires had spread throughout the forest. Trees burned to crisps and splintered like spiderwebs. Above, the skies glowed red. The air no longer had its frigid chill, but a suffocating heat that pressed onto the island.

A wide trunk split in half and crashed, sending another wave of heat. Corin motioned for Elly to follow her. They crawled over jagged roots as thick smoke muffled their violent coughs. She found cracks where the ground split open, the source of the earthquake that had nearly dragged her into oblivion. As they followed the fissure that trailed the earth like open veins, the path led to a wider mouth in the center of the forest, a hole that spewed light and magic.

Dread curdled inside the pit of her stomach as she recognized the smell of blood. Surely the island was playing tricks on her. The earthquake and fires weren't signs of intruders disrupting their dreams, but manifestations of her fears. The prince was not actually here, but a vision she conjured up again, an exhibition of her most selfish desires.

If so, she could not explain the three bodies littered on the ground. The faeries were face down, limbs bent, dresses swallowed up by flames. Elly ran to their side, attempting to put out the fires. She rolled over their bodies to face up and jumped back upon the sight of glass eyes and bloodied chests.

Their stab wounds were the size of her fist. The blood gleamed fresh, the faeries killed immediately upon arrival, as if someone had no use for them anymore once they arrived.

The sisters fell back as the earth shook again. A monstrous scream split the sky, one that chilled Corin's bones. Only one person could make that sound. Elly pointed above the line of trees, where she'd spotted the flicker of a tail and heard the echo of a dragon's screech.

Corin grabbed Elly's hand as they ran inside the sooty heart of the island. Burnt branches scraped their arms as they bounded through crackling woods. She refused to tear her eyes away from the sky, hoping she would catch a flicker of scales again, some confirmation that they hadn't lost Malicine. The farther they ran, the farther the demon crossed off the path, stomping toward a rocky cliffside at the edge of the forest.

They yelled Malicine's name. The demon didn't hear it. The dragon had fixed their vision onto a stone figure at the base of the cliff. Scales shone in the flames, yet below, something burned brighter. A gleaming sword, an angry man. A walking nightmare.

Ezran hadn't changed since the last time Corin saw him. White-blond hair glinted in the fire, as if he were a blinding ball of light, too bright to stare at closely. His ivory armor stayed impeccably clean despite the rainfall of ash, which dissolved upon touching his glowing sword. Weaponry aside, it was his features that intensified his wrath: the tight lock of his jaw, the narrowed slivers of his eyes. He possessed an anger that had been broiling for centuries.

With each step he took, ground crumbled beneath him. White fragments scattered in the trail of his shoes, bursting in flames and ruin. Everything he touched fell apart, as if the world couldn't piece itself together under his ire. A swing of his sword and an entire row of trees sliced open, roots split as if struck by lightning. Heat sizzled the air as Malicine breathed a tidal wave of fire in retaliation. It wasn't enough. He needed only a simple flick of the wrist to tilt his sword and send the flames ricocheting back.

Corin could barely comprehend magic, yet even she knew from the sheen of his blade that the faeries had enchanted his weapon. As he lifted his sword, the blade absorbed the flames and glowed a deadly light. Her eyes burned so bright she didn't realize he'd lunged forward until the sword sliced the dragon's throat.

She knew then that Ezran was real, for Malicine's cry was worse than anything she could have imagined.

The demon plunged down the cliff. She let out a scream and raced to the bottom, trying not to spew her heart out of her chest. The base of the cliff had hollowed out into a jagged cave, where old rainwater filled the space and soaked her pants as she waded through. By the time Elly caught up to her, she found Malicine reverted to their regular form. The demon's body had strewn across rocks, their wings covered in pine needles and dirt. Corin collapsed at their side and didn't stop shaking them until they rolled over and retched into the water.

"You need to run," they groaned.

"No," she argued. "I came here for you!"

They grabbed her hand and squeezed it so tight she thought they would break her bones. When they pulled away, the broken shard of an amulet glowed in her palm.

"Take this to Briar and open a new portal. Run to a place where he will never find you."

"Not without you," she insisted.

Malicine's eyebrow arched, making her overly conscious of the gaping wound in their throat. Desperation overtook logic. Survival required believing they could remain whole, together.

Light glowed from their palm, and she felt the tug of the chain around her neck. The amulet fused inside the hollowed pendant that she carried close to her chest, becoming one. They tucked the necklace back under her shirt, and she felt a heavier weight on her body, as if she held the pain of every past self that had been sacrificed for the amulet. She didn't know if she could carry such responsibility, not when she could barely reconcile her own past.

"The world is falling apart," they rasped. "If you stay here, you will never make it out, and this will all be for nothing. Get out of here. I'll hold him off."

She stared at the dribble of blood down their chin, the fading green of their eyes. Leaving Malicine behind wasn't fair. She had seen the torture they endured in Autumnland, the words and violence hurled at them throughout their life. They had no reason to help anyone but themselves.

"You don't have to be good," she said, fighting back tears.

The ends of Malicine's lips twitched. Long nails scraped her cheek as they cupped her face.

"I was wrong, Corin. I shouldn't have left your world behind," they said. "Some of you are worth the sacrifice after all."

With the last burst of their magic, Malicine pushed a gust of wind that sent Corin and Elly flying off their feet. Their bodies barreled backward into the forest, where the trees sensed their presence and swayed their trunks to clear a path. Corin coughed black flakes of smoke. The fumes cleared when she got up and her line of sight revealed Ezran.

He was too far away to notice her, fixated on the wounded demon at the bottom of the cliff. The man stood in front of the caverns, a gaping hole that looked smaller beside his towering figure. Darkness radiated from his body, as if his presence sucked in all the shadows and left behind a void. With each step he took, fragments of the ground disappeared, the dreamworld they had carefully constructed dissolving like sand. He was stronger than Autumnland, a hero and nightmare in one.

His command was hard as stone. "Let's finish what we started, demon."

"Go to hell." Malicine spat blood at his feet.

Ezran let out a cruel laugh that made the hair on the back of Corin's neck stand stiff. It was the sound one made after waiting over a hundred years for this victory.

"That's reserved for monsters like you," he said, before plunging his sword through Malicine's chest.

Corin clamped a hand over Elly's mouth, dampening her sister's scream so they would not be caught. She bit her tongue so hard it bled as they watched Malicine slump forward. It took all her willpower to hold back from lunging at Ezran and sobbing over Malicine's body. She couldn't. Not if she wanted to throw away everything the demon had sacrificed for her and Briar. Her other hand let go of the amulet before she could shatter it in her tightly wounded fist, letting the gem dangle from her necklace and safely under her shirt.

As they ran, she could only think about how the fairy tales were wrong. There were no heroes to save them. They were only stories written by invaders—not the ones from faraway lands who sought refuge, but the very men who lived beside them and tore down their homes, claiming heroism in their own violence.

CHAPTER 38

100 YEARS AGO

THE NIGHT WAS pitch black as Amelia tore through darkness. She could hardly breathe through ragged sobs, the lump in her throat a burning coal. The sweeping curve of trees was her only semblance of a trail, though she knew Ezran would catch up to her if she stopped. She let the forest eat her whole, hoping the woods would swallow her into darkness and leave no trace of her behind. Thunder boomed from skies as if the clouds lamented with her. The blur of tears delayed her realization that rain had started pouring.

She could hardly feel the pinpricks of ice while running until she collided against a tree. Her body hunched over a gnarled root and vomited in dirt. Rainwater swirled the bile, sticky and rancid. Beneath her enchanted beauty and golden blood, perhaps this ugly mess was truly what she was made of. She no longer wanted to pretend.

She just wanted to disappear.

Bile burned her throat as she turned over her stomach with a low moan. Twigs dug into her skin, scraping to pry flesh open. Rain pounded against her deflated dress, where mud streaked the torn fabric, now a dirty champagne. She could not will herself to move. Her bones weighed too heavy, her heart too fractured. She hoped the rain would pour hard enough to drown her.

There was no way to tell time in the fog of her mind. By the time Malicine found her, she was already half asleep. She woke to the demon shaking her by the shoulders.

"Amelia," they yelled over the rain, "what are you doing here?"

It was strange how seeing a familiar pair of horns and red-eyed raven brought a small sense of comfort. As they examined her injuries, she realized they must have sensed she was nearby and come for her. She thought she'd been running aimlessly, but this was no coincidence. Subconsciously, she had searched for the only creature who'd seen the darkness inside her, because they shared it as well.

She whispered, "I don't want to be here."

"Of course not," they snapped. "You'd barely survive these woods."

She shook her head. Exhaustion ate away her bones. She would have collapsed farther into the ground if she could, sinking so deep her blood would water the roots of trees. "No. I don't want to be *here*."

Understanding slowly dawned on Malicine's face. Before they could reply, a rustle of leaves snapped their attention to the trees. In the distance, the sound of hooves hitting the ground echoed, the neigh of a frantic horse. A torch's flame burned past the thicket, the fiery eyes of a prince with a bloodthirst for vengeance.

Amelia didn't mention Ezran was after her, yet somehow Malicine knew to hide them both. They draped their cape over her like a shield made of darkness. She shrunk into the fabric and watched a sky full of foliage envelop them. The floor shifted from wet mud to bark, as if she were inside a tree. A wall of vines covered her vision as Malicine waved their arm to cast light inside. The dimensions of their cocoon expanded with an orange glow, and she landed on a carpet of moss.

Amelia scanned their new surroundings, where each corner felt less like a dangerous forest and more like a makeshift home. Fire blazed from a hearth made of stone. A driftwood mirror slanted itself to a wall. Across from it was a spinning wheel.

"Where are we?" she asked, watching Talon nestle inside a bed of twigs below the lamp.

"A witch's cottage. I set up this place the night I cursed you. You were to be lured here the eve you turned eighteen, pricking your finger on a spindle I'd sharpened just for you."

Moss had grown over the bobbin like green thread, yet the spindle glinted with a sharp smile as it pointed in Amelia's direction.

"The place has no use anymore since I revoked the curse. But it keeps us hidden, so at least my petty grudge provided some benefit. You left this behind, by the way."

They pointed to *The Book of Samael* nestled between the vines. The relic hardly mattered to Amelia after their failed venture into the Otherworld. Instead, the spinning wheel beckoned for her attention, even though no curse should have compelled her otherwise. She'd never seen the actual contraption before. Her father had banished it across the kingdom. Watching it now, she could understand how the sight was alluring. There was a repetitive motion in the wood spinning, the blurriness of the wheel, the needle dangling.

She didn't notice she was freezing until the warmth of Malicine's staff brought her gaze to the amulet. A scarlet fog spun inside the gem, bright as she'd remembered it from the Otherworld. Malicine appeared familiar with their newfound powers already, pointing the staff at the bark floor and raising a flattened trunk from the ground. They hauled Amelia over the makeshift stool while their staff sputtered magic sparks onto the floor, wiping clean the mud she'd left behind.

She didn't realize how dirty she'd become. Her dress was drenched from the rain, her skin tinged with ice. Malicine's fingers carefully unbuttoned the back of her dress and peeled off the fabric. Lacy undergarments covered her pale skin, and with the cloth stripped away, goose bumps ran prominently down her limbs. Malicine held their breath the entire time they undressed her, as if they thought the smallest gust of air would topple her over. They squeezed rainwater from the fabric, watering the plants buried beneath. Once the clothing dried, they helped Amelia dress herself again.

"What happened?" The demon's voice remained calm like stone. Fire crackled from the hearth, slowly bringing warmth back to her bones. Yet no matter which way she looked, Amelia still saw pale skin tinted blue, the color of a woman's veins left after snake poison.

"Lilith's dead," she whispered. "And so is my father."

Silence filled the air, only disrupted by the muffled sound of rain against the walls.

"What does this mean for you?" Malicine asked.

Blankly, she answered, "I don't know."

"Where are your godmothers?" Rage seeped into Malicine's tone. "They should be helping you."

"I didn't come with them. There's no one I can trust. Except . . ."

She turned silent, feeling foolish for running away and seeking Malicine instead. Of course they could not be her godparent, let alone her friend. When they sent her back to this world, they made it clear they wanted nothing to do with her. And yet, the demon squeezed her arm gently, an anchor to remind her of their presence. It was a gesture so rare and kind that it made Amelia want to cry again.

"I'll make something warm to drink," they muttered, "and we'll figure it out."

They crossed over to the hearth, where fire flickered from the wooden logs. Amelia watched their finger make swirling motions over a cup, guiding black tea leaves across ripples of water. The offer should have comforted her rather than left her skin itching. She didn't need to deliberate her next steps. She already knew what she needed to do. Take over the throne. Rebuild the royal line. Save the kingdom, like Lilith would have wanted.

But Amelia couldn't. To be strong meant enduring the shame of her mistakes, the consequences of her flaws. And she did not want to be strong.

Thunder boomed loud enough outside to shake the foliage. The wooden clock hanging above the hearth rang. Both dials pointed to the top, signaling midnight. Light glowed from her head like a halo. For a moment, she thought a magical part of the curse remained, ready to take her life at eighteen. But sweet fragrance wafted from her hair, and she remembered the moonflowers entwined between her locks. They looked like orbs of light in the mirror, their petals unfurling into full moons. This wasn't a crown, yet it reminded her of royalty somehow. She stared longer into the mirror until she pieced together the answer.

The moonflowers looked like pearls.

Lilith had said they would bloom when Amelia turned eighteen. The flowers would die in a few minutes, while she would keep living, like a cruel miracle.

No, this couldn't be her fate. She didn't want to endure the daily wars in her mind or heal the darkness in her heart. Life was not worth fighting those battles. All the sadness she swallowed threatened to burble up to her chest and spew out. She could hardly breathe as her body gravitated toward the spinning wheel. The corners of her vision darkened, the sharp tip of the spindle the only point of clarity.

"Amelia." Malicine's voice rang like a warning. "I told you I revoked the curse."

The demon's words were like rain, a background noise that muffled her ears. She picked up the spindle and traced her finger over the tip. A trickle of blood slipped down her hand. How easy it was for her thin skin to be sliced open with just a prick.

She turned to her companion, whose face twisted into newfound fear, as if reading her mind.

"I'm sorry, Malicine."

The demon lunged to stop her, but it was too late. She locked her grip onto the spindle with both hands and thrust the sharp end into herself. Pain bloomed from her chest as her vision turned blurry. Malicine's scream sounded like a distant echo, their arms a faraway embrace. She didn't know she had collapsed to the floor until blood stained the moss. There was a soft *thump, thump, thump* of her heart slowing down, like a hummingbird laid to rest, its wings too tired to fly.

Shrill cries muffled behind walls of vegetation, voices she might have recognized if she had the energy to focus. Sparks of light slashed the vines open. Rain descended from the sky once more, their cocoon disappearing and giving way to clearer noises. There was the whinny of a horse, overlapping voices, and shouting, so much shouting. Amelia could not make sense of the cacophony with her ears pressed against soft, blood-soaked moss. She heard Malicine yelling for their raven, the tear of fabric, their flesh splitting apart. A silhouette of a winged creature transformed before her. A monstrous roar shook the trees. The earth erupted into flames. They warmed her bones and covered her like a blanket.

Her pain started to fade. It hurt to breathe, but Amelia wouldn't need to do that anymore. She could feel her potential slipping from her lips, and with a final breath, she closed her eyes forever.

CHAPTER 39

CORIN RAN OFF the island with gritted teeth and a shattered heart. Shadows surrounding the woods stretched tall, rows of swaying silhouettes that reenacted the fairy tale once more: the knight in shining armor, the dragon slain by his strength. A sword raised in the air, a blade plunged through the monster's heart. She pressed her palms to her ears, but she couldn't forget the sound of Malicine's screech as Ezran killed them.

The ocean rolled waves of mist by the time she stumbled to shore alongside her sister. The rowboat looked like a speck in the fog, something Briar Rose must have sent back once she retreated to safety. Corin hauled Elly inside before jumping in the seat, then stopped when she spotted a shadow among the trees.

She wanted to believe the tears she'd been fighting back simply blurred her vision. Yet as the figure approached closer, she couldn't deny the rising panic in her throat from seeing Ezran's ivory armor. Her heart lurched just as her body did over the boat, hooking Elly's neck with her arm to dive forward. Water filled their lungs as she pressed their backs against the bottom of the wooden craft and resisted the urge to choke or risk giving themselves away.

His shadow stretched over the water as he stopped at the shore. The larger his figure grew, the smaller they shrank in hiding. She couldn't tell if the trembling of her skin was Elly's or her own.

While Ezran towered above, pressure built in Corin's chest. Her body screamed for air. She focused so intensely on not passing out that she nearly let out a gasp when a pinprick of something cold hit her cheek. Elly picked the tiny orb from Corin's face and held between her fingers a glistening pearl.

Corin watched in a confused daze as more emerged from the black abyss of the ocean floor. They floated like bubbles, a shining tidal wave of gemstones that reached the surface. Ezran's shadow shifted in the ocean's reflection. His fingers plunged through the water to grasp the pearls.

She watched his shadow go still. A memory she couldn't decipher swirled like air bubbles. Something dark and mournful pressed onto her chest, as if she were truly drowning underwater. But the pain wasn't hers. Neither was the guttural howl that came next.

The sound split the ocean in multiple pieces. Waves ripped her body from the boat, wooden splinters flying in different directions alongside her. Her hands lost grip of Elly's, their fingers ripped apart from one another. Salt poured down Corin's throat as water drowned her yells. They expelled to make room for sand filling her mouth next, and she found herself strewn over a narrow strip of land, where water drained away and left behind barren patches of mineral and earth.

Corin knelt over sand and clutched her burning throat, gasping for air. Without water, the land turned blank, a bright nothingness that set fire to her eyes. She blinked hard, readjusting her vision to find Elly a few feet away from her. Her sister crawled out from beneath the overturned boat, and when she pulled her pant leg up, a large splinter had stabbed through the meaty flesh of her calf. Elly ripped the wood from her leg and let out a cry.

"I can't run," she winced. "It hurts too much."

"Then hold on to me," Corin demanded, already snaking her arms beneath Elly's armpits to hoist her up. She carried her sister on her back, but barely kept balance as the earth beneath them shook. A dark gloom stampeded over the dried well where the ocean once was. They looked up to see what the prince had become. Shadows wrapped around his limbs, turning his figure amorphous. His form was massive enough to puncture the sky, and he absorbed every cloud he touched until they became part of him, rain and lightning swirling inside a chasm of darkness and grief.

With each step he left behind, cracks splintered the ground and opened to swallow what was left into an empty, endless gulf. Corin heard distant animal cries behind her, and as she looked back at Autumnland, the island slowly sank into a white void.

The dreams were collapsing. Creatures that once terrorized her screamed as they tumbled into the void and disappeared forever. Trees that previously shrouded the island and scratched her limbs were sucked into the chasm, leaving no trace behind. The nothingness spread like disease beyond the shores so that even the sand surrounding them crumbled to dust. Corin backed away from the void, realizing it would reach her too. Her hold on Elly tightened as she turned the other way and ran. For the first time in their fragile lives, she didn't want to disappear.

THEY COULD NO longer find Ezran by the time they reached Summerland, and it both relieved and terrified Corin. Her chest wanted to collapse over her entire body from how heavily she panted in exhaustion, but her hand grasped the amulet tucked safely underneath her shirt, a reminder that she needed to find Briar Rose before Ezran would. Yet every time she touched the gem, it became less of a resolution and more of a worry. She could not tell if Malicine's magic contained in this tiny rock would be enough to save them all. It wasn't even enough to heal Elly's wounds.

When they reached the emptied shore, the gash in her sister's leg had widened farther. Her skin had split open not to reveal flesh and bone, but a white mass of space, just like the disappearing land that surrounded them.

No, Elly couldn't disappear. Corin wouldn't allow it.

"You're going to be okay, El," she said, still carrying her sister on her back. Despite her attempt to stay calm, her voice rose in panic as sand dissolved behind her steps. She hauled them both through jungle foliage and tangled vines, sights that should have been familiar, except the picture was now askew. Apricots had fallen from trees and split open to reveal swarms of ants and rot. Tropical flowers had shriveled into wilted petals and sagging leaves. She felt the first chill of Summerland as the sun above the canopy blinked like a dying light, and she knew then she would no longer feel warmth from this land.

In the corner of her bleary vision, apricot juice stained the vegetation like orange paint. She stared at the misshaped circle bleeding into the roots and heard her mother's voice grow fainter in her memory. *Look, Corin. You just made the sun.*

But the sun was dying. Clouds had already choked out the star, leaving them shivering in the cold.

"I'm slowing you down," Elly said. "There's no point in carrying me. We both know I'm not—"

"Just shut up and hold on to me, El!" Corin's voice cracked in desperation.

She soon learned how ill-equipped she was to travel with the added weight on her back and her exhausted condition. Sweat dripped down the side of her temple, and her panting turned to strained breaths. Birds flew over their heads and scattered to dust the moment their wings reached the void. If she could outpace the nothingness, surely she would reach something else. But things were no longer making sense. Rain poured from the ground upward to the sky, and wildflowers sprouted in the air without any roots. Branches grew out of fruit, and when her boots stepped on them, they snapped into crystal fragments and vanished.

The weather jumbled itself together, blazing hot one minute, freezing cold in another. She thought the sky might collapse on them next. If it did, she still would not let Elly go.

DUST PERMEATED THE air to the point where Corin had to instruct Elly to rub her eyes when they reached Springland. The particles came from dandelion seeds whipping through the meadows like a tornado. Fuchsia colors from flowers dulled to browned petals, each one wilted to crisps. Corin struggled to balance her legs on top of rolling hills that swayed like ocean waves. The world could not make sense of itself, and in her dizziness, she collapsed forward.

They both rolled down the hill and thudded against the oak tree that had frozen over in ice. Corin bent over and groaned, fighting nausea in an ever-changing landscape. Elly had to shake her by the shoulders to pull her attention ahead of them.

Across withering fields and dying trees, a cottage had collapsed in a tornado of broken wood and shattered stones. The lace parasol that once acted as a makeshift rooftop had been ripped apart, the strings of fabric hanging on splinters like defeated flags. At the porch, a long table caved in at the center. Neither Briar nor the animals could be seen.

"Check if she's in the dollhouse," Elly urged. "I'll stay here."

"I won't leave you—"

"I know. But you can take a break from carrying me."

Corin couldn't think of a good argument, so she got up to approach the cottage, keeping an eye on Elly and the white void growing in her sister's leg. Her shoes crunched against broken teapots and shattered glass. She called for Briar as she surveyed the debris and sorted through rubble.

A small rumble of stones caught her attention. She lunged toward the noise and dug through the pile until tufts of fur emerged from debris. Penny, once the color of caramel candy, blended far too closely with the dirt surrounding her. Her ears tucked over her snout, her eyes closed in sleep. Only Dime had awoken, barely, his dark pupils glazed in slits.

"Didn't anyone tell you? The tea party is over," he said. "We ran out of time."

"I'll carry you," Corin said, a desperate response that spilled from her lips before logic could fill in the gaps. There was no way she could lift both Elly and the animals to safety. The entire world was collapsing, and she thought she could still carry every burden on her shoulders.

She tried holding Dime until claws scratched her fingers and she yelped in pain. Dime only responded with a hiss.

"I don't know what I'm supposed to do," Corin cried.

She could no longer make out words as he meowed in response. He seemed smaller now, a regular cat with no clothes or human speech. He continued pawing at Corin's hand, trying to communicate something to her, yet hissed if she tried to move him. The cat curled in a ball next to Penny, and Corin realized they'd been nestled in a woven basket. The wood splints were frayed, but they were with each other, and that was enough. Penny never opened her eyes, and Dime refused to leave her side.

"You're ready to go," Corin whispered.

Resignation settled on her shoulders. She watched the void stretch across hills and blossoms turn white before disintegrating to dust. The nothingness loomed over the dollhouse, and still the animals slept in peace together. She scanned the field for the last patches of wildflowers and plucked them from withering grass. Her fingers carefully spread daisies across the basket. Her palm grazed the spot behind Dime's ear, and from his lack of reaction, she knew it was time.

The void streamed toward the dollhouse like a river. Up close, the abyss appeared like light, clear and vivid. Carefully, she placed the basket on the white expanse and backed away. The void cradled Penny and Dime as if the basket floated on invisible water. Waves swallowed them as they disintegrated like starlight, a faint memory that existed once upon a dream.

She vowed to herself that she wouldn't forget. Not the animals, or the cottage, or any of the seasons that disappeared before her eyes. She turned back to Elly, the one person she could count on being tethered to her forever. Panic struck when the oak tree had sank into the white fissure, and Elly was nowhere to be found.

"El?" Corin shouted. "El! Where are you?!"

Her boots stomped over chipped teacups and rotting grass. She raced through the disappearing meadow, her heart wanting to rip from her chest. Elly couldn't be gone. Corin could make her real, as solid as flesh and bone. She clenched her eyes shut and focused on their connection. She had conjured her sister in these dreams, which meant she could do it again and keep her. Her skin, her voice, her heart. Everything Corin was so desperate to hold.

There it was, a tiny drum of a heartbeat. Slow and faint, but enough to pull Corin toward the sunflower maze behind the cottage. Her legs strained to catch up to the endless stretch of stems that continued multiplying. The sunflower stalks had grown thick and tall, blocking the little sunlight left from the broken sky. The haze of yellow turned brown and swallowed her up in dusk. But the dark could not hide Elly. They were tethered, after all, and Corin could tell when she was about to lose a piece of herself.

She found her sister curled over a pile of wilted sunflowers. Elly's black hair looked like roots making their way back to soil. The hole in her leg had grown wider, taking over her torso, then her chest, the fading beat of her heart that never truly existed.

"El," Corin whispered, cradling her sister.

It always came back to this. Finding Elly's body. Not reaching her in time. There was never enough time.

Elly's lashes fluttered as she barely opened her eyes. "Corin," she managed to say. Her breaths came out faint and shallow. Foolish hope rose in Corin's chest anyway.

"El. El, please. Don't leave me." Corin wiped tears from her face and clutched Elly's face with wet hands. "It's going to be fine. I'll find Briar Rose. She'll open a new portal. We'll make a new world, and we'll be safe, and happy, and everything will be okay. I promise, El. I'm never going to let you go."

Corin thought it had been Elly trembling until her sister placed a hand on her arm, stilling her.

"I'm already gone, Corin."

"But you don't have to be," she begged. "We can still be together."

Corin clung tighter, but Elly felt too light, like a candle flame one breath away from disappearing. Her sister gave a tender squeeze to Corin's hand.

"We had fun, but it's time for me to rest." Her voice was so gentle it split Corin's heart in pieces. "You can let go now. It's okay."

Corin could feel her sister fading, yet something pulled Elly still, a taut string. Slow understanding washed over her like an ocean wave. Elly, who never had the patience for anything, had waited for her all this time.

Deep down, Corin knew this moment would come. She had evaded it for so long, distracting herself with fiery anger and self-loathing, petty arguments and desperate promises. Her avoidance had prolonged the inevitable pain. And so, slowly, she loosened her grip. Finger by finger, each bone in her hand that weighed down on Elly's flesh, she forced herself to lift off.

Her tears fell on Elly's cheeks. They pressed into the girl's skin and left tiny holes like constellations. Light poured from Elly's lips as they parted for a whisper.

"I hope someday," she said, "you'll love yourself as much as you loved me."

Corin nodded, quietly weeping, and leaned down to press a soft kiss to Elly's forehead. She placed Elly back in the soil and watched her sister's face shift to permanence. Her lashes drooped over her starry cheeks, and her lips opened to a small part where her last breath escaped.

Elly never opened her eyes again. But she looked peaceful, like she had been tired for a very long time, and could finally sleep.

Withered sunflowers trembled from the wind. Brown petals unfurled and smoothed over their wrinkles, as if waking up to a breeze. Their stalks lifted from the ground and carried Elly's body in a bed of leaves. The smell of fresh soil wafted in the air, and for a moment, the sky washed over in yellow, like sunlight spilling across the atmosphere.

The flowers grew tall enough to reach the sun. At the first trickle of light, they burst into stars. Bright shimmers painted the atmosphere before the fractures of sky appeared again. The last stalk floated toward the void, revealing a fox waiting behind the maze. Cracks formed in his clay skin, but he was still whole, his brown eyes gazing upon Corin.

With the flick of his tail, he turned around and hopped away, melting into the light. So, too, did Springland disappear.

CHAPTER 40

100 YEARS AGO

ONCE PAIN FADED from her chest, darkness came to welcome Amelia in death. It hugged her like a warm blanket, wrapping its arms around her body until fully enveloped as one. There was peace in dying, the kind of serenity that made her forget how she ended up here, but not question how she should go back. Eighteen years of fighting to have some meaning in life, and all she had to do was give up to finally find comfort.

A prickle of light peeked through like holes in a kaleidoscope. The light expanded wider until it eventually swallowed her. Stars exploded in her body, the particles of herself swirling like grains of sand in a windstorm. She hurtled through the air, only slowing to a gradual float, drifting toward nothing.

Then she lay in emptiness.

At first it hurt to open her eyes. The light was too bright, and she had been used to being swathed in darkness. Once her vision focused to clarity, she felt dizzy, stumbling. Her surroundings turned pure, blinding white, an ever-stretching field of nothingness. She looked down and watched her body materialize into existence. Pale limbs filled a white dress, bare feet hovering over a blank abyss. She didn't know where to move, because she had not been standing anywhere. Miraculously, incomprehensibly, she did anyway.

Her first step poured a patch of grass beneath her toes like ink on a page. She took another step and watched the grass expand farther. Daisies sprang from the ground, blades of grass curling around her ankles. The smell of spring wafted in the air, poppy seeds and acorns and sweet florals. She looked up to watch the sky wash over blue like ocean waves. The color stretched endlessly, the horizon never fading.

It was impossible. And yet, as the song of a hummingbird whistled in her ear, it became impossibly real.

"Amelia!"

She spun around to see Malicine and Talon surface from the blank canvas of her surroundings. Relief flooded her lungs as she watched green skin and black ink feathers fill the void. Colors that were once frightening, now familiar and safe.

"Am I dead?" she asked.

"You were close to dying, thanks to that senseless stunt you pulled." Malicine scowled as Talon flew in circles around the emptiness. "The only way I could stop it was restoring the curse so that you'd fall asleep."

Malicine tilted their chin and watched tufts of clouds materialize along Talon's flight path. Blue skies stretched above their heads like paint spilling over a blank board.

"It was our best chance for escape. That prince came looking for you and brought your godmothers for help. I gave them what they wanted: a reason to feel like heroes."

Amelia pieced together vague memories and fragmented

sounds. Shrill voices muffling behind dead foliage. Hooves clopping against gravel. Her heart beat rapidly as the scene turned clearer. Fire crackled the sky, clouds turning into black smoke that shaped into a dragon's silhouette. Smaller tufts of smoke morphed into running figures, shadow puppets that charged toward the winged serpent with raised weapons. As swiftly as he had appeared, the figure riding on a horse threw his sword and pierced the dragon's chest. Smoke dissipated as the creature released an earsplitting scream.

The ground shook. Amelia fell back on the grass while green blades turned into rotting vines, twisting around her wrists to lock her in place. She tried to resist it, but the truth had been painted by the clouds. Ezran was working with her godmothers. He must have fled from the scene so he wouldn't be associated with her father's death. No one had known his whereabouts, and by the time the godmothers realized Amelia was missing, he'd likely looked distressed enough for them to believe his story.

But maybe none of his words were lies. Her godmothers believed they were helping him avenge his true love. They didn't know that meant hunting Amelia.

The ground split open, an emptiness gaping open for Amelia to fall through and disintegrate forever. Malicine seized her by the shoulders.

"Stop it," they demanded. "He's never going to find us."

The demon stilled her long enough for the rocks beneath her to slowly fuse back together. Smoke cleared from the sky, leaving behind white.

"You lost a lot of blood. I did too," Malicine said. "Do you understand what that means? I opened a portal to your dreams."

The amulet in their staff flickered red. Amelia blinked as slow understanding dawned upon her. Pale blue washed into the sky like quiet waves. The world turned quiet, as if waiting for her thoughts. She tried to make sense of the emptiness, but there were no rules to reference. This place was not Gyldan, nor the Otherworld. She was not alive, but she was not dead. She was somewhere in between.

Amelia waved her hand and watched butterflies scatter from her fingertips. Black veins decorated sunny-gold wings, colors swirling like sand in a desert night. She followed their blurry flights. A meadow paved the way for her footsteps, careful and light at first, then quick and manic, bounding across fields as trees sprouted from earth, tangled branches lifting her into the air. Her dress spun daffodils and tulips, petals pressed to fabric, leaves folded into sleeves. A laugh burst from her lips and turned into wind chimes. Rays of light streaked to her fingertips.

She looked down at her hands and saw that her palms shimmered like the sun. This was different from the gold that ran through her veins. This was true magic.

A single sunflower sprung from grass. A memory rooted in her mind. Smells of pastries and apple cakes, an autumn breeze. At Gyldan's marketplace, she'd discovered a miniature cottage house with a sunflower garden. As she recalled that hazy afternoon, gray stones lifted themselves from the ground and hovered in the air. They stacked on top of one another until they were two stories tall. Dry vegetation melded together into a roof, and glass washed over the gaps where windows should be. Behind the house, grass parted ways to create a soil field that stretched for miles. Thick stalks sprouted in rows. Sunflowers bloomed, their faces full of black seeds that shone like oil under the sun.

Her heartbeats raced with her across the field. The fertile soil sensed her footsteps, and another stalk grew beneath her feet and lifted her to the sky.

Malicine called after her. "Amelia, wait—"

But she was already running across the stalks, adrenaline pushing her forward. Black seeds crunched beneath her toes before she leapt into the air. Vines reached to catch her in leafy grasps and settled her on the thatched roof.

"Slow down," Malicine warned.

"How can I?" she exclaimed, arms stretched wide over the straw and heather. The sun's warmth radiated on her skin, freckles blooming like tiny brown flowers. A finch with rainbow feathers perched on her fingertip. "This is everything I've always wanted. A garden of sunflowers. A cottage on a hill. A place where no one knows my name. Just like . . ."

The dollhouse she gave me.

The words died on Amelia's lips. The wind carried it away like dandelion seeds, leaving her mute. She stared into the distance, where a muffled sound of thunder rumbled behind the mountains. Dark patches of gray formed a silhouette of a faceless woman. Small tufts of clouds collected around the silhouette's neck, like a string of pearls. Amelia knew this person. She must have. Long ago, she received a dollhouse for her birthday. Who had given her such a gift?

Someone wise.

Someone kind.

Someone who believed in her—

Someone who died because of her.

Dark clouds advanced toward Amelia. She felt uneasy, the sound of hissing droning in her ears. Then, a strike of blade against flesh. Blood splattered across the pearls. She jolted back, the sudden memory of Lilith hitting her like a hammer to her chest. Tears stung her eyes as she remembered the pearls rolling across dirt, the limp weight of her father's body, her hands drenched in his blood. She tried to forget by looking back at the garden, but the sunflowers began to wilt, their petals shriveled to a muddy brown. Limp birds descended onto fields of dead grass. Gray skies loomed above, growls of thunder reverberating through black clouds.

Wind sliced Amelia's skin. She shrieked and fell backward. The thatched roof turned into brittle straw, and she broke through the flimsy material, falling to the ground. Dirt and bugs crawled over her pale flesh. She shivered in the flimsy fabric of her dress, where flowers died and stank in rot. Snakes slithered around her ears. Their tongues hissed reminders of what she left behind. *Your fault, your fault, your fault,* they said, and each word made her sink deeper, until the roots beneath the soil wrapped around her limbs, squeezing her bones so tight she would break into pieces.

Malicine called for her, but their voice sounded far away and distorted, like Amelia was underwater. Talon dove to the ground and snapped at the snakes and vines, cutting them into ribbons. Once Amelia was freed, Malicine pulled her from the ground and pushed her aside. They swung their staff and sent a ripple of air. The force made the terrain roll over like tidal waves: the bare trees with sunken faces in their trunks, the snakes that coiled and hissed, the mud that had dragged her down like quicksand.

A rift broke through the ground and separated them from a gray mass of land. The terrain warped into a small island, where dark clouds hovered in a circle of fog and broken memories. Water poured into the fracture between them, separating the island with miles of ocean.

In the distance, Amelia could still hear muffled thunder. A menacing fog veiled the shadows living on the island. Gravestones of people she let—

Malicine snapped their fingers in front of Amelia's face.

"I told you to slow down," they said. "This isn't just a world where you can make up whatever you want. It's your dream, which means it'll take pieces of your subconscious."

A storm brewed in the distance, thick gray clouds covering the island filled with bare trees and parched soil. They hovered above the dead foliage, never crossing over the ocean or reaching the rest of the world. A bolt of lightning struck the trees, and an ominous hum reverberated through the misshaped island. The shadow that was once Lilith's silhouette transformed into a larger figure. Its shoulders broadened, and its head grew a pair of horns that pierced through the sky.

A flicker of fear passed through Malicine's eyes before they snapped their head away. "It seems like mine is bleeding over as well."

Amelia watched the horn-shaped clouds before the fog rose high enough to dissipate. Though the island radiated a menacing aura, the grayness was contained behind the ocean and did not seep through water. If she turned her head higher, the skies above remained bright blue, untouched by smog and death.

The nightmares existed. Yet, if she tried hard enough, they could never touch her.

"What if we stayed?" she dared to ask.

"And have an island of doom, quite literally, looming behind us the entire time?"

"We'll do what we always do," she murmured. "We'll bury it all. The memories. The pain. Everything."

A spring's breeze brought the smell of sweet fragranced petals. Fresh grass parted ways to recreate the soil fields, where stalks of sunflowers rose up once again, as if they had never wilted. White and gray stones collected themselves together to rebuild the dollhouse she loved. Its charmingly misshapen roof slanted to the side, like she'd never fallen through it in the first place.

She heard Lilith whisper promises of treasure, but she could not make out the full sentence or meaning behind the words. Not when she was too busy listening to the bees instead, their buzzing drowning out any other sound. Black seeds from the sunflowers dropped like pellets, a few of them turning white like pearls. Amelia spun her dress and swept them away as she continued to dance in blissful ignorance.

Malicine stopped her at the end of the maze. "And what will be left of Gyldan?"

Her fingers curled into fists. The sunflower next to her also began to curl into itself, mimicking the same motion as it withered into a sad, ugly thing. Inside her was a weak soul, one that perished as easily as flowers did.

She replied, "I'm sure it would not make a difference to the world if I existed."

The world would keep turning, the same as it always did. People would mourn the loss of their princess, but they would move on.

Malicine pressed their lips together. Shadowed thoughts passed behind the veil of green eyes as they took in Amelia's words and made sense of them. She knew Malicine felt the same way, for the world had failed them as well. She would never know the true impact of her decision, but she could not will herself to believe there would be any. She would trap herself in a snow globe of her own making, where the scenery never changed unless she willed it, and any chance for true connection would be given up in exchange for comfort.

"You will never want more than this?" Malicine murmured.

"I will never want more," Amelia answered, because she was good at fooling herself too.

She turned her head to the sky, where the shade of blue was so vivid it could only be imagined. Her eyes closed as she inhaled the sweet smell of florals. The sunflowers grew taller around her, their petals grazing her skin and softly bringing her back to the life she envisioned. Even if it wasn't real, it was both of their new lives now. Neither here nor there, they stayed frozen in between. The villain and the damsel in distress had found a hidden pocket between realities to hide, and they would never come back.

CHAPTER 41

CORIN STOOD ALONE in the middle of a white void. The animals, the grass, the house, were all gone. Pieces of meadow scattered across the emptiness, a few flowers clinging onto the soil as temporary survivors, only to wither moments later.

She jumped across small patches of grass to reach the rest of the land that hadn't been wiped away yet. A stream lapped quietly at the bottom of the hill. She splashed her face for clarity, then stared back at her reflection. Water dripped down her chin and slicked the fresh cuts across her flat nose and scratched cheeks. Her eyes were blotted red from crying. This was what someone looked like when they were going to lose everything.

She peered at the snowy mountains in the distance, where Winterland remained. Her wet hands balled into fists. Somewhere out there, Ezran still hunted for Briar. He wouldn't stop chasing, just like how Briar wouldn't stop running. It didn't matter how many portals they created or worlds they left behind. Briar would spend the rest of eternity hiding, even if it meant never finding out what was on the other side.

But Corin had already buried her sister. She didn't want to keep burying more pain.

The stream dwindled itself into nothing more than a trickle before it disappeared. Her hands dried, but a new icy chill ran down her palm. The clear resolution came to her before her subconscious could conjure it in the shape of a dagger in her hand. She grasped the weapon tight. There was only one way for them to move on, and it would no longer be running away.

A SNOWSTORM HAD overtaken the world by the time Corin reached Winterland. The bitter wind howled like a cry. Snowflakes morphed into tiny pins that struck her cheeks. Still she trudged forward in the snow, her own icy dagger in hand. A trail of dead crows paved the way for where Ezran had traveled. He'd gone through the mountains and past frozen lakes, where cracks formed past each footstep.

Some of the ice began to drift upward to the sky, like hail moving backward. Corin dodged the torrent of crystals while jumping between broken pieces of a frozen lake. A chunk of ice flew into the air and cut her shoulder. Her foot slipped on the glacier as she hurtled into water.

The lake was so cold she thought her bones would freeze over. Her blood pressure spiked, her heart beating wild like a hammer. She tried not to let water clog her throat as she gasped for air above the surface. Her hands grasped for the ledge, knuckles turning white to the bone as she struggled to lift her weight. Her wet clothes had gotten too heavy, and the water threatened to drag her down. She stared at the horrified reflection in the ice: face as pale as a sheet, lips turned blue from the cold.

The glacier had also brought something to the surface. The chain around her neck drifted up, the pendant swirling in the water, the amulet glowing red. Corin remembered handing the necklace to Briar, telling her about the sacrifices her family had made. She remembered Malicine giving her their amulet, a relic of their own lineage as well.

Perhaps these tokens were always meant to be given away from one person to another, like a price to pay. There was a reason why, despite her insides screaming to give up, that Corin kept going. For her mother and father. For Harlow and her friends. For Malicine and Elly.

For her.

Corin wanted a better world for every person she ever loved.

She gasped a lungful of air and pulled herself out of the water. Her arms wrestled across ice, the amulet tucked under her vest, glowing through the fabric and shimmering red across glaciers. She dragged herself across the lake until she could reach snow again. Her teeth chattered like they would fall out, and she charged forward, no matter how sharply the wind bit into her skin.

She followed the trail of dead crows leading to the caves. Glaciers glowed a bright blue light, and the open mouth of crystals swallowed her in its entrance. A bitter cold filled the cobalt-colored space. The cavern walls, once glistening like jewels, dulled into a muted gray. Darkness clouded beneath the ice floor, the silhouettes of whales drifting by as limp bodies. The ice no longer vibrated with a rhythmic pulse, but a deep, droning sound of death.

Footsteps echoed from the other side of the cave. She turned the next corner and pressed her back against the wall. The ice felt too cold against her skin, like it was biting through her clothes. Ezran's presence brought a different chill as he roamed down the corridor.

Icicles turned black in his reflection. Darkness spread across cracked ice, but if she stared closely enough, she could make out an expression in the amorphous gloom, the vague silhouette of hollowed cheeks and mournful eyes within the nebula. He drifted through the caverns like a ghost, yet there was a steadiness in every step, a heavy weight he carried like a dragging shadow.

As he moved, the walls beside him glowed with new visions. Scarlet burned across icy rocks and swirled into a kaleidoscope of scenes unfamiliar from Corin's memories. Ocean waves under a colorless sky. A young blond boy sinking alone. The bitter smell of salt and tears wafted through the caves like a crisp morning.

Then ocean hit the walls, and water trickled down the ice, eroding away into a new memory. A necklace of pearls tucked inside wooden cases at a marketplace, a slender hand snatching them amid distracted eyes. The ice fractured, and those same fingers interlocked with another's. Her skin was tinted brown next to his pale hands, yet when the glaciers stretched high enough to reveal the woman with dark hair, the pearls resting on her collarbone made it known that she was his.

She had belonged to him. Until she wasn't anymore.

The walls shattered as hundreds of pearls splashed to the floor like teardrops. Ezran reached to grasp them, but they melted past his shadowy limbs. A sorrowful groan reverberated through the caves. A hollow voice scraped the ice.

"We were supposed to be happy together. Until that family ruined it all."

Though his amorphous form didn't have a face, Corin could tell Ezran had turned to her from the way the shadows shifted. She pulled back to hide behind the wall, but there was no use. In every broken piece of ice, she could see his permeating gloom reflected.

"You destroyed my dreams, Amelia. Now it's time for me to destroy yours."

Ice shattered like starlight across the walls. Water burst through the caves, a typhoon disaster exploding and sending Corin off her feet. As quickly as the glaciers fell, the darkness lunged toward Corin. She swung her dagger, but the weapon caught between his shadowy fingers, wispy limbs curling around the blade and cracking the ice. The dagger shattered in her hand and cut her skin. She yelped in pain before a force kicked her chest to the ground. A heavy weight dropped onto her ribs as his shadow clouded her vision. She choked for air, while his darkness wrapped around her throat, strangling her.

"I assumed you were a petty thief, but it's worse than that. You think you can change and be a hero now. Perhaps that's why you love this fantasy world so much, how it feeds your delusions. But remember this: You ended up here by chance. You took my place that night, and it was never yours to begin with."

His voice was smooth and rich, the kind of sound that lingered on skin in its echoes. It reverberated through the walls even as the cave slowly disappeared into the void. He pushed her skull toward the empty mass beneath the ice, and she could somehow hear the nothingness, the way it was close to taking her with it to nonexistence.

Corin strained to see past his shadowy form for proof that something still existed beyond the darkness, even if they were dangling icicles. A dark reflection in the broken ice stared back at her. She looked like a skeleton, all broken skin and brittle bones. So small and inconsequential that once she disappeared with the rest of this place, she would not even be noticed.

But she wanted to matter. Even if for a moment outside time.

Even in an imaginary world that was crumbling apart.

So she stared directly into the darkness and said, "I didn't take your place. I saw the opportunity to stand where you never did."

Corin grabbed a fistful of broken ice and held it to the void. Refracted light poured from her fingers and tore through the hazy figure. Ezran recoiled under the fluorescence, his wisps shrinking back. Slivers of flesh flickered in his silhouette. She aimed for skin and not shadow, smashing the ice into his head, feeling the crack of bone. Gloom slipped from his figure as blood dripped from his skull and down his cheeks.

Ezran staggered back, which freed up enough room for Corin to get up and jump across the sleet. The ice below her fractured into pieces. Chunks floated to the sky, gravity disappearing as quickly as melting water. She grabbed onto an icicle that floated in the air. Her feet dangled dangerously over the tides, but even more terrifying was the water dissipating below, vanishing into a white void that stretched beyond the horizon.

Corin couldn't cling onto the icicle forever. It melted between her fingers. She swung forward to land on a field from the other side of the caves, where animals made of glass crumbled in the blizzard. Behind her, the caves burst like a dam. She rolled over the snow and crawled as far away as she could to avoid disappearing along with it.

Black branches swayed frantically in the storm, as if beckoning her to hurry. Corin tried to get up before Ezran's hand grabbed her ankle and pulled her down with him. He had blended with the rest of the snow when he jumped with her, his lashes clumped in powder over his pale face and white lips. The pallor made it look like he was decaying, as if the magic that had granted him immortality drained from his bones.

His free hand dragged through the snow until the ice formed a sword as long as his reach. The blade swung at Corin's legs, and the cut was deep, tearing into fabric and bone. She let out a cry and fell. He got on top of her again, locking her body between his knees. The hilt of his sword slammed into her eyes, nose, and teeth. Bones cracked like porcelain, and snow soaked in red. Her vision turned hazy, and she no longer knew if it was the world slipping away or her own life.

Ezran forced her to stay conscious as he gripped her hair and pulled her up to look at him. Silver eyes bore into hers, filled with rage, and yet, somewhere in the dying flecks of light, there was a deep sorrow that had been harvested for centuries.

"When you die, history will forget you," he snarled, "and I'll be the one who fulfilled his promise."

Ezran dropped her limp body to the snow and stood straight. His arm swung back, the blade of his sword pointed to the fractured sky. Corin was too tired to close her eyes. She would not even flinch. Instead, she would let herself see the sword plunge into her chest and meet death face-to-face.

The blade lunged forward before an arrow shot through the wind. It barely missed the space between his sword and arm before landing in snow. Ezran released the weapon in shock, but it did not fall on Corin.

Everything stopped moving. The snowfall. The cracks in ice. The crystals that drifted from a broken sky. They hung suspended, frozen in motion. The sword dangled above Corin's face, yet to drop. The only movement was the breath escaping from Ezran's lips as he stared at the arrow. Corin followed his shifting gaze to the black trees across the field.

Bare-bone branches hardly camouflaged the girl standing

between them. Broken sunlight made her blue dress gleam in the emptiness, a beacon to signal exactly where to find her. Corin had become so used to the different versions of Briar Rose that the real girl looked plain in comparison. Her skin was pallid, her hair limp with uneven shades of dull yellow. Her dress looked too flat, the muddy fabric draped over inelegant limbs. There was no glamor, no magical adornments. Only her.

Amelia dropped her bow. The branches where she stood curled together, and the trunk bent over with a mournful groan. She walked along the trunk like a bridge, finally meeting the man who had been trying to wake her for centuries. But the reunion was no amicable scene, and the prince's distorted smile did not convey love.

"You missed," he sneered. "All these years, and you still can't do anything right."

But Corin remembered the careful balance of the arrow whenever Amelia wielded her bow. She recalled the slow, deliberate breaths Amelia took before releasing the pointed weapon. There was purpose in those long seconds, the decision to tilt her aim elsewhere. Too often people mistook violence for strength and bloodshed for proof of it.

The wood dissolved with each step Amelia took until the only things left in this world were the three of them. Her first and only words came as a single breath, one that she had held for centuries.

"The treasure is Gyldan."

A tense silence passed between them to register her words. Corin didn't move, even as snow melted around her. She watched Amelia's arrow descend through water and into the white void, the dart nothing more than a tiny, dissolving speck.

"You're lying," Ezran hissed.

"Lilith loved Gyldan more than anything. It wasn't perfect, but nothing truly is," Amelia continued. "She wanted to make it better, because she wasn't afraid of the future on the other side. Not like we were."

Ezran snarled. "Don't lump me in with you. She wanted to be with me. She wanted—"

"She wanted so much more, and you didn't see that."

He shook his head with gritted teeth, but the goose bumps on his skin betrayed him, prickling with admission that he refused to voice. Hundreds of years had passed, consumed in revenge and hatred, while kingdoms crumbled around him. Centuries of violent invasions and dying children, bitter poverty and fervid disease. An immeasurable amount of suffering that could have been alleviated by an immortal prince and his loyal faeries, if only they had looked at the world around them and done something.

Corin should have felt vindication, yet grief weighed upon her and spread its mass across the others. As Ezran's face crumpled in agony, so did the dreamscape. Skies crumbled in bits of starlight and dust. The ground broke apart until they stood on nothing else other than a patch of snow. Amelia lifted her chin to the sky, where snowflakes shattered to pieces, their crystals disintegrating into the void. Her eyes turned wet, reflecting oceans long gone in this world.

"But I am worse," she confessed, "because I knew what she treasured most and ran anyway."

A tear slipped from her cheek and plummeted past the snow into nothingness. She swallowed hard and stepped closer to Ezran, who instinctively wrapped a hand around his sword.

"I'm sorry for everything you've been through. I'm sorry I can't bring her back," she said. "No matter how many centuries pass, I miss her every day. Only you know what that feels like."

She reached out a hand to him. There was no bow and arrows, no weapon to defend herself with. Only blind trust.

"I don't know if it's too late to change. Perhaps that's another foolish dream. But maybe the thought of it wouldn't be so terrifying if we helped one another. Maybe it would hurt a little less if we tried."

Corin fixated on the empty palm and bare skin of Amelia's outstretched hand. Guilt twisted her bleeding insides. How quickly Corin had suppressed Amelia's quiet desires when the girl had voiced them in the boat. The love Amelia sought had waited beyond her buried pain, patient through years of silence.

Amelia's trembling fingers told Corin she was afraid. Somehow, Corin knew this did not make her a coward.

She couldn't read Ezran's expression as he closed his lips in resolution, a decision solidifying behind his silver eyes. He reached out for Amelia, and for a moment, Corin thought this would be a peaceful union. But she was behind him and saw the hand that wrapped his sword. She had spotted the grip of his fingers, the whitening of his knuckles, the answer in his eyes.

As he pulled the hilt, she leapt forward. He swung, and there came the slice of flesh, a cut too deep to take back.

Pain bloomed Corin's stomach, searing and heavy. It spread through her body, from her slow-beating heart to the tips of her fingers. The pain became more agonizing as she leaned forward, letting the blade wedge deep into her flesh, and shoved him with all the strength she could muster.

Her full weight pushed him backward, but Ezran never landed in the snow.

The ground crumbled beneath his feet, and he stumbled into the void with a silent scream. In his descent, the emptiness became a part of him. His blond hair turned so white it disintegrated into strands of light. His steel armor dissolved into atoms, exposing his skin and bones before they disappeared as well.

He was nothing. And then, he was gone.

Corin felt the weight of her bleeding body fall forward until Amelia pulled her back. They fell onto the last patch of snow floating in the void. White flakes disintegrated around them as Amelia pressed her hands against Corin's stomach, trying to keep her whole. The ice caps were melting, the sky was fracturing, and Corin, too, was dissolving before Amelia's arms.

Corin untangled the necklace from her vest and showed the amulet locked safely inside the pendant. She placed the glowing orb inside Amelia's palm, sensing her own blood reacting to the mixture that swirled inside, as if it knew the next price to pay.

"Malicine left this," she gasped, "for you to open a new portal."

Amelia stared at the magic brimming inside the amulet. They both understood the unlimited possibilities of what she could do. It was so easy, Corin thought, to continue this for eternity. People in Gyldan would be abandoned for dead, but Corin had fought so hard and for so long to survive too, hadn't she? Surely, she deserved to be selfish once more. She could claim this paradise for herself, a bargain better than anything Woodbine or soldiers or kingdoms could offer her.

Not a roof over her head, but endless blue skies. A stomach that was always full. A love that was guaranteed. A world where she was not a failure.

But Corin could no longer be the same person she was when she had entered Amelia's dreams. Even if it was only imagination, she had to believe she was capable of changing too.

And so, she tightened her grip on Amelia's hand and said, "I don't want to run away anymore."

Tears brimmed in Amelia's eyes. "Corin," she pleaded. "You're going to die."

"I know you want to try again. You don't need him, or anyone, to start over."

"I can't—" Amelia shook her head, sobbing. "I don't want to wake up in a world without you."

Even as Amelia clung onto her tight, Corin's bones eroded away, starting from the tips of her toes as her blood dissolved to particles. She was afraid of dying, while the girl holding her was afraid of living. They had never met each other, not truly, and still, Corin had to believe that their dreams were enough.

"You'll find other things to wake up for," she promised.

The amulet sparked in pure light as the world crumbled around them. Amelia's pleas echoed as Corin's consciousness drifted farther away.

"What if I'm not strong enough?"

What if it doesn't get better?

What if I can't survive this?

What if—

Corin draped the chain around Amelia's neck, choosing a new home for her grandmother's pendant. Amelia's eyes opened, a clear blue ocean in the void, tears lighting up like stars. Her fingers closed around the amulet. The snow beneath their bodies melted away. The amulet's brightness consumed everything around them. Somewhere, beyond sight, a portal opened.

Corin felt herself unraveling. Her flesh was dissolving, her bones decomposing, her memories bleeding away. With the last of her strength, Corin pulled Amelia closer, tasting salt and grief in their kiss. Between their lips, she whispered her answer.

CHAPTER 42

ANOTHER DREAM

ON A WARM SPRING afternoon, Corin and Amelia drank tea with their friends, and nobody died.

The tea smelled like lemon but tasted like sugar. The garden bloomed with marigolds, a vivid orange that shone like sunset. In the kitchen, Malicine brewed a pot over the fire, their raven perched over their shoulder and sniffing for caramel and smoke. Quiet, tinkling sounds of spoons and ceramic rang through the cottage, occasionally interrupted by Corin's sneezes from the marigolds. Amelia laughed at how Corin sounded like a foghorn, yet always kept napkins on hand, silk handkerchiefs that felt plush on Corin's itching nose.

Beyond the porch, where sunflowers grew in the garden and white sheets hung by clothespins, footprints peppered over a winding path. Elly peered behind a stalk, her wild hair spilling over her shoulders in tangled strands of clovers. She brought her pets, a cat and rabbit, to look at the chirping birds. Hats and frilly dresses adorned the animals, a clumsy attempt to make her pets match her own dress made of daisies.

Elly fussed with the sleeve sliding down the cat's arm. She yelped when the cat scratched her hand.

"Ow! Dime, that hurt!"

They spent the afternoon patching Elly's wounds while Dime hid beneath the porch and licked his paws. For the rest of the day, Elly whined that the scratches would leave permanent scars.

Corin rolled her eyes. It was the worst thing that ever happened to her little sister.

ON A COLD winter evening, Corin washed the dishes to the sound of Amelia humming a song, and nobody died.

They did, however, come close to death during dinner with Malicine's sisters. The meal started off seemingly well, as one would expect from family reconciliations: passive-aggressive remarks, false platitudes, empty compliments over tomato stew. One biting remark too many led to screaming arguments, thrown porcelain, and shattered ice. Malicine told their sisters to get out of their face and never speak to them again, or else they'd stab each sister's eyeball with their fork and feed it to Talon.

Corin preferred washing dishes in the aftermath because the activity brought a welcome silence. Amelia was better at soothing Malicine, anyway, as she swept the ice shards in a dusting pan and straightened the dining table.

At some point, Elly pointed out that there was still cake left. Beyond empty glasses and crumb-filled plates, a melted pile of buttercream drooped over a glass pedestal. Blue icing made the cake look like it was frowning, and everyone toppled over laughing from its similarity to Corin. Her glare at them did not help their laughter quiet down.

They ate cake on the floor that evening, deciding the overturned chairs and broken furniture would be dealt with another day. The cake, despite its slush form, still tasted quite good.

Malicine admitted they would never be on good terms with their sisters. They held too much resentment. "It's all right," the demon said, and Corin could tell they meant it. "I know I don't owe anyone forgiveness."

As they savored the last piece of cake, Corin contemplated that the night hadn't turned out so bad. There were more dinners to be had, after all, and other families to celebrate with.

ON A HOT summer morning, Corin showed Amelia her paintings, and nobody died.

This was largely because Amelia restrained Corin from killing her sister when she discovered Elly had left a handprint on the canvas long before the paint dried. Corin had hoped some habits would die with age as Elly turned older, yet even at eighteen, her sister never learned to wipe her hands properly after eating. Sticky fruit, mixed with curiosity about Corin's latest creation, resulted in a red smear across Amelia's face in the painting.

"I love it," the real Amelia said, admiring the glossy paint that streaked golds in her hair, the background of tree foliage and tangled vines.

"It's wrong," Corin hissed, fixated on the red smear.

Amelia plucked a strawberry growing from the garden in their backyard. She tore the flesh with her teeth and let the sticky juice drip down her chin. Her fingers dabbled around her mouth, leaving rose-colored residue.

"Now it's right."

Corin stared at the girl, her painting coming to life. The red hue of Amelia's lips, the strands of golden hair stuck to her cheeks. Her hand cupped Amelia's face and pulled her closer. Their skin was warm with beads of sweat running down their necks. She kissed every part where the stain was, tasting strawberry with each press of her lips.

Amelia did that so well, dealing with Corin's grouchiness, reminding her what was important. Elly was eighteen, the age Corin was when they had first met. She remembered the immaturity she carried back then, and was grateful for the freedom she had now, one that could kiss a beautiful girl without restraint.

ON A CHILLY autumn afternoon, Corin held Amelia's hand along a leaf-covered path, and nobody died.

Corin could tell death was coming soon, for age and time had weathered them both like crumpled plants. They mirrored the dying trees around them with hunched backs and sagging skin. Countless seasons filled with bitter winters and sweltering summers, and they had spent every moment growing old together.

Yes, they were old, but they still enjoyed hearing leaves crunch beneath their boots, even if they had to hold on to each other's arms for balance. The frigid chill hurt Corin's bones a little, but the fresh air was always welcome. They found a bench beneath a maple tree to rest their feet. Bluebirds chirped among the branches. Corin watched leaves change from orange to crumbling brown.

She thought about how sometimes things died and no one could do anything about it but let it happen, grateful that the leaves had once been a remarkable color anyway.

The two of them sat in silence, waiting for the end.

Amelia turned to Corin, her face crumpled in fear. She whispered, "What if I'm not strong enough?"

Corin turned to stare at the sea glass in Amelia's eyes, the snow in her white hair, the golden sun in her freckles. She remembered the years they shared that never existed. Memories of stars and oceans and specks of time where their paths never crossed. A love that had time to bloom even though it could never exist one hundred years apart. The same questions echoed in their minds.

What if I'm not strong enough?

What if it doesn't get better?

What if I can't survive this?

What if—

Corin blinked. *Ah,* she thought. *This is a dream.*

Even dreams must end, and she could feel this one fading. She looked down and saw blood spread from her abdomen. Trees disappeared, and their surroundings turned to white. Amelia could barely hold on to Corin as she was dying. The amulet glowed brighter still, like a light at the end of the tunnel.

With the last of her strength, Corin pulled Amelia closer, tasting salt and grief in their kiss. Between their lips, she whispered her answer.

CHAPTER 43

THE END

"I WANT TO SEE what happens in a world where you don't give up."

EPILOGUE

CORIN OPENED HER eyes to the sound of someone calling her name.

She stared at a thatched roof filled with sunbeams and dust, her limbs twisted in sweat-damped sheets. A gust of air flooded her lungs from an open window next to the bed. Something tickled her cheek. She brushed the sensation away, her fingers wet.

A voice rang in her ear, the sound irritating and comfortable at the same time in its familiarity. "Corin, wake up!"

A round face emerged in her vision. Large brown eyes stared back at her. Elly's black hair grew past her shoulders, a few strands falling on Corin's forehead. Her cheeks were full, her breath warm. The girl furrowed her eyebrows.

"Were you dreaming?"

Corin blinked the last of her tears and scanned the room, her surroundings turning clearer. A hand-carved oak table sat in the corner, the surface completely covered with sketch paper full of drawings and illegible scribbles. A wobbly stool much too tall for the table stood in front, and on top of the seat, a worn-out pillow sat deflated from overuse. She vaguely remembered the soreness of a hunched back and late nights. She did not know where those memories came from, only that they were there.

In the opposite corner, a tall mirror perched against the wall. Corin sat up and gawked at the glass, unable to discern the stranger in the mirror. There were still familiar qualities she recognized: her broad shoulders and dark skin, her thick black hair, which looked like tumbleweed from too much time spent in bed. But other things had disappeared: scars that once nicked her cheeks, broken bones beneath a crooked nose. A gaping wound in her abdomen that should have lost too much blood for her to survive.

She looked clean. More alarmingly, she felt lighter. Like whatever weight she had carried disappeared, a discarded bag of rocks that no longer would have dragged her to the bottom of the ocean if she fell.

Corin wasn't drowning anymore.

Her trembling hand cupped Elly's face. She feared her palm would go through her sister like a ghost. "Is this real?" she whispered.

Elly swatted Corin's hand away. Even their fingers brushing sent a warm jolt through Corin. "You're being weird—"

Corin crushed her sister into an embrace. She hugged Elly so tight that even if the girl were a dream, she would never escape from Corin's arms. But Elly wasn't a figment of imagination. Her heart beat loudly against her chest, and she yelled protests in Corin's ear. Their limbs wrestled as she wriggled her way out of Corin's arms and ran out the door.

"Ma!" she shouted. "Corin's acting strange!"

Corin froze in place. Before she determined if she'd heard Elly correctly, their mother already stood at the door. Her black hair was tied neatly in a bun, a stray strand curled over her earlobe. Faded paint peppered over her apron like raindrops, while new stains of tomato paste streaked across the lower half, like she'd wiped the cloth absentmindedly. Corin remembered their mother using the same apron for painting and cooking, the way that habit created a chaos of colors splattered across her abdomen. That tiny detail, somehow, confirmed she was real. It was more solid proof than her own flesh.

"What's wrong, Corin?" Her voice was rich and warm like toffee. She approached the bed and placed a hand on Corin's forehead, checking her temperature. Corin nearly burst into tears, like a child taken care of.

"I don't understand what's happening."

"Maybe you're disoriented from sleeping too long. You missed dinner when you went to bed early."

Corin stared at the wrinkles etched around her mother's mouth. Years spent laughing at jokes and tasting homemade meals carved into her dark skin. Countless lines traced her face, trailing like a map that proved she lived a long and full life.

"I missed you, Ma," Corin whispered.

Her mother laughed. "You make it sound like you've been gone for centuries."

"But I—" The words were lost upon her. Had she been dreaming this whole time? No, that couldn't be true. They were dreams, yes, but they were real. Her head fell in her hands, straining to piece together a logical explanation. Memories blurred with each passing second, like watercolors washed away before having time to dry. She clung onto broken fragments of snow and ice castles, sunflowers and rolling hills, sticky summers and secret confessions below waterfalls. Hazy visions of Elly with spiky hair, a demon with two horns, a raven as black as night. A girl whose hands Corin wanted to keep in hers forever.

Who had that girl been? There had been a faint taste on her lips, salty with tears and promise. A searing pain in her stomach, like Corin had been stabbed—no, there was a deeper pain than this, clawing its way up to her chest, a beating heart that reached for another.

But Corin hardly remembered her dreams, and she sensed she was already forgetting.

"She was real," Corin insisted, though she couldn't remember who. "I gave her—"

Her hand stopped at a sensation of cold chain around her neck. The familiar shape of a pendant pressed itself underneath her shirt, absent of any amulet. Corin had not given anything away. The necklace had always been here.

Then her father came home, and he was alive as well. He smelled like cedarwood and smoke, and his hands were calloused from work. Corin could not make sense of it all, the familiarity of their skin, the warmth of their breaths. In the kitchen, there were four mugs side by side in the sink, a bowl chipped from when Elly dropped it as an infant, a lopsided table that Corin clumsily put together after splitting one of the legs while playing hide-and-seek. At the entryway, there was ugly wallpaper with plaster cracks, ink marks that measured their heights, drying bunches of lavender and thyme that her mother hung on the door for good luck.

Corin did not know why she broke down crying. She could not explain the feeling of existing with a family that was never missing, while missing another family that only existed in dreams. She could not make sense of spending an entire life thinking how much easier it was to die, and in her final moments, realizing she desperately, truly wanted to live, after all. That perhaps, if she were to keep living, she could have another chance.

IN WINTERS, THE cold was harsh and bitter. It turned the tips of her fingers purple and the skin of her knuckles raw. Corin blew shuddering breaths into Elly's hands to warm her sister. Though their father had covered the window cracks with a heavy tarp, her bones felt brittle, as if they would break under the slightest breeze. Corin hated how powerless she was under the wrath of snowstorms. How easily they could coat her body in white and bury her, forgotten with the earth.

With a shuddering breath, Elly insisted, "We'll survive this."

“How do you know?” Corin hissed.

“Because the ice will melt, like it always does,” she replied, “and there’s so much left to see.”

At the break of dawn, Corin woke to light slipping into the cracks of the window, a fallen tarp draped on the ground, and her sister gone. Panic struck Corin, making her lunge through the door and nearly slip on melted snow. She found Elly kneeling over a shining cold patch. Her boots crunched the snow as she approached the scene and discovered what had caught her sister’s attention.

The ice had thawed into a puddle, revealing a bundle of daisies that sprouted from the ground. The flowers were so small that she would never have noticed them before, or realized they were capable of surviving.

IN SPRINGS, THEIR vegetables struggled to grow. Corin helped her father plant spinach and onions, but their garden was so small it made Pa look like a willow tree, towering over the soil. He was just as she remembered, calloused palms and broad shoulders, a gruff voice that made her strain to hear his murmurs.

She recognized the darkness in his eyes as well. In fleeting moments when he thought no one was looking, in minutes when he had time for himself, his eyes grew distant, a muted sadness that came and left in waves.

Corin knew the look, because she had inherited it from him. There were some things that never went away, no matter what world they lived in. They could not avoid the raging river that called to his darkest desires, the screams that ripped from her throat as she pulled him from the ledge, his tearful apologies for attempting again. Perhaps second chances were burdens too. An uphill battle where one had to fight harder to stay this time around.

One spring morning, she diced the onions and chopped the wilted spinach leaves. She added rice and sprinkled dandelion heads, an embellishment she hoped would incite her father to eat again. Pa took his first bite. He closed his eyes, brows furrowed in concentration, and chewed slowly. At first, Corin thought she must have overcooked the rice. But his lips stretched to a rare smile, and he said he could taste the onions from the garden.

Small pride surged in Corin's veins. She did not like the mornings where sadness dug its fingers into both of them. But their little garden needed to be tended, and so, they would try again.

IN SUMMERS, THE days were too hot and the marketplace was too crowded. There were no warplanes to hide from and no bombs to rattle the earth below her. The first time Corin heard a plane roaring through the sky, she tackled Elly to the ground and covered her sister's ears, exhaling forcibly so that the overpressure wave wouldn't crush her lungs. Instead, the only oppressive air was the humidity.

The breeze was thick with spice instead of smoke, filled with smells of food from faraway places. People shouted to each other in different languages and wore eclectic fashions she didn't understand. Among the chaos, she found a place for her booth, where she hung Ma's paintings and rearranged Pa's pottery while they worked at better-paying jobs. Corin's own art didn't make much money either, and she often found herself hunched behind an easel and painting whichever child asked for a free portrait.

As the afternoon sun reached its peak, she would share her

lunch with other artisans, sitting in one of their booths with the most shade. There was Maggie, the seamstress with calloused hands, who often spilled fabric residue around their shoes. And Rowan, the weaver who insisted on wearing his wool no matter the temperature, which made him look ridiculous. Among their group, however, Corin often bickered with Harlow. A friend she had known for so long that she could hardly recall how they first met.

"Your stamina for always having something to complain about will never end."

Corin had grumbled this as she helped Harlow paint protest posters for their weekly disruption at Gyldan's town hall. Councilmembers convened every quarter to discuss the future of Gyldan under a republic, and for every stride they made, Harlow countered by arguing with their weakest delegate. The woman was never satisfied with any authority, though Corin suspected the right councilmembers would welcome being challenged.

"You are aware our lives are much better compared to other places, right?"

Corin was certainly no patriot, but she'd become accustomed to the comforts of life in Gyldan, where boring days felt like a luxury. She had seen reports about wars in neighboring countries and felt pangs of grief for faceless people, as if she'd felt this once before, the loss of a home. She did not know why these stories made her heart ache, but they made her turn to Harlow like a compass, believing in her friend's missions.

"The fight doesn't end when we live comfortably," Harlow replied. "Not everyone in Zilar wants to flee to Gyldan like our grandparents did. They deserve to stay in their homes. Gyldan owes their neighbors more than one desperate choice."

Despite their arguments, Corin joined Harlow for every duty her friend asked of her. No matter how stubborn they both were, Corin would never leave her side. They stayed past sunset with other artists, gathering supplies and gluing thick placards for signs. One evening, Corin didn't pay attention as she turned around to reach for a poster in her booth. Her hip collided against the table, and the ugly sound of broken ceramic rang in her ears. Pa's hard work shattered across the cement. She cursed loudly and picked up the fractured pieces of a fox figurine.

"Make something new from it," Harlow suggested, much to Corin's dismay. So Corin mixed raw lacquer with flour and water to glue the pieces together. She left painter's tape on it for weeks. The lacquer oozed unevenly from the cracks, so she shaved it off until they were jagged, dark lines. She spent the night mixing paint oils and hunching over the tiny figurine until, eventually, the fox was polished with a vivid yellow filling where the cracks once were.

When the sun came up, Corin squinted at the new figurine she had reconstructed. Under the light, it almost shone like gold.

IN AUTUMNS, THE leaves changed too often. Every time Corin found the right shade in her paintings, the trees morphed colors once more. In a cramped shed behind her family's home, large canvases filled the walls, the old floorboards stained with spilled paint. There were drawings of white gemstones and frozen fountains, ice castles and mountains of snow. Then came more vivid colors, bright fuchsia and chestnuts, seas of wildflowers and blossoms. She sketched ripples from steep waterfalls and spilled black oil for shadows of cloudy islands.

Sometimes Elly pulled a stool next to Corin and watched her

paint. Her sister seemed to be growing every day, her limbs getting longer, her hair growing thicker. A simple chain draped around her neck, one that Corin had given her so that her sister would carry their family's pendant next.

"What's the story behind this one?" Elly asked, pointing at the oil painting of an ocean filled with stars.

At first, Corin could not recall her dreams or explain to her family what happened. Her mind had quickly forgotten the details, like the color of the shirt she was wearing, or the warmth of her lips meeting another's. But when her hand held a brush, and the bristles mixed oils together, memories surged back in paint. Her hands pieced faraway lands and retold the lives of horned demons and ravens, and a girl with sunflowers in her hair, someone she had met once upon a dream.

She told herself these were not fairy tales imagined from her mind. The stories were true. What she felt had been real. In another world, she had rested her weary bones in a haven long enough to heal something broken inside her. She had found some foolish hope in that wretched heart of hers to save others, and in turn, saved herself.

There became new stories for her to paint as well. Drawings of mismatched mugs in the kitchen and crowded marketplaces full of life. Windows with slanted light and dust motes floating in the air like fireflies. Rainy afternoons and quiet mornings and Elly's hair spilling across her pillow. These stories were not epic tales. They had no swords and dragons, no mystical lands or noble battles. Survival did not need to be grand. In these stories, there were tiny plants that survived the harshest of winters, sisters that survived the worst of arguments, and simple relics that survived generations of people, who fought for a reason to keep living.

And sometimes, like on this ordinary autumn day, Corin didn't need to fight at all.

EPILOGUE

100 YEARS AGO

AMELIA OPENED HER eyes to a new reality. Flames ran over her skin, the smell of smoke thick and suffocating. Her hand had gone limp, a sharp spindle left on the ground. Blood soaked her dress and Malicine's hands as the demon's body sprawled over hers. She placed a gentle palm on Malicine's cheek, her fingers slicked with their tears. Regret coursed through her body from causing them pain.

"I'm scared, Mal," she confessed, "but I want to try again."

She gave Malicine the amulet from the dreamworld, which had been hanging from Corin's necklace. The gem unraveled from the pendant and lodged itself onto Malicine's staff. Magic sparked from the demon's skin as familiar blood ran through their veins. Centuries of another life rushed back to them. Their eyes glowed in recognition. Stories cast from generations, birthed from different worlds and times, shared from past lives and histories, all culminated in this very moment.

The flood of memories hit them all at once. They reeled backward, steadying themselves on the overturned spinning wheel. A shuddered gasp escaped their lips before they collected themselves again.

"Are you certain about this?" they warned. "I can't cast the sorrow away from here. If we stay, there will be pain beyond our control. The world will not thank us if we survive it."

Their palm pressed against the hole in Amelia's chest. She winced as flesh materialized in her wound. Her heart slowly pumped into a steady rhythm once more.

"Does it still hurt?" Malicine asked.

Amelia pressed a hand over the closed wound, where her fragile heart solidified.

"It always will," she said. "But I need to know if there's more than surviving the hurt."

The walls surrounding them rumbled with the sound of intruders. A crowd of shrill cries, a strained bray from a running horse. Light sparked behind the foliage that had hidden the two of them, tearing through tangles of vines. The first drops of rain that permeated their barrier felt like tiny knives against her skin. She would see the man who nearly killed her moments ago in her dream. If she didn't die, she would have to face the people of Gyldan, whose fate unfairly rested upon a frightened girl with no readiness to rule a kingdom. This was a world that paved only two paths for her.

The cacophony rang louder as their barricade thinned to a single layer of rotting leaves. Malicine seized Amelia by the wrist. She could feel the scales spreading across the demon's skin, the flare of heat running down their veins.

"Stay back, Amelia." Spikes studded their tongue, and the pupils of their eyes narrowed into slits. Amelia remembered the distant echo of a dragon's roar in another version of this scene. How the stories told of a man who vanquished a monster to save a sleeping princess. That was how the world kept turning: The one who conquered the land and its people became the ruler of all.

But Gyldan had once been nothing more than sand before those rules were made. The seeds of a new path grew in Amelia's mind, one that Lilith had planted long ago.

"No," she told Malicine. "I will be the one who will burn it all down."

And so, the fairy tale went like this: A brave prince battled against a vicious dragon that fateful night. Her faerie godmothers carried her sleeping body to the castle, where Gyldan would mourn and weep.

And then, the ending went like this: After the prince kissed his sleeping beauty, she finally woke up.

Amelia opened her eyes and parted her lips, feigning a full gasp of air, as if life were restoring to her veins. Ezran's silver eyes widened, the first suspicion of her trick, for they both knew that true love did not exist between them. Anger twisted in the snarl of his lips as he realized her pretense. She called for her godmothers before he grabbed his sword. The faeries swarmed her in an embrace, blocking themselves between the two as they cried in celebration.

She let them believe in this fairy tale. The story needed a happy ending, one where the kingdom would come together and celebrate. The couple should announce the wonderful news together, the godmothers suggested. Ezran pressed his lips tight, and behind gritted teeth, new plans formed in his mind. Whatever he considered, Amelia had more than enough time to imagine a different ending.

At the break of dawn, they emerged onto the balcony together. Fractured sunlight glowed across the hopeful faces of Gyldan. The kingdom cried in joy, falling to their knees, their prayers answered. Amelia tried not to think about how the man who wanted to kill her was holding her hand, pretending to be in love, only so that he could pierce his sword through her heart once they were alone. She placed her other hand over her chest, touching the necklace that a girl from her dreams once gave up.

Amelia broke away from Ezran's grasp as she approached the center of the balcony. She scanned the crowd of faces, and for the first time, spoke loudly to them.

"As your new queen of Gyldan, I will make my first order." She pointed to the man standing opposite from her. "Prince Ezran will be imprisoned for murder and treason until proven rehabilitated."

A ripple of outraged gasps surged through the crowd. Amelia turned as Ezran lunged after her in blind fury. His sword aimed for her heart until the blade froze in midair, his limbs locked in position. Confusion spread among the crowd, but the shrill croak of a raven notified Amelia who'd pulled the strings.

Lightning flashed from the sky. A bolt shot from the clouds and shattered Ezran's sword. Malicine flew toward the balcony, their staff gripped in a tightly wound fist. The people of Gyldan screamed in panic as they assumed a second murder attempt. Amelia waved her hands and urged them to calm down, but her voice was mute against the uproar. Malicine snarled for the crowd to silence. Within seconds, their lips sealed shut, their feet rooted to the ground.

The silence made Amelia's breaths too loud. She curled her fingers into fists and tried to still herself before continuing.

"Before I turned eighteen, Malicine revoked my curse. Which means I did not wake up from true love's kiss. I woke up because I decided so." Her voice trembled as she pressed forward. "I do not need a man's love to be the reason why I am alive. And I will not stay married to a man who is too ignorant to realize our family's treasure has always been Gyldan."

She turned to Ezran, waiting for recognition to settle upon his face. His features remained frozen under Malicine's spell, but she could see the war raging in his eyes. She hoped that, over time, he would understand.

"Ezran is unfit to be your king. But the truth is, I am unfit to be your queen as well. No ruler can save Gyldan, no matter how much gold they have in their blood."

Amelia had never been suited for the throne, and yet, she could not think of a single person who deserved to sit there as well. Not her father, whose thirst for conquests only stained blood in his legacy. Not her godmothers, who chose to waste their magic for vanity. Not even Lilith, whose peace and virtues alone could not survive violence.

The gold in Amelia's veins shimmered under the light, and she thought about how useless it was in the end. Centuries of wars and violence for earthly minerals and imaginary titles, all so that the cycle could repeat once more. She remembered the destruction in the Otherworld, how quickly another universe was tarnished under greed and power.

If Gyldan were to avoid the same fate, the kingdom needed something different. She did not know what that would look like yet. But if she could dream impossible things, she could dream this.

"Gyldan was once a kingdom built out of nothing. We welcomed people from all lands and creeds, and that was what made Gyldan today. There were no saviors, kings, or gods. The only thing we have is each other. That is why I will step down as queen and abolish it all. The soldiers, the Fae council, and the monarchy."

Amelia waited for someone to speak before remembering magic had sealed their lips shut and planted their feet to the ground. Malicine raised their hand to the crowd, facing the guards and faerie godmothers.

"Before I restore everyone's bodily functions, know that any mutiny against your former queen will result in dire consequences. As a reminder, I have the capability to create and destroy entire worlds. Rest assured I can make yours a living hell." Their fangs gleamed in a poisonous smile. "If you think my tyranny is a problem, that is all the more reason to find the right leaders."

Amelia felt the braided metal of her necklace slick with sweat. She wished Corin could see this scene unfold, but Corin was not here. It would be a very long time before she would arrive in this world, and Amelia had so much to do before then.

GROWING PAINS CAME naturally with drastic change. Amelia was not fond of pain, and the people of Gyldan were not fond of change. Many left in droves, believing that a kingdom without a proper ruler would result in invasion. Others who couldn't leave remained skeptical. Only a handful expressed interest in serving as officials in Gyldan, hardly enough to decide the future of a former monarchy.

While Ezran remained in prison, her godmothers left the kingdom, refusing to help as advisors so long as Malicine was there. With no offer of wealth or status, the rest of the Fae possessed little interest in meddling with mortal affairs and seemingly disappeared from the human eye. But Malicine was worth more than any faerie, and if Amelia could find any solace in life, it was the steady presence of her companion.

In the remains of an empty castle, she paced the floors with worry.

"This was a mistake," she cried to Malicine. The demon rubbed their forehead, their headache growing both from Amelia's constant panic attacks and the frequent noise of hammering in the background. Workers had volunteered to tear down the castle and make room for town houses. The idea sounded romantic in her mind, but in reality, she spent every day surrounded by rubble and destruction. She nearly tripped over debris before Malicine grabbed her by the shoulders.

"Rebuilding isn't going to look as pretty as your dreams," they snapped. "We don't know if things will get better until we see it through."

"What if it doesn't matter in the end? I can't stop a war. I can't end poverty. It's impossible."

She remembered the stories Corin told her in their dreams. Skies filled with smoke, streets teeming with rubble. Man-made machines that could fly and release weapons that turned bodies and homes into fire. The future would create atrocities beyond her imagination. She could not end the tragedies, for she was only one person, and not even a brave one.

Malicine glanced out a cracked window, where mobs formed outside the castle to protest its destruction. Red-faced noblemen spat curses, while farmers swung pitchforks to riot. A sigh expelled from the demon's lips.

"It is inevitable that humans will do terrible things. But we've learned that there will be humans like Corin and Elly, as well. Perhaps the smallest changes could make their lives a little better."

"I can't change people's lives," Amelia said.

"You changed mine just by being born."

A warmth slowly filled Amelia's chest. Her fingers fidgeted with her necklace. The pendant felt small in her palm, yet its future held a heavy weight. She pictured a child who would learn how to paint from her mother, a small joy that would remain tucked inside that child's heart even as life sharpened her edges with age. She remembered calloused hands holding her own, and how, even in their rough grip, she could still feel that girl's gentleness.

She had learned the answer was not isolation or a lonely throne. For the same reasons that common people had changed Lilith's life, Amelia, too, needed others to depend on for a better outcome.

IN THE END, they did not become heroes. Such were the fates of a frivolous former princess and a wicked demon.

Instead, they left Gyldan to live on the outskirts of civilization. A quiet cottage nestled in the forest, where white crowns of honeysuckle grew through the cracks of windows, their climbing tendrils growing into the light. The grass grew so high they created a wall of green that blinded the porch. Amelia allowed the vines to grow wild, covering the stone walls as if they were encased in their own fortress. They had the occasional animal visitors, a rabbit and cat that wandered through open doors, often paired together.

More frequently came the human visitors, arriving with baked goods and news about Gyldan. The republic had formed over the years, where a council of citizens argued over the kingdom's future. Amelia never had passion for politics, but she'd found people who did. There were craftsmen like Jasper, who started communes for other artists. Translators like Levu and Inya, with rich accents and multiple languages, who traveled between the borders of Gyldan to assist asylum seekers. Apothecaries like Sybil and midwives like Nessa who distributed medicines for the sick. People who reminded her of Lilith so much sometimes that Amelia wanted to cry.

The human visitors rearranged tables and smoothed the linens. Malicine brewed tea over the hearthstone and Amelia mixed her bowl of squash and sunflower seeds. Their friends asked about the flowers blooming in her garden while Talon pecked grapes from their palms. On a warm afternoon, they shared meals with mismatched plates. Between laughter and anecdotes, Amelia scanned the faces of everyone in the room, taking in the friends she never would have made had she decided her life would end at eighteen.

In the evening, crickets chirped outside the window in belated farewell to their guests. Soon, Amelia knew, it would be time for Malicine to say goodbye as well.

"Where will you go after I'm gone?"

Amelia had been washing the dishes when she asked this. Soap bubbles floated toward the exposed wooden beams overhead, where moonlight cast upon the silver streaks in her hair. Her skin had turned thinner, her eyes blurred with a cloudy hue. Time brought changes to her body that she'd never imagined at eighteen. She had become a spinster, a life of peace she had always wanted. She reveled in the variations that came with age, how they proved she'd survived every impossible thing she once feared. Meanwhile, throughout the years they lived together, Malicine's appearance remained the same.

"I see your morbid thoughts haven't disappeared," they replied.

"They're not morbid. It's been a good life. But I'm not leaving until I know what happens to you."

Fire crackled in the stone hearth. Memories flitted by of afternoons nestled in Malicine's overstuffed armchair and Amelia's tufted pillows. Books with crinkled pages lined the shelves, jars filled with jam and marmalade sat on countertops, every relic revealing decades spent with one another.

"I don't know where I'll go. Perhaps that's the thrilling part," Malicine said. "It's a big world, and we only live in one of them. I want to see what Talon and I find next."

Amelia held back her tears, yet the small pinch in her chest came from happiness as well. She'd loved the slow mornings tending the garden in her backyard, filling the beds of her fingernails with dirt, watching the sunflowers bloom every summer. She appreciated having only the company of crickets on quiet evenings and knowing that every day would be the same. But Malicine wanted more, and the demon stayed by her side longer than they should have to watch over her. Despite the good days, darkness always lingered at the back of her mind, a permanent residue of grief she couldn't escape even in the comfort of bedsheets.

But she had survived each time, and she would survive again. She would not let fear hold Malicine back from exploring the rest of the world.

Before they said goodnight, Amelia felt the long arms of an embrace and a soft kiss pressed to her head. She thought about how some curses could become fortunes, and she had all the luck in the world to find her closest companion in this one.

OVER TIME AMELIA noticed fine lines etched in the corners of her eyes and mouth. She marveled at the delicate creases in the mirror. Small moles bloomed on her cheeks after decades spent in the sun. Strands of silver wove through her hair like stars. She moved like the turtles in her pond and thought about how her body was once a blank canvas, beautiful yet empty, before she lived and collected proof of it.

As she grew older, she would wake in the middle of the night, when the moon was out and her thoughts could not be quieted. She could feel the darkness returning to her mind, as it always did. But age gave practice to temper aching sadness and spiraling thoughts until they passed. Her cloak shielded her figure, her footsteps light on the forest path as she slipped out of the cottage while Malicine slept. The night air filled her lungs, and the crickets' chirping followed her all the way to Gyldan.

She visited the republic occasionally to pick up bread from the marketplace and visit her friends. The previous day's rain had slickened the cobblestoned roads and made lampposts reflect a brighter sheen. Clear rivers ran through canals and mirrored the moon in ripples. The night was completely still until a straggler caught the corner of her wrinkled eyes.

The lone figure stood at the end of a bridge, peering into the water. Amelia knew what this person would do, for she remembered the familiar desire she once had at eighteen.

She hurried toward the bridge and called out to the stranger. The woman turned around before Amelia tackled her off the ledge and they fell onto the pavement. Her weary bones ached, yet desperation propelled her forward, grabbing hold of the stranger to make sure she would not jump again. Refugees often fled from other kingdoms to Gyldan, and the council had established temporary shelters for them to stay. Sometimes it wasn't enough. Not when fighting to survive for so long could wear someone down to the bottom of a river.

Amelia brushed black hair away from the stranger's forehead, and the sight of the woman took her aback. Under the moonlight, the woman's features turned clearer: dark eyes, wide nose, a face that Amelia had seen long ago. A rush of nostalgia made her heart ache. She nearly embraced this person, but knew it would only be a stranger's body, one with different angles and shapes that were not the exact match as her dreams.

Weariness dragged the timbre of the woman's voice. "You should have let me go."

Amelia clasped the stranger's hand and gazed at her fiercely. The woman's eyes were dull, like a cloud passed over them, still in the fog of hunger. "No. I need you here."

The woman laughed weakly. "Nobody needs me."

"That's not true," Amelia said, seeing a distant future in the stranger's eyes. "I know you want to run away from the pain. I've run away too. But there will be love on the other side. One day you will see. We cannot survive without each other."

Perhaps the woman would think Amelia was strange. She would never recognize Amelia in the night. It was too dark, and the woman's vision had become so weak that Amelia had to lead her to shelter. But there were no signs of protest, as if Amelia had said things so surely, they almost seemed like they'd become reality.

She clasped the woman's hands in hers, gripping them until they no longer felt like strangers. They never exchanged names, and they never saw each other again. Yet before Amelia said goodbye, she reached for the pendant nestled against her collarbone and wrapped the chain around the woman's neck. The necklace fit over the woman's collar with a natural clasp, as if finding its home.

Afterward, Amelia limped to her woodland cottage with sagging skin and aching bones. The candle in her windowsill had pooled to hardened wax. Her body sank into bed with a heavy heart.

She did not know what tomorrow would bring. There were no promises of happiness or meaning to come. The only thing she knew with certainty was that the morning would cast the sunlight sideways through her windows, the bees would pollinate the wildflowers in her garden, and the seasons would change long after her bones turned to soil.

So for now, Amelia slept.

And when she woke up, the world did not end.

ACKNOWLEDGMENTS

One of the takeaways from this story is that we cannot survive without each other, and that has certainly been the case for this book, which would not have seen the light of day (or at least not in good form) if it weren't for these people:

Marielle Thompson, who was the first person to ever read my manuscript and not only believed in it, but also resonated with the themes of depression and escapism. Thank you for being my writing mentor and pushing the story to be so much better. My publishing journey wouldn't have started without you. Corin also wouldn't have stolen from that poor old lady in Chapter 1 if you hadn't pushed for more agency, so thanks for contributing to elder abuse!

Thao Le, who believed in my story even while the YA market was weak and publishers were looking for either romantic or epic fantasy. Thank you for embracing my dual timelines, dream sequences, and dark themes without diluting the story to fit into a clear category. You once wrote to me saying you felt privileged to have worked on this book, when really it is my privilege to have someone like you behind it.

Zareen Jaffery, who understood this story's message and pushed it further in all the right places. The world-building, character development, and themes were made stronger because of your thoughtfulness. You pushed me to expand these characters and their worlds, making the book better with each round of edits.

Enid Din, Kaitlin Yang, and Asiya Ahmed, who did the artwork, cover design, and interior page design respectively. I had a very specific vision and am grateful that you not only considered all my lengthy notes, but executed them to be even better. Thank you for being the reason that many people decide to pick up this book.

Diane João, Rob Farren, Rye White, Madison Penico, Natalie Melius, Misha Kydd, and Vanessa Robles, for all your help with copyediting, proofreading, and supervising this production. Thank you for lending your careful eyes even in the midst of quick timelines.

Kokila and Penguin Young Readers, who supported me throughout the publishing process and made me feel seen and heard. It is an immense privilege for an author to receive the attention and care you've given to this project. Thank you for being so inclusive and considerate.

Allegra Martschenko, who played a big part in my querying journey with your advice and edit notes. I owe much of Corin's character development to you, particularly with the commune of artists, which led to her having an even more tragic background story. Thanks for helping me make Corin suffer more!

Ali Hazelwood and Kate Goldbeck, because even though my story had no relation to your books at all, you were so supportive of me that it showed how genuine and kind even "big authors" can be. No wonder your books are so damn delightful.

The Dream Girls, Levi, Marialuisa, and everyone I've done writing sprints with, because you know I hate drafting and can barely write a hundred words on a good day. The writing process is torturous, but your company alongside my slow ass helped this book get closer to the finish line. I can't wait to shout about your books when it's your turn.

Annabelle Slator, Mela Rogers, Akana Phenix, Rachel Phan, and every author I've had the pleasure of becoming good friends with. The publishing industry intimidates me because I hate pettiness and competition. It's people like you who make the space so much better with your presence in it.

Victoria, because your unconditional love turned this sapphic story into an Own Voices book and continues to heal me.

Last but not least, everyone who has followed my journey on YouTube and social media. Whether you're an avid commenter or silent lurker, a long-time viewer or a newbie, your support gave me a platform that increased my chances of publishing this book and made the publisher more invested in it. The internet can suck sometimes, but I've received kindness from so many of you during times when I could not be kind to myself. I hope I meet more of you IRL so we can escalate this parasocial relationship even further. And regardless, we'll always have faerie dick jokes on the internet.